PONNIYIN SEL1

CW00551702

PONNIYIN SELVAN

BOOK 1: FRESH FLOODS

KALKI R KRISHNAMURTHY

Translated from the Tamil by Pavithra Srinivasan

ZERO DEGREE PUBLISHING

Original in Tamil, Ponniyin Selvan : ©KALKI R KRISHNAMURTHY
English Translation, Ponniyin Selvan : ©Pavithra Srinivasan
First Edition: July 2019
By ZERO DEGREE PUBLISHING

ISBN: 978-93-88860-02-4
ZDP Title : 21

ZERO DEGREE PUBLISHING
No.55(7), R Block, 6th Avenue,
Anna Nagar,
Chennai - 600 040

Website: www.zerodegreepublishing.com
E Mail id: zerodegreepublishing@gmail.com
Phone : 98400 65000

Typeset by Vidhya Velayudham
Cover Art by Art Muneeswaran

PUBLISHERS' NOTE

Writers are the cultural identity, the memory of the aeon, the conscience and the voice of the society. By the sheer magic of their art, they surpass the barriers of language, land and culture. Any country should pride itself on possessing writers – national assets – whose works in translation have the potential to catapult them into international renown.

The Latin American Boom during the 1960s and '70s was a launchpad era that thrust names such as Julio Cortázar, Gabriel García Márquez, Carlos Fuentes, Jorge Luis Borges and Mario Vargas Llosa into the Anglophone literary world where they enjoyed a plausive reception.

Publication of translated nineteenth-century Russian literature fetched Tolstoy and Chekhov iconic status. Due to the availability of and the demand for their works in translation, Haruki Murakami of Japan and Orhan Pamuk of Turkey have become bestselling writers to watch in the present day and age.

What we understand from all of this is that translation and publication are fruitful endeavors that engage national writers and their oeuvres with the world at large and vice versa.

Zero Degree Publishing aims to introduce to the world some of the finest specimens of modern Indian literature, to begin with, we take great pride in introducing Tamil literature in English translation because, as Henry Gratton Doyle said, "It is better to have read a great work of another culture in translation than never to have read it at all."

– Gayathri Ramasubramanian & Ramjee Narasiman
Publishers

Dedication

To Kalki R Krishnamurthy—who first opened my eyes to the wonderful world of history, and guided my first hesitating steps towards the incredible world of historical fiction. From you I learnt my past; through you, I look to my future.

-Pavithra Srinivasan

CONTENTS

1

Auspicious Aadi

We ask our amiable readers to kindly disregard the present, and climb into the boat of imagination, that we may take a little journey across time, unmarred by beginnings and endings. We shall cross a century in a convenient second, and reach a year roughly nine hundred and eighty two years before our time.* (*Written in 1950.).

Between the hoary lands of Thondai Nadu and Chozha Nadu is placed the kingdom of Thirumunaippaadi; in its southern region, roughly two *kaadhams* west of the famed Chidambaram Temple sprawls the huge Veera Narayanan Lake, as large as an ocean. It measures something like one-and-a-half *kaadhams* from north to south, and half a *kaadham* from east to west. These days, it is known no longer by its full, original name, but by a much shortened, colloquial version— *Veeraanathu Eri*, or Lake.

Those who saw this massive body of water during the months of Aadi and Aavani, when the floods poured in fresh water, its surface churning and tossing, almost overflowing its banks, could not help but marvel in astonishment and heave sighs of delight at the great feats accomplished by their ancestors in ancient Thamizhagam. For, such deeds were not merely for their own advancement, or even the betterment of those of their times, were they? Their benefit was passed down through generations, like the munificent plantain trees bequeathing their resources to their young, enriching their descendents a thousand years into the future, didn't they?

On the auspicious, eighteenth day of *Aadi*, sometime in the early evening, a young man rode his horse along the banks of the Veera Narayana Eri, almost ocean-like in its vastness. A scion of one of *Thamizhagam*'s most distinguished clans—the Vaanar *kulam*—was our young man; by name, Vallavarayan Vandhiyathevan.

They had traveled a great distance without pause; his horse was weary and stumbled slowly, along the path. Not that our young traveller was much distressed by this—he was too fascinated by the lake and its enormous proportions to set much store by his steed's fatigue.

Aadi Perukku was traditionally important for more than one reason—on this day, every river in Chozha Nadu overflowed its banks; consequently, every lake that fed from the rivers was filled to the brim as well, the waters tossing and churning the surface. The river known as Vada Kaveri by devotees and Kollidam colloquially, fed straight into the Veera Narayanan Eri through the Vadavaaru—and the latter was more an ocean in dimensions. Water gushed through the seventy-four canals that ringed the lake, bubbling and foaming, adding to the vast expanse, and irrigating vast swathes of the surrounding land.

Agriculture was the mainstay here; farmers were engaged in ploughing, seeding and planting their respective fields, as the lake's waters flowed into their lands. Men and women, neck-deep in their work went about with sweet songs on their lips to alleviate the burden of labour.

Vandhiyathevan chose to linger on his way, listening to their songs; besides, he was engaged in another, more important task: verifying whether the lake did possess seventy-four canals, as he'd heard tell. Thus far, he had traveled one-and-a-half *kaadhams* – and counted only around seventy.

It was then that the true magnitude, the sheer vastness of the lake burst upon him in all its glory. Ha—such length and breadth! How enormous it was, seemingly endless—why, even the so-called large lakes dug by the Pallava Emperors were nothing but tiny ponds, in comparison! And then, consider the incredible foresight of Prince Rajadithyar, son of Madurai's conqueror, the illustrious Paranthakar, who had conceived the plan of diverting the Vada Kaveri's vast waters into a lake of such proportions! Indeed, who could claim to be his equal when it came to sheer foresight, and execution of plans? For that matter, there was no one who could match his courage and valour, either. Wasn't he the warrior who had chosen to personally lead his armies into battle at Thakkolam? Hadn't he borne an enemy's spear in his chest as he rode his war-elephant, and ascended to heaven as a valiant soldier? Didn't he fully deserve the title "He Who Embraced Death on His Elephant," as a result of his great deeds?

In truth, these Chozha kings were a strange and wonderful breed. They were as outstanding in valour as they were in war; as committed to justice, as they were to God. And he had actually had the great good fortune of mingling with, nay, claiming friendship with them! Vandhiyathevan's shoulders swelled; his heart threatened to burst with pride, buffeted by waves of sheer exhilaration, just as the surface of the Veera Narayana Lake heaved and tossed, striking the banks, whipped by the brisk west wind.

By the time Vandhiyathevan reached this point in his ruminations, he had arrived at the southern end of the lake, and saw the magnificent sight of Vadavaaru emptying itself into it. The lake bed extended for a small stretch between the banks and the water's surface; thorny *karuvela* and *vila* trees had been planted in it to prevent damages to the shore from floods. Sturdy *naanal* bushes clustered thickly at the edges. In all, the sight of the Vadavaaru, with water rushing between tree-laden banks and emptying with a roar into the Veera Narayana Lake made a very pretty, colourful picture indeed, from afar.

Vandhiyathevan was delighted with nature's painting—but there were a few other sights too, that considerably increased his admiration, and joy in his surroundings.

The auspicious day meant that villagers from in and around the lake were in the mood for celebrations—and scores of men, women, children and even a few aged ones took advantage of the festive occasion, dressed in their best clothes and finery, dragging along *sapparams* made of delicate, ivory-white coconut fronds. Women wore fragrant blossoms of jasmine, *mullai, thaazhambu, sevvandhi, iruvatchi* and *shenbagam*, spreading their sweet scent around. Of food, there was plenty as well, in the form of delicious *kootanchoru*, a mixture of rice and various condiments. Some strolled along the banks, having ladled their food into cups fashioned from *kamugu*; other, slightly more adventurous sightseers walked right up to where the Vadavaaru poured into the lake, and ate their food, watching the sight. Children threw their used *kamugu* cups into the canals, watched the flimsy containers tumble through the choppy waters and clapped their hands with glee. Some young men exhibited their playful nature—pulling flowers off their beloveds' tresses without their knowledge, throwing them into the canal and laughing to see them burst through on the lake's side.

Vallavarayan stayed on the banks for a while, enjoying the sights and sounds of celebration. He took in the sweet, appealing melodies of the women—they ranged from boat-songs, to *kummi*, *sindhu* and even some celebrating the floods, in all their delightful variety.

> *"Come, sing in welcome—*
> *The Vadavaaru leaps towards us*
> *Watch, and dance in welcome—*
> *The Vellaaru springs towards us*
> *See, delight and welcome—*
> *The Kaveri rises towards us!"*

These and many more songs were sung with joy, celebrating the new waters and Vandhiyathevan listened for all he was worth, the sweetness in the tone and verses gladdening his heart.

War-like fervour found favour, among other celebrants in the groups. Some women enshrined in song the valour of Vijayalaya Chozhar, who sported ninety and six scars on his battle-worn body, from thirty-two wars; yet another woman chose to sing about the piety and compassion of his son Adithya Chozhar who built sixty-four temples for Siva Peruman all along the course of the Kaveri, from its birthplace to where it merged with the sea. Paranthaka Chozhar's incredible feats as he subjugated the Pandiyas, Pallavas, Cheras, and won massive victories in Ilankai were sung by a young lady with enormous zest and vigour. Everyone's performance was heard with gratifying attention; sometimes, listeners gave themselves completely to them, uttering spontaneous exclamations: "Ah! Ah!"

Lost in the revelry, Vandhiyathevan gradually became aware of an old woman's scrutiny. "You look like you have traveled far and hard, *Thambi*. You must be very tired. Would you like to get down from that horse of yours and share some of our nourishing *kootanchoru?*"

This seemed to be the signal for every young woman in the vicinity to direct keen glances at our young man. Their laughing eyes settled on him; they giggled and tittered among themselves, obviously discussing his appearance.

Vandhiyathevan would have been paralyzed by bashfulness, had not a part of him been overjoyed at the female attention. He wondered, briefly, if he should take up the old woman on her offer and gorge himself on food—but surely, if he did, those young women would surround him on all sides and swamp him with ridicule.

But what of it? Opportunities to be swamped by a bevy of young ladies did not often come by; even if they did ridicule him, surely the sound of their teasing laughter would defeat the mellifluous music of celestial beings!

To Vandhiyathevan's besotted young eyes, every maiden on the shore seemed to be no less a beauty than the divine dancers Rambha and Menaka, who adorned Indra's court.

Before he could accept the old woman's invitation, though— something else caught his attention, and made him hesitate.

In the distance, a heavenly sight met his eyes: seven or eight large boats glided swiftly along the Vadavaaru from the south-west, their white, silky sails fluttering in the brisk west wind, oars spread like the wings of a graceful swan.

Men and women, indulging in celebration along the banks, gradually fell silent, their attention riveted by the approaching spectacle.

One among the cavalcade outran the rest, making its way swiftly towards the northern bend of the lake. Soldiers lined its decks; sunlight caught the glint of their spears and javelins, dazzling onlookers. Some of them jumped on shore and began to herd everyone with alacrity: "Clear out! Move away, all of you!"

The celebrants themselves, obviously, did not want to lay themselves open to such bracing treatment; they were swift to pick up their belongings and move well away from the banks.

Vandhiyathevan watched the boats and warriors, puzzled. Who were they, and what sort of passengers did the boats behind them carry? Were they, perhaps, members of the royal family?

He sidled up to an old man who stood on the banks, leaning on his stick. "*Ayya*, whose men are these? Whom do those swan-like boats belong to? Why do these soldiers drive away the people? And why does everyone obey them?" The questions fairly tripped off his over-eager tongue.

"Why, *Thambi*, do you tell me that you do not recognize them?" the old man raised his eyebrows. "Do you see the boat in the midst of the rest? And the flag that flutters in it? Tell me—what is the emblem it bears?"

"It seems to be a palm tree."

"Indeed. And do you not know that it is the emblem of the *Pazhuvettarayars*, my lad?"

"Good God," Vandhiyathevan exclaimed, startled. "Is it truly him? The great warrior Pazhuvettarayar?"

"It must be. Who else would dare to brandish the palm-tree flag with such authority?"

Vallavarayan's eyes turned towards the approaching boats again, wide with astonishment. Such were the tales he had heard, about the warrior among warriors, Pazhuvettarayar. But then, who had not?

The names and fame of the amazingly valiant Pazhuvettarayar brothers, both Elder and Younger, had spread through the length and breadth of Chozha Empire, from Eezham in the South, to Kalinga in the North. The brothers hailed from the city of Pazhuvoor on the northern banks of the River Vada Kaveri, near Uraiyur; their clan had earned a name for valour from the times of Vijayalayar. The Pazhuvoor family claimed intimate ties with the Chozhas through marital alliances; their royal connections and reputation for courage had made them one of the first families of the land, a clan that was almost, if not quite, the equal of the ancient Chozha dynasty itself. Such an illustrious status also meant that they were among the few who could boast the privilege of a flag of their own.

Of the current duo, the Elder was more renowned, having earned legendary status in twenty-four battles; for sheer bravery, it was common knowledge that he had no equal in Chozha Nadu. More than fifty years old, he no longer graced battlefields but held several truly exalted positions in the Chozha Empire: *Dhana* and *Dhaanya Athikaari*—Treasurer, and Guardian of Granaries. His was the right to guard the resources of the land, both cash and kind; his also, the privilege to assess the demands of the government, decide on the *thirai*, or tax to be levied upon and collected from the people. He could march up to any *kottam* official, affluent landlord or minister, and demand to be paid whatever tax he levied, that year.

In other words, Pazhuvettarayar was considered next in importance to none other than Maharaja Sundara Chozhar himself, in the empire.

Naturally, Vandhiyathevan's heart was filled with the unquenchable urge to catch a glimpse of this supremely important personality, this warrior who claimed the respect of every Chozha citizen.

But then—he remembered the confidential message entrusted to him by Prince Aditha Karikalar, in Kanchi's Golden Palace.

"Vandhiyatheva! I'm well aware of your prowess as a warrior. I'm also aware of your keen intelligence—which is why I'm entrusting this responsibility to you. Here are two palm-leaves: one is to be delivered to my father, the Maharaja; the other to my sister, Ilaiya Piratti. I hear such disturbing tales about even highly-placed officials in the empire—you must, therefore, make sure that my message does not fall into their hands. No matter what position of authority they hold, not a whisper of suspicion must enter their heads that you carry a message from me. Do not, I repeat, *do not* pick fights along the way. It isn't enough if *you* don't quarrel with anyone—make sure that you ignore anyone who forces a quarrel on you. Vallavaraya—I know you to be an excellent warrior, so you may be easy about your reputation. Rest assured that ignoring a few disputes isn't going to be a blemish on your honour." There was a pause. "In particular, my lad—you must be very wary of the Pazhuvettarayars, and my uncle Madhuranthakar. Not on any account must they know the purpose of your mission!"

Such was the message entrusted to him, not just by the Crown Prince of the Chozha Empire, but one who held the vastly important position of *Maathanda Naayakar* of the Northern Chozha Forces. Aditha Karikalar had taken such great pains to impress ways of good conduct and behaviour upon him, not to mention precise instructions to be carried out, that Vallavarayan could not find it in himself to ignore those words of caution. Meeting Pazhuvettarayar, therefore, was a desire he would have to suppress.

Vandhiyathevan heaved a sigh and spurred his horse forward. That noble animal, already worn down by hard travel, could do little more than ooze along the path.

Well, that left him with only one option: he would spend the night at the Kadambur Sambuvaraiyar Palace, and leave the next morning—with a brand-new horse, able and fit for travel.

ॐ

Hidden Meanings and Explanations

Kulam

Clan, or tribe.

Thambi

Literally means "younger brother," but is also used commonly to refer to a young man.

Kaadham

A unit to measure distance in ancient times. One kaadham approximately equals 1.167 kilometres.

Jaamam

A unit of time, measuring 2 hours and 24 minutes.

Naazhigai

A unit of time, measuring 24 minutes.

2

Azhwarkkadiyaan Nambi

Vandhiyathevan spurred his horse down from the banks, towards a path that went south.

His heart, at the moment, was light as a feather, almost tumbling cartwheels in delight—much like the boats that had skimmed forward so effortlessly on the lake's surface. His had always been an optimistic nature, willing to anticipate pleasure rather than pain. Sheer exhilaration bubbled up from deep within, coursing through his veins.

Something whispered to him that he was about to embark on a strange and wonderful journey. Ah, if he could feel such delight just by stepping into Chozha dominions, how much more enjoyable would it be as he journeyed beyond Kollidam? How alluring would he find those lands, overflowing with natural beauty? What would the people, especially the women, be like? Such rivers, streams and delightful, clear ponds! What a magnificent sight would the River Ponni present, enshrined in countless poems and epics? Her lush banks, crowded with *Punnai*, *Konnai* and *Kadhamba* trees, weighed down with their fragrant blossoms would gladden anyone's heart! Doubtless he would be treated to the sight of red lotuses, *kuvalai* and *kumutham* flowers in ponds, enticing him as they unfurled their delicate petals, their subtle scents wafting towards him in welcome. Richly carved temples, built by Chozha kings renowned for their piety would greet him on either side of the river's banks, affording opportunity for quiet devotion.

Ah, Pazhaiyarai—divine, beautiful Pazhaiyarai! The illustrious Chozha capital that had wrested pride of place from such Chozha mainstays as Poompuhar and Uraiyur. The latter cities were nothing more than insignificant villages, at the moment. Such temples, mansions, palaces, wide avenues, soldiers-quarters, magnificently carved stone temples for Siva and *Vinnagara* temples for Vishnu as Pazhaiyarai boasted, were never to be found anywhere else. Vandhiyathevan had heard tales that the simple, charming *Thevaram* and *Thiruvaimozhi* verses, sung with touching devotion by versatile musicians, were capable of melting even a stone. Now, he would have an opportunity to listen to such soul-stirring melodies himself.

That was not all: soon, he would have the honour of an audience with one who was popularly held to be the equal of Manmadhan in beauty and Velan, for courage: none other than Maharaja Paranthaka Sundara Chozhar himself. Even more important—he would meet his daughter, the much loved and revered Chozha Princess Kundhavai Piratti as well.

Provided, of course, he met with no danger upon the way.

What if he did, though? He had his spear; his trusty sword hung sheathed, at his waist; his armour protected his body from injury. Best of all, his heart possessed enough courage to overthrow any calamity.

But then—there were *Maathanda Naayakar* Aditha Karikalar's instructions to him as well: they would prove a stumbling-block indeed. He wasn't to descend to brawling with anyone, no matter what the provocation. Well, that might prove a difficult proposition. Still, he had managed it thus far, a considerable distance, hadn't he? Just two days more. Until then, he would have to keep his temper in check.

It had been Vandhiyathevan's intention to reach Kadambur Sambuvaraiyar's palace by the time *Aadhavan* sank in the west; he set a steady pace and soon, found himself trotting up to the Veera Narayanapura *Vinnagara* Temple.

The *Aadi Thirumanjanam* festivities meant that the already popular shrine was teeming with droves of people, filling even the surrounding groves.

Stalls had erupted in every available corner, selling slices of jack-fruit, bananas, cuts of sugarcane, sweet-meats and savouries; others sold flowers with which women loved to adorn themselves, and lotus buds meant for divine worship. Some stalls were overflowing with heaps of coconuts, *ilaneer*, fragrant incense like *akhil*, sandalwood paste and other necessities such as betel-leaves, jaggery and puffed rice; business was brisk. But fun and frolic had their place as well.

It was not just the vendors who thrived—at certain appropriate corners sat astrologers, palmistry experts, men who advertised themselves as masters at reading signs and divining the future, and slick magicians who swore to remedy any poisonous bite. People milled around all of them, enjoying the sights and scenes.

So did Vandhiyathevan, as he cruised slowly through the organized pandemonium.

At one point, though, the uproar seemed to be at its raucous best. Crowds of people thronged around, and some voices were so loud that they permeated even the festivities. Evidently an argument was in progress—and judging by the heated shouts, a vociferous one.

Every instinct in Vandhiyathevan tugged at him to immerse himself in the dispute; he simply could not help himself. He brought his horse to a halt by the roadside, a little outside the crowd, and climbed down. Communicating to the steed to remain in place was a moment's work; Vandhiyathevan patted the animal, broke into the heaving crowd at an opportune position, and ploughed through its ranks with alacrity. What he saw, when he arrived in its midst, made him stop short in astonishment.

The cause of the massive argument and yells that almost reached the heavens—were just three men.

They might be minuscule in number, but the surrounding crowd more than made up for it. Each verbal combatant, it seemed, had his own ardent following that shrieked its support whenever he put forth a particularly brilliant argument—and this, Vandhiyathevan saw, was the real reason for the clamour.

Once he had taken the time to observe all this, he bent his mind to the dispute on hand.

One of the three men was almost smothered in sandalwood markings that denoted the symbol of Thirumaal, or Lord Vishnu, and wore a top-knot at the front of his head. His short and stocky build proclaimed a hardened body; he held a staff, as well.

The second was a Siva devotee, adorned liberally with stripes of *viboothi*, sacred ash.

The third happened to be clad in saffron and sported a bald head. He, it was soon understood, was neither a Vaishnavite nor a Saivite, but professed to be beyond such definitions: one who followed the tenets of the Advaitha Vedantha philosophy.

"You, Azhwarkkadiyaan Nambi, listen!" announced the Saivite. "Haven't we all heard tales of Brahma and Vishnu searching in vain for the head and feet of Siva Peruman? Didn't they fail spectacularly to bind Him to such pitiful dimensions, and finally fall at His divine feet, begging forgiveness for their transgressions? How, in all honesty, can you argue that Thirumaal is worthier?"

This was the sign for Azhwarkkadiyaan Nambi to brandish his staff in a wide arc. "Stop this instant, you who worship the dust at Siva's feet!" he bellowed. "Your blessed Siva Peruman was the one to rain boons on the undeserving head of Ilankai's demon-king Ravana—but didn't all those ridiculous powers come to nothing, before the divine bow of Vishnu's incarnation, great Rama? How could you possibly argue that Siva is the more powerful?"

The saffron-clothed Advaitha monk barged in. "Really, I fail to see the point of these petty arguments. You may debate the greatness of Siva or Vishnu until the end of time—but there would be no purpose to it.

The only truth, the greatest of them all, lies in Vedantha. You, who still prostrate yourselves at the feet of mere deities, are doomed to follow the paltry *Bhakthi Maargam*; you are too ignorant to understand that the spiritual path, *Gnana Maargam* lies above; and the *Gnyasa Maargam*, even more so. Once you arrive at this point, you will realize that there is no such thing as Siva or Vishnu; everything is Brahmam, the cosmic consciousness. *Sarvam Brahma Mayam Jagath*. I should like to elaborate here on the excellent essay in the *Brahma Sutra Bhashyam* written by Sankara Bhagavadpaatha, wherein he quotes—"

"Cease your ridiculous drivel!" yelled Azhwarkkadiyaan Nambi. "Do you even remember what your sacred Sankarachariyar did after scribbling endless essays and commentaries on the Upanishads, Bhagavad Geetha and Brahma Sutra? Listen to this:

> *Baja Govindham, Baja Govindham*
> *Baja Govindham, Moodamadhe!*"

Hear that? He's instructing mindless idiots like you to chant the name of Govindha and redeem yourselves, *that's* what he says!" And the crowd erupted into jeers, laughter and scornful exclamations.

This comprehensively rude argument did not seem to have any effect on the *sanyasi*. "Indeed, I *have* lost my mind, you top-knotted ruffian! All you do is brandish your ridiculous staff in my face—and I truly have abandoned my senses to even stand here, arguing with the likes of you! I am, in fact, a *moodamadhi!*"

"Oy, I may have just a simple staff in my hands, you saffron-robed hermit, but it has its uses—breaking the heads of the likes of you!" And Azhwarkkadiyaan raised his staff, as though about to bring it down on the monk's unsuspecting skull—which sent the crowd into wild paroxysms of delight.

The Advaitha ascetic, it seemed, was unfazed by such an unbridled enthusiasm to bash his brains in. "My man, kindly rein your fanaticism and keep a hold on your staff. I am disinclined to take offence, even if you *do* wreak havoc on my head. Nothing you do or say will make me angry. I shall not descend to your level and abuse you either. That which strikes me is Brahmam; that which bears the strike is Brahmam as well. If you do break my head, you would only be injuring yourself!"

"Hear, hear, my dear friends," crowed Azhwarkkadiyaan Nambi. "The sacred staff will now descend upon Brahmam's head, duly wielded by the supreme Brahmam itself. I'm going to bash myself up!" And he stalked towards the monk.

Vandhiyathevan, watching the altercation, felt an overwhelming desire to wrench the staff from the excitable Nambi and deal him a few well-placed, sacred blows upon his revered person, himself.

But stay—the monk was nowhere to be found! He had taken advantage of the Nambi's antics, the general distraction, and made his swift escape through the crowd.

Azhwarkkadiyaan's devout supporters roared in approval.

It was now the turn of the Veera Saiva Pathadhooli Battar, to face the Vaishnavite's ire. "Well, my beloved Siva devotee, what say you? Prepared to go head to head with me in an argument? Or would you prefer to make a speedy escape, like our friend the monk?"

"Ha, certainly not! I, unlike that verbose idiot, am no coward. Or, perhaps you thought I might ape your blessed Kannan, stealing ghee and curds from the homes of the Gopis, getting thrashed with churners and—"

Azhwarkkadiyaan butted in before he could finish. "And your Siva was utterly without blemish, I suppose? Who was the man who played around instead of carrying earth to build a bund for River Vaigai, and got caned for it?" And Azhwarkkadiyaan advanced upon the Saivite, brandishing his staff once again.

It must be mentioned here that while the Nambi was a stout, muscular fellow, the Pathadhooli Battar was built along gaunter lines.

This seemed to be the sign for the surrounding crowd to promptly gird their loins and prepare for all-out battle, in support of their respective idols.

For some reason, Vandhiyathevan felt an instinct to end this ridiculous bout, and stepped forward.

"Why do you fight amongst yourselves over such silly things?" He said, in his clear voice. "Don't you have anything better to do? If battle is what you want, Eezham is in the midst of war and has plenty of opportunities to test your mettle. Couldn't you take yourselves there and fight to your hearts' content?"

Nambi turned to him in an instant. "Who's the man who dares to teach us *our* business?"

The crowd was now inspecting Vandhiyathevan. His bearing, which suggested valour and a certain nonchalance appealed to them—not to mention his open, handsome countenance.

"You are very right, *Thambi*—do teach these quarrelling men a lesson," they offered. "We will support you!"

"I shall tell you whatever I know, about such things," Vandhiyathevan elaborated. "It doesn't seem to me that Siva Peruman or Narayanan are fighting amongst themselves; from what I can see, they're on very friendly terms. Why, then, must this Nambi and Battar try to break each other's heads over them?"

This very reasonable explanation drew a round of laughter from the crowd.

"You seem sensible, at any rate," acknowledged the Battar. "But charming speeches will not serve to end this argument, you know. Tell me, young man, who is the greater god: Siva Peruman, or Thirumaal?"

"Both," was Vallavarayan's reply. "They're equals, and everyone is free to worship whomever they please. Why must we fight over them?"

"How dare you?" bristled Azhwarkkadiyaan. "What's the proof that they're equals, eh?"

"You want proof? Well, *that* I can offer in plenty. You see, I was a guest to Vishnu's divine abode Vaikuntham yesterday, and whom should I see there but Siva Peruman, also there on a visit! They seemed to be great friends. I saw them seated on similar thrones, side by side, and their height was exactly the same. Still, I didn't want to entertain any doubts and decided to verify it myself. I used my arm as a measure—"

"Boy—how dare you make a mockery of us!" Azhwarkkadiyaan fairly growled.

"Go on *Thambi*, go on!" cheered the crowd enthusiastically.

"—and found that my measurements were accurate; they *were* of the same height. But I didn't stop there, and decided to clarify the issue once and for all, and asked them, Which of you is the greatest? Do you know what they said?

"Sivan and Vishnu are like as peas in a pod,
If anyone disbelieves this,
Fill their silly mouths with mud!"

They didn't stop with that. If anyone was stupid enough to still fight over them, they gave me this, and ordered me to throw it in their mouths!" Vandhiyathevan opened his right fist. In it was a handful of earth—which he flung out.

The crowd went into a frenzy at once: people began to scoop up and fling handfuls of mud at the Nambi and the Battar. Some tried to prevent them from descending to such vulgar antics.

"Ha, scoundrels! Unbelievers!" shouted Azhwarkkadiyaan, ploughing into the crowds. "Infidels!"

The scene seemed ripe for a full-fledged riot—but something occurred, thankfully, to put a stop to the mayhem.

"Make way! Make way!" announced a voice in stentorian tones. "Warrior among Warriors, the Most Valiant Udaiyar who broke the ranks of Pandiyas and beheaded Maara Pandiyan; He Who Sports Sixty-four Scars from Twenty-four Battlefields; the Treasurer of the Chozha Empire and the Guardian of their Granaries; the Lord Who Levies Taxes; the Most Illustrious and Noble Periya Pazhuvettarayar comes among us! *Parak! Parak!* Make way!"

Once the *kattiyakkaran's* thunderous voice died away, the sounds of a *murasu* took over, its loud beats echoing around, followed by those who bore the Pazhuvoor standard, the palm-tree flag. Warriors bearing spears marched upon the heels of these men.

And finally, in the wake of such pomp and glory appeared the warrior himself; a dark man, proud of bearing and majesty in every glance, seated atop a richly decorated elephant. It was a sight for sore eyes, akin to a dark cloud nestling atop a craggy, jagged cliff.

The jostling crowd parted obediently to let him pass; Vandhiyathevan followed suit, craning his neck to catch a glimpse of the warrior. There was no doubt that it was Periya Pazhuvettarayar himself.

A palanquin covered with silk-screens followed upon the heels of the elephant. Vandhiyathevan felt a prick of curiosity about its occupant— but before he went any further, two things happened.

A slender hand, tinted a delicate shade of ivory appeared from within the palanquin. It pushed away the silk-screen slightly, bangles clinking melodiously.

A dazzlingly beautiful young woman's face appeared from behind the screen—like a radiant, pearly moon from behind a dark, rain-laden cloud.

Now Vandhiyathevan was not, in the usual way, averse to womenfolk, or impervious to the charms of a pretty face. The opposite in fact, was true. The lady he saw possessed a brilliant complexion and sculpted features; she shone like a golden, full moon, in the velvety night sky.

And yet—Vandhiyathevan's heart did not leap for joy at this undoubtedly ravishing countenance. Instead, he was conscious of a vague fear; an indefinable disgust.

The lady's eyes alighted on something by his side; her eyes narrowed as she stared hard. The next instant, a horrifying *Screech*! could be heard— and the palanquin's silk-screen fell back into place.

Vandhiyathevan glanced all around; his instinct warned him that she had shrieked at something she saw, in his vicinity.

It was then that he caught sight of Azhwarkkadiyaan Nambi, a little behind him—leaning against a tamarind tree. The staunch Vaishnavite's face was almost unrecognizable, distorted with fury and hatred.

Vandhiyathevan stared at him, astonished and somehow, repulsed.

3

The Vinnagara Temple

They say that life is an unpredictable journey that surprises one at every turn. That trivial incidents are often the catalysts to significant, life-altering events that turn the world upside down.

Such an experience occurred to Vandhiyathevan, at that moment.

He had been staring, slack-jawed, at the Pazhuvettarayar procession as it wound its way through the crowd; his horse had been standing just a little further away.

The last of Pazhuvettarayar's cavalcade, marching behind their mates, caught sight of it. "*Adei*," exclaimed one. "Look at that *kurudhai*!"

"That's a horse, not a mule, dimwit," corrected another.

An acid comment intercepted them. "Will you two scholars kindly set aside grammar lessons and find out if that animal is a horse or an ass?"

"Now *this* is a mission more to my liking," agreed a third. He promptly set off towards the steed and attempted to clamber on its back.

That intelligent animal, realizing instinctively, that the newcomer was not his master, shook him off. It flounced away, obviously distressed.

"Well, well, would you believe the temper of this one!" chuckled the soldier who had taken a tumble to the ground. "The mule won't let me mount. It's a respectable animal, you see—wants a member of an ancient royal clan for its master." He appeared to ponder this deeply. "In that case, no one less than a prince of the Thanjavur Mutharayar dynasty would do!" he quipped—and the soldiers around him cackled appreciatively.

There was reason for their derisive laughter: the Mutharayar dynasty of Thanjavur had been crushed out of existence a hundred years ago; the Chozha Empire's tiger flag fluttered triumphantly, in its place.

"Who cares what the horse thinks?" put in one. "I'd say that our Thandavaraayan right here is a thousand times better than some descendent of long-dead Thanjavur Mutharayars!"

"Thandavaraayaa, you'd better make sure this animal really is a horse and not a false-legged prop for the temple festivities," mocked another soldier. "After all, it refused to let you mount, didn't it?"

"An excellent idea," agreed Thandavaraayan, and proceeded to put this to the test. He approached the horse and this time, caught its tail—giving it a vicious twist. That much-afflicted animal decided enough was enough, kicked its hind legs three or four times, and galloped away.

"Ah, look at it run! It really is a mule, then—how wrong we were!" yelled the soldiers, carried away by what was, to them, a hilarious sight. They whistled and screeched "*Ui! Ui!*" and crashed behind the horse as it stumbled through the festival crowd.

People milling about tried to get away from the terrified animal as it ploughed through them. Most managed to escape, but some were still caught under its thundering hooves, and suffered injuries. The horse galloped on, meanwhile, maddened out of its senses.

All of this had happened in moments, before Vandhiyathevan could gather himself and take any action. Azhwarkkadiyaan, who had caught sight of the young man's expression, guessed that the stallion was his.

"Saw the antics of those Pazhuvoor oafs, *Thambi*?" His voice was suave. "Why couldn't you teach them the lesson you promised me?"

The smoothly delivered taunt found its mark; Vandhiyathevan's face turned crimson with fury. He grit his teeth, however, and forced himself to keep calm. The Pazhuvoor men had turned out in full force; there was no point in trying to take on hundreds of them in a fight. They had not stayed behind to look for a quarrel with the horse's owner either, marching away after cackling at the animal for a while.

Vandhiyathevan chose, instead, to go after his stallion, which had slowed to a stop after a while. He had not been much worried about it; the horse was well-trained, he knew, and would not wander away too far. No, what he was itching to do was teach those arrogant Pazhuvoor idiots a lesson—but now was not the time. He would have to wait.

The horse had come to a halt in a tamarind grove, away from the milling throngs. Sorrow practically dripped off its drooping mien, and it neighed a little when Vandhiyathevan approached. *Why did you leave me alone, among those louts?* It seemed to ask, and Vandhiyathevan applied himself to the task of soothing its lacerated nerves. He patted its back, and managed to calm it down enough to walk it back to the thoroughfare. The crowd caught sight of him, and impaled him with criticism. "Why did you bring this unruly animal to the festivities, boy?" They complained. "Look at the number of innocent people who have suffered its kicks!"

Others were slightly more charitable. "Not the poor boy's fault at all. What could he do? What could the horse do, for that matter? It was just the mad, vulgar antics of those Pazhuvoor men."

Azhwarkkadiyaan stood waiting as Vandhiyathevan returned with the horse, and the young man's face narrowed with irritation. *Why won't this quarrelling idiot leave me alone?*

"What's your direction, *Thambi*?" asked the Vaishnavite.

"Er—ah—well, I fully intend to travel to the west and then turn south and then, perhaps, take a stroll to the east and double back to the south-west," Vandhiyathevan rattled off.

"That wasn't what I meant. Where do you intend to stay, tonight?"

"Why do you wish to know?"

"If you were, perhaps, intending to lodge at the Kadambur Sambuvaraiyar Palace, I have a commission for you."

"Well! Are you an expert in the black arts or magic? How on earth did *you* know where I was headed?"

"Hardly something that warrants the expertise of a magician. Dozens of visitors will arrive today from all over the country, and stay at the palace."

"Is that so?" murmured Vandhiyathevan, surprise colouring his voice.

"Indeed. Don't tell me you didn't know this—to whom else could the palanquin, royal umbrellas, elephants, horses, drums, conches and trumpets belong, but the Kadambur royal family? They were here to welcome and escort Pazhuvettarayar to the Palace. He would expect, and settle for nothing less."

This was news indeed. Opportunities to stay in the same place as Chozha Nadu's greatest warrior would not be easy to come by; who knew? He might even chance upon a God-given excuse to actually meet him, and introduce himself, perhaps. All this was highly tempting—but recent experience with Pazhuvettarayar's brutes had soured his expectations, a little.

Lost in reverie, Vandhiyathevan came to himself at Azhwarkkadiyaan's voice.

"*Thambi*—will you do me a favour?" Azhwarkkadiyaan's tone was filled with pleading.

"What sort of favour could I offer you? I'm a stranger to these parts, myself."

"I wouldn't ask you anything beyond your means. Take me to the Kadambur palace with you, tonight."

"Whatever for? Do you expect to meet a Saivite, there? Perhaps you're eager to debate with him about the respective merits of Siva and Thirumaal?"

"Of course not. Did you really think I picked quarrels for a living?

See, my lad, the palace will resound with celebrations tonight—they are sure to hold an enormous feast which will be followed by *kaliyaattam*, *saamiyattam*, a delightful *kuravai koothu*, dances and songs. I've never seen a *koothu*—and this would be a perfect chance."

"Be that as it may—how would *I* be able to escort you?"

"You could introduce me as your servant."

Every suspicion that Vandhiyathevan had entertained some time ago returned in full force, and grew in strength. "Look, you'd better play off your petty tricks on someone else. I'm not the man to fall for them. The last thing I want is someone like you as my servant—and who do you think will believe such a thing? No one would, even if I were stupid enough to take you with me. Besides, judging by everything you say—I doubt if even *I* will find a place to stay there, tonight."

"Then—you're not traveling to Kadambur by invitation?"

"I am, in a way. Sambuvaraiyar's son Kandan Maaravel is a very dear friend of mine, and has often insisted that I visit him if I'm ever in these parts."

"Is *that* all? You won't find it an easy circumstance to enter the palace tonight, then!"

They walked together in silence, for a while.

"Why do you follow me?" asked Vandhiyathevan, finally.

"I could ask you the same thing. Why don't you go your own way?"

"Because I don't know my way around, of course. Nambi, do you go to Kadambur, as well?"

"No—you've refused to take me along, haven't you? I'm on my way to the Vinnagara temple."

"To the Veera Narayana Perumal Temple, you mean?"

"Yes."

"I would like to visit, too."

"Would you, now? I wondered if you might object to entering Vishnu temples. This one has an excellent history and is worthy of worship, as well. There's a Battar, a priest here, by name Eswara Munigal, who serves at the temple. A great man, indeed."

"I've heard of him too—but the shrine's so crowded today! Is it some sort of auspicious occasion?"

"Of course—today is the birth star of the lady Andal, one among the twelve Azhwars, the chief of Thirumaal's devotees. And then, it's *Aadi Perukku* as well, which explains the teeming crowds. Hardly surprising, is it?" Azhwarkkadiyaan changed tack. "*Thambi,* have you ever listened to any of Andal's songs?"

"No."

"Don't. Never, never make even the attempt!"

"Why this hatred?"

"I cherish neither hatred nor loathing for her *pasurams*—all I wanted was to warn you about their fatal charm. My lad, if you ever had the misfortune of listening to her exquisite poems, you'd throw away your spear and sword; swear off your military lifestyle and wander away on a pilgrimage through all the *Vinnagara* temples in the land!"

"Do you know any? Can you sing them?"

"A few. I've learnt some of Nammazhwar's divine verses as well. I intend to sing them at the temple; you may listen, if you wish," answered Nambi. "Ah, here we are!"

And, in truth, they had arrived at the Veera Narayanapura Temple.

—

Paranthaka Chozhar the First, the grandson of Vijayalaya Chozhar, carried the magnificent title of "The *Kopparakesari* Who Conquered Madurai and Eezham" —and it was he who laid the foundations for the empire, the Chozha kingdom would later become. Paranthakar was also the bearer of other, grand titles: he it was who had fitted Thillai Chitrambalam, or the Chidambaram temple with a golden roof; he possessed the titles of *Chozha Sigamani, Soora Sigamani* among others— not to mention Veera Narayanan, as well.

The Rashtrakuta kings of the Rettai Mandalam kingdom in the north wielded considerable power during his time; Paranthakar suspected that they might cherish designs on the Chozha territories as well and stationed his firstborn, Prince Rajadithyar, in the Thirumunaippaadi country, with a large army at his disposal.

Rajadithyar was loath to let hundreds of thousands of warriors lounge about with nothing to do, and hit upon a plan: they would work towards something that benefited a large swathe of the local population. Well aware that copious amounts of water overflowed the banks of the Vada Kaveri, or Kollidam and drained into the sea with no use to anyone, he made arrangements for his men to dig a massive lake, to collect it. He named it the Veera Narayana Eri in honour of his beloved father, and raised a *Vinnagara* Temple, as well—it was common for Vishnu Temples or Vishnu Grihas, to be known in Thamizh as *Vinnagaram*, in those days.

Thirumaal, or to address Him by another name, Sriman Narayanan Murthy was the Protector, the Supreme Guardian of all life as he lay on his snake-bed, in a sea of milk. It was only appropriate that temples in his name were often raised on the banks of lakes; this was also the reason for the presence of the Veera Narayana Temple, on the banks of this one, too.

Azhwarkkadiyaan and Vandhiyathevan entered the sacred precincts of such a hoary temple; once they approached the sanctum, the Vaishnavite cleared his voice, and began to sing. He worked through a few of Andal's divine *pasurams* or songs, and finally touched upon Nammazhwar's work, commonly referred to as the *Thamizh Vedham*:

"*Poliga poliga poliga*
Poyitru valluyir chaabam
Naliyum naragamum naindha
Namanukingu yaathonrumillai
Kaliyum kedum kandu kolmin
Kadal vannan boothangal manmel
Maliyap pugundhu isai paadi

Aadi uzhi tharak kandom!
Kandom kandom kandom
Kannukkiniyana kandom
Thondeer elleerum vaareer
Thozhuthu thozhuthu ninraarthum
Vandaar thannan thuzhaayaan
Maadhavan boothangal manmel
Pandaan paadi ninraadip
Parandhu thirigindranavae!

[*Behold, behold, the shining grace of the Lord who redeems us of our curses; Behold the light that banishes the darkness of hell; that releases us from the yoke of death; the age of kali is at an end, and those who worship Lord Vishnu will rise again, upon this earth; sing and dance, to glory! Behold, behold, the sight that gladdens our hearts; to see the prayers of His servants rise to reach Him; we, who sing His praises are lost in the ecstasy of His grace, as bees drunk on the nectar of His thulasi garland!*]

Tears gathered in Azhwarkkadiyaan's eyes, rolling slowly down his cheeks as he gave himself up to the beauty of the divine. Vandhiyathevan listened carefully as well, and though he shed none, his heart melted at the simple beauty and pure emotions that were their essence.

His sentiments towards Azhwarkkadiyaan underwent a change, as well. *This man*, he thought, *is a true servant of God.*

Others besides the young man, immersed themselves in the songs: the *mudhalimaar*, the temple authorities lost themselves in it, as did the priest, Eswara Battar, who stood by the sanctorum, tears brimming in his eyes. By him stood a fresh-faced youngster, his attention entirely on the singing Vaishnavite.

Azhwarkkadiyaan sang ten *pasurams* with the utmost feeling, and finished with one more:

"*Kalivayal thennan kurugoor*
Kaari maaran sadagopan

Oli pugazh aayirathu ippathum
Ullathai maasarukkume!"

[*Sing these songs, devout ones, composed by Kari Mara Sadagopan of Kurugoor in the divine lord's honour—and thy heart will be cleansed of every blemish!*]

When he finished, the youngster leant towards his father and whispered something into his ears. The Battar, who had bent down, straightened and wiped his eyes. "*Ayya*, hasn't the revered Nammazhwar, Sadagopan of Kurugoor sung a thousand songs in praise of our Lord? Do you know them all?"

"This servant hasn't had that good fortune," answered Nambi. "I am acquainted with a few, though."

"Pray, teach this youngster of mine whatever you know," requested the Battar.

—

Veera Narayanapuram was to be honoured with a great many more accolades in the coming years: the young Battar's son who now stands beside his father, listening to the chaste *pasurams* of Nammazhwar, his face a picture of innocence and the radiance of youth, would grow up to become Naadamunigal, the first and most illustrious of many Vaishnava Acharyas; later, he would journey to Kurugoor, also known as Azhwar Thirunagari, and gather all thousand of Nammazhwar's beautiful verses, adding even more acclaim to the great devotee who had composed the *Thamizh Vedham*. Naadamunigal's many disciples would painstakingly catalogue these verses, memorize them, and sing them all over the country.

His noble work would not stop there: Naadamunigal's grandson Alavandhaar would lead a life rich with destiny and far more miraculous events than even his grandfather.

More praise would pour in: Udayavar Sri Ramanujar himself would visit this, the birthplace of such greatness, and stare in astonishment at the Veera Narayanapuram Lake and its seventy-four gushing canals. He would ponder upon the endless grace and compassion of Thirumaal who showered his blessings upon his devotees, just as the canals that poured water into the lake. This would lead the saint to conceive of setting up seventy-four Acharya *peedams* or Vaishnavite centres for devotees; these would, one day, lead to the establishment of seventy-four *Simmasanadhipathigal* or Vaishnavite leaders, who would dispense knowledge and grace to devotees in their turn, and begin a rich tradition that would continue over centuries.

But such things do not come under the purview of this tale; we shall let the richly compiled tomes of *Vaishnava Guru Parambarai* to recount their lives, and return to Vandhiyathevan.

Once they had completed their worship and walked out of the temple, the Vaanar warrior turned to Azhwarkkadiyaan. "Nambi, I must beg your forgiveness. I had no idea that you were such a devout man, or that you were so well learned. You won't hold my ignorant words against me, will you?"

"By all means, you have my forgiveness, but tell me—will you do me a favour?"

"I said that I couldn't do what you wanted—and you agreed, didn't you?"

"Ah, but what I wish you to do now is something else altogether. I shall give you a tiny note. Should you have the opportunity to stay in the Kadambur palace tonight, you must deliver it into the hands of a certain person."

"Oh? To whom?"

"The woman who followed Pazhuvettarayar, in her closed palanquin."

"Nambi, what sort of a man do you take me for? Do I really seem like the kind that delivers notes to women? Had it been anyone but you who asked this of me—"

"If you're unwilling, *Thambi*, leave, by all means. There's absolutely no need to fly into a passion. The thing is—if you'd helped me with this, I might have lent you my assistance at some point. Never mind."

Vandhiyathevan lingered no more. He leapt on his horse and galloped towards Kadambur.

4

The Kadambur Palace

The many minutes of repose seemed to have done Vandhiyathevan's horse plenty of good; the young man set an excellent pace and reached the entrance of Kadambur Sambuvaraiyar's Palace within a *naazhigai*'s time.

Many were the leaders of ancient clans that wielded authority under the banner of the imperial Chozhas; Sengannar Sambuvaraiyar was one among them. The entrance to his palace rivaled that of a city's massive gates; the walls that rose beside them resembled a thick and unyielding fortress *madhil* as they wound their way on both sides.

The entrance was teeming with activity. Elephants, horses and bulls stood cheek by jowl while their trainers jostled for space with those who brought water for steeds; men who held aloft torches to see by in the fading light, and those who poured oil for said torches. The place reverberated with enthusiastic exclamations and celebratory shouts.

Vandhiyathevan paused before entering the clearing, hesitation and a hint of despondence in his heart. Obviously, he had arrived in the midst of revelry—and this was not, he felt, a circumstance in his favour. And yet, he felt a keen desire to know the cause for the festivities. The gates did stand open, but were guarded by armoured soldiers who held swords and spears in readiness. Tell the truth, they looked more like demons in death's abode than mere men.

Hesitation would serve no purpose, decided our valiant young man; he would be sure to be noticed, and stopped at once. No, riding full tilt at the soldiers and dashing through was the only way in. To think was to do, in Vandhiyathevan's book—and he suited thoughts to action.

But ah—what a disappointment! The moment he reached the entrance, two of the sentries barred his way, crossing their long spears. Four more grabbed hold of his horse's reins. One of them craned his neck and stared at the intruder; another raised his oil-torch against the young man's face for better visibility.

"So!" Vandhiyathevan's voice rang with fury. "This is how you treat your esteemed guests, is it? Is this your idea of hospitality?"

"And who might you be, *Thambi*, with such an unruly tongue in your head?" queried the sentry.

"You wish to know *my* name and designation? You may have them!" bellowed Vandhiyathevan. "Vaanagappadi is my country; I claim Thiruvallam as my city. Once upon a time, your men took pride in tattooing my valiant ancestors' names on their chests! I am called Vallavarayan Vandhiyathevan. Does that satisfy you?"

"How impressive!" exclaimed a guard. "Pray, why not bring along a *kattiyakkaaran* to bellow your titles before your arrival?"

The rest cackled in merriment.

"Whatever your title, you cannot enter the palace precincts at this hour," declared the Chief of Guards. "All our expected guests have arrived; our master has issued orders not allow anyone else!"

By this time, the altercation at the palace entrance had attracted attention; some of the guards who stood chatting just within the gates ambled forward to meet the feuding men. One of them directed a keen glance at the new arrival, and perked up. "*Adei*, this looks like the mule we chased from the temple grounds this evening!"

"Call it an ass, idiot," supplied a jester.

"Ah, my friends—do but take note of the proud bearing of the noble ass's owner!" declared another.

Even as Vandhiyathevan listened to these taunts, his mind spun through his options.

Was there even a point in braving these men and entering the palace? Wouldn't a better purpose be served if he just turned away at this point?

Perhaps he ought to just pull out and display Prince Aditha Karikalar's royal insignia to these idiots. That would certainly shut them up. Who, after all, would dare to stop a man who bore the emblem of the Commander-in-Chief of the Northern Chozha Armed Forces? Surely no one from Vada Pennai to Kumari, the tip of Thamizhagam, would dare to even think of such a thing!

The last of the Pazhuvoor men's heckling fell on his ears as he thought this—and he came to a swift decision.

"Let go of the reins; I'm leaving," he announced, and the soldiers released him.

Vandhiyathevan pressed his heels into the underbelly of his steed; at that very instant, he unsheathed his sword with a hiss, from his scabbard. The flickering lights caught the metal; he swung the weapon with such force and dexterity that for a moment he resembled Thirumaal, wielding the divine discus with supreme confidence.

The sword cut through the air with finesse. Vandhiyathevan's horse sprang through the gates. Soldiers standing on either side sprawled on the ground in an ungainly fashion. A dozen spears, supposed to be held in readiness, clattered to the earth, wholesale.

The Pazhuvoor men stood gaping as the horse bounded forward. A lightning-fast counter-attack was the last thing on their minds and when it seemed likely that their skulls would be broken, they scattered in every direction.

Other events happened at almost the same time: the fort's enormous gates banged shut—shouts rang all over the entrance— "Get him! Now!" Metal bruised metal as spears were picked up; swords were unsheathed, and the *Clang*! *Clang*! of weaponry rang through the courtyard. The Palace drums scented danger and banged their warning through the land: *Daddam*! *Daddam*!

Twenty, thirty, fifty soldiers surrounded Vandhiyathevan and his horse in an instant; the young man lost no time and jumped down at once.

"Kandamaaraa!" he yelled, brandishing his gleaming sword in a wide arc. "Kandamaaraa! Your soldiers are murdering me!"

The converging men stopped and fell back, suddenly hesitant.

"Stop this instant!" A stentorian voice thundered above them, from the upper balconies of the Palace. "What is all the commotion down there?" A few men could be seen in the vicinity of the voice, peering down at the palace entrance.

"Master—a man has just broken through the guards, into the palace grounds," explained a soldier from below. "He mentions the name of our Young Master!"

"Kandamaaraa!" bellowed that stentorian voice, again. "Get down and see what the uproar is about!" That bellow, Vandhiyathevan speculated, probably belonged to Sengannar Sambuvaraiyar.

He and the men surrounding him stood in place, for the next few minutes.

"What's happening here?" came a considerably youthful voice. The men promptly stepped aside and made way. A young man strode swiftly through the ranks and stopped at the extraordinary sight, taken aback.

Vandhiyathevan stood in the midst of the soldiers, twirling his sword like the valiant lord Subramanya, brandishing his divine weapon.

"Good God, my dear man—is it really you?" And Kandamaaran almost ran forward, folding his arms around the warrior in a crushing embrace.

"You've insisted time and again that I visit you, but when I finally do—look at the hero's welcome I get," Vandhiyathevan pointed at the men still surrounding them.

"Thick as posts and just as intelligent," Kandamaaran chided them. "Get lost, you idiots!"

—

Kandamaaran lost no time in grasping his friend's hands, and dragging him through the entrance, into the palace. His feet barely seemed to touch the ground; his heart fairly danced with enthusiasm as he rushed about, eager to point out the sights.

Such, after all, is the case when one finds a friend after his own heart, in one's early years. Oh yes, there *was* such a thing as romance— but love, even if it brought ecstasy, also came with its fair share of trials, tribulations and heart-aches. But the friendship of youth—ah, nothing existed then but joy and happiness; not even the shadow of sorrow intruded upon it.

"By the way, Kandamaaraa," Vandhiyathevan began, casually, as they raced along. "I see the palace overflowing with guests and their entourage—what seems to be the special occasion? Why this security and guards all over the place?"

"I'll come to that in a minute, but first—remember our days at the military encampment on the River Pennai? You'd go on and on about how you wished to meet Pazhuvettarayar, Mazhavarayar, that warrior, and this one—now you can see them all, right down to their staff, bodyguards and every stick and stone they own. Right here, in this palace!" Kandamaaran exulted.

The first place he took his friend to, when the first ecstasies of meeting were done with, was the section of the palace reserved for esteemed visitors. But before that, came the host.

"*Appa*, haven't I mentioned often my dearest friend, Vandhiyathevan of the Vaanar clan? Well, here he is," announced Kandamaaran, standing the young man in front of his father. Vandhiyathevan, true to his birth and breeding, bent low and folded his hands in respect.

For some reason, Sambuvaraiyar did not seem very happy with his presence. "Is that so? Were you the reason for all the mayhem below?"

"No—our so-called soldiers were," Kandamaaran explained.

"Indeed?" Sambuvaraiyar raised an eyebrow. "If you must know, Kandamaaraa, I see no reason for your friend's arrival half a *jaamam* after sunset, today—and in such a chaotic fashion too."

Kandamaaran's face grew pinched, but it was obvious that he did not want to argue with his father. He took his friend aside and made haste to present him to Pazhuvettarayar, seated majestically in a richly decorated throne in the midst of them all. "Uncle, here is my dear friend Vandhiyathevan, descended from the illustrious Vaanar dynasty. We served together on the border, in the military encampment on the banks of the River Pennai. It's been his greatest ambition to meet you, Warrior among Warriors, for long time. I remember; he'd ask me if you really did sport sixty-four battle-scars on your body," laughed Kandamaaran. "And I'd often reply, Well, if you're really that doubtful, you could count them yourself!"

"Indeed, *Thambi*?" Pazhuvettarayar looked him up and down. "So, you don't believe that my scars do exist? Or is it your contention, perhaps, that no clan but the Vaanars is capable of possessing such courage?"

The friends stared at him, aghast. Neither had intended the words as anything but extravagant praise—and it had never occurred to them that the warrior would take offense.

Vandhiyathevan felt irritation burgeoning within him, but quelled it before his face revealed it. "*Ayya*, the Pazhuvettarayars' fame has spread through the length and breadth of our land, from Imayam to the tip of Kumari," he said, in his most respectful voice. "Who am I to entertain the slightest doubts about their valour?"

"Not bad at all," Pazhuvettarayar acknowledged. "You do possess brains, I see."

There was nothing more to be said; Vandhiyathevan and Kandamaaran made their escape, more relieved than they could say. Sambuvaraiyar took his son aside at the first opportunity. "You had better feed your precious friend and put him to bed somewhere out of everyone's way," he whispered. "He is bound to be exhausted after a long day's travel."

Maaravel nodded roughly, plainly furious.

Later, Kandamaaran shepherded his friend to the *anthappuram*, the ladies' quarters, where the women of the royal household were assembled in full force. Vandhiyathevan paid his respects here too, falling at the feet of his friend's mother and gaining her blessings. The young woman standing well behind the older lady, overcome by shyness must have been, Vandhiyathevan guessed, Kandamaaran's sister.

The Kadambur prince had described his young sister in such glowing terms that she had, in his over-active imagination, acquired the status of nothing less than a goddess. Now that he had seen her in person, Vandhiyathevan was conscious of some disappointment.

His eyes roved over the women present, gazing keenly at them. Which of them, he wondered, was the woman who had followed Pazhuvettarayar in her palanquin?

જી

Hidden Meanings and Explanations

Imayam: The Himalayas.

"Ungal arivu ulakkaik kozhundhudhaan!"

The phrases Kalki used to describe his characters and move the story along are almost as interesting as the story themselves. He wrote *Ponniyin Selvan* in the 1950s, which means that many of the *Thamizh* phrases he used then are out-of-fashion, today. Take, for instance, the phrase Kandamaaran uses in Thamizh, when he's telling off his stupid soldiers: *"Muttalgala! Ungal arivu ulakkai kozhundhudhaan!"* An *ulakkai* is a wooden cudgel bound by iron on both ends to pound grains; there's no chance of it coming alive, or sprouting leaves. The soldiers' intelligence was much the same—non-existent.

5

THE KURAVAI KOOTHU

The friends had strolled out of the *anthappuram* when a feminine voice reached them. "Kandamaaraa! Kandamaaraa!"

"That's my mother—wait a while here, will you?" and Kandamaaran vanished within the ladies' quarters again. Vandhiyathevan, left to cool his heels in the corridor, could not help but listen to the muffled sounds of women throwing a barrage of questions at his friend, who stammered and stuttered his answers. A burst of tinkling laughter assaulted him, as well.

Perhaps they were laughing at him, Vandhiyathevan wondered, and felt his face grow hot with shame and anger. But there was no more time to be wasted on such thoughts; Kandamaaran re-appeared that very instant. "Come on," he grabbed his friend's hands and dragged him away. "There's a great deal I must show you!"

While they made a duly thorough inspection of such grand sights as the Kadambur Palace's moonlit courtyards, dance and music halls, large granaries, marble terraces, beautifully carved alcoves and balconies, towers, commemorative plaques, *kalasams* and royal stables, Vandhiyathevan put forth his question as nonchalantly as he could. "The ladies seemed to be very merry when you left me to answer their questions—were they so very overjoyed at my arrival?"

"They certainly were happy to see you—my mother and the rest liked you very well. But you weren't the reason for their laughter—"

"Oh? Who, then?"

"You know, don't you, that Pazhuvettarayar has married a young woman after all these years, at this advanced age? He's brought her here with him in a closed palanquin—but listen to this: he won't send her to the women's quarters! He chooses, instead, to keep her locked up in his own apartment. One of our maids happened to catch sight of her as she peeped into their rooms through the *palagani*, and described her in such glowing terms that no one knows what to make of it. They're now speculating about her birth and identity—maybe she's from Ilankai, Kalingam or perhaps even the Chera kingdom! You're aware, I suppose, that the Pazhuvettarayars originally hail from those parts?"

"Of course; you told me so, yourself," Vandhiyathevan waved a careless hand. "Be that as it may—how long has it been since the old man married this mysterious beauty from who-knows-where?"

"Not more than two years, I should think. Rumour has it that he doesn't leave her alone for a moment; takes his beloved lady with him in a palanquin wherever he goes. People have been trading gossip about his marital escapades for quite a while now. What else do you expect when a man of his age and standing gives in to temptation and stoops to spending all hours with a young girl?"

"That's no reason for such widespread talk about old men and their predilection for young women; shall I tell you the truth about such gossip? Women, my dear Kandamaaraa, are jealous creatures. I'm not putting down your family—merely commenting about their nature, in general. Kadambur's royal ladies are dark-complexioned beauties; Pazhuvettarayar's young wife is a golden nymph, with skin like a delicately tinted lotus! Hardly surprising, is it, that they should comment about her in such terms—"

"Golden—but how on earth would *you* know? Have you seen her, then? Where, and when? If Pazhuvettarayar ever caught wind of it, you'd be dead in moments—"

"You know me, Kandamaaraa—I'm hardly the man to be terrified about such things. In any case, it wasn't what you think. I was part of the crowd at Veera Narayanapuram, watching the Pazhuvettarayar cavalcade as it passed by me. By the way, I did hear that the elephants, horses, palanquins, *parivattams* and everything else were part of your welcoming committee—"

"True enough. What of it?"

"What, indeed? I merely compared his magnificent entry, with mine –"

Kandamaaran chuckled appreciatively. "We gave Pazhuvettarayar the welcome due to the Empire's Treasurer—while you, as a warrior staunch and true, deserved something a little more spontaneous, shall we say? If, by Muruga Peruman's grace, you should happen to become something more—such as the Kadambur royal family's son-in-law, for instance— you'll find that your welcome changes entirely!" He paused. "But you were about to speak of something else, weren't you? How did you ever know that Pazhuvettarayar's beautiful wife was a golden nymph?"

"Ha, there I was, gaping at Pazhuvettarayar as he passed me by, majestically seated on his elephant—truth be told, Kandamaaraa, he seemed more like Yamadharman on his terrifying black bull—and lost in daydreams about how, one day, I should like to ascend to his height. A closed palanquin followed him. I was wondering about its occupant, when a slender hand crept out and pushed away its silk-screen a little, allowing me a glimpse of a golden face. And that was all I saw. From what you've been telling me now, she would seem to be his young wife."

"You're a lucky man, my friend. Word is that no man has ever managed to catch the smallest glimpse of her—but you saw an arm and her face, didn't you? What country did she seem to be from, did you think?"

"I'll confess that I didn't really bend my mind to it, at that moment. From what little I saw, though, I wonder if she might be from Kashmir? Or one of those lands beyond the seas, such as Saavakam, Kadaaram, Misiram—or even Greece? Perhaps she's from the Arab lands? I've heard tales that they cover their women from head to toe the moment they're born—"

From far away, the sound of instrumental music fell on their ears. The beats and notes of *Salli, Karadi, Parai, Udukku* and a flute blended together as they reached the friends.

"What's happening?" asked Vandhiyathevan.

"It looks like the *Kuravai Koothu* is about to begin—they're playing the prelude, I think. What's your pleasure? Would you like to watch? Or prefer to have your meal and make an early night of it?"

Azhwarkkadiyaan's enthusiastic words about the celebrations at Kadambur, that night, echoed in Vandhiyathevan's ears. His mind was made up in an instant. "I've never seen a *Kuravai Koothu*, Kandamaaraa—I should like to, now."

The friends turned a corner in the long corridor, to find the glory of a stage set for the performance in front of them. And in truth, they were just in time: spectators had begun to arrive.

The stage for the *Kuravai Koothu* was set in the midst of a vast space, a white-sand strewn courtyard, enclosed on one side by the palace and the fort's thick walls on the other. Drawings of roosters, peacocks and swans were set up on the stage at appropriate positions; various colourful decorations consisting of puffed rice from roasted red grains, glossy red and black *kunrimani* beads, fragrant flowers and turmeric-smeared *thinai* rice were sprinkled liberally. Large lamps or *kuthuvilakkus* and oil-torches burnt bright in an effort to dispel the encroaching the darkness—but smoke belched by said torches and the fog-like density of various incenses like *akhil* dimmed the light, producing a dramatic effect. Musicians had seated themselves in front and by the sides of the stage, and begun their performance with alacrity.

The thunderous beats, scented flowers and aromatic incense wended their way into Vandhiyathevan's brain and for a moment, the world seemed to spin.

Once the chief guests arrived, there was no more reason to tarry. Nine women gathered on the stage, prepared to begin their performance. In accordance with the *Koothu* tradition of those times, they wore garments moulded to their figures and jewellery that set off their charms to perfection. *Silambu* anklets clinked on their feet; their tresses fairly glowed with red flowers such as *kanni, kadamba, kaandhal, kurinji* and *sevvalari*—all blooms set to gladden Muruga Peruman's heart. In addition to wearing them, they had woven the flowers into a long garland as well, and themselves into it. Some held parrots in their hands gracefully, fashioned from sandalwood and painted in a riot of colours.

They paid their respects to the gathered audience; the *Koothu* began in earnest.

The women sang songs in praise of Muruga Peruman, his courage, the valour that led to confront demons such as Soorapadman and Gajamugan; the stirring tales of his battles against them; the enormity of the divine power he wielded that vaporized entire seas and oceans, and his complete annihilation of evil forces. They spoke of his beauty, his many attractive charms, his compassion, and of the celestial women who, themselves the epitome of beauty, yearned for the love of such a warrior; of Muruga's magnanimity in refusing the hands of such high-born damsels and journeying to the wild mountains of *Thamizhagam* where he wooed and won the heart of a simple tribal girl, who shooed birds as she guarded *thinai*.

The stories they told; the songs they sang, and their beautifully coordinated dances, not to mention the steady beats of the *parai* and the melodious notes of the flute, set pulses racing and nerves jangling in anticipation.

They finished, finally, with the age-old, traditional blessing:

"*Pasiyum piniyum pagaiyum azhiga!*
Mazhaiyum valamum dhanamum peruga!"

[*Woe to Famine, Disease and War! Welcome, welcome, to Rains, Wealth and Fortune!*]

Their departure was the sign for the next, and more important part of the *Koothu* to commence: the *Velanattam*, the dance of Velan. Accordingly, the principal players, the Devaralan and Devaratti, the male and female components of the dance, arrived on stage. True to the roles they were to act, each was dressed in blood-red garments and had twined gloriously red *sevvalari* flower garlands around them. Their foreheads were smeared thickly with red *kungumam*; their mouths glistened red with the juice of betel leaves and areca-nuts. Their eyes, when they cast them around the audience, glowed a bloodthirsty red.

It began, to tell the truth, in a subdued fashion; man and woman danced away on stage—by themselves, at times; in tandem, hands interwoven, at others. As the minutes went by, the crashing beats of instruments picked up pace—and their dance turned turbulent, reverberating with emotion. The Devaratti danced to a corner of the stage and picked up a spear; the Devaralan pranced to her and did his best to wrest the weapon from her. The Devaratti protested and tried to fend him off; the Devaralan, after a prolonged effort, finally grew tired of her refusal and delivered a mighty leap that set the stage quaking. He grabbed the spear from his mate, upon which the Devaratti crept away from the stage, as though trembling in fear at the sight.

The Devaralan grasped the spear and began to dance; a dance that grew in frenzy and mad, mad energy by the moment. A dance of annihilation, of destruction, that razed down the pride and arrogance of the demon Soorapadman and his evil cohorts. Velan hacked away each of the demon's heads but—lo and behold—they simply grew back! The more they did, the more did Velan's wrath boil over. His fury reached enormous proportions; his eyes spit sparks of fire. And finally, the demon lay dead at his hands. The spear dropped from the Devaralan's nerveless fingers.

Suddenly, every instrument stopped its agitated performance; none but the *udukku* could be heard, rattled furiously by the head priest. The Devaralan quaked and shivered on stage; every pore in his body jangled with a sparking energy that seemed to fire up the nerve-endings in his brain.

"The *Sannadham!*" whispered his audience, comprehending his state as almost God-like, filled with the power of divine perception, and the ability to foretell the future. "It is time!"

And indeed, so it seemed, as the priest rattled his *udukku* with more energy than ever. Presently, he focused his attention on the quivering Devaralan: "Vela! Muruga! Commander of the Divine Armies!" he entreated. "Kandha! Destroyer of the Demon Soora! Grant us your pearls of wisdom! Give us knowledge of what is to happen!"

"What do you wish to know?" growled the Devaralan, shaking in the grip of the *Sannadham*. "Tell me!"

"Will the rains come on time? Will our lands never lack wealth and water?" asked the priest. "Shall the empire flourish? Would all our desires be fulfilled?"

"The rains shall come! The land shall flourish! All your desires shall be fulfilled! But you—you have failed—failed to satisfy my Mother—failed to worship Her! You have not given Her Heart's desire!" shrieked the Devaralan, caught in the grip of other-worldly power. "She asks for blood—my Mother, the fearsome Goddess Durga, Mother Kali wishes for a sacrifice! She Who Guards the World, the Supreme Goddess Chandikeswari, who vanquished Mahishasuran wants a sacrifice!"

"What kind of a sacrifice?" asked the priest.

"Are you prepared to offer what She wishes?" The Devaralan shook and quivered in frenzy. "Will you give what Her Heart craves?"

"We will; we will!" yelled the priest.

"Blood! The blood of kings!" The Devaralan screamed, catastrophe colouring his voice. "My Mother craves the blood of a royal dynasty that spans a thousand years!"

Firelight cast strange, vaguely terrifying shadows on the faces of Pazhuvettarayar, Mazhavarayar, Sambuvaraiyar and other dignitaries, seated directly across the stage. They glanced at each other upon the Devaralan's startling words; their bloodshot eyes, already swimming with the mad fervour of the evening's events, traded furtive glances.

Sambuvaraiyar directed a quick look at the priest and gave a barely perceptible nod.

The *udukku* stopped, abruptly. The Devaralan, shaking on the stage, dropped like a felled tree. The Devaratti ran up, managed to scoop him into her arms and made a hasty exit. The audience dispersed in silence.

Somewhere, far away, jackals howled into the night.

Vandhiyathevan, whose nerves were almost as jittery as anyone else's, what with the excitement of the *Koothu* and its attendant emotions, pricked his ears at the animals' inhuman howls. His eyes strayed almost involuntarily, to the fortress walls.

Azhwarkkadiyaan's head rested there.

Vandhiyathevan almost jumped out of his skin, horrified. His skin broke out in goose-pimples; the hairs on his neck rose, prickling in terror. It looked as though—as though—someone had cut off Nambi's head and stuck it on the wall!

He blinked and stared at the fortress wall again—to find it empty.

Vandhiyathevan shook his head, ashamed at his morbid fancy. Nameless fears and conjectures filled his heart; he could not find it in himself to shake them off.

ॐ

Hidden Meanings and Explanations

Parivattam

An ancient honour usually conferred by tying a richly decorated turban upon the recipient's head. The roots of this custom lie in the fact that these were conferred upon lords and other privileged men, often during ceremonial affairs. These days, one can see the custom followed during elaborate temple festivities.

6

A Meeting at Midnight

A royal banquet was on the agenda once the *Kuravai Koothu* and Devaralan's frantic dance came to an end; the Sambuvaraiyar clan well-nigh outdid itself.

Vandhiyathevan, sitting down to the feast, found that the food turned to ashes in his mouth. None of the dishes spread out for the guests' edification delighted him. His body was exhausted; he felt a mixture of worry, confusion and a vague disquiet that he was hard put to explain. Still, he could hardly ignore his friend, and listened with a very creditable assumption of enthusiasm as Kandamaaran who, brimming with justifiable pride at the honoured guests, listed every single one of them.

Aside from Pazhuvettarayar and host Sambuvaraiyar, there was Mazhavarayar, known by his proud title of Mazhapadi Thennavan; Mummudi Pallavarayar was present as well. Kandamaaran took care to whisper about other renowned guests in Vandhiyathevan's ears, and point them out subtly: Thanthongi Kalingarayar; Vanangamudi Munaiyaraiyar, Devasenapathi Poovaraiyar, Anjaatha Singam, or the Lion-hearted Mutharaiyar, Rettai Kudai Rajaliyaar and even the Kolli Malai Peru Nila Velaar, amongst others.

None of these men could be termed ordinary in any sense of the word; it was no easy task to gather them under one roof, either. All were rulers of their own dominions, large or small as the case may be—or had earned the status of kingship through their valorous deeds and service to the country. The word "Raja" or "Arasar" had, by continuous usage, morphed into "Araiyar;" it was the norm in those days to refer to the chiefs of important clans, or those equal to such chiefs in stature, by that prestigious title—a nod to their ruling capabilities; sometimes, "Araiyar" was added to their respective seats, as well. In truth, these warriors were treated more as kings themselves rather than chieftains, or feudal lords.

Not for nothing were they awarded such privileges. Princes and kings born in royal families, lounging in luxury, and enjoying every comfort were not the only ones to be addressed with respect; their titles would serve no meaning if they could not defend themselves or their people.

The men assembled in Sambuvaraiyar's palace were all warriors of repute; sporting numerous scars on their battle-hardened bodies as evidence of distinguished war service. Each had proven himself, time and again, as capable of guarding his fort and country with his life, if necessary. All had pledged their unconditional support and submission to Pazhaiyarai city's Sundara Chozhar, ruling their territories under his suzerainty. Some occupied positions of great authority in the Empire as well, and carried out their respective duties in administrative or other capacities.

By rights, Vandhiyathevan's heart ought to have been leaping with wild joy at the sight of such august personages at the same banquet—but he felt not the slightest enthusiasm.

Why are so many of these kings gathered here, he wondered, more than once. *Why now?* Vague suspicions and conjectures cropped up in his mind, confounding him.

The sense of disquiet had not abated by the time he finished his meal and retired to the isolated space Kandamaaran had shown him to, for the night. Sambuvaraiyar's royal palace was swamped with esteemed guests; it meant that Vandhiyathevan was allotted a mere mandapam in one of the upper balconies, open to the elements.

"Sleep well—you must be exhausted. I'll join you here, once I've seen our other guests to their rooms," Kandamaaran assured him, before leaving.

—

Drowsiness assailed Vandhiyathevan the moment he set his head on the floor; Nithradevi swept him into her arms almost at once.

And yet—not even the Goddess of sleep can exercise much control over the mind. The body might be at rest; the eyes closed in repose, but thoughts that crawl in the subconscious choose these moments to reveal themselves. Dreams rise, shaking off the suppression of a conscious mind, looping unconnected thoughts, fears and experiences to form surprisingly disturbing pictures.

Far away, in the distance, a jackal began to bay. One multiplied into ten, hundred, and a thousand—raising their voices in a howl that made his skin prickle in terror. And that was not all; they were approaching him, step by excruciating step. In the deep, stifling dark, their little eyes smouldered in their faces like bright, red embers of burning coal.

There was only one way of escape; Vandhiyathevan turned in the opposite direction—and stopped abruptly. A thousand shrieking hounds accosted him, their sharp teeth practically dripping with the urge to tear him apart. Their eyes gleamed, spitting sparks of fury in the pitch blackness.

Vandhiyathevan shuddered, barely able to string a thought together as he contemplated his terrible fate, caught between slavering hounds on one side and a pack of jackals on the other. But then—oh, thank God, there appeared a temple almost in front of him. Vandhiyathevan shook off his terror, practically flew into it, and locked the doors behind him.

When he turned to finally take in his surroundings, he found that his refuge was a Kali temple. The fierce Goddess seemed to be at her terrifying best, teeth descending in fangs; tongue hanging out in bloodthirsty fashion. Before Vandhiyathevan could do little more than gape at the statue, a priest danced out from behind it. He gripped a fearsome scythe in his hands. "So—finally arrived, have you? Come here!" And he sidled closer—closer—closer to our young man. "You are a prince, are you not? Recite your family history!" he demanded. "How long did your ancestors rule? The truth—now!"

"The—the Vallavarayars of the Vaanar clan ruled for three hundred years," Vandhiyathevan stammered. "We lost our kingdom because of the Vaithumbarayars, in my father's time."

"You are not a sacrifice worthy of the Goddess," roared the priest. "Leave!"

Abruptly, Kali's form changed into that of Krishna. A couple of young women danced around the idol, garlands in their hands, and Andal's melodious *pasurams* on their lips. Vandhiyathevan almost smiled, mesmerized at this appealing performance, when he heard someone else singing behind him: *"Kandom, kandom, kandom ..."*

He turned and saw Azhwarkkadiyaan Nambi. No, not the man—but just his head, stuck on the temple's *bali peedam*!

Unable to stomach this truly hideous scene, Vandhiyathevan turned abruptly, and struck his head on a pillar. The misty wreaths of dreamscape dissolved—but he happened to see something else that seemed to bind the terrible strands of a nightmare with reality.

The Kadambur fort wall circled the palace at a little distance, and a head was stuck on it, directly opposite the balcony Vandhiyathevan lay in. And yes, it happened to belong to Azhwarkkadiyaan. This time, though, Vandhiyathevan was sure that the sight was neither a nightmare, nor the product of an over-active imagination: no matter how many times he blinked or shook himself, the head remained in place. It was equally obvious that this time, said head was attached to a stout body;

Nambi's fingers clutched the edges of the wall in a death-grip. His eyes were focused downwards, observing something below him.

What on earth was he watching, face furrowed with concentration? Something was terribly wrong here. Azhwarkkadiyaan could not have arrived out of the goodness of his heart; he had some nefarious intention tucked away; some evil plan in mind, Vandhiyathevan was sure.

And wasn't it his duty, as Kandamaaran's dearest friend, to save Kadambur from harm? What kind of a man was he to loll about in bed, when the people who had offered him such a magnificent feast were about to be wounded?

Vandhiyathevan sprang up, tucked his sheathed sword into his waistband, and began walking towards where he had seen Azhwarkkadiyaan's head.

His makeshift bed had been in a corner of an upper balcony, well away from passages in use; Vandhiyathevan had to pass through, skirt around and walk by a great many corridors, pillars, the tops of *mandapams*, benches and *sthubams*, to find his way to the fort wall.

He had been walking for a while along one such eternally meandering passage when he heard voices.

Vandhiyathevan paused. He tiptoed towards a pillar, concealed himself behind it, leant forward and gazed down.

Below him lay a narrow courtyard, enclosed on three sides by towering walls. Ten or twelve men were seated within. The fort wall, rising high, failed to let in the half-moon's pearly rays—but a strategically placed iron lamp managed to shed some light.

The courtyard's occupants were none other than Kadambur's esteemed guests; Vandhiyathevan had seen these men—kings, lords and officials of the Empire—at the banquet barely hours ago. Obviously, they had foregathered this late to discuss matters of great importance; Azhwarkkadiyaan was probably doing his best to eavesdrop on their conversation. His position was strategically advantageous; the fort and palace walls met in such a way that he could see the gathering below and listen to their speech, but the reverse was not true. Ah, Azhwarkkadiyaan was clever indeed—no doubt about it.

But he had reckoned without the Prince of Vallam, the valiant Vandhiyathevan! No one could palm their clever tricks off him, least of all this stout scoundrel! He would catch the wily Nambi by the scruff of his neck, stop him from spying on people, march him straight to his hosts and—but how?

He would have to jump into the courtyard and walk across it to get to Azhwarkkadiyaan—and he could hardly do so without attracting the attention of the warriors gathered. God knew there were dangers enough in attempting *that*.

Sambuvaraiyar's morose words, "I see no reason for your friend's arrival today!" echoed in his ears. These men, these pillars that upheld Chozha Nadu in every way, were keen on discussing gravely important matters of state; that they wished to do so in secret, was obvious from their location. His sudden arrival in their midst would rouse all their worst suspicions. It would be impossible to explain his real motives; Azhwarkkadiyaan would be long gone, by then. He, Vandhiyathevan, would be chastised as the spy; the one to suffer the ignominy of an interrogation. And, in truth, what possible answer could he give, should they ask him about his nocturnal wanderings? There would be only one possible outcome: Kandamaaran would be put to the blush. Ah, there he was, seated at the periphery of the crowd! He too, seemed to be a part of this discussion. No matter; Vandhiyathevan would ask him all about it, in the morning.

His attention wandered, at that moment, to a closed palanquin that sat towards one side. Ah, wasn't this the one that had followed Pazhuvettarayar on his way to Kadambur? The lady within—the one who had pulled aside the screen with her silken, golden hands—where was she, in this sprawling palace? Hadn't Kandamaaran mentioned that the old man didn't even dare leave her in the *anthappuram*? Ah, such was the case when men married so late in life—and it was a thousand times worse when the bride happened to be ravishingly beautiful. Men such as

Pazhuvettarayar were reduced to the pathetic state of dragging their wives along wherever they went; so tortured were they, by wild suspicion and doubts. Now here was this grand old warrior, reduced to the disgrace of being hopelessly infatuated by a pretty young woman; he was little better than a slave to her beauty. And she was no Rathi, Menakai or the celestial Rambhai, at any rate; Vandhiyathevan hadn't forgotten his revulsion when he'd caught sight of her. God knew what the great Pazhuvettarayar saw, in this supposed beauty. Even worse was Azhwarkkadiyaan's fascination with her; why else would he eavesdrop so desperately on this gathering, if not for the palanquin's presence?

But then, who knew what their relationship was, to each other? Perhaps they were siblings—or lovers? Had Pazhuvettarayar, perhaps, taken her by force? He was certainly capable of such cavalier treatment. If so, that would explain Azhwarkkadiyaan's preoccupation with the lady; possibly, he was seeking an opportunity to speak with her. Ah, what did any of this matter? Sleep beckoned; there was nothing to be gained by poking his nose into affairs that did not concern him.

Just as the young man decided that his bed looked more inviting by the moment, a stray word from the conversation below, reached him. Someone had mentioned his name.

Vandhiyathevan paused—and listened to the speech with all his ears.

"The young man who arrived today, claiming to be your son's friend—where has he been quartered? It is of the utmost importance that not a whisper of our conversation tonight reaches him. Remember, his master is the *Maathanda Naayakar* of the Northern Chozha Forces; the last thing we need is for word of our plans to leak. Should any of us suspect that boy of the slightest knowledge of our meeting—make sure that he does not leave this fort. In fact, it would be better if he is silenced, once and for all …"

Our readers may well imagine Vandhiyathevan's sentiments, upon this speech. He decided, then and there, that he was going nowhere, and settled down to listen to the rest. Aditha Karikalar happened to be the

Commander-in-Chief of the Northern Chozha Forces; the firstborn of King Sundara Chozhar and heir apparent to the Empire. What was their objection to Vandhiyathevan's serving under him? And what were they discussing, that the crown prince could not know of, at any cost?

"Vandhiyathevan is fast asleep in a balcony above-stairs," Kandamaaran's voice floated up to him, defending his friend. "Not a word of our conversation is bound to reach him. He isn't the kind that pokes his nose into business that doesn't concern him, anyway. Even if he should get wind of our meeting, somehow, I'll make sure that he doesn't prove a hindrance to your plans. You may rest easy—he's my responsibility."

"Such faith in your friend, Kandamaaraa! —touching indeed. For your sake, I am glad of it; we know nothing of him, after all. These warnings are necessary; we are about to speak on a supremely confidential subject; one that will decide the fate of this very Empire. Our purpose in gathering here is to discuss the succession to the Chozha throne. Remember—the slightest whisper of our meeting would end in disastrous consequences for all of us!" warned Pazhuvettarayar.

கை

Hidden Meanings and Explanations

Bali Peedam

A slab of rounded stone, sometimes carved around the sides and placed in front of the sanctum sanctorum of the temple. Originally intended for sacrifices in times long gone, the practice was discontinued. These days it is used more for offerings, or rice.

7

OF MIRTH— AND CONSEQUENCES

The moment he heard the words "succession to the throne," Vandhiyathevan decided that he would listen to the entire conversation. What were these men about to discuss regarding the succession? What right did they have to do so, anyway? No, his duty was clear: he would have to do some eavesdropping himself, and there was no better place for it than his current location. Azhwarkkadiyaan could go hang himself; who cared what became of him?

Something was about to happen here: something mysterious and disquieting enough to ruffle the realm, if possible. For quite some time now, Vandhiyathevan had been plagued by the niggling suspicion that the Kadambur Palace was the nerve-centre of strange happenings: Azhwarkkadiyaan's odd little speeches; the palace sentries' heavy-handedness; Sambuvaraiyar's belligerent welcome— if, indeed, it could be called that—the Devaralan's frenzied call for sacrifice … all of these had sparked a discomfort in him that could not be alleviated. Now here was a God-given opportunity to rid himself of conjectures, and find out exactly what was happening. Why on earth would he waste it?

Ah, not even his beloved Kandamaaran could find it in himself to confide about the evening's activities—here he was at this clandestine meeting, having persuaded his friend to sleep in an isolated balcony! Vandhiyathevan would be sure to give him a piece of his mind, tomorrow.

By this time, Pazhuvettarayar had begun to speak; the Vaanar warrior concentrated on every word.

"My purpose in journeying here is to give you news of great import; it is also the reason for why Sambuvaraiyar has gathered us all. King Sundara Chozhar's state of health is extremely precarious. I have made enquiries of the royal physicians; they are all decided in their opinion: there is not much hope—his days are numbered." Pazhuvettarayar paused. "It behooves us now, to come to a decision on a future course of action."

"What do the astrologers say?" came a voice from the midst of the gathering.

"Why consult them about this?" put in someone else. "Haven't we all seen a comet late at night, for a while now?"

"The astrologers' prognosis is merely to postpone the inevitable by a few weeks," answered Pazhuvettarayar. "Whatever the outcome, it is upon us to decide the heir to the Chozha throne—"

"What would be the use of contemplating such a thing?" asked a hoarse voice. "Aditha Karikalar was announced Crown Prince more than two years ago, was he not?"

"True—but I should like to know which of us, if any, were consulted before such a peremptory decision was taken. All of us here have pledged body and soul to the Chozha dynasty for more than a hundred years; our clans go back centuries, and have been in service to the Empire for more than four generations. My great grandfather sacrificed his life in the Thiruppurambiyam battle; my grandfather in the conflict at Velur; my father in the battle at Thakkolam. Everyone here has lost a valued family member, our sons even, guarding this Empire—today, the war raging in

Eezham has our youngsters standing shoulder to shoulder, destroying our foes. And yet—none of us were asked for our opinions when it came to choosing the successor to the throne. You will recall that even King Dasarathar called for a council to choose the Crown Prince for Ayodhya; he sent for his ministers, commanders, aides, generals and feudal lords, convened a *mandhiralosanai* and made sure their concerns were heard. Sundara Chozha Maharaja, on the other hand—"

"... may not have asked our advice, it is true—but our illustrious Treasurer is not quite correct to presume that *none* were consulted. After all, Periya Piratti, the noble Sembian Mahadevi, and Ilaiya Piratti, the honourable Kundhavai Devi were both taken into his confidence, were they not?" asked a faintly mocking voice. "Can Pazhuvettarayar honestly claim, now, that Sundara Chozhar made an arbitrary decision about his heir?"

A wave of mirth flowed over the audience.

"Ah, you laugh! —*how* you can find it in yourself to be amused at this pathetic situation, I shall never quite understand. My heart burns, my blood boils; I am moved to wonder at the purpose of my pitiful existence on earth! The Devaralan demanded the sacrifice of a royal whose dynasty has flourished a thousand years—do me a favour, all of you, and offer *me* up to Durga! My clan has made Chozha Nadu its home for more than a thousand years; you may all cleave my head from my body with your swords; the Goddess is bound to be pleased with my blood—and my soul will find some measure of peace!"

Pazhuvettarayar came to a stop, finally, chest heaving, voice shaking with as much frenzied emotion as the possessed Devaralan that evening.

Silence reigned for a while. The west wind whirred through the courtyard. Trees outside the fort swung madly in the stiff breeze, their branches rustling and whispering against the fort walls.

"The King of Pazhuvoor must pardon our thoughtless speeches and laughter—ridicule was very far from our minds; such was not our intention. You are our peerless leader, and each one of us here is willing to deem your smallest wish, our command," supplicated Sambuvaraiyar, at his humblest. "Yours is the right to lead us; yours is the path we seek to follow. Pray accept our apologies, my lord."

"I beg your pardon as well, for having lost my temper. Do, but listen: this time, a hundred years ago, Vijayalaya Chozhar reduced the Mutharayar dynasty to dust and captured Thanjavur; he ranged himself on the side of the Pallavas and destroyed the Pandiyan armies in the Thiruppurambiyam Battle. Ever since, the Chozha Empire has grown by leaps and bounds—I doubt if it possessed the territories it does today, in the times of great Emperor Karikalar, who raised the banks of the Kaveri. Today, our magnificent *samrajyam* stretches from the tip of the Kumari, to the banks of the River Thungabhadhra and Krishna. We have Pandiya Nadu, Naanjil Nadu, Thondai Mandalam, Paagi Nadu, Gangapadi, Nulambampadi, Vaithumbar Nadu, Seetpuli Nadu, Perumpaanappadi, Kudagu Nadu, the birthplace of Kaveri, paying tributes as our vassals. Even Chera Nadu, which has a history of never submitting to others, acknowledges our suzerainty. Our glorious tiger flag flutters in all these countries, proclaiming our superiority; by rights, Eezham in the south, Vengi and Rettai Mandalam in the North ought to have fallen to their knees, before our onslaught. As to why they have not—surely my friends here are aware of the reasons?"

"Indeed. There are only two: one is Aditha Karikalar, the *Maathanda Naayakar* of the Northern Chozha Forces; the other is his young brother, the Commander of the Southern Armies, Arulmozhi Varmar—"

"Mazhavarayar speaks the truth. All the kings I knew favoured time-honoured methods of choosing their generals or commanders; warriors who had excelled in wars and sported their scars proudly, with years of experience at their backs were usually deemed most suitable to lead armies; such was the custom in our Empire too, for the last hundred years. But now—now, we have the Crown Prince, quartered with vast armies in the North, supposed to reap victories against Vengi and Rettai Mandalam—and what does he do, instead? Squats on his hind-quarters in Kanchi, building a palace of gold. I ask you, respected members of this gathering, scions of *Thamizhagam*'s oldest and most valiant families— which of the rulers of this land has ever built himself a golden palace?

Not even Paranthaka Chakravarthy who vanquished Madurai, Eezham, and now resides in resplendent glory in the heavenly abode of *Kailasam*, ever wished such an extravagant residence for himself. What he did accomplish, was to present the Chidambaram Temple with a roof of gold. But witness, if you please, the lofty aims of our revered Crown Prince! Apparently, the hoary palaces of the Pallava Emperors are not quite suited to the status of the heir to the throne; he builds a palace of gold and embeds diamonds and precious stones into its walls! Not a single measly copper coin of the treasures he carried away from Nulambampadi, Gangapadi or Kudagu has made it back to the Chozha royal treasury—"

"The Golden Palace is complete, then?"

"I have reliable information from my spies that work is, indeed, at an end. Sundara Chozhar has received quite a few missives from our Prince as well. Apparently, his beloved and dutiful firstborn wishes his father to reside in his obscenely opulent edifice, for a while."

"Is the Maharaja to stay in Kanchi?" asked a worried voice.

"Never fear. My trusted brother and I, together, shall make sure that such an eventuality will never come to pass. None can enter the Thanjai fort without our express approval, seek an audience with the King or present any kind of *olai* to him. I have, in fact, made sure that two or three such palm-leaves have been successfully intercepted."

"Ah! Long live Pazhuvettarayar! Praise be to his strategies!" rose several voices in a shout. "May his valour rise to greater heights! Truly, you are a Chanakya among us!"

"There is more, my friends. If you thought the Crown Prince off his royal mind—wait until you listen to the antics of Prince Arulmozhi Varmar, sent to fight in Ilankai. Reflect, if you please, on the methods of waging war: on our own experiences thus far and on traditions that have been in place for a hundred years. Should we ever march into an enemy's lands, our armies seize what food they can from the surrounding areas; our rewards are the loot plundered from their treasuries—and they are the chief source of payment to our soldiers. The surplus must be transferred to the royal treasury in the capital. But listen to Prince

Arulmozhi Varmar's high-flown sentiments, if you please: he believes that plundering conquered land is a despicable act, and wishes for food to be sent from *Thamizhagam!* The good God above knows that I have sent more than ten shipments of grains and pulses—"

"What idiocy is this!" "Such foolishness!" rose outraged voices. "Such things have never been heard of!" "Why must we put up with this injustice?"

"Do but listen to Arulmozhi Varmar's odd explanation for his outlandish conduct: he refuses to seize local sources as that would lead to discontent and misery among the populace. Our battle, he believes, is with Eezham's rulers; the people should not be made to suffer for his sake. Once he has vanquished them and their armies, he would much prefer to secure their approval and happiness, before he establishes his rule over them!"

"I have seen and heard many unnatural things in battle, but to acquire the goodwill of the people about to be invaded ..." mumbled one member of the gathering, disbelief evident in his voice. "What does he wish us to do—fall at their feet?"

"Witness the result of these hare-brained tactics: both our princes have ensured that the treasury and granaries are almost empty. And I am placed in the uncomfortable position of heaping taxes on you, to make good the deficit! Such is my duty, after all—and if it were not for the fact that the Empire's fate weighs heavily on my conscience, I would have resigned this revolting post years ago!"

"Never—never! The Pazhuvoor King is the only reason the Empire has not crumbled into dust, by now; your iron will and conscience ensures our protection. But have you not sought an audience with the King, regarding such pressing concerns?"

"A thousand times have I tried—only to be repulsed categorically. Should I ever require His Majesty's advice, I am, if you please, supposed to bow down to the superior guidance of Periya Piratti or Ilaiya Piratti! I tell you, the King has lost the will or ability to think for himself—at no moment does he seek our opinions in vital matters. His beloved Sembian

Mahadevi stands in the role of a mentor; her words are as holy as the Vedhas, to him. That, or he wishes us to seek the opinion of his beloved daughter Kundhavai—he believes her understanding to be most superior, and capable of addressing all our concerns. I! —I and other ministers who have grown grey in our service, are expected to stand at attention in front of this chit of a girl—a sheltered girl whose dainty feet have not stepped beyond Kollidam in the North and River Kudamurutti in the South—and beg her precious indulgence! Have you ever heard of women being allowed such free rein in matters of state, in any kingdom? How long do you expect me to bear such insult to my name and fame? But there is a way out: you could come to a unanimous decision and demand my resignation; I should be very glad indeed to free myself from these stupid affairs, and consign myself to my home—"

"Never! The Pazhuvoor King must not even think to utter such terrible words," Sambuvaraiyar called out. "The Chozha Empire stands today on the shoulders of thousands of warriors, strengthened by the blood of four generations of our men; nothing will induce us to see it ground into dust in our lifetime!"

"My friends and compatriots—I rest my case," finished Pazhuvettarayar. "Our Empire is now governed by females; we have a veritable *Alli Rajyam* on our hands. How do we rectify this terrible state of affairs?" He paused. "What do we do?"

Hidden Meanings and Explanations

Kudagu

Today's Coorg, in Karnataka

Alli Rajyam

Said to be a legend in the Mahabharata, Alli was a Pandiyan queen who harboured such hatred for men that every single official in her kingdom, administrative or otherwise, was a woman. Men, it is said, were little more than playthings in her rule and she treated them with contempt – until, of course, her nemesis arrived in the form of Arjuna, the most macho of the Pandava brothers, who subjugated her and "made her a true woman." The tale was all the rage, re-told in street-plays and theatres among the general populace; the "*Alli Kadhai*," and "*Alli Arasaani Maalai*" were and are, popular folk versions.

Eezham, Ilankai

Today's Sri Lanka

8

"Who is in the Palanquin?"

A confused babble of voices arose from the men gathered in the courtyard, as everyone seemed to speak at once. Discussions, opinions and arguments erupted in a dozen corners and for a while, Vandhiyathevan was hard put to understand a single word or recognize the man who uttered it.

Sambuvaraiyar, who seemed to come to his senses first, spoke up. "Aren't we required to furnish Pazhuvettarayar with some sort of answer?" His voice rang in strident tones around the courtyard. "What is the purpose of arguing endlessly amongst ourselves? The night is into its third *jaamam* as it is; the moon swims in the night sky. We must come to a decision—quickly."

"I am plagued, if you will pardon me, with a doubt. Perhaps others harbour the same sentiments as I," came the hoarse voice that had spoken earlier. "Should the Lord of Pazhuvoor not object, I should like to voice it and seek clarification."

"It is Vanangamudiyaar who speaks, is it not?" said Pazhuvettarayar, in a tone that brooked no argument. "Let him rise and come to the light."

"It is I, indeed. And here I am."

"I reserve my fury for battlefields and enemies—not those I consider my allies and friends. You may speak your mind without any scruple."

"I believe I will. The King of Pazhuvoor lists certain crimes against King Sundara Chozha Maharaja, but is it not true that some level the same charges against Pazhuvettarayar, as well?" asked Vanangamudiyaar. "I do not say I believe it—indeed, I do not—but I should like to know the truth, in any case."

"Pray, enlighten me: what is the truth that you wish to know?"

"This assembly is well aware of the fact that the Lord of Pazhuvoor married a young woman a few years ago—"

Sambuvaraiyar's voice cut in at this point, burning with anger. "This is outrageous—I am sure I speak for everyone here when I say that we object to Vanangamudiyaar's tactless comment. To address our peerless leader in such a way—to level such an accusation against our general, our leader who has our best interests at heart is akin to blasphemy! In short—"

"Much as I appreciate the sentiment, I entreat Sambuvaraiyar to remain patient, and allow Vanangamudiyaar to ask his questions. There is nothing more poisonous than a mind riddled with suspicion; far better to lance the boil and relieve oneself of unending doubts. I did, at the late age of fifty-five and more years, marry a young woman—I admit this with no qualms whatsoever. But when, my friends, have I ever declared myself an incarnation of Lord Rama, in this Kali Yuga? Neither have I claimed to be an *Ekapathni Viradhan*; bound to one wife. I fell in love with her and she with me; we found our hearts united, and wedded each other according to ancient Thamizh customs. Pray, is this a crime?"

"No—not at all!" rose several voices in unison.

"It was never my intention to accuse you of matrimony, My Lord. Who, amongst us, has bound himself to merely one wife, after all? And yet—yet—"

"Yes? There is no reason to hesitate. Ask what you will."

"There is talk that Pazhuvettarayar listens far too much to his young queen, the Ilaiya Rani. Worse—that he consults her even regarding affairs of state and royalty. That he takes her with him where he goes."

A mocking cackle erupted in the crowd.

"Stop!" Sambuvaraiyar sprang up again, voice shaking with fury. "Who dared to laugh, just now? Show yourself! What gives you the right to jeer at our leader?" He unsheathed his sword, almost growling.

"If it is any consolation, it was I," admitted Pazhuvettarayar. Then, he turned to Vanangamudiyaar. "Tell me—is it such a crime to take my lawfully wedded wife, who bears my *thaali* around her neck, wherever I go? It is true that I rarely stay away from her—but to accuse me of consulting her regarding state affairs is unjust. I have not done so, and never will."

"If that be the case, I pray that Pazhuvettarayar answers just one more question—and I shall pronounce myself satisfied. What does a closed palanquin, meant to stay within the walls of an *anthappuram*, do here? What is its place among those who are involved in discussing such serious matters as the succession? Is there anyone within? If not, whose are the bangles that clinked a while ago—or the throat that cleared itself?"

A strange, uneasy hush settled over the courtyard. Since everyone present had entertained Vanangamudiyaar's suspicions at one point or the other during the meeting, no ringing protest rose against him. Sambuvaraiyar's lips did, in fact, mumble a few words, but they were too indistinct for anyone to understand.

Pazhuvettarayar it was, who chose to cleave the stifling silence with his strong, confident voice. "An excellent question, and one that deserves an explanation. Be sure that I shall give it when this meeting is at an end. May I have half a *naazhigai* more? Surely my esteemed friends trust me enough to grant me this favour?"

"We do, we do!" exclaimed many voices. "We have complete faith in you!"

"I assure you that I cherish as much regard for Pazhuvettarayar, as anyone assembled here," explained Vanangamudiyaar. "I posed these questions only because he bade me clear my mind. I swear, here and now, that his every wish is my command, and I am prepared to do anything to carry it out. Should I be required to sacrifice my life in his service, so be it!"

"I have the greatest faith in Vanangamudiyaar's loyalty; in fact, I am aware of every one of your trustworthiness, and I cherish your regard. For that very reason, it becomes all the more important for us to remember why we chose to meet, and come to a decision about several important affairs. King Sundara Chozhar may live long and rule his Empire as he wishes—but we are here to consider the possibility that that rosy future may not come to pass. If the royal physicians were to be proven right—if the comet in the sky proves to be a portent omen—it behooves us to decide on the rightful successor to the Chozha throne."

"We request Pazhuvettarayar to give us his honoured opinion, on these matters. None of us would venture a word against yours."

"On the contrary—at no other time has it been so important for all of you to speak up, and inform me of your views. At this juncture, I should like to take the opportunity to remind ourselves of certain events in the past. Twenty four years ago, the great warrior, saint and pious ruler, King Kandaradhithar ascended the heavenly abode; his son, Madhuranthaka Thevar was a mere infant, a year old, at that time. It was for this reason that Kandaradhithar wished to place his brother Arinjaya Thevar on the Chozha throne and rule after him; we were informed of his sentiments by his devoted wife, Empress Sembian Maadevi. And it was loyalty to our king that made us agree to such an arrangement. Unfortunately, cruel destiny did not allow Arinjayar to rule for more than a year. His son Paranthaka Sundara Chozhar was a strapping young man of twenty years; we, the empire's pillars, the ministers, aides, chieftains, lords, *kottam* and *kootram* officials gathered, discussed the best interests of the country, and crowned him king. There is no doubt that this was an excellent decision; until two years ago, Sundara Chozhar gave us no cause to doubt his rule. He consulted us upon royal matters and events prospered as ever before. Now however, his health is deteriorating—and that circumstance leaves us with certain questions. Kandaradhithar's honoured son, Madhuranthaka Thevar is now an extremely capable prince; his piety, accomplishments, intelligence and character make him an eligible contender for the throne. In the meanwhile, Aditha Karikalar, Sundara Chozhar's firstborn is stationed in Kanchi as the Commander of the Northern Chozha Forces. My friends—who, among these two men, is worthy of being the heir? I ask you to consider royal tradition and practice, thus far; to consult what *Manu Needhi* tells us. What, according to the dictates of fairness and justice, would be your decision? Would you choose Madhuranthaka Thevar, son of the elder Kandaradhithar? Or Aditha Karikalar, the grandson of the younger Arinjaya Chozhar? Think—think carefully; search your mind, and give me your opinion …"

"Kandaradhithar's son Madhuranthaka Thevar is the rightful heir to the throne," answered Sambuvaraiyar promptly. "That decision, my lord, is according to the dictates of justice, fairness, and righteousness."

"True!" "This is my decision as well," "I agree!" murmured the others, one by one.

"Your opinion is mine; the Chozha throne does, indeed, belong to Madhuranthaka Thevar. But such a decision, although easy to make, will entail enormous difficulty if it must be enforced. Tell me—is everyone here prepared to undergo any hardship, to make it so? Do we swear to sacrifice our body, soul and wealth in fighting for Madhuranthakar's rights, and to restore them to him? Do I have your assurance that you will all pledge yourselves to this noble cause at the sacred feet of Goddess Durga?" Pazhuvettarayar's voice fairly rang with a new fervour.

Silence descended on the gathering again.

"We are prepared to swear, in the presence of God, that we shall sacrifice anything to uphold Madhuranthaka Thevar's rights," Sambuvaraiyar, finally, spoke up. "All of us do wish, however, to ask you something before we do: what are the Prince's own sentiments? Is he prepared and willing to ascend the throne? Many are the tales of the piety of Kandaradhithar's son—that he takes no joy in worldly pleasures and devotes himself completely to the worship of Siva Peruman. We have heard, too, that nothing could be farther from his desire than to rule this empire. In addition, his mother Sembian Mahadevi does not wish it either. We should like to know the truth of such statements, if you please."

"An excellent question—asked at the right time too. I shall answer it in a way satisfactory to everyone. In point of fact, it ought to have been answered much before. I beg your pardon for not doing so," Pazhuvettarayar began, with a preamble. "The whole country knows that Sembian Mahadevi has done everything in her power to turn her son from thoughts of the throne and towards worship of the divine. What neither the country, nor its people know, are her reasons for doing so. Should it ever become known that Madhuranthakar wished to ascend the throne, Periya Piratti feared that such knowledge would put a period to his existence—"

"Ah! Is that so?" exclaimed several voices.

"Indeed. Any mother worth the title would wish her son alive and uncrowned, rather than see him rule and be assassinated. Madhuranthaka Thevar, to whom his mother's words are as sacred as the Vedhas, duly devoted himself completely to God, spurned all worldly pleasures and spent his time in worship of Siva Peruman. For some time, though, his sentiments have been undergoing a steady change. He has begun to feel that he has a right to ascend the throne, and to wish to govern the country in the best way possible. He is prepared to voice his sentiments in public, once he is secure in the knowledge of your fealty to him—"

"And what is the proof of this?"

"Certainly, I am prepared to provide as much and more proof, as you wish. But if I do—will you all swear to pledge yourselves to his cause and rule?"

"We will! We will!" The gathering assented vociferously.

"I hope no one entertains any further doubts?"

"No, none at all!"

"In that case, there is no reason to delay—here is the proof you have all been waiting for. And I have an opportunity to clear Vanangamudiyaar's suspicions as well." Pazhuvettarayar rose, walked majestically towards the palanquin in a corner, and stopped beside it.

"My Prince—we require your presence amongst us," he said, in his humblest voice. "Do step out of the palanquin and cast your eyes on these warriors, these pillars of strength who are prepared to lay down their lives to uphold your noble cause!"

Vandhiyathevan, who had been listening to the courtyard conversation with all his ears from behind his pillar above-stairs, now leant forward carefully, and peered down.

A slender golden hand—the same, delicate, rose-leaf complexioned limb he had seen that evening—crept out of the palanquin, and gently pushed aside the screen. Except that, what he had believed to be a woman's bangle was in fact a *kanganam*, an ornament usually worn by princes. The next instant, that face, the one that resembled the golden fullness of a radiant moon, appeared from behind the screen. A man with a form that rivaled the beauty of Manmadhan himself stepped out, smiling at the warriors in the courtyard.

Ah—wasn't this Prince Madhuranthakar, the son of King Kandaradhithar? His presence within a palanquin had made Vandhiyathevan mistake him for a woman. He threw a swift glance at the fort wall—was Azhwarkkadiyaan, who had committed the same error, still eavesdropping on the scene?

Tree branches shadowed that section of the fort wall, however, and nothing could be seen.

By this time, the courtyard below was resounding with ferocious shouts and chants: "Long live Madhuranthaka Thevar! Long live the Crown Prince!" Men unsheathed their swords, raised their spears, and their voices to the heavens. "*Vetri vel! Veera vel!*"

To remain here anymore would lead to complications; Vandhiyathevan slipped away from the pillar, returned to his bed in the isolated balcony, and lay down.

ॐ

Hidden Meanings and Explanations

Manu Needhi

According to Hindu tradition, the one who is the at the head of mankind, and created a set of laws and rules, for humankind to live by.

Manmadhan

The god of love, and a celestial being who is, according to Hindu mythology, the most beautiful being ever to be seen on both heaven and earth.

Vetri vel; Veera vel

Literally, *May the Spear be Victorious*. An ancient war-cry which has its roots in the mythical battle waged by Lord Muruga against his demonic enemies, where he used his weapon, the spear, to great success.

9

CONVERSATIONS BY THE WAYSIDE

Much of Vandhiyathevan's life had been spent in the arid lands north of the River Paalaaru. Swimming in a river, therefore, was a skill unknown to him. Once, stationed as a sentry on the banks of the Vada Pennai, he had stepped into its swirling waters for a quick dip. Too late, he realized his mistake and ignorance in even attempting it: the wicked current grabbed hold and simply pulled him under. Vandhiyathevan thrashed round and round, limbs paralyzed by the sheer force of the water. Fatigue settled over him like a stifling blanket. Just as he decided that he was done for and the Vada Pennai was going to be his watery, unmarked grave—a sudden swirl caught him, and practically threw him out. Vandhiyathevan praised every deity he had ever heard of as he washed upon the shore in an exhausted heap, and made a miraculous escape.

Lying on his bed in a balcony of the Sambuvaraiyar palace that night, he was conscious of the same, helpless feeling—caught unawares in a crippling whirlpool. Except that this time, it was not a river—at least not in the literal sense—but an enormous, vicious royal conspiracy. Would he be able to escape this one's clutches the same way?

What he had learnt, eavesdropping on the meeting that night, almost overwhelmed him. It had been only a few years after all, since the Chozha empire shook off endless onslaughts from external factors; for a while now, its people had been able to breathe easy, unafraid of invasions. Crown Prince Aditha Karikalar was responsible a good deal for this state of affairs: a soldier through and through, an expert in war strategies, and almost a Chanakya when it came to battling enemies, he utilized Chozha armies and resources to their fullest, and released Thondai Mandalam completely from the shackles of Rettai Mandalam's King Krishna. That had taken care of foes from without.

What though, of the enemies who threatened the empire from within? Weren't they a great deal more dangerous? What would be the result of this battle that had erupted within Chozha factions?

Ah, weren't the *samrajyam*'s own warriors, ministers, lords and officials a part of this terrible conspiracy? The reputation, resources and power that the Pazhuvettarayar brothers commanded—was there anyone else, except perhaps the Maharaja, who could rival them? And what of the other kings and lords present? Each was powerful in his own right, lord of considerable territories and man-power. Not to mention their fame in battle, as well. Was this the first time they had gathered? Or had there been other clandestine meetings, with Madhuranthakar hiding away in closed palanquins? Ah, Pazhuvettarayar's marriage at such a late date *had* had its uses!

Until that evening, not the lightest doubt had invaded Vandhiyathevan's mind about the succession. Aditha Karikalar was the undisputed Crown Prince, the choice of both King and country; it had never occurred to him that there might be competition from other quarters. Like most citizens, he knew of Madhuranthakar of course, and had heard tales of Kandaradhithar's son immersing himself in worship and saintly pursuits. Not for an instant had he entertained the suspicion that Madhuranthakar might have an actual claim on the throne—or that he might consider himself a contender for it.

But—to quote someone in the meeting itself—what was right, as per the dictates of justice and fairness? Was Aditha Karikalar the lawful heir to the throne—or Madhuranthakar?

The more Vandhiyathevan mulled over it, the more did he feel that both claims had equal merit. If they did decide to contest each other's rights, who would win? And what would be his own position, if it came down to a pitched battle?

Ah, the dreams Vandhiyathevan had cherished when he first set out from Kanchi! The castles in air he had built, hoping to ascend to a great position in the empire under the aegis of the Crown Prince— why, at one point, he had even nurtured hopes of winning back the Vaanar's ancient kingdom, and restoring them to their former glory! And now—now the very branch he had chosen, to clamber onto a magnificent tree, seemed about to splinter.

Vandhiyathevan tossed and turned in his bed for a long time, plagued by doubts and conjectures. The fourth *jaamam* had arrived and with it dawn, when he finally succumbed to sleep a second time.

The result of all this was that he did not wake up early; not even when the sun's red-hot rays scorched him the next morning. It took Kandamaaran's good-natured slap to bring him to awareness; Vandhiyathevan jerked awake, startled out of his wits.

"Slept well?" enquired the Kadambur prince, after the usual practice of hosts. Then he volunteered, "I did come here late last night—but you were so immersed in your worship of Kumbakarnan that I didn't have the heart to disturb your penance," he grinned.

It took a great deal of forbearance for Vandhiyathevan to clamp down the words that bubbled up his throat, but he did. "I remember lying down here after the *Kuravai Koothu*, but nothing else. Ah, it looks like almost a *jaamam* has passed since daybreak—I must start at once. Kandamaaraa, do instruct your men to saddle my horse!"

"Well, here's a good one! What do you mean, you have to leave at once? There's no hurry; stay a while, perhaps ten days."

"I'm afraid I can't, my friend. I've had news that my uncle is in a very bad way, in Thanjavur—apparently, he's on his deathbed," Vandhiyathevan rattled off, perjuring his soul without a qualm. "I must set off at once if I ever hope to see him."

"In that case, you must promise to stop here, on your way back."

"By all means. Now, please let me take my leave."

"Such haste! Do but settle down for a while, until at least morning meal. I'd like to accompany you as far as the Kollidam."

"But—how can you? With so many important visitors vying for your attention—"

"No one here is more important to me than you –!" Kandamaaran bit his lip, and paused. "It's true that we're entertaining esteemed guests at the moment, but they have my father to play host and the palace officials, besides. I couldn't talk to you for even a while last night. I was hoping we might, on our way to the Kollidam. I shan't rest until we do— and I'm coming with you, no matter what!"

"I've no objection, in that case," Vandhiyathevan acquiesced. "Do as you please."

A *naazhigai* later saw the two friends canter off on their horses from Sambuvaraiyar's palace. Their pace was slow; the morning, mellow and peaceful. So engrossed were the young men in reminiscing their past that neither paid any attention to the rustling west wind, showering them with clouds of dust.

"I may have stayed at your palace just for a night, Kandamaaraa— but it's done me a world of good," Vandhiyathevan remarked casually, after a while. "I'm a little disappointed about just one thing, though. All those endless descriptions you gave of your sister's remarkable beauty on the banks of Vada Pennai—and I could barely catch a glimpse of her, last evening! All I could see when she peeped from behind her mother, was an eighth of her face. My friend, I'm frustrated! Thamizh girls ought to behave with decorum and a proper degree of bashfulness—but your sister has a little too much of them, I tell you!"

Kandamaaran's lips trembled with the urge to speak—but not a word came out.

"Never mind, though," Vandhiyathevan prattled on. "You've invited me to stay for a few days on my journey back home, after all. Be sure that I'll take every opportunity to remedy these shy silences! Your sister wouldn't think of hiding behind her mother's back when she's known me for a while, would she? By the way—what did you say her name was?"

"Manimekalai."

"Ah, a truly sweet name! Now, if she were only as pretty and good-humoured as her name suggests—"

Kandamaaran cut in, at this point. "My friend, I beg of you—forget my sister. Forget what I said about her as well. Don't ever bring her up, again!"

"Good God, this is a turnaround! What on earth happened to last evening's speeches about offering me a son-in-law's welcome?"

"I don't deny that I said a great many things—but do ignore them, for my sake. Things … have changed. My parents have decided to give her in marriage to someone else. Manimekalai has accepted, as well."

Well done, my girl, mused Vandhiyathevan. It did not seem difficult either, to guess the identity of the probable groom—who else but the royal Madhuranthakar, occupant of a closed palanquin, would do for them? It was obvious that they were garnering as many profitable alliances as they could, for the prince. Ha, Pazhuvettarayar's cunning surpassed all! "So you've decided on one of your royal guests as her husband? To tell the truth, Kandamara, I'm neither disappointed nor surprised. I expected something of the kind—"

"You did?"

"Think, my friend—an orphan is hardly the first choice for parents with hopeful daughters. I have neither home nor country; my ancestors may have ruled these parts once, but they've been dust on the ground for years. I'm not surprised that no girl wishes me for a husband—"

"Stop, please—! If you truly think I and my parents would descend to such lowly conduct—but we wouldn't. And it isn't what you think, either. There are reasons for our decision. You'll realize how important they were, soon enough. I'm afraid I can't say any more— but I hope to, some day."

"You're very mysterious all of a sudden, Kandamaaraa. What's happened?"

"Forgive me—I know I'm talking in riddles, but it can't be helped. Do believe me when I say that you're as much my friend now, as you were before. When it's time, you'll be the first person I shall open my heart to! Trust me to do the right thing until then. Know that I'll never betray you, whatever the cost."

"I'm happy to hear it—but I fail to see the point of all this talk of betrayal and trust. You do realize that I depend on my own sword and spear for my protection, and not others?"

"Soon, there will come a time when you'll need to use that very sword and spear in battle. And by God's grace, we will stand shoulder to shoulder on the same side, and who knows, your ambitions might be fulfilled as well—"

"Battle? Do you expect there to be one in the near future? Or were you, perhaps, intending to join the war in Eezham?"

"Eezham? Good God, you'd laugh to know the spectacle they're making of themselves, there! Do you know that Chozha forces require food and grains to be sent to them, from here? Ridiculous, is what I say— but that's not what I'm talking about. No, don't try to get anything more out of me. Stay patient; you'll know everything in due course."

"As you wish. You needn't tell me anything you don't want to," soothed Vandhiyathevan. "And there's the Kollidam, at last."

The river did indeed grow visible with every step; within moments, the friends had arrived on its banks.

The month of *Aadi* had arrived in a truly auspicious fashion; the river almost broke upon land as waters rushed by. So vast were the river's dimensions that trees on the other side looked like tiny bushes. Red-brown waters thundered past, swirling and dimpling, the currents causing deep whirlpools, frolicking on their eager way to join the sea in the east.

Vandhiyathevan stared at the sight, bewitched, listening to the floods trying to break the banks and the deafening sound of crashing water.

A boat bobbed alone in the ferry; two men stood in it as well, oars in their hands. They had a passenger already and by the looks of it, he seemed to be a man steeped in Siva worship.

One of the boatmen craned his neck and peered at the newcomers. "Master, would you be wishful of coming with us?"

"Not I, just him," answered Kandamaaran. "Wait a moment."

The friends descended from their steeds. Vandhiyathevan clucked his tongue in dismay. "Ah, what a fool I am—how will I get my horse into this boat?"

"Unnecessary—here are two men, behind us. One will take your horse back to Kadambur. The other will accompany you in the boat, and procure another for you on the opposite bank."

"Such forethought, Kandamaaraa! I'm impressed. You're a friend indeed."

"You might have believed the Kollidam to be along the lines of the smaller Paalaaru or Pennai, perhaps. It probably didn't occur to you that you couldn't just walk your horse across."

"Indeed. I crave pardon for having underestimated your Chozha country's magnificent rivers. Ha, would you just look at these thundering waters? Why, it seems more an ocean!"

It was time for farewell; the friends embraced each other warmly. Vandhiyathevan walked along the shore and climbed into the boat. One of Kandamaaran's men did so, as well. Everything appeared to be in readiness; the boatmen lowered their oars into the water.

Abruptly, a voice called out to them, from afar. "Stop! Stop the boat!"

The men paused in their rowing. The one who had shouted approached the banks, running helter-skelter. Vandhiyathevan recognized Azhwarkkadiyaan the moment he set eyes on the heaving, gasping figure.

It seemed his co-passenger had, as well. "Row, row away at once," he yelled. "I will not stay in this boat an instant if that Vaishnavite gets into it!"

Vandhiyathevan, though, would not hear of it. "Stay, if you please. There's plenty of space—we may as well take him along."

His motives were not all altruistic. In truth—he wanted, very much, to pick Nambi's brain about last night's mysterious happenings.

ॐ

Hidden Meanings and Explanations

Kumbakarnan

Younger brother of the Demon King Ravanan, Lord of Lanka. A giant known for his skills as a warrior, he had one great weakness: sleep. It was a Herculean task to wake him up and he was generally ravenous when he did, but his expertise in war more than made up for every lack. This predilection for sleep was, legend says, the result of a wrongly-worded wish: when, after prolonged penance, Brahma offered him a boon, Kumbakarnan asked for *Nidravatvam* (sleep), instead of *Nirdevatvam* (destruction of the Devas). This, it's said, was because of the intervention of Goddess Saraswathi, who scrambled his mind (and tongue, it appears). Unlike his many demon contemporaries, Kumbakarnan seemed to possess a conscience—he actually protested Sita's abduction, and advised his brother to restore her to Rama. His loyalty to his brother still won out, though; when Ravanan refused, Kumbakarnan went to war on his behalf, and was killed in battle.

To this date, anyone with a predilection for sleep is still teased with his name.

10

THE ASTROLOGER OF KUDANDHAI

Beautiful River Ponni claimed the Kudagu Mountains as her birth-place and spent her infancy trickling through its fastnesses. But time passed; she grew to womanhood, and the time came for her to join her beloved, the Ocean. She gurgled over rocks, flowed through forests, tumbled off hills and gushed into vales, her eagerness to reach her destination growing each moment. As she poured over the plains, it occurred to her that she was closer than ever to her loved one. Her heart trembled; she swelled with sheer delight. She went further—two limbs branched out from her, eager to embrace her lover. She leapt forward, hands stretched in front—but they simply seemed not enough. How could they, when such love overflowed in her heart? Her hands grew from two to ten, twenty, a hundred; she extended them all in a bid to touch Samundra Rajan, the Ocean King.

Ah, how the mothers of Chozha Nadu delighted in decking out their daughter, the bride, in nature's finery! They laid out lush, green sarees to wrap around herself; threw fragrant blossoms from every flowering tree they could find, and scattered breath-taking incense to welcome her arrival. The sight of *Punnai* and *Kadamba* trees lining her banks, showering the river nymph with their pearls and rubies—was there anything to ever equal it? Not even the divine blossoms of the Devas could compare!

Ponni! No maiden could fail to be captivated by your charms; no woman would fail to lose her heart, dazzled by your bridal finery! And it only natural, after all, that they surround you with laughter and delight when they set sight eyes on your magnificent beauty.

One of the slender golden limbs that Ponni reached out to embrace her consort, was the *Arisilaaru*. Tucked away to the south of the vast river, she flowed silently, concealed by a lush avenue of shady trees. Indeed, those approaching from afar rarely knew of her unless specifically informed. Hers was a sweet, shy presence; a princess leading a sheltered life in her *anthappuram* from birth, never to appear before strangers. There is nothing on this earth that can compare to the exquisite loveliness of this virginal maiden.

May our readers kindly tear themselves away from the lures of the *anthappuram*, and follow us between the dense trees on the banks, towards the *Arisilaaru*. Ah, what is this sight that greets us—sweeter than nectar, and adding charm to such divine beauty?

Who are these young women on a richly carved boat, shaped like a graceful swan? And who is the lady seated in the very midst of them? Ah, she is as a golden moon amidst twinkling stars, with the presence of one born to rule not just this land, but all the seven worlds! And who might be this tranquil young woman, seated by her with a *veenai* in her slender arms? Each of them, it seems, possess a feature that adds to their loveliness. One is a *meenalochani* with bewitching eyes; another is a *neelalochani*, her eyes an appealing blue-black. A third's face glows like a lotus in full bloom; a fourth's eyes are of a graceful shape that would put that very same lotus's petals to blush. As for the one who plays the *veenai*—one could spend days just watching her fingers, as delicate as the soft *kaanthal* flower, dance upon the instrument.

And what, indeed, of their charming songs! The river flows softly, listening to their merry voices; even parrots and nightingales nestling in trees on the banks have fallen silent in deference. It is no surprise, therefore, that humans, much more capable of appreciating such fine music, should lose themselves in ecstasy.

But what do they sing? Ah, here it is:

Marungu vandu sirandhu aarppa,
Manippu aadai athu porthu

Karungayarkkan vizhithu olgi
Nadanthai vaazhi Kaveri

Karungayarkkan vizhithu olgi
Nadantha ellaam ninkanavan

Thirunthu sengol valayamai
Arinthen vaazhi Kaveri

Poovarsolai mayilaadap
Purindhu kuyilkal isaipaada

Kaamarmaalai arugasaiya
Nadanthai vaazhi Kaveri

Kaamarmaalai arugasaiya
Nadantha ellaam ninkanavan

Naamavelin thiramkande
Arinthen vaazhi Kaveri!

Now where have we heard these charming words, before? Indeed, yes—they are verses from the *Silappathikaaram*, praising the divine Kaveri and her peerless beauty. And yet, sung by these young women, they possess an allure that holds listeners in thrall. They must be Ponni's beloved hand-maidens; no one else could sing about her with such fervour. The melody, expression and emotion that flow from their voices! But no, that is all nonsense. No one could possibly pick these songs apart and examine them for what makes them beautiful—it is sheer magic, sorcery that well nigh bewitches both singers and listeners!

The boat floats along the river, gradually sidles towards a gap in the trees, and stops at a landing. Two women step out; one is the majestic young lady we saw before, who possesses the aura of an Empress; the other is the one who played the *veenai* with delicate fingers. Both were beautiful—but in their own way, with classic features. One's face resembled a lotus in full bloom; the other had a countenance that was more akin a gentle *kumudha* flower. One had the radiance of a full moon; the other, the translucent beauty of the crescent moon at dawn. One looked stately, like a magnificent peacock; the other was a mild nightingale. One was Lord Indra's divine consort Indrani; the other possessed the fragile beauty of Manmadhan's beloved, Rathi. One was the royal River Ganga, a *vegavahini* in her grace and majesty; the other the gentler, bashful Kaveri.

We shall not test our readers' patience any longer, and reveal their identities: the regal young woman was King Sundara Chozhar's daughter, Princess Kundhavai; beloved sister of Arulmozhi Varman who would later gain immense fame as Raja Raja Chozhan. Her titles included that of Ilaiya Piratti; she was to become a pillar of strength that the Chozha Empire would one day lean on. She it was who would also raise her brother's son, Crown Prince Rajendra Chozhan into the warrior and great Emperor he was destined to be.

The other was a princess of the Kodumbalur clan, a faithful vassal of the Chozha Empire; she resided with Princess Kundhavai, as was the custom of young women of her state. Fate was to bless her with a destiny beyond her wildest dreams—but that lay in the future. At the moment she was a demure, gentle young woman, as yet unaware of the part she would be called upon to play.

When they had stepped out of the boat, Kundhavai turned to look at the others, still in it. "Stay where you are. We shall return in a *naazhigai*."

All the young women in the boat belonged to one royal clan or other in the empire; they resided with Princess Kundhavai in Pazhaiyarai as was the custom; all hoped for her patronage, as princesses of various vassal kingdoms. To see her now stroll away with just one among their group, was galling. Disappointment and jealousy warred in their narrowed eyes.

On the banks stood a chariot at the ready, horses harnessed. Kundhavai glanced at the young woman beside her. "Vanathi, get in." When she obeyed, Ilaiya Piratti followed. The chariot set off at a spanking pace.

"*Akka*, may I know where we're off to?" asked Vanathi.

"Indeed you may," answered Kundhavai. "We're about to visit the Kudandhai astrologer, of course."

"But—why? What do you wish to ask him?"

"What else but about you, my dear? You've been looking pale and dispirited for months now—not to mention thinner than ever. I'd like to consult him about your health, and find out when you'll be better."

"*Akka*, if you please—there's nothing the matter with me. If this is all you wish to ask him, may we turn back? Please?"

"No, my girl, we won't. I promise that I shan't utter a word about you. Shall we say, instead, that I wish to consult him about *my* future?"

"You? But—why would you consult an astrologer about yourself?"

"Why would a girl ever want to consult one? I wish to ask him about my marriage, of course. Will I ever wed anyone? Or is it my fate to spend my days as a virgin?"

"*Akka*, wouldn't you rather ask that of your heart? All you have to do is nod—princes from all fifty six kingdoms from Imayam in the north to Kumari in the south, would be ready to fling themselves at your feet! I daresay they'd arrive in droves from even beyond the seas. I wonder which prince would be fortunate enough to claim your hand? But that decision is yours, isn't it?"

"Let's say for the sake of argument, that you're right—but I see obstacles there as well. Should I ever marry a royal, I shall have to make my home with him, in his kingdom. Vanathi, I'd hate to leave Chozha Nadu, made lush and beautiful by the River Ponni. You see, I've made a pledge to never depart these lands—"

"I confess I don't see the problem. The one who marries you is bound to fall at your feet, slave to your every whim and fancy. Order him to make his home here, and he'll be happy to do so."

91

"Ah, talk about bundling a rat in your waistcloth! Do you truly wish me to confine a prince of another kingdom here? Are you aware of the serious consequences *that* might have, my girl?"

"But—every woman *must* marry some time, mustn't she?"

"And which scripture lays down such a rule, I ask you? Take the poet Auvaiyaar, for instance. Wasn't she a virgin unto her death? Didn't she live a long life, unattached to any man, and yet reap such fame? A *kaveeswari*, in fact?"

"Auvaiyaar was blessed by God, *Akka*—she received the boon of growing old in her youth. You haven't a single wrinkle."

"Have it as you please, then. But I shall marry only a poor soldier in this very Chozha Nadu—such a one will have no kingdom to rule, no people to govern. He wouldn't pose conditions about taking me away, either. He would make his home here, in this empire, quite happily ..."

"Then—you wouldn't leave Chozha Nadu, *Akka*? Ever?"

"Never. Not even if they promised to make me the Queen of Heaven."

"Now, I'm truly happy."

"You are? Why?"

"If you leave, you see, I shall have to accompany you—for I can't even imagine living anywhere in your absence. But I don't wish to leave Chozha Nadu either—"

"But you'll have to, wouldn't you? Once you're married?"

"I'm never going to get married, *Akka*."

"Good heavens, girl—what of the reams of advice you've been giving *me*, about women and matrimony?"

"Our positions are hardly the same, are they?"

"Why, you imp —! Did you really think to fool me with your little ways, my girl? I know for a fact that you don't care the slightest about these lands; the Chozha Nadu you desire is now in Eezham, fighting with swords and spears. Vanathi, you didn't really believe me to be so ignorant, did you?"

"*Akka*—do you truly think me so silly? How can I—how can an insignificant little dewdrop on the grass ever aspire to the sun? How would it ever come to pass?"

"Indeed; there's no comparing them, after all. But the tiny dewdrop does capture the vast, seething ball of fire within itself, doesn't it?"

"Truly, *Akka*? Do you really believe that it may claim the sun?" Vanathi asked, all eagerness and delight. But then, abruptly, depression set in. "The dewdrop does cherish desires; it succeeds in capturing the sun too. But what's the use? The dewdrop receives the punishment it so richly deserves for such outrageous daring—it melts within moments in the scorching sunlight!"

"Wrong, Vanathi. The sun does return the dewdrop's affections—he loves her in the only way possible; he takes her to himself and never lets her return to the earth again. You see, he doesn't really want other men to cast their lustful eyes on her, for she belongs only to him. When night falls, he releases her—don't we see fresh dewdrops on the grass each morning?"

"These are merely words to pacify me, *Akka*."

"So you do admit that something troubles your heart—while insisting all these days that it was nothing of the sort! Now you know why I wish to consult the astrologer."

"And if I *am* troubled," Vanathi stared at the scenes outside, and heaved a great sigh. "What would be the point of asking *him* about it?"

—

The astrologer had chosen to live in the vicinity of a Kali temple in a corner of Kudandhai, well away from the bustle; it was possible to arrive at his home without entering the city at all. The chariot followed a well-appointed path; from the ease with which the charioteer negotiated the route, it seemed fairly obvious that he had done so many times, and knew it like the back of his hand.

Their arrival appeared to be expected; the astrologer and his disciple stood in readiness at his home's entrance. The moment the princesses alighted, he came forward and bade them welcome, deference in every pore of his body. "*Perumaatti*, Your Gracious Highness! This humble abode of mine is honoured to welcome you, the embodiment of *Kalaimagal* and *Thirumagal*—that you should grace this hut once again with your noble presence is truly a privilege!"

"*Ayya*, may we be sure that no one else will try to visit you for the duration of our consultation?" asked Kundhavai.

"Certainly, my lady. Nobody seeks me, these days. And why should they? Your father, the illustrious King Sundara Chozhar rules with such benign grace that there is no want, need, hunger or disease. His subjects lead a happy and fulfilling life. Why would they need to consult astrologers?"

"In other words, I'm doing so because I'm in difficulties."

"Never, *Thaaye*! Who in this land would ever dare to imply that the Pazhaiyarai lord's noble daughter, blessed with the *navanidhis,* the nine kinds of wealth, is plagued by trouble? Doubtless, it is to succour *me* that Goddess Ambigai has decided to visit this pitiful dwelling—for, with every citizen of Chozha Nadu living a satisfying life, it is I who am now deprived of an income and therefore, in great difficulties," the astrologer recovered, with considerable aplomb. "May I request the princesses to kindly step inside? It is an insult to your noble selves to stand at my entrance for so long!"

Kundhavai turned to the charioteer. "Make sure the *radham* stands under the banyan tree by the temple." She and Vanathi entered the residence.

The astrologer paused for a moment to speak to his disciple. "My boy, guard the door with your life. Make sure that not a soul trespasses, until our visitors leave."

The home itself might be of humble dimensions, but it was obvious that the astrologer had taken great pains to appoint it in a manner suitable for his royal visitors. A charming painting of the Goddess was placed in an alcove in one wall; two seats were placed on the floor, in readiness. A *kuthuvilakku* cast its golden light around the hall; artistic *kolams* were drawn along the walls and floor. In addition, palm-leaves with intricate drawings of astrological signs were strewn about everywhere.

The astrologer took his seat, once the princesses had done so. "My lady must graciously apprise me of the reason for her visit."

"Wouldn't you be able to glean that from your palm-leaves?"

"Very well." The astrologer duly closed his eyes. His lips mumbled something, as though he were chanting mantras. "You are here, *Thaaye*, to consult me about this maiden's horoscope," he said a while later, opening his eyes. "Goddess Parasakthi's divine grace informs me so. Is this true?"

"Wonderful! Words fail me, Ayya, when I try to praise your powers. Indeed, yes—my purpose in visiting you today was to seek a consultation about this young woman. She came to the Pazhaiyarai palace a year ago, and you would have been hard put to find a more carefree, happier girl— she sang and danced all day. For the first few months, she was the most cheerful among my handmaidens; full of spirit and enthusiasm. But something changed: she hasn't been the same for the past four months. She tires easily and sits as though in a trance, for hours. There's never a smile to be seen on her face but when I ask if something is wrong, she insists she's fine. I daren't face her family if they visit us and make enquiries about her health!"

"My lady, this young woman is the beloved daughter of the illustrious Kodumbalur Velir the younger, is she not? Is her name Vanathi?"

"Why, you seem to know everything about her!"

"I have her horoscope too, somewhere about. I remember collecting it, amongst others. Just a moment *Ammani*, while I find it." The astrologer opened an old box nearby and began rootling about in it. Soon, he picked up a few palm-leaves from within, and read their contents carefully.

Hidden Meanings and Explanations

Silappathikaaram

One of the five great epics of Tamil, this work is supposed o have been written sometime around the 5th or 6th century AD, by Ilangovadigal. The story revolves around the lives of Kovalan and Kannaki, a young couple whose lives go haywire upon Kovalan's liaison with a courtesan, Madhavi. *Silappathikaaram* derives its name from the ornament *Silambu* (in fact, it is often referred to, thus), which is a central part of the story, and is renowned for its classic verses of romance, betrayal, tragedy—but also for its descriptive verses on nature, particularly the Kaveri.

Akka

A term used to address elder sisters, both biological and otherwise.

Kuthuvilakku

Large lamps usually made of brass, and with five or seven lamp-wicks.

Kolam

Intricate rice-flour drawings usually drawn at the entrance of homes and sometimes, within as well.

Thaaye

Although it literally translates to "Mother," it was also used as an honorific towards women.

Ammani

Another honorific to address women.

11

EXPLOSIVE ENTRANCES

So famous these days that it has earned a place even in English dictionaries, the Kumbakonam of today went by the name of Kudandhai or Kudamooku at the time of our story, and was much renowned for its temples and religious connections. In addition to these attractions, there was the fact that our astrologer had chosen to make it his home, as well.

A little to the south-west lay Pazhaiyarai—provisional capital of the Chozha Empire, a magnificent sight with towers, *maadams* and temple *gopurams* piercing the sky.

It was one of the astrologer's missions in life to collect and analyze the horoscope of every royal in this majestic city's several palaces; accordingly, the Kodumbalur Princess's birth-chart had made its way into his collection as well.

He gazed down at this important document for a while. He looked keenly into Vanathi's face. Then, he went back to gazing at the horoscope, and again, at the young woman. But though he spent a good many minutes switching endless gazes between palm-leaf and princess, not a single word did he utter.

"Well, *Jothidar*?" asked Kundhavai, finally. "Are you ever going to grace us with your predictions?"

"What do I say, my lady? I recall picking up this particular horoscope once before, but was so astounded by what I saw in it that I could not believe my eyes. I doubted that such things could even exist. But now—when I look at both the gracious lady in question and her birth-chart, I cannot help but gape at it!"

"Do, by all means, to your heart's content—but will you deign to tell us *something* when you're done?"

"Ah, this is a horoscope that fairly overflows with good fortune, my lady. If you will not mind my telling you so—it is, in several respects, a shade better than even yours! I have never seen destiny and fortune come together in such an excellent fashion!"

A smile appeared on Kundhavai's face; Vanathi went pink with embarrassment. "*Akka*, I don't see how he can call this ill-fated creature the world's most fortunate woman! Is this how he usually predicts anything?"

"What is this that you say, *Amma*? I declare—if any of my predictions are wrong, I shall give up my profession!"

"Kindly don't swear any such pledge, *Ayya*—if only to mumble a few kind words to anyone who comes to you. Vanathi's seized by doubt, as all your predictions so far have been vague in the extreme."

"You wish for something specific, my lady? Here it is, then: four months ago, an event happened that could have been misconstrued as a terrible omen—but it was no such thing. In fact, that very event laid the foundations for this fortunate damsel's magnificent destiny!"

"There! —what did I tell you, Vanathi?" exulted Kundhavai.

"It looks like you've already informed him of everything that needs to be said," murmured that young woman.

"Would you just listen to this one's words, *Ayya*?"

"Indeed, she may say whatever she pleases. When she marries the king of kings—"

"Now *that* is the way to talk. What young woman wouldn't be delighted to learn about her marriage?"

"Precisely my opinion as well, my lady—but I could not very well begin with marriage, could I? You would chastise me a lecherous old man, then!"

"When and where is this gracious young lady's husband to be found?" queried Kundhavai. "How may we identify him? Would you be able to predict all this?"

"Why not, *Amma*? All things are possible when it comes to horoscopes!" And the astrologer bent his head studiously towards Vanathi's birth-chart once again. Of course, he may have just been pretending to study it—but of that, we shall never know the truth.

Presently, he raised his head. "*Ammani*, the one who is to wed this young lady does not need to come from very far away; he lives very near her, to tell the truth. But this warrior of warriors is not in this country at the moment—he has journeyed to a land beyond the seas."

Kundhavai glanced at Vanathi, who lowered her head in a bid to contain the thrill of delight that coursed through her. She was not very successful; her face gave away her ecstasy.

"And—? Who is he? What is his clan? Is there any way to know from her horoscope?"

"Indeed there is. The man fortunate enough to wed this young lady would be blessed with the lines of a conch and discus in his palms, *Amma*!"

Kundhavai glanced at Vanathi again. That young woman stared studiously, at the ground.

"In that case, wouldn't *her* hands have some sort of sign too? Lines that corresponds to his?"

"My lady, I wonder if you have ever had occasion to look at her soles—"

"Good grief, are you suggesting that I fall at her feet?"

"No, that was not what I meant. But it is entirely true that thousands of well-born ladies, crown princesses, queens, empresses and others will perform penances, some day, for precisely such an amazing honour!"

"*Akka*, did you really bring me here just to listen to this old man make fun of me?" retorted Vanathi, this time, genuinely angry. "Let's leave, please!"

"Hush, now. Why do *you* fly into a rage? What does it matter what he says—?"

"But it does, my lady. I do not forecast indiscriminately— only what this horoscope says. You may have heard court poets sing of "lotus feet" —and perhaps you thought they were merely soft words of gratification. But do, if you can, look at this young woman's soles. You will find the lines of a red lotus adorning them."

"Enough, *Jothidar*! Any more and she might grab my hands and drag me from here by sheer force of will. Do tell us something now, about her husband."

"Ah, certainly! The man who weds this damsel is a warrior among warriors; he will meet his enemies face to face, and destroy them in a hundred battles. *Vaagai* garlands of victory will descend upon his neck by the dozens, and he will be an Emperor among Emperors. Thousands of kings will lay their heads at his feet, and he will rule from his bejeweled throne for years—"

"I don't believe you," put in Kundhavai, her face a tumultuous blend of eagerness, delight, doubt and concern. "How can this ever come to pass?"

"He's just rattling off the first thing that comes into his head," interjected Vanathi. "Perhaps he believes these predictions will make you happy."

"Your disbelief does not matter in the least, *Amma*. One day, you will realize the truth of my predictions. All I ask is that when that time comes, kindly do not forget this poor astrologer—"

"*Akka*—shall we leave?" Tears trembled on the lashes of Vanathi's dark eyes.

"Just a moment—you may do so, once I have told you this: the warrior who weds this princess is about to face a great many dangers and untold disasters. He will incur the ire of powerful enemies—"

"*Ayyo!*"

"But in the end, every single one of his foes will be defeated; every calamity will dissipate like dust in the wind. This young lady's prince will vanquish all obstacles and ascend to greatness unheard of, among men. My lady—do not take offense at what I am about to tell you; I am an old man, and believe I have the right denied to youth. Do, please, observe this young woman's abdomen, if you can. And if you do not find the lines of an *aal* leaf in it, I swear I shall give up my profession!"

"What is its significance?"

"Do we not know the Lord who rests on a banyan leaf, my lady? The Kodumbalur princess is truly blessed; she is to have the honour of giving birth to a boy who will be the image of *Thirumaal* Himself. Her husband might be burdened with obstacles, catastrophes and disasters but her son—ah! He shall be the very incarnation of God on earth! Nothing shall be beyond him. Everything he touches will turn to gold; he shall own and rule all the lands on which he sets foot; the tiger flag will flutter gloriously, wherever he casts his sight. The young man borne of this princess will lead armies that flow over countries in vast numbers, just as the Ponni overflows its banks and washes over the land. Goddess Jayalakshmi, Divine Benefactor of the Victorious, will bow to him with respect; his will be the hand that brings prosperity and fame to this land; this empire will know its greatest glory under his magnificent reign; the Chozha dynasty will be renowned all over the three worlds—and *he* will be the reason for its magnificence—!"

Kundhavai sat opposite him all this while, her eyes burning into his, drinking in the astrologer's every fervent word as though her life depended on it.

A feeble voice brought her back to earth. "*Akka?*"

Kundhavai turned, startled.

"I—I don't feel—I can't—" Vanathi stuttered, and crumpled to the floor, unconscious.

Kundhavai sat up briskly. "*Ayya*, some water, if you please." She raised Vanathi and settled her in her lap. The astrologer duly arrived with water; Ilaiya Piratti received it, and sprinkled a few drops on her companion's face.

"Nothing to worry, *Amma*," reassured the astrologer.

"Indeed. She's been making a habit of fainting away—it's been five or six times already. Mark my words: she'll wake up in a few moments, and ask me if we're on earth or *Kailasam*!"

Then, she turned her attention to him—and her voice went very low. "I came here, *Ayya*, to consult you about something important. I've been hearing disturbing talk among people, lately; towns and cities are full of news that upsets me. I see a comet in the sky too, these days—do such omens have any import? Will they truly spell calamity for the empire? Perhaps—perhaps ill fortune truly is upon us?"

"My lady, kindly do not ask me about empires, affairs of state or kingly dominions. Such things do not possess horoscopes; neither do they lend themselves to forecasts. Perhaps the only men who can divine their futures are sages, saints and other yogis with the power to predict such things. I am but a poor astrologer with meager resources; such things are beyond me. Stars, charts, planets and moon become powerless before the might of an empire and its machinations ..."

"How very diplomatic, *Ayya*. Cleverly phrased, too. Predicting an empire's future might be beyond your meager means—but surely not those of my father and brothers? Divining their futures would be the same as divining the empire's, wouldn't it?"

"Certainly, *Amma*, but that is a task for another day. In general, these are hazardous times for all, filled with confusion and danger. It would serve us well to exercise great caution."

"My father's move from Pazhaiyarai to Thanjavur worries me greatly."

"I said this before, *Amma*; a great adversity is about to befall the

Maharaja—indeed, these are trying times for everyone in your family. They will face the gravest dangers. By Goddess Durga's grace, though, every single stroke of ill fortune shall dissipate, and the fates will smile again."

A frail voice reached them, at that moment. "*Akka?* Where are we?" Vanathi gazed up from where she lay in Kundhavai's lap, eyes wide, like a flower unfurling its delicate petals, lids fluttering like a bird's.

"My heart's dearest! The celestial *Pushpaka Vimanam* hasn't arrived to whisk us to heaven, unfortunately; we're doomed to be on earth for a while; more's the pity. Do get up, now—we'll have to do with our own paltry chariot and horses, to return to the palace."

Vanathi sat up slowly. "Did I faint?"

"Certainly not, my love. You simply decided to take a nap in my lap for a while. I even sang a lullaby—didn't the lilting notes fall on your charming ears?"

"Pray—pray don't be angry, *Akka*. I couldn't help myself. My head spun so—"

"I'm not surprised your head spun a pretty dance—mine would have too, if this wily astrologer had rattled off such dazzling predictions to *me*."

"Dazzling predictions—*Akka*, you don't really think I'd believe such things, do you?"

"Regardless of what you believe, my dear, you did succeed in frightening him out of his wits! I've decided never to take such a little coward anywhere, ever again—"

"I did tell you that I didn't want to come here, *Akka*. But you said –"

"My fault, of course. Now, get up. Will my lady take a few steps to the front door—or must I tuck you onto my hip?"

"Oh, no, please! I can walk by myself."

"Just a moment, *Amma*. Kindly accept Devi's *prasadham* before you leave." The astrologer began to gather his palm-leaves and tie them up.

"*Jothidar*, you've predicted so much about me—but you haven't said anything about *Akka*'s future," spoke up Vanathi.

"*Amma*, I have forecast hers, as well. Besides, there is nothing I can tell Ilaiya Piratti that she does not already know. What more?"

"The warrior of warriors who is to wed *Akka*—"

"A Nightmare to Foes!" cut in Kundhavai. "An *asakaaya soorar*—"

"And why not? Of course he would be the greatest of them all, a *paraakramasaali*; a mighty prince who is—"

"—so handsome that he's the embodiment of all thirty-two aspects of the *Saamudhrika Lakshanam*; rivals Brihaspathi in brains, equals Saraswathi in arts; would compete with Manmadhan for his looks—wait, no, Arjunan!"

"Ilaiya Piratti's prince, this *sukumaarar* is to come soon, isn't he?" asked Vanathi eagerly. "When? And where will he be from?"

"Indeed, he will arrive, my lady. Very, very soon."

"Ah, but the question is—*how* will he make his superb entrance? Will he stomp in on an elephant? Trot in on a horse? Clatter by in a chariot? Tramp by on foot?" quipped Kundhavai, gaily. "Or simply crash through the roof like a God and reveal his divine presence?"

"There —! I can hear hooves!" exclaimed Vanathi.

"Such excellent faculties, my dear, to catch something that doesn't exist."

"I'm not teasing you, *Akka*—do listen!"

And indeed, they did hear hooves clattering along the street at a furious pace.

"What of it? This is Kudandhai city, after all; horses must be commonplace on the streets," explained Kundhavai.

"No *Akka*—I believe this one's coming here!"

"You and your silly fantasies. Get up now; time to leave."

Precisely at this moment, a clamour of voices reached them from the entrance. A fierce altercation seemed to be in progress, interspersed with shouts and a cacophony of sounds.

"This is the astrologer's home, isn't it?"

"Yes—and you are?"

"Is he in?"

"You can't enter right now."

"I will."

"I won't let you."

"I *must* see the astrologer."

"Later."

"I have no time for later—I will see him *now*!"

"*Dei—dei*—stop! Stop at once!"

"Shoo! Get away—or I'll mow you down—!"

"*Ayya*, please do not enter the house! Please do not—!"

Dadaar! The door was flung open with a crash. A young man made an explosive entrance into the room. Another was almost at heels, catching him by his shoulders in a vain bid to pull him away. The young man wrenched himself from the latter and took a forceful step across the threshold, and into the room.

Our readers may have guessed the identity of this intrepid youngster by now—it was, indeed, our valiant Vandhiyathevan.

The eyes of all three within the room, focused themselves on the new entrant at once.

Vandhiyathevan, in turn, directed his attention on those within. No, that would not be quite correct. His eyes fastened onto only one person in the room—and even then, he did not quite manage to see Princess Kundhavai all at once.

He took in her fair countenance, radiant as the golden full moon. Ah, but not even all her face at the same time! He saw her lips, gleaming red corals, parted slightly in surprise; he saw her eyes—large, brilliant and brimming with laughter, mischief, astonishment and yes, the aura of majesty that pervaded her; every perfect eyelash, and brows that curved gently over them; the forehead, delicately tinted in ivory; rosy cheeks, dimpling in a smile; a slender neck, with the silken smoothness of a conch, translucent in its beauty.

He saw all these at the same, as separate images. And that was how they fixed themselves in his mind, as well—with startling, brilliant clarity.

All this had happened within the space of a few seconds. Now, Vandhiyathevan seemed to shake himself, and turned to glare at the astrologer's disciple. "Why, you little—why couldn't you have warned me that there were females inside—! I wouldn't have barged in if I'd known –" and he pushed away the man almost roughly, retreating in some confusion towards the entrance.

He did, however, seize the opportunity of darting one last glance at Kundhavai, before he left.

"Good grief—it sounds as though a tempest had just wrecked its havoc and blown itself out," sighed the princess.

"Not yet—do listen," pointed out Vanathi.

Vandhiyathevan, it seemed, was still locked in a fierce verbal duel with the disciple.

"*Ayya*, who might this be?" asked Kundhavai.

"I do not know, my lady. He does not seem to be from these parts. Looks to be quite a ruffian too."

Abruptly, Kundhavai seemed to recall something—and went into merry peals of laughter.

"Why do you laugh, *Akka*?"

"If you must know, I remembered what we'd been discussing about my future husband and his entry—if he would stomp by in an elephant, come in a horse, or drop through the roof!"

This time, Vanathi was hard put to control her laughter as well.

Their collective mirth rang through the hall, flowing in merry waves through the doorway, and drowned the argument outside.

The astrologer seemed lost in thought, as he provided the princesses with *kungumam*.

The ladies rose, took their leave, and walked out of the house; the astrologer followed.

Vandhiyathevan, who moved aside the moment they appeared upon the entrance, snatched the chance to explain his behaviour. "My apologies," he announced, in a loud voice. "I did not realize that there were ladies within—this idiot never thought to mention it. Had I known,

I would never have made such a hasty entrance—I apologize, once again!"

Kundhavai glanced up at him, face alight with good humour. Mischief and laughter mingled with a certain undeniable dignity, in her expressive eyes. She spoke not a word but took one of Vanathi's hands instead, and walked towards the chariot, under the banyan tree.

"Kudandhai's womenfolk don't seem to have a smidgen of manners," Vandhiyathevan's loud complaint floated towards them, from a distance. "Not even a pleasant word to a man who takes the effort to speak to them? Terrible!"

The charioteer stood in readiness, having harnessed his horses. The princesses climbed into the *radham*; he took his place at the front. The equipage sped away, towards the banks of the *Arisilaaru*.

Vandhiyathevan stood watching the chariot, until it vanished into the distance.

৪৯

Hidden Meanings and Explanations

Kailasam

Heavenly abode of Siva Peruman.

Prasadham

Offerings placed before the deity, and later distributed among devotees, or visitors.

Kungumam

Vermilion. Equated with all things auspicious and feminine, it was (and still is) the practice to offer it to women, both virgins and married, when they took their leave after a visit. It is also considered *de rigueur* to offer it before they rise from their seats—which explains why Kundhavai and Vanathi rose only after they accepted the *kungumam* from the astrologer.

12

NANDHINI

Ah, yes. We left Vandhiyathevan on the banks of the Kollidam, safely inside a boat, didn't we? Now we're honour-bound to tell our readers how he made an explosive entry into the Kudandhai astrologer's home, of all places.

The Saivite who had objected in no uncertain terms to Azhwarkkadiyaan's getting into the boat, preserved his silence until they were well across the river, and then turned to our young man. "*Thambi*, it was on your account that I even let this one get into the boat. Order him never to utter that eight-letter word in my presence—or I shall task these boatmen to push him into these waters! They are my men, you see."

"Well, honoured Nambi?" queried Vandhiyathevan. "Did your sacred ears get the message?"

"I am content never to mention the blessed eight-letter name—as long as that one never utters the five-lettered blasphemy," retorted Azhwarkkadiyaan.

"Who is this idiot, who dares me to never chant that divine five-letter word, the Panchakshara Mantram of Siva Peruman Himself?" thundered the Saivite in righteous anger, proceeding to recite in majestic tones:

"Katroonaip pootti kadalir paaichinum
Natrunaiyavadhu Namachivayave!"

[*Bind me to a stone pillar and throw me into the oceans—and I shall still chant Namachivaaya, in praise of Siva Peruman, who is always by my side!*]

Azhwarkkadiyaan, never to be outdone, sang in turn:

"Naadinen naadi naan kandukondein
Narayana ennum naamam!"

[*I searched within myself, and I found—the blessed name of Narayana, the Supreme Being!*]

"*Siva Siva!*" growled the Saivite, and stuck his fingers in his ears. He took them out only when the Vaishnavite was done.

"Do listen to this fanatic go on and on about his precious God, *Thambi*," began Azhwarkkadiyaan. "He complains so much about Thirumaal's name even falling on his ears—but doesn't this very Kollidam come down to us only after washing the divine feet of the Lord Who Resides in Srirangam? And Siva Peruman, of course, realizes how blessed these waters are, which is why he practically submerges himself in them to perform penance in Thiruvaanaikkaval temple, grateful for the high honour—"

The Saivite pounced on Nambi with a roar, barely allowing him a word more. The two began a wild tussle in one end of the boat; when it looked like it might capsize, Vandhiyathevan and the boatmen intervened, pulling them apart.

"It seems, my devout men, that you wish to dive headfirst into this raging Kollidam and ascend *moksham* straightaway," admonished Vandhiyathevan severely. "I, however, still have a great many things to accomplish in the world and wish to stay, if you please."

"I am not sure about *moksham*," averred one of the boatmen. "But they are sure to reach the stomachs of crocodiles. Look over there!"

They followed his finger—and saw one gaping wide, its terrifyingly sharp teeth clearly visible.

"I'm not afraid of them in the least," declared Azhwarkkadiyaan. "Don't I have the divinely powerful Narayanamurthy who rescued the elephant Gajendra from the clutches of a crocodile, to sweep me away from danger?"

"Only if he finds the time to actually tear himself away from the saris of Brindavan's Gopika women," snapped the Saivite, tone dripping with sarcasm.

"Or, perhaps, Siva Peruman is caught in difficulties, like the time he granted all those silly boons to the demon Basmaasuran, and came whining for assistance. And perhaps Thirumaal has hastened to his help," mused Azhwarkkadiyaan.

"This Vaishnavite does not seem to remember how Thirumaal's arrogance was destroyed during Siva Peruman's annihilation of the Three Worlds," retorted the Saivite.

"I really don't understand why you must quarrel endlessly, this way," complained Vandhiyathevan. "Why don't you choose your favourites and worship them in peace?"

—

As to why exactly the Saivite and Azhwarkkadiyaan were at each other's throats, or the religious argument that ended almost in a full-fledged fight at Veera Narayanapuram—perhaps it would be better to reveal to our readers the reason for such fervour among the local populace, in those days.

For more than six hundred years, Jainism and Buddhism had reigned supreme as the religions of favour, in the Thamizh lands. Many were the benefits reaped as a result of their prevalence: sculpture, art, poetry, dance and prose flourished. Later, it was the time of Azhwars and Naayanmars belonging to Vaishnavite and Saivite traditions respectively, to begin the Bhakthi movement in earnest with their divinely beautiful songs in simple, chaste Thamizh.

Their campaigns to popularize their faiths with the masses proved to be extraordinarily powerful: sculpture and music were put to great use in their work; many chose to sing the Azhwars' beautiful *pasurams* and the work of three celebrated saints of Saivism, compiled as *Thevaram* verses, set to charming music, almost celestial in their beauty. Such songs melted the hearts of listeners with their exquisite loveliness, raising religious ardour to almost fever-pitch. Those temples that had songs of Azhwars and the three Saivite saints dedicated to them attained a new degree of respect, conferred as they had been, with a signal honour. Many were the houses of worship that had been built with wood and bricks thus far; now, they were rebuilt in stone, never to be destroyed. It was Vijayalaya Chozhar who took up this monumental work; his heirs and others of the royal family would later expand upon it.

Meanwhile, neighbouring Kerala was not exempt from momentous events either. A tiny village called Kaaladi witnessed the birth of a saint; at a very tender age, he renounced the world and became an ascetic. The pursuit of knowledge drove him to learn the languages of the North; soon, he was an expert in the Bhagavad Gita, the Upanishads and Brahma Sutra—which formed the basis for his much acclaimed treatises, especially when he later hoisted the flag of Advaitha philosophy victoriously upon the peak of theological debates, besting his peers. His proficiency in the Northern languages aided him in travels across the length and breadth of Bharathavarsha; he established eight seats or monasteries that propounded Advaitha philosophy in earnest. Monks and ascetics, captivated by his theories and treatises, traversed the lands, expounding them to eager audiences.

Approximately 980 years ago, around the time this story was set in Thamizhagam, religious fervour had peoples' imaginations in a feverish grip. As much as this was advantageous in some ways, it cannot be denied that a good many adverse elements also found a way to twine their poisonous tendrils around the population. Fierce Vaishnavaites and

Saivites rose everywhere with thorny arguments; Advaitha philosophers pitched in to add their mite. Religious debates often turned into ugly fist-fights.

There is, in fact, a rather quaint story that illustrates the Saiva-Vaishnava skirmishes of those days beautifully:

Once, a staunch Vaishnavite walked along the towering temple walls of the Siva abode in Thiruvaanaikkaval. Suddenly, a stone dropped on his head. It was a sharp one, and the resulting gash began bleeding at once. The Vaishnavite craned up his neck—to see a crow perched on the temple tower. He guessed, at once, that the bird's awkward perch must have dislodged one of the stones in the aged, crumbling *vimanam*.

Instantly, every sign of distress left him; he even forgot the blood flowing freely from his head. "Devout crow, you must be a staunch Vaishnavite from Srirangam!" he crowed. "Destroy this Thiruvaanaikkaval temple tower at once!"

This was how things stood at that point, in Thamizhagam. Learning these circumstances will aid our readers immensely, in understanding this story.

The boat reached the opposite banks. "Go to hell!" The Saivite hurled a last, liberal curse at Azhwarkkadiyaan's head and went his way. The Kadambur soldier who had accompanied Vandhiyathevan departed as well; he would procure a horse in nearby Thiruppanandaal.

Left to fend for themselves, Vandhiyathevan and Azhwarkkadiyaan sat down on the banks, under a sprawling *arasu* tree. Hundreds of birds perched in its numerous branches, chirping and twittering in enthusiastic tones.

Both felt that the other possessed a good deal of information; both tried to get the other to blurt out what he knew. The result was that each spent a good deal of time talking in endless circles, circumventing one topic after another, yet moving inexorably towards the other's secrets.

"Well, *Thambi*?" Azhwarkkadiyaan made the opening gambit. "You did go to the Kadambur palace, didn't you? And you never thought to take me along!"

"It was all I could do to get in myself, Nambi."

"Indeed? How did you enter, then? Or perhaps you never did?"

"Oh I did, all right. When have I ever backed out of something I set my heart on? The sentries at the gates did their best to throw me out — but I spurred my horse and practically dashed in. They tried to bar my way, but every single one of them crumpled to the ground in a heap. And my friend Kandamaran arrived to escort me before they could gather their simple wits and close in."

"I thought that it might have happened that way. You're courageous, *Thambi*! And then? Who were the guests? Did you see?"

"So many that I lost count. And such great men too! I couldn't recognize all of them. There was Pazhuvettarayar, though. And his wife. Ah, the beauty of that young woman! Where am I to find the words to describe her?"

"You saw her, then?"

"Did I *not*! My friend Kandamaran practically dragged me to his palace's *anthappuram*. That's where I caught sight of her—and let me tell you: she fairly dazzled down every other woman in that place. Her face shone like a radiant full moon amongst those dark-skinned ladies. All the celestial beauties—Rambhai, Urvasi, Thilothamai, even Indra's queen Indrani, Chandrani, hah, they're all nothing to her!"

"Well! This is describing her indeed. And what happened next? Did they perform the *Kuravai Koothu*?"

"Indeed. And very well too. I thought of you, then."

"How unfortunate that I couldn't attend! What else?"

"Well, the Velan Dance, for one. The Devaralan and Devaratti came on stage and put up an aggressive performance."

"What about the *sannadham*? Were they possessed? Any predictions?"

"Ah, certainly! "There will be rains; the land will flourish; all our deepest desires will be fulfilled ...""

"Is that all?"

"I believe there *was* something about royal matters—but I wasn't really listening."

"Ah, but you should have, *Thambi*! How unfortunate that you didn't. See, you're a youngster; a valiant and intelligent one at that. You must keep your eyes and ears open when it comes to royal affairs."

"Indeed, you speak the truth. I thought so myself, this morning."

"Eh? Why only this morning?"

"Because Kandamaran and I were chatting as we traveled towards the Kollidam, and he happened to mention something about their famous visitors. Apparently they gathered after I'd gone to bed last night, and discussed some very secret royal matters."

"What royal matters?"

"Kandamaran was very vague about it, so I've really no idea. All he would say was that something momentous would happen soon, and he'd tell me all about it. Very mysterious, he was. Nambi, would *you* happen to know anything about it?"

"What about?"

"There's been talk everywhere about strange things happenings, hasn't there? About the comet in the sky—and how that portends terrible misfortune to the Chozha throne … people are discussing all this as far away as Thondai Mandalam. Apparently, several great men have been gathering and considering who might be next in line to the throne. What about you, Nambi? Who do *you* think will be the next Emperor?"

"I'm afraid I'm not knowledgeable about such things, *Thambi*. What have I to do with royalty? I'm a Vaishnavite; the servant of devout Azhwars who sing the praises of Thirumaal. All I do is follow in their footsteps and go on pilgrimages."

As if on cue, he began to sing *Thirukkanden Ponmeni Kanden*—upon which Vandhiyathevan cut in without compunction. "Do me a favour, Nambi, and kindly shut up."

"This is a divine Thamizh *pasuram*—why would you tell me to stop?"

"Devout Azhwarkkadiyaan Nambi—I find myself entertaining a suspicion. May I reveal it?"

"By all means."

"You wouldn't take a swing at me with that stick of yours, will you?"

"Dare I even think of such a thing?"

"All this devotion—your piety, arguments about Thirumaal, being a staunch Vaishnavite, these *pasurams* and the sacred symbols on your body—I say that every single one of these is just a clever disguise."

"*Ayyo!* How could you? Good God, sacrilege! Blasphemy!"

"Blasphemy indeed! Ah come now, Nambi—all this is just a ruse to cover up your lust, isn't it? I've come across men like you—insanely enamoured of women. I wonder what you see in them? I confess your obsession is beyond me. For myself, I hate their very sight."

"It's true that certain men have nothing on their minds but women—but kindly don't lump me with them, *Thambi*. I'm no lecherous idiot masquerading as a devotee. Your assumption is unjust."

"In that case, why ask me to deliver a message to the lady in the palanquin? Harbouring romantic feelings for a married woman too! That's why you wanted to come to the Kadambur palace, didn't you? It wouldn't do to deny it."

"I won't. What I do deny is your rationale for why I wanted to come to the palace. I had my reasons—but that's a very long story indeed."

"Well, considering the horse isn't here yet, you may as well begin."

"If you think it's just an amusing fable—don't. Every part of it is true. Are you sure you want to listen to it?"

"Only if you wish to tell me."

"I believe I will, even if I'm in rather a hurry at the moment. After all, I may need something else of you, some other time—and then you'll help me, won't you?"

"If it's an honourable request, yes. However, you needn't share anything if you don't want to."

"But I must. The young woman caught in the terrible clutches of that ogre Hiranyasuran—I mean Pazhuvettarayar—is named Nandhini. Her tale will astonish you, I promise. You will practically explode with anger at the injustice of it —!"

With this preamble, Azhwarkkadiyaan began Nandhini's history.

—

A village on the banks of the River Vaigai in Pandiya Nadu was Azhwarkkadiyaan's birthplace; his family was steeped in poverty— but for all that, every one of them was a staunch Vaishnavite.

Once, his father went to the flower gardens on the river banks, and stumbled upon an infant girl, lying all alone. No one claimed her; he brought her home. She was a charming, lovely child, and the family instantly fell in love with her. They had found her in a beautiful *nandhavanam*; the name Nandhini thus suited her and she swiftly became a much-loved member of their home. Azhwarkkadiyaan, for his part, considered her his own sister, and cherished her.

As Nandhini grew, so did her devotion towards Thirumaal. Neighbours predicted that she would become another Andal, following in the footsteps of that devout lady; she would give herself up to God and a life of divine service.

Azhwarkkadiyaan believed in this more than anyone else. Such was his affection towards the young girl that he took the responsibility of raising her, upon his father's death. Brother and sister went on pilgrimages, visiting temple after temple on a mission to spread Vaishnavism. The sight of a young Nandhini wearing a simple *thulasi* garland, singing *pasurams* in her exquisite voice, was enough to melt the hardest heart.

Once, Azhwarkkadiyaan left on a journey to Thiruvengadam. It was a while before he returned—and this was when disaster struck Nandhini's life.

The unceasing war between Pandiyas and Chozhas had escalated to one final, bloody battle in the vicinity of Madurai—and the former suffered a crushing defeat. Veera Pandiyan lay on the battlefield, grievously wounded; some of his closest aides unearthed him among the massacred bodies and tried to save his life. In the thick of the night, they brought him to Nandhini's home. The young woman saw the badly wounded king and felt her heart stir with pity. She tried her very best to succour him—but Chozha soldiers had already caught the scent of the hidden Pandiya king, and surrounded her home. They stormed the dwelling, killed Veera Pandiyan—and Nandhini, whose luminous beauty had bewitched Pazhuvettarayar, was promptly imprisoned.

Three years had flown since these events. Try as he might, Azhwarkkadiyaan had never been able to see Nandhini again. Ever since then, he had used every means in his possession to meet her at least once, to speak with her, and if she were unhappy, to rescue her somehow, from her present circumstances. Until this moment, though, all his efforts had been in vain.

Vandhiyathevan's heart melted at this moving recital. For one brief moment, he even considered revealing to Azhwarkkadiyaan that the palanquin's occupant had actually been Prince Madhuranthakan and not Nandhini—but some instinct seemed to prevent him. What if, he wondered, this entire tale had been one of Azhwarkkadiyaan's carefully constructed fantasies?

The thought made him refrain from saying anything about the events at Kadambur, and his own midnight adventures.

In the distance, they saw the soldier from Kadambur approach, horse in tow.

"Will you help me, *Thambi*?" entreated Azhwarkkadiyaan.

"But what can I do? Pazhuvettarayar is among the most powerful men in the empire, capable of making anyone dance to his tune— while I'm just one man without any connections. How am I supposed to help?" Vandhiyathevan's words were cautious. "Nambi," he began, after a pause. "Do you really mean to say that you know nothing about royal affairs? Can't you truly make a guess about who might ascend the throne, if something should happen to Maharaja Sundara Chozhar?"

And he gazed intently at the Vaishnavite, seeking some sort of reaction. Azhwarkkadiyaan's face, however, remained as placid as ever.

"Again—what do I know of such matters, *Thambi*? Now, if you were to ask the astrologer of Kudandhai …"

"Ah—and is he truly that skilled?"

"Indeed. He happens to be an expert in not just astrology, but divining your innermost thoughts. He can even deliver predictions according to the state of current affairs!"

I certainly must pay this paragon a visit, resolved Vandhiyathevan to himself.

Humankind has been obsessed for millennia, after all, in learning about the future. Prince or pauper, intellectual or idiot—no one is exempt from a deep curiosity in glimpsing what time holds for them. It's hardly surprising that our young warrior, entrusted with the weight of royal duty and forced to chart a perilous course for himself, should wish to know as well, is it?

જી

Hidden Meanings and Explanations

Moksham

Salvation

"Approximately 980 years ago..."

This story was written in 1950.

Thiripura Samhaaram

The destruction of the Three Worlds. Like many Hindu mythological stories, this one too, has its roots in a legend: The demon Taraka had three demon children: Taarakaaksha, Kamalaaksha and Vidyunmaali, who were the lords of three moving cities or forts and wreaked destruction, buoyed by their boons from Lord Brahma. Siva Peruman destroyed them in summary fashion with his destructive powers.

Brindavan-Gopika Women

One of Lord Krishna's favourite pastimes was to play with the women of the neighbourhood, or even to steal away the clothes as they bathed. When people wished to deride Lord Vishnu, they alluded to this often—as only the weak-willed, supposedly, appreciated the company of women.

13

The Waxing Moon

Once the princesses had vanished in their chariot, the astrologer escorted Vandhiyathevan within his home, took his seat, and bade the young man, who was staring around him with wide-eyed curiosity, take one as well. Then, the older man subjected him to a keen scrutiny.

"Well, *Thambi*? And who might you be?"

Vandhiyathevan chuckled; the astrologer frowned. "What amuses you?"

"You're supposed to be famed for your skills, aren't you? Why must you ask me anything, then? Surely you can predict my name and purpose of visit?"

"Ah, it would be no hard task to divine anything about you; such a thing is well within my means. But if I do everything for myself, what about my *dakshinai*, my fee? That is my only concern, you see."

Vandhiyathevan smiled a little. "*Jothidar*—who were your visitors?"

"Ah, you ask about the people who just left, do you? The ones who were here when you came in? The ones who climbed into their chariot and drove away in a cloud of dust? You *are* enquiring about them, aren't you?" asked the astrologer in as roundabout a fashion as he could.

"Yes, they're the ones I'm talking about."

"Ask away, by all means. You have every right. And I shall tell you, of course. The people who just left were two young women."

"Wonderful. I saw that, myself. I do have eyes after all, and I frequently use them. I'm capable of distinguishing men from women. I can even tell if a man is masquerading as a woman."

"What, then?"

"Women, as in who they are, their designation, their caste, perhaps—"

"Ah, as to that, you do know that women can classified into several types, don't you? Padmini, Sidhini, Gandharvi and Vidhyaadhari are the four kinds. You seem to be acquainted with the *Saamudhrika* laws, *Thambi*. Well, one is a Padmini, while the other is a Gandharvi—"

"Good God!"

"Yes, my man?"

"Why do *you* answer if I call out to God?"

"And what if I did? You have heard, I hope, that He is omnipresent? You do not seem to have been fortunate enough to benefit from the knowledge of your elders. See, my boy—God resides in me, and in you as well. He dwells even within my young disciple, whom you dragged into my home—"

"Oh, enough, please—stop."

"God is the one who has been speaking all this while; God, it is, who wishes me to stop!"

"*Jothidar*, all I wanted to know were the names, clan and whereabouts of the women who just left. Do please stop beating around the bush, and provide me the details. And if you will—"

"What would you offer me, exactly?"

"*Vandhanam*; my eternal gratitude, of course."

"You may keep it. I much prefer *pon-dhanam*."

"Fair enough. Would my gold overcome your scruples?"

"That would depend on my discretion. Listen, *Thambi*. An astrologer has many visitors; we must not divulge information about one to another. I should never, for instance, reveal anything about the women who just left, to you. Neither will I betray information about you, to anyone who asks!"

"Ah, Azhwarkkadiyaan Nambi was right about you!"

"And who would that be?"

"Don't you know? He spoke of you as though you were a long-lost friend. And here, you don't even seem to have heard of him."

"Perhaps I know the man, but have forgotten his name. Describe him to me, if you please."

"Short and squat, with a top knot. He's got quite a paunch, and wears his *veshti* tight, around it. He bears the Vaishnavite mark all over his body in broad stripes, and quarrels with Saivites every chance he gets. As for Advaitha philosophers, he beats them with his trusty stick. A few moments ago you declared that God resided within you and me, didn't you? Well, had Azhwarkkadiyaan heard it, he'd have yelled: *God now attacks God*, and gone at you with a will!"

"Judging by what you have said so far, this would seem to be Thirumalai."

"Does he have more than one name, then?"

"That staunch Vaishnavite has a name for every town he visits."

"And a disguise to suit every person too, I suppose?"

"To every situation, as well."

"And his words are a clever mixture of truth and lies, aren't they?"

"Three fourths, and three-and-a-half *veesam* might be lies and fantasies but the last, tiny half-*veesam* would be the truth."

"A thorough rogue, you say?"

"Not at all. He returns kindness with kindness, and villainy in like."

"But you can't really trust him, can you?"

"That would depend on his speech."

"He said, for example, that you'd deliver an accurate prediction about my future."

"I did mention that there would half a *veesam's* truth in his words, didn't I? There you are."

"In that case, do please predict something. Time's running out, *Ayya*—I must leave."

"Where would you be going in such a hurry?"

"Couldn't you divine that as well? After all, that was what I wished to ask you about—my journey, destination and the success of my mission."

"We need just a little more information even for such predictions, *Thambi*. A horoscope, for example; if not, your date of birth and star—or, failing that, at least your name and hometown."

"My name is Vandhiyathevan."

"Ah! A descendent of the Vaanar clan?"

"Yes."

"You are Vallavarayan Vandhiyathevan?"

"Indeed I am."

"Excellent! Now, why couldn't you have mentioned this earlier? I may have to search my collection—but I believe I actually do have your horoscope."

"You do? How come?"

"Astrologers such as myself survive with such stock-in-trade, *Thambi*. We collect birth-charts of descendents of great clans and tribes to study them—"

"But I'm hardly one, am I?"

"Good God, my man. What is this that you say? Your dynasty is amongst the greatest that have ruled—why, so many poets have sung the praises of your ancestors in such glowing terms as to put others to shame! But perhaps you have not heard any."

"Why don't you recite one, then?"

The astrologer began at once:

"Vaanan pugazhuraiya
Vaayundo Maagadharkon
Vaanan peyarezhudhaa
Maarbundo vaanan
Kodithaangi nillaatha
Kombundo undo
Adithaangi nillaa
Arasu!"

["*There is none who does not speak of the Vaanar clan's glory; no chest that does not inscribe their valiant name; no staff that does not have the Vaanar flag flying proud; no ruling dynasty that is greater than theirs!*"]

Judging by his performance, the astrologer was no singer—but what he lacked in voice, he more than made up for in spirit and execution.

"Well?" he asked, when he finished.

"It does sound very well, I admit. But to tell the truth, *Ayya*, there's no staff that will carry my ancestor's flag unless I tie it on one, myself. And there's certainly no land, no *arasu* that bears our rule anymore—the only one I can hope for is if I stand on an *arasu* tree. And even that might collapse under my weight and fling me to the ground!"

"That might be the case today—but who knows what might happen tomorrow?"

"Why, I thought you'd know," put in Vandhiyathevan.

"How could I, *Thambi*? This astrologer is but an ordinary mortal, like everyone else. Stars and planets chart our lives and futures; all I do is use my meager skills to divine their course and inform others who seek such knowledge."

"And what do they say about me?"

"That you grow with each passing day."

"Good grief. My height is a hindrance already—I had to duck, just to enter your home. What am I to do with more? Do let's not be vague, but more specific, please."

"Only if your query is precise, as well."

"Fair enough. Will my mission to Thanjavur succeed?"

"If it is on your account—then yes, for your stars are on the rise, my boy. If it is on behalf of someone else, though—I shall have to look at their horoscopes to determine its fate."

"Good God, *Ayya*," Vandhiyathevan shook his head, and touched a finger to his nose in an expression of surprise. "I have never, in my life, met anyone quite as clever as you."

"Flattery will get you nowhere, *Thambi*."

"Be that as it may—I shall make myself clearer. I wish to seek an audience with the Emperor in Thanjavur. Will I?"

"For that, you may have to consult two far greater astrologers in Thanjavur."

"And who might they be?"

"One is Periya Pazhuvettarayar. The other is Chinna Pazhuvettarayar."

"I've heard it said that the Emperor's health is rapidly failing. True?"

"Gossip is untrustworthy at the best of times, *Thambi*. Who cares what anyone says? Do not believe everything you hear. And do not repeat it either."

"And what about the succession to the throne? Who do you think will be the Chakravarthy's heir?"

"Considering it is unlikely to be either you or me—why must we concern ourselves with such things?"

"Why indeed," sighed Vandhiyathevan. "We're certainly spared that."

"True. It is no easy thing to be the heir to an empire, *Thambi*. Far too dangerous, in fact."

"*Jothidar*, you recall that Prince Aditha Karikalar is in Kanchi at the moment."

"I do. You are here on his behalf, aren't you?"

"Finally! You've certainly taken your time guessing the truth. Now, what about his future?"

"I am afraid I do not have his horoscope. Any prediction I make can be done only if I have a copy."

"Well, what about Prince Madhuranthakar's fortunes?"

"A strange horoscope, that one, *Thambi*. Almost feminine in its characteristics. His is a life that will always be under the influence of others."

"Isn't that how affairs are, these days? Everyone vows and declares that the empire is ruled by a woman—that we've knuckled down under a veritable *Alli Rajyam*?"

"Do they? Where?"

"North of the Kollidam."

"Perhaps they speak of the domineering young queen of Periya Pazhuvettarayar."

"Not to my knowledge."

"Oh? Who else, then?"

"Supposedly, it's the Chakravarthy's daughter Princess Kundhavai, who rules the land with an iron hand."

The astrologer subjected Vandhiyathevan to a careful scrutiny: did the young man know, perhaps, that it was Princess Kundhavai who had just left? Were all his questions a result of that knowledge, and the desire to dig deeper?

Vandhiyathevan's face, however, remained guileless.

"That is ridiculous, *Thambi*. The Emperor resides in Thanjai, whereas Kundhavai Devi has made her home in Pazhaiyarai. Moreover—"

"Well? Moreover … what? What were you about to say?"

"One should look around well, when speaking of such things in broad daylight—and never even think to utter them at night. However, you seem trustworthy enough. These days, the Emperor has no powers, does he? Aren't the Pazhuvettarayars the ones truly holding the Empire's reins in their hands?"

And the astrologer stared hard at Vandhiyathevan, again.

"Never fear—I'm not their spy. You needn't entertain any suspicions on that score. You spoke, a while ago, about the fragility of kingdoms and dynasties, about how vulnerable they were. You even quoted the Vaanar dynasty as an example. I request you now—please tell me what the future truly holds, for the Chozha Empire."

"Very well. Listen, and I shall tell you this without the slightest shadow of doubt: By the end of the month of *Aani*, Kaveri and her sister rivers will overflow, almost breaking their banks with fresh floods. People familiar with Ponni will know that these are new waters and that they will only increase, as the days pass by. And that is how it will be through the months of *Aavani* and *Purattasi*. From *Kaarthigai* to *Margazhi*, the floods will begin to subside—and people will understand then, as well, that such is the way of nature. That, *Thambi*, is the Chozha Empire, now: it grows and grows, like the new floods of Ponni and it will continue to expand for the next few hundred years. At the moment, the Chozha Empire is like that of a waxing moon. It expands evermore. But there are days, yet, for it to become a radiant full moon. And so it shall be."

"Thank you. I'm glad, at any rate, that you've told me this much in all this time. Just one thing more: I've longed to go on a sea voyage for a while now ..."

"You will. You possess, you see, the *sakadayogam*—you are destined to travel the world as though your feet were on wheels. You will walk, ride horses; elephants—and even travel aboard a ship. Oh yes, I certainly predict a sea-voyage in your future."

"*Ayya*, the Senapathi of the Southern Chozha Forces, Prince Arulmozhi Varmar who wages war in Eezham at the moment—what can you tell me about him? How do the stars and planets chart his future?"

"*Thambi*, you have heard, I suppose, that sailors use compasses to tell direction, mid-sea? Lighthouses are of great assistance as well. But do you know the greatest and most valuable aid to any sailor in choppy waters? It is the pole star, the *Dhruva Natchathiram* that glows in the northern horizon. Other stars and planets may change position often; even the Seven Sages shift their paths. But the Dhruva star never moves; it shines steadily, always holding its position. That, *Thambi*, describes Emperor Sundara Chozhar's youngest son, Prince Arulmozhi Varmar. Nothing can shake his courage and determination; he is as valiant as he is compassionate, and trustworthy. His knowledge of the world is as deep and thorough as his education; those who look upon his innocent, radiant face will feel their sorrows and hardships vanish, and contentment fill them; he is, in fact, the cherished son of good fortune. Young men like you, who wish to make something of their lives, would do well to take him as their idol, just as the sailors guide their ships with the help of the Dhruva star."

"Good God—*how* you do portray Arulmozhi Varmar! As though a young woman describing her beloved?"

"Anyone who claims the lands of Ponni as his home, *Thambi*, will say the same."

"Thank you, *Ayya*. If ever I have the chance, I shall certainly put your words to good use."

"Your stars are on the ascendance as well, *Thambi*—that was why I predicted what I did."

"I shall take your leave, then. And with my thanks, I give you what gold I can afford, as well. Do please, accept it."

And Vandhiyathevan set down five gold *kazhanjus*, or coins, as his fee.

"The Vaanar dynasty's reputation for philanthropy remains untarnished!" The astrologer duly accepted them.

ℛ

Hidden Meanings and Explanations
Veesam
A measure.

14

THE CROCODILE ON THE BANKS

In those days, it was the custom among travelers from Kudandhai to Thanjavur to journey along the Arisilaaru or the banks of the River Ponni, towards Thiruvayaaru, from whence they turned south, towards the capital. The reason for their choice was simple: it was on this route that ferries were plentiful to cross the rivers that cut across their path: Kudamurutti, Vettaru, Vennaru and Vadavaaru.

Vandhiyathevan was no different. The first thing he did when he left Kudandhai was to strike out towards the Arisilaaru—and it would be safe to say that everything he had seen so far, of Chozha Nadu's splendour far exceeded his expectations. It is quite natural, isn't it, to gasp in amazement at any vision of beauty, when one first lays eyes on it?

He cantered past lush green farms flourishing with the rich scent of ginger and turmeric; sugarcane and plantain fields; groves of coconut and areca-nut; gentle streams; burbling brooks; placid ponds and canals that seemed to follow on one another's heels in quick succession. Hyacinths and lilies grew in profusion in the brooks, while the ponds practically overflowed with red and white lotuses, *sengazhuneer* and *neelothpalam* flowers, in a riot of colour and scent. Flocks of storks flew into the sky, large off-white patches in contrast to the vibrant shades on earth; *Naarai* birds stood on one red leg in the waters, lost in meditation. Smaller canals crisscrossing the fields gushed with water; the fields themselves, enriched by manure, leaves and shoots were a deep, earthy colour, overflowing with mush. Farmers worked these lands from dawn to dusk, tilling the soil; women bent towards the earth, engaged in planting, even as they raised their voice in glorious folk songs.

Lush, fully grown sugarcanes from the previous year were cut in the fields and transported to mills nearby, where they were promptly pressed for their sweet juice; jaggery was boiled in their vicinity as well and the scents mingled, assaulting the senses in tantalizing fashion.

Tiny, charming huts, some with thatched roofs, others with tiles, peeped out from the midst of luxurious coconut groves; their entrances, washed and paved with fresh cow-dung were in pristine condition, almost gleaming like mirrors. Some had paddy strewn across their front-doors; roosters often pecked the grains, crowed a lusty "*Kokkorakko!*" before prancing away. Children supposed to be guarding the grains, barely glanced at them; they went on playing with shells or the fascinating game of *pallanguzhi*. *Those roosters can't possibly eat all that much*, seemed to be their stance, and the thieving birds were largely ignored.

Fragrant smoke billowed above the huts; the aroma of boiling rice, frying *kambu* grain and roasted meat wafted around them; Vandhiyathevan's mouth fairly watered. Most warriors of those times were carnivores; the young man was no different.

Smithies dotted the roadside at regular intervals; glowing coals burnt fiercely within. *Danaar! Danaar!* There—that was the din of iron being forged. Along with farming implements such as ploughs, spades and crowbars were littered swords, shields, bows and spears in large heaps; farmers and soldiers alike jostled with each other, eager to claim their implement of choice.

The tiniest of villages boasted temples that matched their stature;

they resounded with the auspicious sounds of clanging *semakkalams*, the beats of the *nagara*, sacred chants and sweet *Thevaram* hymns. Local deities such as Mariamman were placed on soft cushions and paraded while priests danced in the procession, often carrying colourful *karagams* on their heads or beating tiny percussion instruments known as *udukkai*, a sign of their devotion. Some received liberal offerings of paddy, as well.

Cows ambled through the villages, the bells around their necks tinkling musically while boys drove them towards pasture, some even playing accompaniment on their flutes. Farmers mopped sweating faces as they worked, and rested in the cool shade of trees during intervals. These were the times they enjoyed ram-fights, setting the horned animals against each other and egging them on.

Peahens shrieked lustily from their perches atop huts; peacocks, fascinated by their calls, dragged their magnificent plumage with difficulty and swung through the air, settling down among them.

Beautiful doves stalked here and there, twisting their necks to look about them.

As for the parrots and nightingales, locked away in cages—ah, those pitiful creatures sang sorrowful songs from within their prisons.

Yes, there was plenty to see. Vandhiyathevan drank in the sights, clip-clopping slowly on his horse, his mind engaged in capturing and storing away as much as he could.

But even as he tried to lose himself in the outside world, he was aware, deep down in his subconscious mind, of a picture—the picture of a beautiful young woman, shrouded in the mists of his memory.

Ah, why couldn't she have parted her coral lips and addressed a few words to him? Surely that would have been no loss to her? Who could have she been? No matter—obviously, someone not very conversant with good manners. Else, she'd have paid some attention to him, wouldn't she? Was he, Vandhiyathevan such an insignificant specimen that she must ignore him so completely? And that wily astrologer hadn't breathed a word about her identity! Clever, cunning old man, diverting his attention so well, to other concerns. How perceptive he had been—how vast, his experience of the world! To tell the truth, he's managed to escape saying anything of worth; his predictions about royal affairs were vague in the extreme, filled with caution. The things he did reveal were already public knowledge. Still, he *had* mentioned that Vandhiyathevan's stars were on the rise, hadn't he? For that alone, he deserved some good fortune. Long live the Kudandhai astrologer!

Vandhiyathevan traveled thus, his mind occupied with everything he had heard and seen, so far. Sometimes, the outside world caught his attention and he gave his mind to it as well, in brief intervals. Eventually, he reached his destination, the Arisilaaru.

In the distance, he heard a few sounds, and stopped.

Feminine laughter—and the tinkling of bangles. Vandhiyathevan stared at the banks, intrigued, but the dense foliage screened the ladies effectively. The urge to seek them out struck him and he trotted along the riverside, peering through the trees, trying to find where they might be.

Abruptly, he heard a scream. "*Ayyo! Ayyo!* A crocodile—help, please!"

Instantly, Vandhiyathevan spurred his horse towards the frightened voice. There! He could see a few women through a gap in the trees. Terror painted their faces vividly—ah, what a surprise! Two of them were the young women he had seen at the astrologer's home.

It took only a few moments for Vandhiyathevan to take all this in—but this was not the only thing he saw.

Underneath a large tree, clothed in deep shadows, lay a large crocodile, half on land and half in water, almost part of an enormous tree's thick roots. Its mouth gaped wide, teeth jagged and sharp. Vandhiyathevan had seen one such terrifying reptile himself in the Kollidam; he had also heard what frightening predators they were.

This one particularly, brought his worst fears to the surface and set his nerves jangling with tension. Not only did it seem ready for a human feast, it was very near the laughing young women as well, mouth open wide as if to chomp upon them. All it had to do was pounce forward—and they would be torn to pieces! The banks were thick with clusters of trees; there was really no way for the women to break through and escape.

His heart may have been murky with confused feelings, but Vandhiyathevan's resolve did not falter an instant. Neither did he spend time pondering his course of action: he hefted his trusty spear, took aim and threw it. The weapon cleaved through the air and struck the crocodile, sure and true, penetrating its thick skin and plunging in a little. At once, Vandhiyathevan sprang forward with his sword, fully intending to rip it apart, once and for all.

But—but why were these women laughing, just like before? Vandhiyathevan could barely stomach it. Why were they giggling? He stopped short, suddenly unsure. Not a vestige of fear was on the faces of the women around him; they looked amused, eyes gleaming with mirth. Certainly, they did not seem to be the young ladies who had shrieked with terror just a few moments ago.

One of them—the majestic young woman he had seen at the astrologer's home—spoke in a melodious voice. "Girls, quiet, all of you! Laughing at such a moment—!"

Her stern words echoed vaguely in Vandhiyathevan's ears as though in a dream.

Sword still held aloft, he directed his attention to the crocodile. Then, he stared hard at the chuckling women. A suspicion reared up its head—a suspicion that froze him, mind and body curling in acute embarrassment.

The young woman walked forward again and stood opposite the crocodile, as though guarding it. "Many thanks to you, *Ayya*—but there's no need to trouble yourself."

ஜீ

15

Vanathi's Deceit

Some time ago, we saw Princess Kundhavai and her companion Vanathi climb into their chariot and set off for Kudandhai, did we not? It now behooves us to see what the young women left behind in the boat were up to, and listen to their conversation.

"Talk about that Kodumbalur girl's luck!" spoke one. "Tharakai, my girl—why on earth does our Ilaiya Piratti favour her so much?"

"Favour, my foot. Nothing of the sort, Vaarini. That little idiot has been wandering like a lunatic for the last four months, fainting all over the place. She has no parents—*of course* you'd expect Kundhavai Devi to be worried about someone completely entrusted to her care. That, I suspect, is the only reason for her concern, and she's taken the girl to the astrologer to—to instate enquiries, as they say," said Tharakai, decidedly. "Perhaps she's afflicted by ghosts or spirits? They'd have to employ a good many chants and rituals to drive them out of her, wouldn't they?"

"Ghosts and spirits!" spat Vaarini, with terrible scorn. "Which of those pathetic things would get hold of *her*? That one is capable of banishing a hundred ghosts all on her own!"

"Vanathi's fainting fits? All an act," supplied another. "It's her plan to cast a net and slowly reel our Prince into her scheming, greedy clutches."

"Niravathi is right," concurred Vaarini. "Remember that day when she actually dropped her sacred *aarathi* plate, with its flame glowing bright? I'm quite sure that was just a ploy to get his attention. How do you think a sturdy plate, held with both hands could possibly slip and fall? Shaking and shivering at the sight of our Prince too—as though he were some sort of wild animal, a tiger or bear. Really?"

"And to actually faint away gracefully once she did let the plate fall—imagine the cunning of that woman! She pulled that off quite neatly, I must admit."

"What angers me is not even her sly act, but that Kundhavai Devi and our Prince were taken in so completely," exclaimed one, called Senthiru. "How *could* they?"

"Truly, these are the times of liars, cheats and those who employ cunning and wiles without a speck of remorse," mourned a young lady named Mandhakini.

"But it worked, didn't it?" queried Vaarini. "The Prince, who'd almost started for battle, returned and made enquiries about Vanathi, didn't he? Her deceit actually served its purpose."

"Not at all. The fact that he asked after her only shows how solicitous he is. Did you really expect him to just walk away without a backward glance, once he'd seen a girl faint right in front of him?" countered Tharakai. "You needn't make it out to be something it isn't."

"I'm not. But you're right about the Prince—he's *quite* the most compassionate person in all the fourteen worlds. There's no one to equal him, not even in our epics and tales!" enthused Vaarini. "But that's not what I'm talking about. This one—Vanathi—do you know why she faints so much? There's no need to tramp all the way to an astrologer about it. I could have told Kundhavai Devi myself!"

"Do you know what ails her, then?" questioned Senthiru. "Well?"

Vaarini leaned forward and murmured something into her friend's ears.

"What are you whispering about?" asked Niravathi. "Why couldn't you tell us all, too?"

"Vanathi's illness isn't an ordinary one, it seems," revealed Senthiru, mischief gleaming in her eyes. "She faints of desire!"

The boat rang with peals of merry laughter; birds, roosting contentedly in the trees around, flapped away at the sudden sound.

"This wily one might try some of her sorcery on the Prince again; sprinkle him with magic dust, maybe, when he returns from battle in Ilankai," said Niravathi. "We're not going to let her get away with it, are we?"

"I can tell you this: by the time he does return to Chozha Nadu, Vanathi is likely to tear all her hair out and run completely insane," predicted Tharakai. "Or I shall change my name to the demoness Thadagai!"

"Forget her for the moment and bend your mind, if you please, to the task Ilaiya Piratti set us. Oughtn't we to complete it before she returns?" Mandhakini cut in. "Quickly!"

Two of the young women bent and pulled up a plank at the bottom of the boat, which was a little askew. Underneath was a space the dimensions of a long box, and in it lay a crocodile! One long dead and gone, which had been preserved, stuffed with cotton and fibre, and now looked as real as a live one. They placed it above board carefully, released the boat from its moorings and rowed slowly, until they came to a huge tree on the banks, its thick roots crisscrossing heavily over each other. They threw the crocodile out, placing it strategically half in and half out of the water. Lying motionless on the roots, it looked every bit as menacing as a real one, mouth open wide. To keep it from getting washed away, one of the reptile's legs was tied to a root with a slender rope which the young women made sure, lay submerged in the water.

"Mandhakini, my girl," began Tharakai. "Why do you think Ilaiya Piratti asked us to set up this elaborate charade?"

"Didn't you know? It's to stop Vanathi from being such a terrible coward. Kundhavai Devi wishes her to screw up some courage, I gather."

"Why—it almost looks like …" Niravathi paused, and pondered. "Has she decided, after all, that Vanathi will make our Prince the perfect wife?"

"If there's any such scheme in the offing, I shall poison that sly wretch with my own hands, see if I don't!" swore Vaarini, who was inclined to harbour a jealous nature.

"Don't let such thoughts upset you, my dear. I've heard that everyone from the Rettai Mandala Chakravarthy in Maniya Kedam; the King of Vengi; the Emperor of Kalinga, to the rulers of Empires as far away as Kanauj, are fighting over themselves to get their daughters married to our Prince. Why would anyone waste time upon an insignificant Kodumbalur girl when so many other such favourable alliances glimmer upon the horizon?" spoke Mandhakini, reassuringly.

"Every Emperor in the world might await the Chozha dynasty's pleasure—but surely our Prince's opinion is the only one that matters the most? I've heard it said that he has very definite ideas about wedlock. *If I ever enter upon marriage, it will only be with a girl from Thamizhagam,* he seems to have said," informed Senthiru. "Surely you all know this?"

"Excellent, then. We'll all work some sorcery on our own and show everyone what we're capable of, one by one. If that little witch Vanathi can play up to the Prince so much, surely we can, too?" announced Tharakai. "Even better, perhaps. We've all got our share of magic dust, haven't we?"

There was reason enough for such vitriolic speech from every young lady on the boat—a particular incident that had roused the worst in them. An event that we shall now explore.

৯৯

Hidden Meanings and Explanations
Aarathi
A sacred ritual usually performed by the women of any household to drive away evil spirits, before embarking upon any important event.

16

ARULMOZHI VARMAR

Around 980 years ago, the southern lands flourished under the inimitable rule of Emperor Rajakesari Varmar, Sundara Chozhar, who had ascended the throne approximately twelve years before this story opens. In the last hundred years, the Chozha Empire had grown by leaps and bounds; its dominions expanding with every generation— and yet, affairs were in a tumultuous state when Sundara Chozhar came to power; foes were gaining in strength to the south and north of the empire. Sundarar's predecessor Kandaradhithar had pledged himself to Siva Peruman, and lost himself in worship; such was his piety that he had even earned the respectful title *Siva Gnana Kandaradhithar*. Deep devotion aside, this meant that the Empire's administration suffered, as he had little time to spare for affairs of state; nor did he bend his mind or energy towards expanding existing dominions. Arinjayar, who succeeded his brother to the throne, stayed on it for merely a year before breathing his last in Atrur in Thondai Mandalam, thus earning a unique sobriquet—

Atruril Thunjiya Thevar—which meant that his son, Paranthaka Sundara Chozhar was his heir and successor.

The young ruler seemed to posses every characteristic that defined an Emperor, destined to raise his people and lands to great heights. Naturally inclined towards battle and proficient in martial strategy, one of the first things he did upon ascending the throne, was to go to war in the south. Chozha and Pandiya forces clashed in a terrible battle in Sevur. Despite the assistance of Ilankai King Mahindan's army which had journeyed all the way from Ilankai, Veera Pandiyan's hordes suffered a crushing defeat at the hands of the far greater Chozhas. Lost, without his crown, kingdom and cohorts, Veera Pandiyan managed to escape with just his life and hid himself away in a mountainous cave in arid lands, nursing his wounds in humiliation.

The Eezham forces suffered heavy casualties as well; those few who managed to survive decided that glory and valour were much too large a price to pay and took to their heels, back to Ilankai.

Such had been the situation for at least a while now: it had become almost an acknowledged practice of sorts for the kings of Eezham to aid the Pandiyas, whenever the latter tussled with the Chozhas. Sundarar, not unnaturally, wanted to put a stop to this: he decided that the Sinhala kings needed to be taught a lesson and sent a large force under the command of Commander Paranthaka Velaan, the Younger of the Kodumbalur dynasty, to teach it.

Their intentions may have been exceptional, but the army failed when it came to strategy and execution. Despite their huge numbers, the Chozha forces did not reach Ilankai at the same time; a lack of ships forced them to stagger their approach. The first lot, instead of waiting for the rest to arrive and regroup, took a decision to advance alone. They paid for their lack of forethought dearly: Sinhala forces, led by Mahindan's trusted Commander Sena, surrounded them. Bloody battle broke out and raged furiously—and it was here that Paranthaka Velaan the Younger lost his life, carving a name for himself in the history and stone inscriptions of Thamizhagam forevermore with this valiant title:

Eezhathu Patta Paranthakan Siriya Velaan, or *Paranthaka Velaan the Younger, Who Embraced Death at Eezham.*

No sooner did Veera Pandiyan, hiding in his cave, hear this news than he gathered forces again to battle the Chozhas, renewed with a fresh burst of courage and hope. He was destined to taste a defeat far worse than the previous time: not only was his army routed out but he himself lost his life. This was the battle that saw the emergence of Sundara Chozhar's son Aditha Karikalar as a decisive warrior: he took charge, decimated the enemy and performed a great many valiant deeds which earned him the prestigious title of *Veera Pandiyan Thalaikonda Kopparakesari*—the *Kopparakesari Who Beheaded Veera Pandiyan.*

They might have proven their point with the Pandiya forces—but the urge to teach Sinhala king Mahindan a lesson still burned fiercely, not just in Sundara Chozhar's heart but also that of his commanders, aides, right down to the last, raw soldier. Accordingly, a huge army was assembled once again—but this time, an important question cropped up: who would lead them?

Sundara Chozhar's firstborn, Crown Prince Aditha Karikalar was stationed with his forces at the northern frontiers, at this time. Lately, the Rashtrakuta forces had been usurping power in Thirumunaippaadi and Thondai Mandalam; the Prince had taken them to task severely, and driven them out. His mission complete, he had made Kanchi his headquarters and was immersed in preparations for further war, in the north.

This being the case, it was obvious that there was now a chance for others to prove themselves. The commanders of the Chozha forces now began to compete among themselves in earnest for the honour of leading their army to Eezham. Much jealousy was roused; many, the incidents of back-stabbing and resentment. In those hoary days, it was more the norm among warriors to fight for the honour of leaving for the battlefield, than staying behind. Many were the quarrels and disputes that often rose, when it came to expressing valour in war.

One man, however, came forward to hush them and avoid further altercations: Sundara Chozhar's younger son, Prince Arulmozhi Varmar.

"*Appa*," he addressed his father. "I've spent enough time being coddled by my aunts and grandmothers at Pazhaiyarai. Kindly appoint me the Commander of the Southern Chozha Forces. Allow me to leave for Ilankai—and I shall lead our men to victory!"

Barely nineteen at that time, he was the cherished youngest child of the Emperor; adored by the many queens and royal ladies at Pazhaiyarai—and indeed, the much beloved son of Chozha Nadu itself.

Emperor Sundara Chozhar was a handsome man. His father Arinjayar, infatuated with the luminous beauty of Kalyani, a princess of the Vaithumbarayar clan, legendary foes of the Chozha dynasty, had married her forthwith; their son had been named Paranthakar. Chozha subjects, however, who were dazzled by his chiseled features and good looks, promptly renamed him Sundarar—The Beauteous One. The name found favour and was adopted, henceforth.

It was only natural that all his offspring be famed for their looks— but the last, Arulmozhi Varmar outshone them all. His features possessed a beauty that seemed not merely human but almost divine, in their perfection. As an infant, he was coddled and petted endlessly by the royal women; so many were the kisses showered on his chubby cheeks that they were almost blistered red. But the one who cherished him the most, perhaps, was his elder sister Kundhavai.

She may have only been a couple of years older than him but somehow, the idea that *she* was responsible for her young brother's wellbeing had lodged itself firmly in young Kundhavai's consciousness. Even more astonishing—Arulmozhi Varmar cherished an equal, if not greater regard and affection, for his sister. Not a thought or word would he entertain that might displease her. Kundhavai's slightest wish was his command; her every word carried almost divine authority. Not even the combined forces of the holy trinity, Brahma, Vishnu and Siva could serve to turn him against her, or ignore her instructions. The very thought was repugnant to him.

She, for her part, spent many *naazhigais* watching him keenly—not just when he was awake, but asleep as well. *He possesses divine gifts, this boy—a strange power; a magnetism,* she would muse often, as her eyes scrutinized his chiseled features. *It is my duty to ensure that his potential is nurtured to fruition!*

She turned his palms upwards often as he slept, and gazed keenly at the lines that crisscrossed them. In her imagination, they resembled the divine conch and discus, symbols of the supreme Thirumaal himself. Ah, this young man was obviously meant to bring the whole wide world under his benign rule! But then—there seemed to be no indication whatsoever that he would ever ascend the Chozha throne. There were already two contenders to the Empire, senior to him—where was the question of Arulmozhi ever becoming a ruler? Which throne would he ever grace? On the other hand, humans were incapable of understanding God's will or His divine plans. The world was huge; thousands of *rajyams* and empires dotted its surface. There were wondrous tales of heroes traveling from one kingdom to another, winning each and ascending thrones with incredible courage and indomitable will, weren't there? Hadn't a young prince from the country of Vanga, practically thrown out from his own fertile, Ganga-enriched plains, made his escape on boat, reached Ilankai, and managed to rule that island-country wisely and well? Hadn't his descendents, the proud Sinhala royal family, carried his name for a thousand years?

Thus, Kundhavai Piratti spent her days, foreseeing and planning endlessly, her young sibling's future. Eventually, when discussion about commanding the forces to Eezham came up, she decided that Arulmozhi was the best contender for the position.

"*Thambi*, it hurts me greatly to be parted from you, but I'm afraid I must be the one to send you away," she said. "You must go to Ilankai— you will be the Commander of the Southern Chozha forces!"

The Prince submitted to this dictum with great enthusiasm. Hitherto, he had been stifled among the overpowering affection of the royal mothers; when, oh when would he ever be rid of their smothering ties? And now, his very sister had given him permission to leave—what more did he need?

There would be no obstacles to his going either; was there a soul in the Chozha Empire who could gainsay her? Did she not reign supreme in Emperor Sundara Chozhar's heart? And did not *he* think the world of his daughter's good sense?

In due course, Prince Arulmozhi Varmar was appointed the *Thenthisai Maathanda Naayakar,* the Commander of the Southern Chozha forces; he left for Ilankai, and did head the armed forces for an appreciable time. War, however, was not finished with him; there seemed to be a great deal of difference between his, and others' approach to it. There were a good many equipments and implements he had considerable difficulty in procuring, in this war-torn land; he needed these from his home-country for which he duly made a visit, petitioning his father the Emperor. Having made arrangements to suit his purpose, he soon prepared to set off for Ilankai again.

Princess Kundhavai made sure that her brother departed Pazhaiyarai in pomp and splendour: she had organized quite a few events in the principal palace for his edification. When Arulmozhi stepped out into the royal courtyard, conches blew deafeningly, *murasu* drums thundered victoriously accompanied by the smaller *siru parai* beats; chants of triumph cleaved the very skies.

Every one of the royal mothers blessed their favourite son, applied sacred ash on his forehead, uttered many blessings to ward off evil spirits and gave him leave to return to battle.

At the palace's main entrance, as Prince Arulmozhi Varmar prepared to step from within the complex towards the street, stood Kundhavai Devi's handmaidens, each with a golden plate in her hand and on it, a lamp burning bright. No ordinary young women either, these; each was a member of some of the land's most prominent royal families; each considered it the epitome of good fortune to serve at the feet of Periya Piratti Sembian Mahadevi, and be the friend and confidante of Kundhavai Piratti. One among them was the Kodumbalur princess, Vanathi, daughter of Paranthaka Velaan the Younger.

The prince neared them; the young ladies felt their hearts flutter in excitement and delight. They raised their golden plates and began to perform an *aarathi*.

Abruptly, for some reason, Vanathi's slender frame shook and shivered. *Danaar!* The plate slipped from her nerveless hands and fell to the ground in an explosion of sound.

Ah, how inauspicious! —was the thought that flitted through the minds of everyone present. And yet, despite the plate having crashed down in such a terrible fashion—the wick continued to burn steadily. An almost audible sigh of relief swept in a gust through the gathering. This, pronounced many elders, was an excellent omen indeed.

A smile blossomed on the face of Prince Arulmozhi Varmar at the terrified young woman who had let slip her plate in such inexplicable fashion. He moved beyond her—and the next instant, Vanathi, who was obviously overwhelmed with embarrassment at her clumsiness, crumpled to the ground, unconscious.

The rest of the women, following Kundhavai's command, swiftly carried her into a room and laid her on a platform. Ilaiya Piratti herself stayed with Vanathi, trying to bring her around in vain; so absorbed was she in this task that she did not even watch her brother take his leave. Arulmozhi Varmar, who had caught sight of Vanathi fainting at the doorstep, paused before climbing onto his horse and sent a messenger to his sister: "What ails the young woman who fainted just now? Is she better?"

"Ask the Prince to step in here for a moment," was Princess Kundhavai's terse reply. Accustomed to obeying her every command, Arulmozhi Varmar returned to the palace at once. He walked into the room Vanathi was laid in, and saw his sister trying desperately to bring that young woman around as she lay against her shoulder. The sight was enough to melt his heart.

"Who is this young woman, Akka?" asked the Prince. "What's her name?"

"Vanathi—she's the daughter of Kodumbalur Paranthaka Velaan

the Younger," answered Kundhavai, almost abstracted. "She's frightened easily."

"Ah—*now* I understand the reason for her weakness. Wasn't her father the warrior who led Chozha forces to Ilankai and embraced death in battle? Perhaps those memories were too much for her."

"Perhaps—but I shall take care of her, never fear. May you be victorious in war, *Thambi*! Return to us safely, and keep me apprised of everything through messages," advised Kundhavai.

"As you wish," acknowledged the Prince. "Please do the same for me as well."

Perhaps it was the effect of his melodious voice—but Vanathi began to regain consciousness by degrees. Her eyelids fluttered; the sight of the Prince in front of her made them open very wide. Her face bloomed with unexpected delight. Lips as red as coral parted a little, and a shy smile appeared on her face, dimpling her cheeks.

With consciousness returned awareness; she rose, suddenly bashful, and realized that she had been lying against Princess Kundhavai all this while. Embarrassment overwhelmed her as she remembered all that had happened, in an instant. "*Akka*, what have I done?" she whispered, eyes brimming with tears.

The Prince cut in, before Kundhavai could. "There's no need to fret, Vanathi—these things happen to the best of us. And you, in particular, have more reason than any to be overwhelmed. In fact, I was saying as much to Ilaiya Piratti."

Vanathi could barely believe her ears. Was it really the Prince, widely reputed to have never even glanced at any woman, consoling her thus? Was it really he who was soothing her with sweet words? Ah, how could she bear such good fortune? What had she done to deserve this? Why, her skin was breaking out in goose-bumps. Her head spun—she was about to faint again …

"*Akka*, my men await me," the Prince spoke once more. "When next you send a missive, kindly inform me about this young woman's health as well. Do take care of her—she has no one else, you see." He was gone on the words.

The rest of Princess Kundhavai's handmaidens observed this exchange with keen interest, watching from various balconies, and through windows that liberally dotted the palace. A spark of jealousy was kindled in their hearts—which swiftly burst into a roaring flame.

For, ever since then, Kundhavai made Vanathi her especial friend, and began to take a keen interest in that young lady. The two were inseparable; Kundhavai showered Vanathi with affection. Fine arts, music or skills—she taught her everything she knew, and the two were rarely apart. Kundhavai often took her young friend to the royal gardens where she spoke at length about her brother's fortunes, her own dreams, and the grand future she had imagined for him. To all this, Vanathi listened with rapt and gratifying attention.

The Kodumbalur maiden fainted four of five times more, after this incident; Kundhavai attended to her always, and brought her back to consciousness.

The younger girl would come to, sobbing as if her heart would break, each time. "Silly girl!" Kundhavai would remonstrate, and console her as best as she could. "Come, now—dry your tears, do. Why do you weep this way?"

"I—I don't know, Akka," Vanathi would sob more. "Forgive me, please!"

And Kundhavai would embrace her, soothing her with soft words of reassurance and comfort.

All this, of course, only served to fan the flames of jealousy even more, in the hearts of the other handmaidens. Considering everything that had occurred so far, wasn't it only natural that they behave the way they did, once Kundhavai and Vanathi had set out for Kudandhai?

Hidden Meanings and Explanations

I. *"... uttered many blessings to ward off evil spirits..."*

The royal mothers bless Arulmozhi thus on the eve of his departure to Ilankai, described by Kalki as *"dhrishti kazhithu."* *Dhrishti*, although generally meaning sight, here indicates the evil eye. Simple rituals to remove such nefarious karmic ills involved one or all of the following:

circle the recipient of the evil eye with fire (usually lit camphor);

circle the recipient with a fistful of salt and chillies, and then carefully throw said fistful either in a kitchen fire or at a crossroads;

touch the face of the recipient and crack your knuckles against your forehead. Said to be the simplest and most effective of removal procedures, and followed almost unanimously by most mothers.

Variations include applying a dark mark of *mai* (*khol*) on the face but in Thamizhagam, this was usually reserved for babies and very young children. As Arulmozhi was considered a child by the royal ladies, one isn't quite sure if he was subjected to this treatment as well.

II. *"...widely reputed to have never even glanced at any woman..."*

This is how Kalki describes (through Vanathi's thoughts), Prince Arulmozhi Varmar: *"Pengalai saadhaaranamaaga erittup paarkkaamale pogum vazhakkamudaiya ilavarasar ..."*

To someone unfamiliar with ancient Thamizh codes that defined manliness, this description might prove befuddling. The trick is to look beyond the literal meaning: women were not looked upon as lustful objects. This evolved into a social construct: unfamiliar women were not to be gazed at, as a mark of respect and graciousness.

Clearly, in this context, Vanathi doesn't mean that Arulmozhi Varmar never looks at women; only that he doesn't treat them as objects of desire, since he respects the royal ladies—not to mention the greatest influence in his life, his mentor, advisor, guide and the one he reveres more than anyone: his sister, Kundhavai.

17

OF GALLOPING HORSES

Quite simply, matters stood thus: only the best of women could make an excellent bride for her brother who was destined to achieve greatness; who had no equal among men. This, Kundhavai had decided, was none other than Vanathi.

There was only one obstacle to her ambition: the one fault, in the Kodumbalur princess's disposition—Vanathi was much too much a coward for Kundhavai's taste. Surely a young woman about to wed a warrior among warriors; a princess destined to give birth to the emperor of emperors, could not afford to quake in fear at the slightest pretext?

Plainly, there was only one thing to do: Vanathi must be transformed into a fearless maiden at all costs. It was with this praiseworthy intention that she had arranged for the charade with a fake crocodile—but the Kodumbalur princess managed to exceed all her expectations and emerge victorious in her trial.

Once the princesses had returned from Kudandhai, they climbed into the boat, which cruised along the little river for a while. It was their custom to halt along the banks where trees grew in profusion; the young women would then play about in the water to their heart's content. They did the same today as well, and descended from the boat into the river.

Abruptly, one of them set up a yell. "*Ayyo*, a crocodile!" She pointed at the opposite side of the tree they stood beside. "A crocodile! *Ayyo!*" she screamed again. The rest promptly took up the refrain, shrieking in terror, and began to scuttle in every direction.

The only exception was Vanathi, who did not seem fazed in the least at the commotion. The sight of the predator a few bare feet from her, straddling tree roots and gaping it jaws wide, seemed to inspire no fear in her; neither did her obviously petrified friends, acting, as per their 'chief's instructions. "*Akka*, a crocodile is fearsome only when it's in the water," she explained to Kundhavai Devi. "This one's only on land. Do tell the others not to be scared, do!"

"Why, you little devil! You *knew* that it wasn't real, didn't you?' accused one of the girls. "Someone must have told you the truth!"

"I wouldn't have been afraid even if it *had* been a real one," confessed Vanathi. "You see—I'm terrified only of lizards and cockroaches."

It was at this moment that our hero Vandhiyathevan crashed through the trees and reached the river, eager to perform a daring rescue. He took a look at the fearsome crocodile, and threw his spear at it.

Then, that majestic young woman who had captured his fancy so much came forward, shielding the crocodile, and said something in a rich, melodious voice. Ah—one, at least of Vandhiyathevan's desires ever since he had seen her at the astrologer's home, was now fulfilled: she had parted her coral lips and spoken to him!

And yet—that crocodile bothered him considerably. Why was she standing in front, as though guarding the reptile? Why was she beseeching him "not to trouble himself"? And why, oh, why hadn't the ferocious predator in question moved an inch? Why did it lie so still?

Meanwhile, that young lady continued to speak. "*Ayya*, you apologized about barging into the astrologer's home in Kudandhai without so much as a by-your-leave—and I'm afraid we walked away without a word. Perhaps you think Chozha women are ill-mannered, but nothing could be further from the truth. My friend was feeling faint—and I was intent on caring for her. That, I assure you, was the only reason for my behaviour—"

Ah, what a musical voice! Why does my chest heave and flutter as she speaks to me? Why does a lump lodge itself into my throat? Neither flute nor the melodious veenai have ever inflamed me thus; the mathalam and drums of war have never roused me to such frenzy—not shaken me so! Why can't I interrupt her? No words rise to my memory—my tongue cleaves to my mouth—why? Why doesn't the wind rustle through the trees? Why do the waters of the Arisilaaru no longer flow? And that crocodile—why is it so still?

Even as his heart rose and fell with the tumult of emotion, the young woman who had mesmerized him continued to speak. There was a dream-like quality to the scene; her voice reached him as if through a mist: "*Ayya,* your intentions were most honourable—you threw your spear at the crocodile to save us helpless females from its terrible clutches. And I assure you, your valour is undisputed; such unerring accuracy is a very rare feat indeed—!"

The rest of the handmaidens, who had gathered under a tree, observing them, broke into a peal of merry laughter.

And Vandhiyathevan's beautiful dream crashed to an abrupt halt. The strands of the magical web her melodious words had woven around him broke with a snap.

He stared hard at the crocodile. Then, he stalked past the giggling maidens by the tree, and approached it. He placed a hand on his trusty spear, embedded in the reptile's body, and pulled hard. The spear, yielding to such robust treatment, came away—but what was this that spurted out of the gaping hole left behind? Blood and gore? Indeed, no—just lumps of cotton and plantain fibre!

Those girls—wretched, unfeeling girls—laughed again. And this time, they clapped and almost danced with unholy glee.

Vandhiyathevan wished the ground would simply open up and swallow him. Never, in all his years, had he ever suffered such crushing embarrassment. Why, *why* must he be subject to this crippling humiliation in front of these laughing girls? If they were, indeed, girls—no, little demons! He wouldn't spend a moment more, in their company. Ah, my trusted spear—to suffer such an ignominy! How am I ever going to cleanse this blemish, and avenge you?

All of these thoughts flitted through his mind in a matter of moments. Had those who dared to mock him been men—ah, things would have been mightily different, then. These banks would have seen a ferocious battle; none would have been alive to laugh at him! This pretty little Arisilaaru would have carried their blood to the seas instead of red, rich water! But these were women. What could he do but give them a wide berth and walk away?

Vandhiyathevan stepped away from them—ignored even the majestic young woman who had captured his attention—and sprang upon the banks, almost leaping towards his horse. That noble animal neighed when it saw its master; to Vandhiyathevan's furious ears, it sounded as though even his faithful steed was laughing at him. He treated it the way he could not treat the women: leaping onto its back, he delivered two stinging slaps with his reins. The horse, roused to fury, practically galloped along the riverside road.

Kundhavai stood staring for a while as stallion and soldier set off at a ferocious pace. She continued to watch as they disappeared in the distance, until the dust settled.

Then, she turned to her handmaidens. "Really, girls—you need a lesson on manners, all of you. You have every right to act any way you wish when we're alone—but kindly do, do strive for some decorum in front of others. And you shouldn't have laughed at him. Why you couldn't have kept your silence in the presence of a young man, I shall never know. What do you suppose his opinion will be, about the morals and manners of Chozha women?"

ॐ

18

IDUMBANKAARI

We shall now return to Azhwarkkadiyaan, also known more respectfully as Thirumalaiyappar, whom we left destitute on the banks of the Kollidam—and learn his fate.

He stared after Vandhiyathevan as that young man leapt on his horse and galloped towards Kudandhai. *The lad's a wily one,* he murmured to himself. *No matter how I try and trick him, he manages to evade my questions like a slippery eel. After all that—I couldn't find out a thing about his master or mission. And what was his part in the midnight conference at Kadambur? Was he even there? I don't know anything about that, either. Ah, well, at least I've bundled him off to Kudandhai—perhaps the astrologer can accomplish what I couldn't.*

A voice right by his ear made him jump. "Are you speaking to the *arasu* tree, *Swami*? Or to yourself?"

Thirumalaiyappar turned—to see, standing by him, the Kadambur soldier, who had brought Vandhiyathevan a horse.

"You, my man? I hate to disappoint you, but I wasn't talking to either—just a ghost that resides in this tree," was Azhwarkkadiyaan's repartee. "We happen to be old friends, you see."

"Ah—and would it be Saivite or Vaishnavite, your ghost?"

"That was *my* question too, but the dratted thing vanished before I could wring an answer. Never mind; what are you called?"

"Why do you wish to know, *Swami?*"

"You saved our boat from capsizing in the middle of the Kollidam, didn't you? Don't I have a sacred duty to remember you and yours?"

"My ... my name is—is Idumbankaari, *Swami,*" stammered the other.

"Why—it seems familiar to me, somehow ..."

Idumbankaari did something strange at that moment: he splayed out his fingers, turned palms towards the earth, placed one on top of another and waggled his thumbs on either side. All the while, he stared hard at Nambi.

"I'm afraid I don't understand—what sort of a sign is this, my man?" queried Thirumalaiyappar.

Idumbankaari's pinched face darkened further; his brows drew in a frown. "I? But I did nothing."

"Oh yes, you did. You placed your palms and brought them together in a gesture that Bharathanatyam dancers use, to depict Thirumaal's first incarnation, didn't you?"

"Thirumaal's incarnation? I really don't understand, *Swami.*"

"No? But how surprising! It's the *Machavatharam.*"

"*Macham*—do you mean a fish, perhaps?"

"Indeed, I do."

"Good heavens; such peculiar sight as you have! You see ghosts on empty trees, and fishes on my bare hands! Perhaps you're a little over-fond of sea food, eh, *Swami?*"

"*Chee!* Pray do not talk this way, my man. Be that as it may—

remember that staunch Saivite who traveled with us? Do you know which way he went?"

"Don't I, now? He joined me on my journey to get a horse and called you every name he could think of, all the way, not to mention heaping abuse—"

"If you'd be kind enough to be specific—"

"That if he ever saw you again, he would shave off your top knot; make sure you were bald—"

"Ah, so he's trained in that sort of work too, is he?"

"—and he would rub off every vestige of Thirumaal's sign, the *naamam* on your body and smother you in Siva Peruman's sacred ash, as well!"

"Ha—in that case, I really must meet him. Where does he hail from, do you know?"

"He mentioned that he was from Pullirukkum Velur, himself."

"A reunion with this old and valued friend is certainly in order. And where would you be off to, my man? Perhaps your way lies in the same direction?"

"Oh no, *Swami*. Why should it? I'm off to Kadambur again, once I cross the Kollidam. Else the master would gouge my eyes out."

"In that case, time you left. Look, the boatman is about to push off."

Idumbankaari turned, and saw that Nambi was right. "Very well, *Swami*, I shall take your leave, then." And he began to make his way towards the ferry. Halfway there, he looked back once again.

But Azhwarkkadiyaan had done something peculiar in his turn: he had clambered swiftly up the *arasu* tree and secreted himself amongst its thickest, leafiest branches. Idumbankaari, thus, saw nothing of the Vaishnavite.

One of the boatmen called out to Idumbankaari. "Are you traveling to the opposite shore?"

"Perhaps in the next boat," answered the menial. "You may leave."

"Well! What with you scampering up, I really thought for a moment that you were in a hurry to cross," grumbled the boatman. "And I actually waited to take you on board!" He began to paddle across the river, shaking his head.

So I was right, after all, mused Thirumalai, who sat well concealed in the *arasu* tree's thick foliage. *He isn't returning to Kadambur, after all—he has a few tricks up his sleeve, this one. And I shall watch which way he goes. After all, didn't I see him make the sign of the fish with my own eyes? What would that mean? A fish—what does a fish represent, now—ah, could it possibly—surely not? But what else could it be? A fish is the much-vaunted symbol of the Pandiya flag—why not, then? Ah, it certainly could be! In which case, I must be just a little more patient. After all, patience begets kingdoms; while impatience inherits a forest—but then, these days, it's far better to rule over trees and animals than a country. Still, I may as well wait and watch.* Thus Thirumalai, mumbling his thoughts to the invisible ghost in the tree.

His patience paid off; soon enough, Idumbankaari, he was gratified to see, did not climb into the boat but walked back, staring hard at the *arasu* tree all the while. Then he looked in all four directions keenly, as though to ascertain that Azhwarkkadiyaan truly had left—and arrived at the bottom of the tree himself. He glanced around him once again and then made himself comfortable underneath it. Judging by the number of glances he cast about, he seemed to expect someone, or something—but the one place he never did check was above. It was doubtful if he would have seen anything, even if he had—Thirumalai had concealed himself so perfectly that neither hair nor hide could be glimpsed.

Approximately a *naazhigai* passed, thus; Nambi's legs had gone to sleep. He was not sure how long he could stay this way, lodged within the cramped confines of a tree—but Idumbankaari seemed to have no intention of budging. Thirumalai considered his options: there was no way to leave without rousing his attention; no matter how stealthily he clambered down the other side, some little noise was sure to be heard. Idumbankaari had the ears of a lynx cat—and a sharp little knife, to boot. What was the guarantee that he would not hesitate to plunge it in Thirumalai's chest?

Well, what else was he supposed to do, then? Could he, perhaps, jump down on Idumbankaari himself, screaming like the ghost that was supposedly possessing this tree? The man *might* be fooled— even faint from horror. Or Thirumalai might just make a run for it—

At this moment, his penance seemed to come to an end.

A man approached the tree from the southwest—that is, from the road to Kudandhai. Some instinct warned Thirumalai that this was whom Idumbankaari had been awaiting, all this while. He was right. The latter stood as the man neared.

The new arrival mimicked the hand gesture Idumbankaari had made some time ago, palms on top of each other, thumbs moving—depicting a fish. Idumbankaari did the same.

"Your name?" asked the man.

"Idumbankaari. And yours?"

"Soman Saambavan."

"I've been expecting you.

"So have I. In fact, I came here to meet *you*."

"Which path do we take?"

"The one to the west, of course."

"Where to?"

"The foe's *pallipadai*."

"You mean the old monument near Thiruppurambiyam—"

"Quiet! What if someone's eavesdropping?" And Soman Saambavan stared hard around him.

"Not at all—I checked quite carefully."

"No possibility of anyone hiding around hereabouts, is there?"

"Absolutely not."

"Time to start, then. I'm not very familiar with the paths so you'll have to lead the way. Go on, first—I'll be right behind you. Just ... wait every few paces and see if I'm following."

"It isn't a very good path—cuts through the jungle, and is littered with sharp stones and thorns. You'll have to be careful."

"Never mind; get going. And remember—it might be a forest track but you must conceal yourself the instant you see someone. D'you understand?"

"Yes, yes, I do!"

Idumbankaari went west, skirting the banks of the Kollidam; Soman Saambavan followed him after an interval.

Azhwarkkadiyaan stayed on the tree all this while, listening and watching with keen interest. *Ah, these truly are terrible times,* he reflected. *God has given me an unimaginable opportunity to learn something incredibly significant! Now it is up to me to use it wisely, and find out exactly what these men might be up to. Kadambur proved something of a disappointment—I couldn't discover much. This time—ah, this time, I will make sure I divine everything I can. They are going to the pallippadai at Thiruppurambiyam— certainly it can be nothing but the Ganga king Prithvipathi's monument. Ah well, it was built a hundred years ago; no wonder it lies in ruins now. It's situated in deep forest too; the village is some distance away. But why are these men journeying all the way into dense jungle to converse within the ruins of a monument for the dead? Surely anything they wish to discuss can be done right here. Perhaps there are others joining them? Why, though? And didn't one of them mention something about "the foe's pallipadai?" Who had Prithvipathi been the foe of? Ah, surely it couldn't be what I surmised!—still, I shall have to see it for myself. These men have taken the path that runs by the Kollidam; I shall choose the one that skirts the Manni River. True, that route is even more densely forested than this one—but when have forests, hills, sticks, stones and rocks ever mattered to me? I'm the one to be feared more!*

Azhwarkkadiyaan mumbled all this and a great deal more to himself as he slipped down to the ground, from the tree. He walked steadily to the south, reached the Manni River, turned left along its banks and picked up his pace

He journeyed through dense jungle, through endless paths without meeting a soul. Hours later, he finally reached the temple-monument at Thiruppurambiyam.

Dusk had set in—and the sun was slipping down the horizon.

ஃஐ

Hidden Meanings and Explanations

The phrase Kalki uses at the beginning of this chapter, when he writes about Azhwarkkadiyaan's thoughts about Vandhiyathevan, is this:

"Indha vaaliban mikap pollaadhavanaayirukkiran; naam thattiyil nuzhaindhaal, ivan kolathil nuzhaikiraan ..."

Such were the words commonly used to describe someone's cunning. A *thatti* is a closely-packed fence made of twigs; so dense that no one can get through. A *kolam* is a rice-flour drawing, at the entrance of Thamizh homes, usually geometrical. To slip into someone's home through a *kolam* is well-nigh impossible. But Vandhiyathevan, according to Azhwarkkadiyaan (who is no dud himself), seems to possess even this fantastic talent.

19

MURDER, MAYHEM, AND A FOREST OF TERRORS

It was the custom in ancient Thamizhagam to erect memorial stones in honour of men who had embraced a warrior's death in battle. Were it just a stone, it would be called a *Nadukal Koil*—a simple monument erected in their memory. Were a deity to be installed within its confines and the precincts made a temple, however, it was the norm to refer to it as a *pallippadai*.

Such a monument existed a little away from the village of Thiruppurambiyam on the northern banks of the Manni River—roughly half a *kaadham* northwest of the city of Kudandhai; it had been established in memory of the fallen Ganga king, Prithvipathi.

Historians are often wont to describe the battles of Waterloo, Panipet and Plassey as critical events that changed the very course of world history as we know it; the battle at Thiruppurambiyam was one such, when it came to Thamizh history. Having taken place a hundred years before this story opens, it is important that our readers understand its significance.

The Chozha dynasty which boasted such great Emperors as Karikal Valavan, Perunarkilli, Ilanjetchenni and Thodiththot Sembian was fated to be shrouded in darkness around five or six hundred years after their glorious rule, eclipsed by the steady rise of Pandiyas down south and the Pallavas to the North. Struggling to breathe, crushed as they were by these mighty giants, the Chozhas were forced to do the unthinkable: leave behind Uraiyur, their capital for centuries. Eventually, they traveled in the direction of Kudandhai and settled upon Pazhaiyarai in its vicinity and soon established themselves in this capital city—but never, for a moment, did they forget that it was Uraiyur that had possessed this distinction in the first place. Neither did they give up their claims to the honorific "Kozhi Vendhar," which had connections to that famed city.

Among the Chozha kings who rose to prominence in Pazhaiyarai, Vijayalayar could, perhaps, be said to be among the greatest: a veteran of many battles, ninety-six scars anointed his body, proclaiming his valour.

Many were the songs sung in praise of this warrior, who thought nothing of his life and body, when he faced his enemies.

> *"Enkonda thonnootrin melumiru moonru*
> *Punkonda vetrip puravalan ..."*

went one, while another said,

> *"Punnuru thanrirumeniyir poonaagath*
> *thonnoorum aarum sumanthonum!"*

Thus did poets sing of his scars and battle prowess, years later. His son Adithan was equally famed for his valour, and earned honours in a good many engagements on his own account.

Having lived a full life, Vijayalaya Chozhar had just carried out his biggest duty in crowning his son as the next king and was finally prepared to enjoy some respite. That, however, was not to be.

The Pallavas and Pandiyas, not content with ruling their respective kingdoms, were now engaged in ferocious warfare. The Pandiya scion was called Varaguna Varman; the Pallava ruler was honoured by the name Aparajitha Varman. Famed Emperors in their own right, neither would concede victory; they clashed again and again on the battlefield—which, as it turned, out, was always on Chozha soil.

This was, naturally, a distressing circumstance; Chozha Nadu was strangled like a rooster caught between mammoths; its people struggled to survive.

Even here, though, Vijayalayar found a way to turn the clash of titans to his favour. He would gather his meager forces and join either the Pandiya or Pallava forces during each altercation. Victory and defeat came to him alternately—but it could not be denied that Chozha men were rapidly becoming infected by a fierce, martial spirit.

It is common knowledge that Chozha Nadu is enriched by River Kaveri and her many tributaries that crisscross the land; all of them split away, south of their mother. One and only tributary flows away from the Kollidam and passes between that great river and Ponni: River Manni.

And it was on the northern banks of this river that the Pallavas and Pandiyas fought a last, decisive, bloody battle. Both armies were almost equal in strength; the Ganga king Prithvipathi had joined hands with Pallavas' Aparajitha Varman; so had Aditha Chozhan with his men.

The Chozha Prince was well aware that his forces were paltry when compared to the colossal armies under the command of the Pandiyas and Pallavas; were the former to win, the Chozhas would be decimated. It was a gamble, therefore, to attach his own tiny army with the Pallavas but he did so, anyway—like the smaller Kaveri merging with the vast ocean.

Endless *kaadham* after *kaadham* resounded with the fury of bloody battle. Armies, each comprising of *Ratha*, *Gaja*, *Thuraga* and *Pathaathi* regiments surged like massive oceans. Elephants crashed into each other like mountains, shaking the very earth; the cavalry stormed their enemy while the spears borne by the warriors on their mounts glinted like shards of lightning. Chariots rammed into one another, splintering in all directions; the deafening clangs of the infantry's swords and spears reverberated to the heavens; the very earth quaked and shuddered.

Three days did war rage without respite; by the end of that time, the battlefield was submerged in an ocean of thick, red blood; elephants and horses lay in lifeless, rotting heaps; broken chariots littered the red field like wrecked ships floating in a dead sea. Thousands of soldiers had fallen on both sides.

Only a section of the Pallava forces remained after such gory battle; even this were exhausted, the men practically drooping with fatigue. The Pandiya *maravar* soldiers, on the other hand, seemed to have gained a boon to never tire in battle and advanced upon their enemy with ill-concealed glee.

A hasty conference was convened in Aparajitha Varman's tent: the Pallava King, Prithvipathi of the Ganga kingdom and Aditha Chozhan huddled together to discuss the next course of action. It was obvious that they could not hold out for long; a retreat to the northern banks of the River Kollidam stared them in the face.

And then—a miracle occurred.

Vijayalaya Chozhar, scarred with endless wounds from battle, practically bed-ridden with infirmity and almost unable to stand on legs riddled with injuries—had somehow managed to arrive onto the battlefield. Should the Pallavas ever retreat to the north of the Kollidam, the Chozhas were doomed; it would be centuries before there would be any hope of regaining lost glory. Well aware of these circumstances, the old battle-hardened lion had arrived on the field—and now growled a ferocious oath that lent new life to the faltering Pallava warriors.

"An elephant—give me an elephant!" he pleaded.

"They have been completely decimated; we have none left," came the answer.

"A horse then—just one horse!"

"There are none alive," was the depressing reply.

"Does Chozha Nadu possess at least two true warriors?" cried Vijayalayar, desperate.

Two hundred answered his clarion call.

"Two—two of you who possess a warrior's heart and strength, may hoist me onto your shoulders and march into battle. The rest—follow us in pairs," commanded that warrior among warriors. "Should the men who bear me fall, the ones behind them shall carry me in turn!"

Thus, two soldiers, each with the height and build of the famed Pandava wrestler Bheemasenan, promptly stepped forward and hoisted Vijayalayar onto their shoulders.

"Now! Carry me to battle, now!" roared the man.

Battle still raged furiously in a corner of the field; the *marava* warriors of the southern lands were engaged in beating back the eastern soldiers.

Vijayalaya Chozhar thus entered the battlefield, to almost certain defeat. He marched on the shoulders of two men, bearing a gleaming sword in each hand, twirling it around with supreme confidence like Thirumaal wielding his discus. He ploughed through enemy ranks, lopping off heads without pause or hesitation; no one, it seemed, could stop him.

And yes—his incredible courage had its effect: soldiers who had hitherto withdrawn, fatigued with battle, now began to creep forward. They stood still, gaping at Vijayalayar's almost inhuman strength and valour. Slowly, they encouraged each other, patted each other's backs— and began to enter the battlefield with renewed vim and vigour.

In an instant, Jayalakshmi, the Goddess of Victory, had turned her compassionate gaze towards the advancing warriors.

The Pallava commanders gave up on withdrawing towards the north of Kollidam. The three kings now joined hands and along with their personal regiments, re-entered the battlefield with new strength. Their concerted attack had its effect: the Pandiya soldiers turned their backs and retreated, stopping only until they reached the frontiers of their own kingdom.

It was in this battle that the Ganga king, Prithvipathi embraced death, having performed a great many valorous deeds. His men raised a memorial stone in his honour and later, a *pallippadai* as well.

For a while afterwards, the battlefield lay bare and empty; not even a weed straggled along the massacred ground. No one went there if they could help it and soon, the forest began to creep over the land. Slowly but surely, the jungle reclaimed the scene of bloodshed and with it, the monument. Jackals made their home among thick bushes; owls and other night-birds roosted in the dark, gloomy trees. In course of time, the memorial lost the few visitors who had braved jungle and wild animals for worship; the temple began to fall apart. At the time of our story, it was practically in ruins.

It was here that Azhwarkkadiyaan arrived, at dusk. Terrifying demons, carved in glorious detail guarded the crumbling wreck and glared balefully at Nambi, from atop the edges of the temple's *mandapam*. Their stony stares bounced off the rotund man harmlessly—he was hardly the type to be nervous at their presence. Azhwarkkadiyaan sprang as nimbly as he could onto the roof of the monument's *mandapam* and scrambled to hide himself among a few tree branches. His sharp eyes were capable of cutting across the dense gloom; his ears perked, ready to catch the slightest sound.

The sun sank beyond the horizon. A *naazhigai* passed—then two, and three. Night lay on the forest like a heavy blanket; to Azhwarkkadiyaan, the murky darkness was stifling. Occasionally, something rustled through the undergrowth—*ah, there is a weasel, climbing up a tree! And here, an owl screeches through the night. Some kind of bird flutters agitatedly up to another branch, alarmed by the approaching weasel. And yes—jackals have begun to howl.*

A muted noise sounded above; Azhwarkkadiyaan craned his neck up. A squirrel or a chameleon—he was not quite sure which; some small animal—scrambled up the tree.

He could see patches of the night sky through the thick, leafy branches. Stars winked down at him. Struggling to be comfortable among the stifling foliage in splendid isolation, waiting for God knew what, these stars in the heavens seemed to be the only friendly souls within sight. Azhwarkkadiyaan began, it must be admitted, a one-sided conversation with them. "Ah, beloved stars that swim in the waters of the night! You look like you're laughing at the stupidity of us humans down here. I suppose you have reason to. After all, you were witness to the bloody battle that was fought at this site a hundred years ago, weren't you? And the rivers of blood that bathed this very earth. I'm quite sure you're wondering why men should be at each other's throats all the time, or be so fond of spilling blood. You see, most would call this valour.

A man has been dead for a hundred years—and yet, they call him their foe! This, you see, is apparently the enemy's monument. They're going to confer about destroying those alive—in a temple dedicated to a dead man! Why wouldn't you laugh, oh twinkling stars? Of course you will—by all means, do!"

Good God, is all this a wild goose chase, then? Am I doomed to be cramped between these branches all night? Are those men never going to arrive? Perhaps my ears were at fault, and I heard them wrong? Or, perhaps those fish-signing men had simply changed their minds and gone elsewhere? Ah, what a disappointment, if so? Should nothing happen here tonight, I shall never forgive myself—wait! There—there's a light. Ah, now it's gone. Now I see it again. There's no doubt about it; someone approaches with a torch. No, there are two men. My wait was not in vain—!

The two newcomers walked a little beyond the *pallippadai*, towards a little clearing in the dense jungle. One sat down; the other held aloft the torch and looked around, obviously expecting someone else. A while later, two more arrived—fearless men and obviously, no strangers to this place. Else how could they possibly find their way through well-nigh impenetrable forest in pitch darkness?

The latest arrivals spoke something to the men already assembled— but Azhwarkkadiyaan heard nothing of their conversation. *Adada*, what a waste of all his efforts—why, it looked like he wouldn't even be able to recognize these plotters!

Two more men arrived; the group conferred amongst themselves again. The last of the newcomers held a bag in his hand; he turned it, mouth towards the ground—and gold coins tumbled to the earth, glinting in the torch-light.

"My friends!" The man with the bag let loose a maniacal chortle. "Witness the beginning of Chozha Nadu's destruction at our hands— with gold from her own coffers! Excellent, wouldn't you say?" And he laughed even more.

"Lower your voice, Ravidasar," advised one. "Let's not scream everything to the high heavens."

"Ah, but who is going to eavesdrop on us in this desolate jungle? Jackals, owls and weasels, perhaps?" snorted the afore-mentioned. "But they won't tell on us, thankfully."

"Even so, it's safer to talk in low tones, isn't it?"

And then they really did begin to converse in murmurs—which, unfortunately, did not bode well for Azhwarkkadiyaan at all, whose ears were not sharp enough to divine their words. There was no point, he thought, in staying atop the monument—perhaps he ought to climb down and approach them. For he had to know what they spoke—he *had* to. And if there be any danger that came with eavesdropping on them—so be it.

Azhwarkkadiyaan duly made an attempt to slip down from his perch—but his body brushed against the tree, rustling the foliage.

Two of the men sprang up with a growl. "Who is there?"

Azhwarkkadiyaan's heart skipped a few beats. There was no way out, now, but to make his escape. And even then, they would certainly hear him blundering through the jungle, wouldn't they?

Just at this moment, an owl spread out and flapped its wings. "*Oom—oom!*" it hooted ominously, in the still night.

ॐ

Hidden Meanings and Explanations

Vinmeen

This is a beautiful Thamizh word to describe stars. Literally, it means "sky-fish" —fish swimming in the ocean that is the sky.

20

"THE FIRST FOE!"

Azhwarkkadiyaan delivered a deeply heartfelt thanks to the owl that had just fluttered through the trees—for, the men gathered in the clearing promptly assumed that it had been responsible for the noise.

"*Adei*, how dare this stupid bird startle us? Slay the wretched thing at once!" exclaimed one.

"No, stay! Let's keep our swords and knives sharp for other, worthy purposes—such as beheading our enemies and destroying their very roots," advised Ravidasan. "What have owls and night-birds ever done to us after all? They are, in fact, our friends—unlike other men, they're awake all hours of the night, aren't they? Just like us?

Azhwarkkadiyaan, listening to this speech, crept forward on noiseless feet towards a towering *marudha* tree. More than a hundred years old, the ancient one's thick roots had sprawled all over the ground. There were large spaces between one gnarly limb and another, and even a cozy hollow underneath the trunk. Azhwarkkadiyaan made the best of his hidey-hole, leant against the tree and eavesdropped for all he was worth.

KALKI R KRISHNAMURTHY

"Where gold is concerned, we're secure as long as Thanjavur's royal treasury continues to patronize us," began Ravidasan. "All we need, now, is the courage to fulfill our pledge and the strength to keep our secret until our work is done. Hear this: we must split ourselves into two groups—one will leave for Ilankai; the other will journey towards Thondai Mandalam and await the right opportunity to carry out their task. And remember—both must be complete at exactly the same time! Should there be the slightest lapse after the first foe's demise, the second will be on the alert. And that, we must never allow. Now—which of us is prepared for the task in Ilankai?"

"I will!"—"No, let me!" clamoured several voices all at once.

"We'll decide that by and by, at our next meeting in Pandiya Nadu—but there are a few things that must be completed before we get to it."

"Which would be the best route to Ilankai?" queried someone.

"Kodikkarai is an excellent option, should we choose the sea-route. But traveling there, in the first place, would be perilous—a great many enemies abound, not to mention every spy in the land. Far better to journey towards Sethu instead, cross the sea and land at Maathottam or thereabouts. Those who opt for the Ilankai mission must be prepared to row a boat, a canoe, and swim in the sea competently. Which of us here can do the last?"

"I can!"—"So can I!" came several enthusiastic answers.

"Our first task there would be to call upon King Mahindan—nothing can be decided without an audience with him. Therefore, it becomes important that at least one of those journeying to Ilankai knows the Sinhala language. Ah—but where's our Soman Saambavan? Hasn't he arrived yet? Did anyone amongst us see him, before this?"

"Here I am," came a voice very near Azhwarkkadiyaan, and he almost jumped out of his skin.

Nambi practically plastered himself to the tree, mourning, not for the first time, his rotund physique that simply would not let him conceal himself anywhere in peace.

He was just in time to notice two more men join the gathering.

167

Azhwarkkadiyaan peered around the tree a very little, and caught sight of them: they were, indeed, the ones he had spied talking under the *arasu* tree on the banks of the Kollidam.

"Welcome!" exulted Ravidasan. "I was concerned that you might have been in danger—that perhaps you wouldn't arrive at all. Which path did you choose and from where?"

"The one along the Kollidam—but a group of jackals surrounded us on the way and we had a difficult time escaping them," explained Soman Saambavan.

"I can understand fearing lions and tigers—but why be terrified of jackals?" mocked one of the men. "What can we expect of those who falter at the sight of *them*, pray?"

"Ah, but that's where you're wrong. One can confront ferocious lions and tigers—they attack alone, face-to-face, and it's easy to get the better of them. Jackals, now—those wretched animals always hunt in large groups and are stronger, as a result. Wasn't that how those Chozhas hunted down our illustrious king, who was caught all alone? Would he have lost his precious life if he hadn't been mown down by those cowardly scavengers?"

"We shall hunt down and destroy those dastardly jackals—right down to the last little pup!" Soman Saambavan growled an oath.

"And behold!—the tools of such destruction," and Ravidasan displayed the heap of gold coins glinting in the torch-light.

Soman Saambavan picked up one, and inspected it carefully. "The emblem of a tiger on one side—and a palm-tree on the other!" he exclaimed.

"Indeed. Chozha gold—with the Pazhuvettarayar's emblem. I, as you see, have kept my promise," announced Ravidasan. "What about you, now? I expect Idumbankaari has some news for us?"

"He has, and is quite ready to tell you."

Idumbankaari, accordingly, began his tale: "I have duly followed your instructions, and am now employed in the Kadambur household as a servant. But it was only yesterday that I had the chance to stumble upon something important. The Sambuvaraiyars hosted a banquet last night, and a great many lords were present—Pazhuvettarayar, Vanangamudi Munaiyarayar, Mazhapaadi Mazhavaraiyar and the like. The Velan Dance and Kuravai Koothu were performed, and the Devaralan delivered a few predictions that will aid our mission very well. Everyone believed that Pazhuvettarayar's young queen had accompanied him in her closed palanquin. Pazhuvettarayar gave the news that King Sundara Chozhar was quite ill, and not likely to survive much longer. Then, all of them decided that Aditha Karikalar did not deserve to be crowned king but Madhuranthaka Thevar, in his place. Some of them entertained doubts about the pious prince's willingness to become heir. Pazhuvettarayar declared that they would receive Madhuranthakar's answer from his own lips, and threw open the palanquin's curtains—and the prince himself stepped out! He was very eager to ascend to the throne, too …"

"And so, they're falling all over themselves to crown a warrior who travels in a closed palanquin like a woman? Excellent! Everything aids our plan, I believe—it suits our purposes very well to have unrest among the Chozhas. No one will ever suspect *us* at any point, will they? You've brought great news, Idumbankaari, but tell us—how did you learn of all this? How did such a circumstance ever come about?"

"It was me they placed as a sentry, while they talked among themselves at midnight about their precious royal affairs. I did guard, all right—but I used my eyes and ears as well."

"And did you manage to learn anything more, while you did?"

"Yes. Someone else was watching the midnight meeting and learning all he could—from the top of the fort-wall!"

"Ah—and who was he?"

"A top-knotted Vaishnavite—"

"Him! And what did you do? Turn him over to Sambuvaraiyar?"

"No—you see, I thought he might be one of ours. I even wondered if *you* had sent him."

"A very grave mistake. He isn't ours—that short, stout man who picks quarrels with everyone he meets. His name is Thirumalaiyappan, although he's been known to call himself Azhwarkkadiyaan on occasion."

"Yes, that's him. And I realized my error this very afternoon."

"Did you? How?"

"One of Kandamaaran's childhood friends arrived last night as well—but I learnt that he had nothing to do with Pazhuvettarayar's meetings; he went to bed in a corner and slept the night away. This morning, I knew that the young master was due to escort his friend to the banks of the Kollidam, and I crossed his path a few times. My ruse worked—he asked me to accompany him. He stopped on the north bank, but asked me to cross the river and get a horse for his friend. I asked him permission to visit my aunt in Kudandhai—which is how I was able to buy the time to come here."

"This is all very well—but how did you learn the truth about that Vaishnavite?"

"He clambered into the boat just as it was about to leave the north banks, and made some sharp speech with Kandamaaran's friend. Something in his conversation made me suspicious. I wondered if he was perhaps, part of our group. He was loitering about on the south bank too, and I believed that he might have been waiting for me. I showed him our secret sign, but he didn't recognize it. That was how I understood that he had nothing to do with us—"

"You did *what*? Ah, what a grievous mistake! You shouldn't have shown him our secret sign, never. Listen carefully, my friends—our tasks are defined in both Kanchi and Ilankai, for that is where our enemies reside. But there is one who is far more dangerous than either of them—who would destroy us in a moment. And that is Thirumalaiyappan, who wanders about under the false name of Azhwarkkadiyaan. He's sworn to ruin us and our mission; he will do everything he can to spirit away our beloved protector, our queen, from us. Should any of you ever meet him at any time, anywhere, do not hesitate even for a single moment: take your knives and plunge it into his heart. Should you have no weapon, use your hands and strangle him. Poison him if you can; fling him into a river as a meal for crocodiles; sweet-talk him to some cliff-top and shove him to his death! Treat him as you would a poisonous snake, scorpion or insect, and crush him mercilessly under your feet. It would be best if you could actually manage to sacrifice him to Goddess Durga or Kannaki Amman. Do not hesitate or pity him for even a moment—for he will continue to hinder us in every way he can, as long he's alive—!"

"He must be a vastly cunning creature for you to deliver such a horrible death sentence, Ravidasar. Who *is* he?"

"Who, you ask? A Chozha spy, unmatched in skills and treachery."

"Yes, but—*whose*?"

"Now that's something I've been wondering about for quite a while, myself. I speculated that he might be spying for Sundara Chozhan or Aditha Karikalan perhaps, but that was not the case. Now, I suspect he might be working for that old hag in Pazhaiyarai, the Periya Piratti."

"Truly? Ah, but isn't she supposed to have dedicated all her time to Siva worship and temple renovation? Why would such a lady need the services of any spy?"

"All a pretense, I tell you. That woman play-acts with her devotion to Siva Peruman just as that Vaishnavite does, with his precious Thirumaal. What sort of a demon turns a vengeful *sathru* against her own son? Why, her brother Mazhavaraiyan doesn't see eye to eye with her and has joined Pazhuvettarayar, hasn't he?"

"Ravidasar, are there any others like this top-knotted devil?"

"I have my suspicions about an astrologer in Kudandhai. He lures people under the guise of predicting their futures and picks their brains, I've heard. Remember—none of you must ever set foot within his home. He's sure to trick you into revealing something."

"Who do you think *he* spies for?"

"I haven't been able to find that out, yet. Perhaps he answers to the false prince in Ilankai? But no matter—the astrologer is of little account. I do not count him a danger. It's the Vaishnavite I'm worried about—as I said, crush him without remorse the instant you see him!"

Perspiration drenched Azhwarkkadiyaan, who stood behind the *marudha* tree, listening to this terrifying speech, quaking with terror. Was he even going to escape here with his life? Somehow, the possibility did not seem to exist at that moment.

As if to make matters worse, something had gotten into his nose—and he felt the overpowering urge to sneeze. Nambi tried desperately to stop it; he even stuffed a cloth up his nostrils—to no avail. Sneeze he did—a tiny, muffled sound.

The west wind no longer whirred through the foliage. The forest was still. Not even the trees murmured.

Azhwarkkadiyaan's hastily suppressed sneeze, therefore, actually did fall on the men's ears.

"I hear something behind that *marudha* tree," said Ravidasan, at once. "One of you—take a torch and see what it might be."

Someone obligingly did so; Azhwarkkadiyaan could hear him walk towards him. The torch's light began to glow steadily brighter. Ah—he was almost at the tree—the light would fall on him—and—and—what next? If Azhwarkkadiyaan ever managed to escape this terrifying ordeal—

His heart fluttered madly; Nambi glanced around him, looking in vain for some means of escape. Nothing seemed to offer a way out. He looked up—and glimpsed a giant bat hanging upside down from one of the branches, seemingly lost in penance. An idea tickled his fertile brain; he came to a swift conclusion. To think was to act; Azhwarkkadiyaan reached up, grabbed the bat and held it in his hands. The instant the scout appeared around the tree—he threw it in the man's face.

The torch fell to the forest floor and began to dim. The man who had received a face full of bat floundered, slurring various unintelligible phrases: "Ei—ei—what—where—!"

Sounds of many feet thundering towards him—and Azhwarkkadiyaan decided that this was his moment. He ran for all his worth and disappeared, into the dense forest.

"What is it?" —"What happened?" came a barrage of questions, and the man who had sustained a bat-attack began to recount his terrifying adventure in some detail.

For quite a while after he had made his escape, their speech echoed in Thirumalaiyappan's nervous ears.

21

THE RUSTLING CURTAIN

Could two minds exist within a man at the same time? To Vandhiyathevan, it seemed that they could.

At the moment, he was journeying through some of Chozha Nadu's most flourishing landscapes. It was the time of the year when rivers overflowed; canals, streams and brooks bubbled and gushed with fresh water that poured into fields; water seemed to overwhelm every part of the land. Ah, truly, the name *Vala Nadu* suited this country—for it well nigh burst with nature's bounty. And it was appropriate, thus, to call the King of this realm Valavan, too.

Speaking of land and kings—his mind flew, at once, to the various perils that seemed to threaten the one he was traveling through, and its ruler. He couldn't help but wonder about his mission and its consequences. What was he supposed to do, now? Deliver Prince Aditha Karikalar's palm-leaf to King Sundara Chozhar and wash his hands off this terrible business? Why must he poke his nose, after all, into this royal quagmire of cousins, kingship and conspiracies? What did he care about Sundara Chozhar's successor, after all? Weren't they, in a way, the sworn enemies of his clan? Hadn't it been a coalition of the Chozhas, Gangas and Vaithumbars that had destroyed the Vaanar dynasty? Aditha Karikalar might consider him a friend today—but did that mean that he, Vandhiyathevan must forget every injustice the Chozhas had perpetrated in the past—ah, no, no, this was ridiculous. To call invasion and war unfair was, well, unfair. Which king, after all, hadn't tried his very best to conquer his neighbour? Every ruler in history had tried to subjugate another; victory and defeat were very much a part of their lives. It was entirely natural too, for those vanquished to cherish the deepest hatred towards their victors—even if such hatred was rather pointless. Good heavens, hadn't Vandhiyathevan's own ancestors committed every atrocity known to them, during their own quest for greatness? Weren't they guilty of the same unjust practices in their time? What was that song that used to be so celebrated, once …? Ah, there it was:

> *"Senai thazhaiyakki senguruthi neerthekki*
> *Aanai mithitha arunchetril—Manaparan*
> *Paavendhar thamvendhan Vaanan parithu nattaan*
> *moovendhar thangal mudi!"*

His own people had once engaged in fierce battles; destroyed men and beasts; roared in approval as they decapitated enemies gleefully and planted their skulls in the bloody morass of battlefields, churned by war-elephants. Truth be told, dishonour was always the fate of those vanquished in battle. Not every king could be as gracious and compassionate as King Rama or Yudhishtra of the Pandavas, surely? And if one were honest with himself—wasn't their compassion the very reason for their terrible sufferings in jungles? What had these warriors lacked, after all, when it came to soldiers, kingdoms or riches? Their benevolence had yielded nothing but penury and anguish. Ah, no—there was no room for pity in royal affairs. In fact, the Chozhas were, if anything, rather inclined to lenience: they much preferred diplomacy and tact rather than deadly war with their enemies. Witness their many alliances forged through marriage with various, supposedly enemy clans? King Sundara Chozhar's father Arinjaya Chozhar had wedded ravishing Kalyani, a princess of the Vaithumbarayar dynasty—which explained the beautiful features and good looks of Sundarar and his children—

Speaking of exquisite beauty … memories floated up, of the young woman from Kudandhai whom he had seen again, on the banks of the Arisilaaru. Well no, not really. He hadn't *just* thought of her— her memory had been smouldering deep within, all this while.

Thus far, he had been gazing open-mouthed at Chozha Nadu's natural beauty and musing over the many dangers that seemed to surround their royal family—but underneath had been thoughts of the bewitching young lady who had captured his imagination so completely. Now, he gave up all pretence of plodding over conspiracy theories and engaged himself in the far more appealing task of thinking of *her*. Everything of Chozha Nadu, now, seemed to remind him of her beautiful features. Smooth bamboo shoots put him in mind of her slender shoulders; dark *kuvalai* blooms, flowering in profusion in the many ponds he passed recalled to him her large, limpid eyes; he wondered, quite seriously, if the pink and white lotuses he spotted were any match for her golden countenance. And the musical buzz of honey-bees in the trees he rode under—could they possibly rival her sweet voice? Certainly, poets did their best to compare nature with women, but truth be told—such comparisons were ridiculous. How could flowers, bees and bamboo shoots possibly equal her unbelievable *soundharyam*, her stately beauty? Ah, the thrill in his veins when he first set eyes on her charming face! How his heart flutters even now, just at her memory? No bud or bee could ever inspire such a thrill in him, could it?

Now this was madness in the extreme. His elders had warned him again and again, of the wiles of women—it took a great man to escape their cunning lures. All the more reason why he should steer clear of them, if he ever hoped to make something of his life. Why, he didn't have to look far—there was Kovalan of the epic *Silappathikaaram*, whose life was destroyed because of women. Or wait, why take him as an example, anyway? There was Periya Pazhuvettarayar, warrior among warriors, Treasurer of the Empire— and the laughing-stock of his people—all because he had tumbled into love, recently. Ah, but people were silly and ignorant—they little knew who he squired around in his closed silk *pallakku*. If they but guessed—

And why must Prince Madhuranthakar demean himself this way? *Chee*! Was this the way a man behaved—shutting himself in palanquins and traveling around the country in the guise of Pazhuvettarayar's young wife? Did he really cherish ambitions to ascend the Chozha throne with such humiliating tactics? If so, how could he ever hope to rule this empire? Anything he did would have to be under the aegis of Pazhuvettarayar and his lordly cohorts—but then, why blame only Madhuranthakar? If anything, it was Sundara Chozhar who had committed a grievous blunder by allowing them such power and authority—especially when he had two excellent sons who were more than capable of ruling the country. Not to mention a lovely daughter, famed far and wide for her intelligence and good sense ...

Ah, that majestic young lady—she whom he had marveled at, both on the river's banks and the astrologer's home—her face seemed strangely familiar, somehow. Why—could it possibly be—no; that was silly, it couldn't—but oh, what if it were?

If his sudden suspicions were true—ah, then Vandhiyathevan was certainly a fool to beat all fools ... and possibly, the most unfortunate among men, too. For he had just met the young lady whose fame was spread everywhere from the hoary Vindhya mountains to the tip of Ilankai—and had behaved like the most ill-mannered lout.

Good heavens, he certainly hoped she wasn't who he suspected she was. How could he ever dare to even look at her, when he tried to deliver her brother's *olai*?

Vandhiyathevan trotted along the road edging the Kaveri, pondering over everything from sky to earth, until he reached Thiruvaiyaaru.

Ah! Truly, it had no equal when it came to prosperity and beauty! He confirmed with passersby that this was indeed that temple-town and discovered that in this case, rumour had done a grave injustice to its charm and loveliness. Why, the boy-saint Gnana Sambandhar's description of it in the divine *Thevaram* stayed true even now—three hundred years had made no difference whatsoever. Witness the glorious foliage along the banks of the river; the luscious jack-fruits that hung heavily from their trees! Such richness was a rare sight indeed, in Thondai Nadu. And here were monkeys, eager to sample nature's delights—how they ever caught the scent of fruits, one never knew. He could never grow tired of their antics. Now, what was it that Sambandhar had sung—ah, yes, he remembered it now:

In Thiruvaiyaaru, young dancers performed on appropriately placed platforms at street-corners; drums beat a glorious rhythm to match their song and dance. Now the monkeys, playing among trees mistook the muffled roar of drums for thunder—and clambered up the highest branches, craning their necks in vain, searching for dark clouds, heavy with the promise of rain! Ah, those words were true even now: monkeys still scampered along trees and that was not all; faint musical strains floated out from within the town as well. There—he can hear instruments playing: the *yaazh*, *kuzhal*, *muzhavu* and *thannumai*—accompanied by the gentle tinkling of anklets. Obviously, these dancers weren't the possessed, frantic *Kuravai Koothu* performers of Kadambur; their song was far more melodious, and their Bharathanatyam aspired to far better standards. Why, he could even hear their teachers, who beat a steady rhythm with their little batons:

> *"Kolodak kolvalaiyaar kuthaadak*
> *Kuvimugaiyaar mugathininru*
> *Selodach chilaiyaada seyizhaiyaar*
> *nadamaadum thiruvaiyaare!"*

Ah, Saint Sambandhar was undoubtedly a great Saivite—but even more important, he understood and appreciated beauty in all its forms. The Thiruvaiyaaru he had described stayed true to his description even today.

Vandhiyathevan decided that he would stay a day here, and spend it looking at the sights to his fill. He would also take the time to visit the renowned temple and worship at the feet of Aiyaarappar, Lord of the Five Rivers, after whom the town took its name—and his divine consort, *Aram Valartha Nayaki*, she who was the very form of righteousness. Ah, the very sight of so many Siva devotees praying along the banks of Kaveri, their bodies covered in sacred ash, was calming indeed. Why, sometimes, their chorus of heartfelt chants, "Namachivaaya!" rose and drowned out the songs from the town itself. Ah, there went someone singing Sambandhar's *Thevaram* songs, in a melodious voice. Truly, this town was blessed by the very Siva Peruman to be the abode of culture and piety. Yes, he certainly would stay here a day and take in the sights! After all, where was the guarantee that he could enter the fort of Thanjavur? And even if, by some hook or crook he did, how on earth would he ever gain an audience with King Sundara Chozhar? Wasn't the man well nigh imprisoned by the Pazhuvettarayar brothers, after all—a bird in a golden cage? Well, well, his way was clear: he would cross over to the Kaveri's north banks, and—

Just as Vandhiyathevan arrived at this part of his ruminations, something occurred to distract him: from the west arrived a palanquin along the path edging the Kaveri, with an escort of soldiers, front and back.

Suspicion touched Vandhiyathevan's mind; he waited until it came closer—and it was just as he had thought: the thick curtains that covered the sides of the palanquin bore the emblem of a palm-tree. It probably came from Kadambur—he had arrived here from Kudandhai, while they had probably chosen another path. But where was Pazhuvettarayar? Perhaps he had opted to stay somewhere on the way?

The palanquin turned south, towards the road to Thanjavur—and Vandhiyathevan changed his mind in an instant. Thiruvaiyaaru could wait; he would follow this palanquin. As to why he made that split-second decision, he did not quite know. All he was sure of, at that moment, was that the palanquin bore Madhuranthaka Thevar—and his scorn for that man grew.

Still, that was not important, now. Perhaps he would gain an opportunity to meet the prince, later on. The palanquin-bearers may set it down at some point; Madhuranthaka Thevar may step out. He, Vandhiyathevan might have a God-given chance to make his acquaintance with the prince—which might serve some purpose, later. Why, it might even gain him entrance into Thanjai and an audience with the King! He might have to resort to subterfuge to make it work—but then, such stratagems and tactics were highly necessary to gain his own ends. After all, he was on a royal mission, wasn't he?

To think was to act: Vandhiyathevan let the palanquin go forward a distance, before following them. He was doomed to disappointment, however; none of the circumstances he had anticipated presented themselves. Four more rivers on the route between Kaveri and Thanjavur came and went but so far, the *pallakku* had shown no signs of a halt. The bearers seemed bent on going ahead without a pause, in fact and—there, the turrets and fort-walls of Thanjavur could be glimpsed, towering above the trees. Vandhiyathevan could even see the gates, at one point. If the palanquin entered the fort, he might as well give up all hopes of acting upon his ruse! He'd have to gather his courage and hit upon some clever ploy to accomplish his aim. After all, what could he possibly lose? His head? What of it? Where was the purpose in returning home without accomplishing his mission? And then, he was furious with Madhuranthaka Thevar as well—his hands fairly itched to throw open the palanquin's silk screen and expose this imposter; his heart raced with the desperate need to tell the world that within was not a dainty woman, but a grown man.

Even as he was thinking of a way to do all the above, one of the soldiers, part of the vanguard of the palanquin, fell back and subjected Vandhiyathevan to a keen scrutiny. "Who might you be, my man? Why do you follow us?" came the sharp query.

"I'm not," answered Vandhiyathevan. "I'm traveling to Thanjavur myself—this *is* the road to the city, isn't it?"

"Yes, but it may be used only by dignitaries and other such personages," shot back the soldier. "There is another path for commoners."

"Indeed? Well, I happen to be a very important personage indeed."

"Are you, now?" the soldier smiled a little. "What is your purpose in Thanjai?"

"I've received news that my uncle is very ill," Vandhiyathevan gabbled. "I wish to visit him."

"Indeed? And what is he? An employee in the royal palace, perhaps?"

"Not at all. He's a caretaker in an inn."

"Oh? But in that case, why lag behind us? You could have gone forward, couldn't you?"

"My horse is tired, *Ayya*. Do you really think I *like* staring at your backs?"

Vandhiyathevan had trotted forward even as this conversation took place—and now, the ruse he had been searching for in vain, burst in upon him in all its glory. Instantly, he pressed upon his steed, reined it in and then let it loose upon the palanquin-bearers in the back. They stared at him, startled.

At once, Vandhiyathevan set up a yell. "*Ayyo*! Maharaja—my king! Your palanquin-bearers are attacking my horse! *Ayyo, ayyo!*"

The silk curtains adorning the palanquin rustled.

ᎧᏋ

Hidden Meanings and Explanations

Yudhishtra

First of the five Pandava brothers, and who, reputedly, never told a lie. True to the mien of such noble men, he and his brothers suffered greatly.

Kovalan

The hero of Ilangovadigal's famous epic, *Silappathikaaram*, Kovalan, a merchant, was married to Kannaki, when he fell for the lures of the courtesan Madhavi. He ignored his new bride and worshipped at Madhavi's feet, but she, at one point, tired of him. Kovalan came back to his senses and returned to his wife, who urged him to travel to Madurai, that they might make a new beginning. Fate had other things in store for him, though, and he met his death.

Of course, Kalki shows how Vandhiyathevan, like many men (and according to the lessons many elders had imposed upon him), believes that it was a woman who destroyed Kovalan's life— forgetting, quite conveniently, that it was Kovalan himself who let his wife languish in misery, and enjoyed a courtesan's company, thus destroying not his own life, but his wife's as well. So much for being ruined by a woman, indeed.

"Within was not a dainty woman, but a grown man ..."

These are Vandhiyathevan's self-righteous instincts when he follows Pazhuvettarayar's palanquin en route to Thanjavur; when Kalki describes Madhuranthakar's treachery, he says that within the *pallakku* was a *"meesai mulaittha aanpillai ..."*— literally, a moustached man.

Technically, the Madhuranthaka Thevar of this story is described as having feminine features; the artist's illustrations featured in the original, serialized version of the novel show a clean-shaven man wearing a crown. So, why describe him as someone with a *meesai*, a moustache? Simple. It was then (and is still now), the custom, when referring to a male, as someone with a bushy moustache, as this was considered a testament to masculinity. It later became a commonly accepted and used phrase.

22

The Velakkara Regiment

The first to move was the outer curtain, etched with the palm-tree, emblem of the Pazhuvettarayars. The next to rustle were the silk curtains within. And before Vandhiyathevan's fascinated eyes, a golden hand crept out—just as he had seen, once before. It would not be appropriate to royal status for him to remain on his horse, he decided. He leapt down at once and practically ran towards the palanquin.

"Your Highness! My Prince!—your palanquin-bearers—!" he yelled and looked up. He stared at the face above him. Blinked, and stared even harder.

For, the vision that met his startled gaze well nigh blinded him with its radiance.

"No, no—I—" Vandhiyathevan's tongue slipped and slurred; his throat went dry. "I mean—no, it's—you're the Pazhuvoor Queer—er—Paluvoor Prince—your—er—your bearers' horses knocked into my palanquin!" he finished in a magnificent display of supreme stupidity.

All this, naturally, had taken place within moments; the Pazhuvoor guards surrounded Vandhiyathevan almost at once. In the subconscious way that is practically second nature to warriors, our young man too, was aware of the soldiers around him; his hands crept to the sword at his waist almost without his knowledge. And yet—and yet—he simply could not take his eyes off the golden, radiant countenance of the young woman who peered at him from within the palanquin.

For it was not a prince as he had fully expected, but a young woman— and what a woman, indeed! Not in all his years had Vandhiyathevan ever imagined that such beauty—beauty that might well madden men— could exist.

Fortunately, some part of his brain seemed to retain its faculties—or at least one nerve, which was sane enough. A strange impulse stole over him, and he decided to act upon it at once.

He gathered every ounce of courage he possessed, and made a monumental effort to work his tongue into speech. "I beg your pardon— but I am in the gracious presence of Pazhuvoor's Ilaiya Rani, am I not? It was in the hope of an audience with your highness that I traveled all this way!"

The young queen of Pazhuvoor fixed her lovely gaze on him. Her golden countenance blossomed into a little smile—and it was as though a lotus bud had unfurled its delicate petals, revealing a row of beautiful, glittering white pearls. The sheer beauty of it dazzled Vandhiyathevan into speechlessness.

The soldiers surrounding the palanquin hesitated, seemingly waiting for their young queen's command. She waved a regal hand at them, upon which they retired to a discreet distance. Two soldiers reined in Vandhiyathevan's horse, which still butted against the palanquin.

The young woman turned her gaze on the Vaanar warrior again; two sharp spears pierced his heart at once.

"I *am* the Pazhuvoor Ilaiya Rani," spoke the lady—and oh, what was it that made her voice so exquisite? This inebriating quality that made his head spin?

"Didn't you complain about something, just now?" she continued. "About my palanquin-bearers?"

The velvety smoothness of the famed silks of Kasi—the beguiling intoxication of spirits—the silky sweetness of forest honey—the brilliance of lightning in the lowering monsoon sky—*could* a young woman's voice possibly be the alluring combination of several such incredible splendours?

"What was it that you said—something about my bearers knocking the palanquin into your horse?"

A mocking smile widened her coral lips; obviously, she appreciated the absurdity of it all.

Vandhiyathevan felt his courage rise at her reaction. "Indeed, yes, my queen. That's exactly what they did—witness my steed's terror!"

"It isn't just the horse that's terrified, I think—you had better ask the priest at Goddess Durga's temple to cast away the evil eye with a clutch of neem leaves."

By now, Vandhiyathevan had recovered his wits completely, and even let himself laugh a little at her words. But this, it seemed, was the sign for the Pazhuvoor Queen's own mood to change. Her radiant smile vanished; her face was now suffused with anger. The golden moon had vanished behind storm-clouds.

"Keep the jests for later, and answer me: why did you let your horse run into my palanquin? The truth now—or else …!"

Fortunately for Vandhiyathevan, he had hit upon an explanation and gave it, now. Glancing around to make sure that there was no chance of being eavesdropped upon, he lowered his voice as though sharing the most intimate of secrets: "Devi—Nandhini Devi? It was Azhwarkkadiyaar—I mean, Thirumalaiyappar—who charged me with a message to you. He wished me to meet you, and that was why I had to devise such a ruse. Again, I do beg your pardon!"

And Vandhiyathevan gazed into her face keenly, eager to know the effect of his unexpected answer. To be sure, it was a little like throwing a stone at a fruit-laden tree: what would he receive for his pains? A ripe fruit? Or a sour one? The stone itself, perhaps—or some other, severe blow?

The Pazhuvoor queen's dark, shapely brows rose; her beautiful eyes stared at him, brimming with surprise and suspicion. The next instant, that lady seemed to have arrived at her decision. "Very well, but the middle of the road is hardly the right place for a conversation. Our palace, tomorrow evening—you may seek an audience, and we shall speak more of this."

Vandhiyathevan's heart practically sang with delight. Ah, it looked like his hoax had been a complete success! He had crossed three-quarters of the well, as the saying went—all that remained now, was just a quarter.

"But, but—Devi, they're not likely to let me into the fort—or the palace," he lamented, eager to cross this last hurdle as well. "How may I see you?"

The Ilaiya Rani turned at once to a small silk pouch by her side, opened it and took out an ivory ring. "Show this, and you will gain admission at once—both into the fort, and our palace," and she gave it to him.

Vandhiyathevan received it reverentially, sparing it a quick glance as he did—the ring was etched with the emblem of a palm-tree. By the time he looked up again, the palanquin's silk curtains had fallen shut. Ah—even the celestial snake Rahu eclipsed the moon so very slowly in the heavens, but these wretched curtains had closed over her fair, golden countenance within moments!

"Take care, and don't follow us from hereon—it's far too dangerous," came her low voice from within. "Wait a while and enter the fort later."

The palanquin went on and with it, the soldiers. Vandhiyathevan stood by, his horse's reins in his careful hands, allowing them to pass. On a subconscious level, he did not fail to notice that one of the Pazhuvoor guards—the one that had spoken to him—cast more than one glance at him as he went by.

Consciously, however, he was still fascinated a great deal by the exquisitely lovely Pazhuvoor Ilaiya Rani, journeying towards Thanjai in her palanquin. Had his meeting with her truly happened? Had he really stood in front of her and spoken a few words? And even more importantly—was it possible for such astounding beauty to even exist on earth?

There were tales galore of celestial dancers such as Rambhai, Urvasi and Menakai, who, it was said, adorned the abode of the Devas, and made even sages and saints who had renounced the world, unhinged with their beauty. In this world too, there was a great deal of mocking talk about Periya Pazhuvettarayar and his infatuation with his charming young wife—but now, it seemed there was nothing surprising about it. Not the most biased of men could ever call the battle-scarred, rugged warrior a handsome man—while his young wife was a fair vision of beauty! It could hardly be wondered at, if the old man was willing to sacrifice heaven and earth just to win a smile from her.

Having spent a good deal of time by the roadside, immersed in thought, Vandhiyathevan finally climbed on his horse and set it trotting slowly towards the Thanjai fort. The sun was sinking to the west, when he arrived at the main gates.

The origins of Thanjai might be within the fort—but the straggling fingers of civilization had stretched forward and the city proper now spread outside, as well. Street upon street surrounded the fort, filled with vendors selling mouth-watering foods, or workshops and smithies full of labouring workmen. Thoroughfares thronged with people buying, selling, all hurrying upon important business, and almost choked with bullock-carts and horse-drawn chariots. Vandhiyathevan felt an intense desire to plunge into the milieu and observe the lifestyle of those who lived in this sprawling, new capital of the Chozhas—but this, he regretfully decided, would have to wait. There was work to be done, first; amusements could come later.

With this very creditable impulse, he approached the imposing main gates of the fort—only to find that they were closed, firmly. Guards at the entrance were moving people to the sides of the road; even more importantly, the milling population obeyed. Far from going about their business they waited patiently, men, women, oldsters and even children, as though keen on watching a procession of some sort.

The space directly in front of the fort's main entrance remained clear save the guards; Vandhiyathevan was filled with the urge to know what was about to happen, but it was not his intention to stride up to the sentries and demand an explanation—especially when the rest of the public stood by the side, pliant and subdued. Such a confrontation would only lead to arguments and anger, and there was nothing he wished to avoid more, at this point. His mission was his priority now—not mad bouts with wayfarers or random soldiers.

Accordingly, Vandhiyathevan made himself merge with the people by the roadside—yet, at a vantage point that would enable him to watch the proceedings.

The strong scent of flowers assaulted his nose. He turned, and saw a young man holding two full baskets of blooms. Liberally adorned with sacred ash and rudraksha necklaces, he looked the very picture of a devout Saivite.

"*Thambi*, why is everyone gathered by the road at this hour?" Vandhiyathevan asked. "Is there about to be a procession or something?"

"Are you not from these parts, *Ayya*?"

"No—I come from the Thondai Mandalam."

"That explains your question. Also, it would be better if you got down from your horse, as well."

It *would* be easier to talk to the youngster if he did, Vandhiyathevan mused, and descended—but that did not explain the young man's suggestion. "Why didn't you want me to stay on my horse, *Thambi*?"

"The Velakkara regiment is in audience with the Emperor now, paying their respects to him. Soon, they will pour out of the fort. That is why everyone has gathered here."

"To watch them, I suppose?"

"Yes."

"I too, might do so from my horse then, mightn't I?"

"You may, but beware of Velakkara soldiers who might spot you. It might get—difficult."

"Difficult, how? Will they steal my horse, do you mean?"

"Horse—and the rider, on occasion. One never knows. They are rogues, those men."

"Is that how it is? And does everyone here put up with their antics?"

"What choice do they have? The Velakkara regiment rules everyone and everything these days. Their word is law. Not even the Pazhuvettarayars interfere in their affairs."

Commotion erupted within the fort walls, at this moment. Trumpets and conches blew with abandon; *nagara* and *parai* drums thundered enthusiastically, while several hundred voices shouted praises that echoed to the skies.

Vandhiyathevan had heard a great deal about these valiant warriors. Their fame had spread far and wide in Chozha Nadu, especially, as a force to reckon with. In name, they were bodyguards to rulers—but there was an important difference between them, and the Velakkara warriors. The latter had taken a blood oath; they were sworn to protect kings with their own lives. Should any calamity befall those they had pledged to protect due to some error or oversight on the part of the Velakkara regiment, they would kneel in the presence of Goddess Durga, and behead themselves with their own hands.

It was only natural, therefore, that warriors who had taken such a terrifying oath be allowed a few privileges denied to others.

Padaar! —Padaar! The fortress gates swung open with a resounding crash.

Two soldiers rode out first on horseback, holding aloft a flag in their right hands. Quite peculiar, its emblem: on a blood-red background was a tiger and below it, a crown. Underneath was an offering platform, a *balipeedam*, a decapitated head, and a large sword. In all, the flag presented quite a gruesome picture.

An imposing bull followed the horsemen, carrying two enormous drums also known as the *perigai* upon which two men beat out a steady, thundering rhythm.

Behind them came around fifty men, striking upon instruments such as the *siruparai, perumparai* and *thambattam*, announcing their arrival in stentorian tones. Fifty more followed them, blowing upon huge, curved horns: *Baam—Baam!—Ba-baam!*

A thousand men marched upon their footsteps; most of them chanting praises lustily until the very air rumbled around them, crackling with their energy.

"Long live the illustrious Paranthaka Chakravarthy, Lord of the World!"

"*Vaazhga vaazhga!*"

"Long live King Sundara Chozhar!"

"*Vaazhga vaazhga!*"

"Long life to the Kozhi Vendars!"

"*Vaazhga vaazhga!*"

"Long live the Lords of Thanjai!"

"*Vaazhga vaazhga!*"

"Long live the Lord Who Brought Veera Pandiya to his Knees!"

"*Vaazhga vaazhga!*"

"Long live the Rajakesari Who Conquered Madurai, Eezham and Thondai Mandalam!"

"*Vaazhga vaazhga!*"

"Long live Karikala Chozhar's illustrious descendents!"

"*Vaazhga vaazhga!*"

"May Goddess Durgai, Maakaali, Paraathpari Paraasakthi be Victorious!"

"*Velga! Velga!*"

"May the tiger flag fly proud all over the world!"

"*Velga! Velga!*"

"Vetrivel!"

"Veeravel!"

Those who heard these valiant chants from a thousand throats felt their skin prickle with emotion. The soldier's rousing shouts were echoed by other voices as they marched out of the gates; a good many people thronging the roads joined in as well.

Thus it was that the route taken by the Velakkara Regiment overflowed with emotion and energy as they marched from the gates and through the streets of Outer Thanjai, and disappeared into the distance.

ॐ

Hidden Meanings and Explanations

Kalki's Note

The Velakkara Regiment, it's said, took its name from Lord Murugan, one of whose titles was Velakkaran—He Who has Sworn an Oath to Protect his Devotees.

Mohanangi; Sukumari; Bhuvana Mohini; Sundharangi

These are words Kalki uses in the Thamizh original, in his description of Nandhini. They naturally mean a woman of bewitching beauty and are sometimes used as proper names; the interesting part is that they are no longer in vogue, in today's colloquial or literary Thamizh. These are words that have their root in Sanskrit and belong, therefore, to a bygone era. They are also an excellent indicator of the timeline of the stories and writers, themselves.

23

Amudhan's Mother

The Velakkara Regiment passed in grand fashion through the Large Market Street—and the soldiers forming the tail-end indulged in a great many "good deeds" as they went. One, for instance, barged into a sweetmeats shop, hoisted a whole basket of luscious, round *adhirasams* and distributed them to his friends. Then, he returned to the shop dutifully and crowned the aghast shop-keeper with the empty basket, thereby earning raucous appreciation from his mates and the watching passersby.

Another grabbed a flower-basket from an old woman walking by, and began to pull apart the blooms in earnest. "Look—look—it's raining flowers!" he yelled as everyone rushed about, trying to catch a few swirling petals. Yet another halted a cart mid-street, yanked the bulls out of their harness and broke a stick over their backs: the animals stomped and bucked madly through the crowd, as the soldiers romped about in glee.

Vandhiyathevan watched their antics, carefully cloaked by the milling throngs by the road. *Ah, these men aren't very different from the Pazhuvoor ruffians,* he mused. *They run amuck through the crowd and are every bit a nuisance to the people—what a good thing that I'm tucked away from their sharp eyes! Else, there would have been a very pretty tussle and my mission, in ruins.*

And yet, he had not failed to notice an important difference as well: the people gathered here did not really seem irritated by the Velakkara soldiers' antics; if anything, they joined in and romped around, as well.

Vandhiyathevan opened his mouth, prepared to comment about this peculiar behaviour—but when he turned around, the youngster had vanished, blooms, basket and all. He had probably wanted to get on with his work and walked away.

Apparently, the Thanjavur fortress gates closed for good once the Velakkara Regiment passed through in the evenings and did not open for anyone except members of the royal family, ministers and *Thandanaayakkas*—who alone, it seemed, were privileged to enter and exit any hour, day or night. The Pazhuvettarayars too, were proud possessors of that concession, Vandhiyathevan learned. That could mean only one thing: there was no point in trying to enter the fort tonight. The last thing he wanted was to display his newly acquired palm-tree insignia and be subjected to the scrutiny of sentries, at dusk. Or even to find out its unique gate-opening powers. Far better to stay the night here, take in the sights, and enter the fort next morning. Besides, even if he did gain admission into the city tonight, somehow, he could hardly demand an audience with the king right away and hand over his palm-leaf, could he?

Having made up his mind, Vandhiyathevan ambled through the streets edging the fort-walls, drinking in the bustling city. His horse had traveled many *kaadhams* that day and was exhausted beyond belief; he knew that it could not be expected to carry him any further. He would have to find some food and shelter both for himself and his steed—or it would be completely useless to him, next morning.

And Thanjai was such an attractive city, besides! Newly established, it was beginning to expand very quickly, thriving and flourishing with business and people. And with twilight falling as well, hundreds of lamps, lit by the roadside, transformed it into a glittering fairyland.

The streets were practically bursting with people; many had arrived from other towns and villages, bent on transacting business and went about looking very important. Most were residents of Chozha Nadu, but Vandhiyathevan's keen eyes spotted men who were obviously from territories newly brought under Chozha dominions, as well. Travelers had converged here, everywhere from the River Porunai to Paalaaru; from the east to west coast. Why, some had even arrived from north of the Vindhya Mountains, or from lands beyond the seas.

Customers attached themselves like demented flies to stalls that sold savoury *aappams* and sweet *adhirasams,* buying them in dozens; other shops had bananas and a variety of fruits heaped in little mountains. As for the flower-stalls—those fragrant corners were frankly, beyond description: jasmine, *mullai, aathi* and *shenbagam* flowers rose like little hillocks; women buzzed around them like bees drawn to nectar.

Riding past them, Vandhiyathevan remembered the youngster and his baskets of blooms. Ah, an acquaintance with him would have proven convenient indeed; he desperately needed food and lodgings for the night.

Even as he thought this, he glimpsed the young man approaching in the distance, and jumped down from his horse at once. "Why, *Thambi*— you don't have your baskets with you. What about the blooms? Sold them all?"

"Oh, those weren't for sale. I was taking them to the temple nearby, for the evening's worship. I've delivered the flowers so I'm on my way home, now."

"And which is the shrine that benefits by your service?"

"Have you heard of the Thalikulathaar Temple?"

"Ah—would that be the Thanjai Thalikulathaar? I've heard much, indeed. And is it a large shrine?"

"No, only a small one. But these days, it's the Durgai Temple that receives all the honours. That's the one where everyone celebrates all the festivals, offers Pongal and other sacrifices, and generally worships. Even the royal family and the Pazhuvettarayars patronize it. Not so for the Thalikulathaar Temple. In fact, not many people even come there—"

"Ah, but you offer it flowers everyday, don't you? Surely you're compensated in some form for your service?"

"My family received a grant for the purpose—it was offered to my grandfather during the reign of Emperor Kandaradhithar. These days, I and my mother serve the temple."

"Is the Thalikulathaar Temple built of brick? Or stone?" asked Vandhiyathevan. All along the way, he had seen many formerly brick temples freshly renovated with stone and this divine work had prompted his query.

"Brick of course, but I've heard that they're going to rebuild it with stone. At least, they say that Pazhaiyarai city's Periya Piratti wishes to begin work right away, but—" and the youngster hesitated.

"But—what?"

"What's the use of discussing rumours? I've heard it said that one must look around before speaking in daylight, and not even that, at night. Besides, we're surrounded by people, in the midst of a city—"

"I would've thought this the best place to discuss secrets. With all the noise and hubbub, no one's likely to hear a thing."

"Oh?" The youngster glanced at Vandhiyathevan, suddenly uncertain. "What secrets are we supposed to discuss?"

Well, here's an intelligent young man, mused Vandhiyathevan. *This one might prove useful to ferret out information. All the more important that I don't arouse the worst suspicions in him.* Aloud, he spoke in a reassuring voice. "What, indeed? Nothing at all. Be that as it may—*Thambi*, I've traveled far today and desperately need a place to rest for the night. Would you help me please, by suggesting a good inn?"

"Thanjai doesn't lack for accommodation, *Ayya*. There are a great many *chathirams* about, not to mention royal lodgings for foreign visitors. But if you wish—"

"What's your name, *Thambi*?" asked Vandhiyathevan abruptly.

"Amudhan; Sendhan Amudhan."

"What a beautiful name! As sweet as nectar, to be sure. But you were about to invite me to stay at your own home, weren't you?"

"Yes—but how did you guess?"

"I'm a magician, *Thambi*; I've quite a few tricks up my sleeve. Where do you live?"

"Our garden is a shout away from the city; we live in a house within."

"That does it; I'm spending the night at your home. I couldn't get a wink of sleep in this noise and commotion, anyway. In any case, I also wish to make the acquaintance of the gracious lady who bore such a splendid son—your mother."

"She's certainly gracious—but also, unfortunate."

"Why do you say so? Perhaps your father—"

"My father is no more, it's true—but her misfortune dates from her birth. You'll understand when you see her. Come, now."

Half a *naazhigai* beyond the city limits and they arrived at a beautifully tended garden. The heady scent of night-flowers delighted Vandhiyathevan's senses, providing unexpected comfort and a sense of well-being. The tumult and roar of the city had receded significantly, and the garden was shrouded in comparative silence. In the middle, stood a tiled cottage. Two thatched huts flanked it, occupied by families that assisted Amudhan in tending the garden. The young man tasked a member of one to stable Vandhiyathevan's horse and feed it.

They entered the house—and as soon as Vandhiyathevan set eyes on Amudhan's mother, he realized the true extent of her misfortune: the lady was deaf and mute. What she lacked in these senses though, she more than made up for in others: her face fairly brimmed with compassion and gentleness; her eyes gleamed with the light of intelligence. And is it not one of nature's quirks that those who lack a faculty are often blessed more, in others?

At Amudhan's sign, she understood that their visitor had arrived from foreign parts, and her smiling face revealed her welcoming, hospitable spirit.

In a few moments, a dining leaf was duly set on the floor, for the night meal. The first to arrive, as befitting royalty, were fluffy white *idiyappams* and coconut-milk; Vandhiyathevan had never, in his life, tasted anything so delightfully light and sweet. He demolished ten or twelve and half a measure of the milk in short order. Next to make an appearance were thick, savoury tamarind stew and corn-flour cakes; Vandhiyathevan did very well by them as well. Still, his appetite seemed unsated—it took a quarter measure of rice and half a measure of creamy curd to staunch the fire in his belly. Then, and only then did he finally rise from his leaf.

He did make good use of the time his meal afforded him, talking to Amudhan. In particular, he was keen on learning of those who dwelt within the Thanjai fort at the moment, aside from Sundara Chozhar and his retinue.

The Pazhuvettarayar brothers for one, in their various palaces, not to mention their own entourage. The Royal Treasury and Granaries too, which meant that an assorted number of officials and accountants connected to these departments lived in Thanjai. In addition, the Chozha Minister Aniruddha Brahmaraayar, who also happened to be the Emperor's confidante, had made his home within the fort, as well as the *Thirumandhira Olai Naayakar*, the Royal Scribe. Then too, there were all the guards and soldiers under the command of Chinna Pazhuvettarayar whose warrior duties made it imperative that they and their families reside within the fort. Silver and goldsmiths, precious metal and gemstone merchants had been given places as well. Hundreds of clerks belonging to Periya Pazhuvettarayar's tax department lived there. The Durgai Temple was situated in a corner of the fort; this meant that priests, other menials belonging to the temple and courtesans resided in its vicinity.

"And the ministers?" asked Vandhiyathevan, once he had divined all the above information. "Are they all within the fort, as well?"

"No, how can that be? They come and go as and when duty demands. Aniruddha Brahmaraayar, for example, hasn't been in the city for quite some time. They say he has journeyed to the Chera country. Periya Pazhuvettarayar left the city four days ago, as well—possibly north of the Kollidam, to the Mid-Lands."

"But perhaps he's returned? Or don't you know?"

"I did see the young queen of Pazhuvoor's palanquin arrive at the fortress gates this evening, with my very eyes. Not Pazhuvettarayar, though. Perhaps he stayed somewhere along the way. He *might* return tomorrow."

"*Thambi*—Prince Madhuranthakar resides within the fort too, doesn't he?"

"Of course. Next to Pazhuvettarayar's palace, to tell the truth. He's married to Chinna Pazhuvettarayar's daughter, isn't he?"

"Indeed? But this is news to me!"

"Not many people know of it. The Emperor's health being what it is, it was decided that wedding celebrations were unwarranted."

"Excellent. In other words, Prince Madhuranthakar *is* within the fort?"

"He must be. I'm not sure, however, as no one is familiar with his whereabouts; he doesn't venture out, much. Word is that he spends much of his time in worship, meditating upon Siva Peruman and other attendant concerns."

"And yet, he's married at such a late date."

"Surprising, but true. And they say the new groom has changed a great deal, after his wedding! But these are royal affairs—far better that we don't discuss such things."

The urge to pick Amudhan's brain and learn more was almost overpowering, but Vandhiyathevan managed to tamp it down. There was no point in asking endless questions and arousing his worst suspicions. After all, one never knew—this naïve youngster might prove to be of immense value, some day. And this charming little cottage so near the city was a great convenience, as well. Why ruin such excellent arrangements?

Conspiracies and intrigues aside, the day's hard travel and the previous night's adventures had taken their toll; Vandhiyathevan felt drowsiness creep up upon him. Amudhan noticed that his newfound friend was practically falling asleep where he sat, and swiftly laid out a bed for him.

Even as Vandhiyathevan dropped off to slumber, it was the Pazhuvoor Ilaiya Rani's radiant face that he saw. Ah, such an exquisite beauty—a dazzling form and face! He remembered the paralysis that had stolen over him at the sudden sight of the vision of beauty bursting upon him. Recalling the evening's incident awoke a vague, long-lost memory.

He had been walking along a forest path once, in his childhood, when he had encountered a hissing cobra. Ah, the slender beauty of its form—the sinuous grace of its movements! Vandhiyathevan had not been able to take his eyes off the beautiful creature, not even to blink. The snake wove about, dancing gracefully; his own body mimicked its actions. It is impossible to guess what might have happened next—but a mongoose leapt up from nowhere and sprang upon the cobra. The two began a furious battle to the death. Vandhiyathevan came out of his trance suddenly, and took to his heels.

Chee, what a terrible comparison! How could he ever compare that ravishing beauty with a terrible cobra, in a forest? Why, one look at her fair countenance, radiating innocence, and you could forget hunger, thirst and every other bodily instinct! Well, he was about to meet her again, tomorrow, wasn't he? Ah, her voice—silky and smooth all at once—he had never heard anything quite like it. But that majestic young woman he had come across on the banks of the Arisilaaru and the Kudandhai astrologer's home—*she* had been exquisitely lovely as well, not to mention the unearthly beauty in her glowing face! Both were stunning, but ah, how different were their features?

Even as he lay dreaming about these two women, a third intruded upon his ruminations, fury radiating in every step. Nithra Devi, that ferocious Goddess who exerted complete and merciless control over the realm of sleep, overwhelmed him swiftly.

24

Crows and Nightingales

Vandhiyathevan slept like a log all night and woke the next day, well after sunrise. Even at that advanced hour he lay in bed, feeling too lazy to stir. The west winds blew briskly around the cottage; leaves and branches rustled against one another in a low murmur that sounded remarkably like rain. As if in tune to nature's music came a sweet voice, singing one of saint Sundaramurthy's *Thevaram* hymns, set to a lilting melody:

"Ponnaar meniyane pulith
Tholai araikasaithu
Minnaar senjadai mel—milir
Konrai anindhavane!"

At this praise to the "golden hued one who wears a tiger's skin at his waist, and lustrous *konrai* flowers in his tresses," Vandhiyathevan deigned to open his eyes. Sturdy *konrai* trees met his sight outside the cottage, with golden yellow blooms hanging off them in long strands. Sendhan Amudhan stood underneath, a basket in hand and a hook in another, singing hymns as he plucked them, one by one. The young man had obviously bathed very early that morning and now, liberally coated in *vibuthi*, looked the very incarnation of Markandeyan. A pity indeed that his mother was fated to never know what a beautiful voice her son possessed!

Vandhiyathevan rose with the thought, and felt a strange yearning for the peace and simplicity of a life spent gathering and offering flowers to deities in temples. Why couldn't he do the same? What was the point in wandering with a sword and spear, looking for someone or something to hunt? Or be hunted, in turn?

In a little while, though, his sentiments underwent a change: not everyone was a model citizen like Sendhan Amudhan; thieves, murderers, bullies and cheats abounded in this world. And one needed a government to put them in their place. Kings and ministers to form such a government; Velakkara Regiments to ensure their safety—and men such as himself, if only to go about carrying messages in palm-leaves. Ah yes—he would certainly have to seek an audience with Chakravarthy Sundara Chozhar today; should he postpone it, Periya Pazhuvettarayar would soon return and then he may as well give up any chance of entering the palace ...

Vandhiyathevan bathed in the lotus pond near the garden, returned to the cottage and dressed in his best clothes and ornaments. To be sure—he was going to see the Emperor himself, wasn't he? If this was not the perfect opportunity to array himself in fine garments, he didn't quite know what else was. At least, that was the principal reason. If he had another motive to look his best—such as meeting the Pazhuvoor Ilaiya Rani, later that day—that was something he kept to himself.

Once the morning meal was done, Sendhan Amudhan made preparations to depart for the afternoon's worship with his baskets of flowers and Vandhiyathevan, for his royal visit. Both started on foot.

Vallavarayan had made a decision to leave his horse in the cottage. There was no point in risking a riot, should he bring it into the fort.

Besides, his steed needed the rest; he might have need of it very soon —
who knew? It was best that it stayed here.

He engaged in some light-hearted banter with Amudhan on their
way to the fort, and gleaned a little more information.

"Any relations, besides your mother?" he asked.

"Yes—her elder sister, and brother. Her sister is no more, but her
brother lives in Kodikkarai, and delivers flowers to the Kuzhagar Temple.
And he tends to the lighthouse as well. He has a son and daughter. She—
" he began, and paused.

"What of her?"

"Nothing at all. You see, nature has seen fit to bless our family with
strange quirks. Some of us are mute, but others possess beautiful voices.
They sing extraordinarily well, too …"

"Your cousin isn't mute, is she?" put in Vandhiyathevan.

"Good heavens, no."

"In other words, she sings very well. Better than you, perhaps?"

"Why, what a question—you might as well ask if a nightingale's voice
is sweeter than a crow's! When Poonguzhali begins to sing, the very king
of oceans bids his waves fall silent, to listen to her song. Cows, goats and
even animals of the forest stay still, spellbound—"

"She's called Poonguzhali, then? The very essence of a flower's
fragrance! A beautiful name."

"That's not the only thing that's beautiful."

"*She* must be, as well—or you wouldn't go into such ecstasies, would
you?"

"Deer and peacocks are supposed to be the very image of beauty—
but even *they* can't hope to rival hers; no, not even if they beg and plead
for it! And as for Rathi and Indrani, those celestial women will have to
do penance for several lifetimes in a vain bid to match her loveliness—"

Sendhan Amudhan's heart was not completely lost at Siva Peruman's
divine feet, Vandhiyathevan noticed.

"The perfect bride for you, in fact!" he enthused. "And as she's your *muraippenn*, your cousinly claims possess even more merit—so, when's the wedding?"

"I would never dare to call her my equal—it is I who am not in any way worthy of her. If they ever held *swayamvarams* for Poonguzhali like in the earlier days, I'm sure kings from all fifty-six kingdoms would fall over themselves, in a vain bid for her hand! Even the Devas might descend from their celestial abode, perhaps, like they did for Princess Damayanthi. But then, this is the Kali Yugam, so such things mightn't happen—"

"Well! It almost looks like *you* wouldn't want to marry her even if she did."

"Now *that* would be too much. If Siva Peruman were to appear before me this instant and ask, *Do you wish to ascend to Holy Kailasam with your human body intact, like Sundaramurthy Naayanar—or wed Poonguzhali and live on earth?* I would certainly wish the latter. But—what's the purpose in just my yearning for it?"

"Why ever not? *You* wish it—and isn't that more than enough for a wedding? How many, do you think, actually ask for the girl's consent? Take Pazhuvettarayar, for instance, who's married at the advanced age of sixty-five; do you think he made a petition for and received the assent of that young queen, before making her his wife?"

"*Anna*—these are royal affairs. Why must we discuss them at all? If you wouldn't take offense, I should like to warn you: you're about to enter the fort; it would best if you didn't speak of the Pazhuvettarayars. That's just asking for danger—"

"You quite terrify me, *Thambi*."

"I'm merely stating the truth. It's the Pazhuvoor brothers who rule the Chozha Empire right now. There's nothing and no one to gainsay them."

"What—not even the Emperor?"

"Who is ill and abed. If the Pazhuvettarayars drew a line all around him, he wouldn't even dare step across it, they say. He never utters a word against them, nor countermands their commands. Why, he doesn't even listen to his own sons!"

"Indeed. They must be extraordinarily influential, then. Surely they didn't command quite so much power even two years ago?"

"No; all this has come about only after the Emperor took up residence in Thanjavur. Now, their authority knows no boundaries; there's no one to raise a voice against them. It's said that that was why Aniruddha Brahmaraayar departed to Pandiya Nadu—disgusted with their power-play."

"Why did the Emperor move from Pazhaiyarai to Thanjavur in the first place? Do you know?"

"Bits and pieces of news have been floating for a while—I'll tell you what I know. Three years ago, Veera Pandiyan lost his life in battle. Word is that the Chozha forces wrecked havoc in Pandiya lands, during those times. Such is war, isn't it? And so, Madurai came under Chozha rule, but there were certain of the Pandiya king's aides who swore revenge. They have sworn an oath to destroy their foes—and this is why the Pazhuvettarayars insisted on bringing the Emperor here. The Thanjavur fort is far more secure, and there are more warriors to protect his noble self. Also, the physicians say that this city is far more conducive to His Majesty's health, than Pazhaiyarai."

"And that's another thing: everyone talks a great deal about Sundara Chozhar's health, but no one seems to know exactly what ails him."

"But they do. Both his legs have been struck by paralysis; they are useless, now."

"Ah—then, he can't walk? At all?"

"No. Neither can he climb an elephant or ride a horse. He's bed-ridden, for what it's worth—even traveling by palanquin is very painful, although it could be attempted, if need be. That's why he never ventures outside the palace. And of late, there have been rumours that he's—well … not himself."

"What a pity!"

"I'm not sure you can even voice such sentiments, *Anna*—for fear of being tried for treason by the Pazhuvettarayars."

Pazhuvettarayar—Pazhuvettarayar! Wherever he went, whatever he did, they seemed to loom large, taking over everyone and everything. Not to be borne, that—no matter their great valour; Sundara Chozhar should certainly never have allowed them such complete and unquestioning authority over the Treasury, Granaries, the Thanjai fort and indeed, the security of the entire land. All this power and authority had undoubtedly gone to their collective heads—would they even dare think of conspiring against him, else? And now, the tendrils of their treachery were spreading further and further—how far would they go? What destruction would they wreak? It was up to him to do what he could to halt its progress. And if he could—seize an opportunity to warn the Emperor, as well!

Thanjai's imposing fortress gates came into view. Sendhan Amudhan took leave of his new friend, and went his way towards the Thalikulathaar Temple.

Vandhiyathevan, in the meantime, approached the fort—with a great many castles in the air of his own.

ॐ

Hidden Meanings and Explanations

Markandeyan

The son of a *rishi*, Markandeyan was born with a strange Damocles' Sword over his head: his parents, who had longed for a child, had been given a choice—they would either beget a hundred stupid sons who might live to 100—or a single, intelligent son who would only live to 16. His father chose the second option, with the result that Markandeyan was everything a parent could wish for: intelligent, loving, and a staunch devotee of Siva Peruman. When he turned 16, however, Yama, the Lord of Death came to claim him— but Markandeyan won over him by appealing to Siva Peruman, and cheated death and infirmity. He is thus held as an example for anyone who appears to have defeated old age, and retains youthful good looks.

The Muraippenn Custom

From ancient times, a man's elder sister's daughter, or even his aunt/uncle's daughter— i.e., his cousin, has been considered a perfect matrimonial match, in Thamizh Nadu. The girl is referred to as his *Muraippenn*: literally, one on whom he has a claim. This custom is the stuff of legends and folklore; stories abound of young men or heroes who carried off girls in the teeth of opposition, because she happened to be his *muraippenn*; sometimes, it also gave way to intense strife and conflict between entire generations of families. In the west, marriage between cousins is considered almost incestuous now, but the practice is still widespread, and approved by families in Thamizh Nadu— largely because cousinly marriage is authorized only amongst different bloodlines. There are many who firmly believe that the *muraimaaman*, or *thaimaaman*, the girl's cousin or uncle is the only one with the right to wed her; marriage outside the family was and is severely discouraged. Naturally, this custom was even more rigidly enforced in earlier centuries, and even Kalki's times. These ties have loosened, now.

Swayamvaram

An ancient practice among royalty, when princesses were either so beautiful/intelligent that it was thought mere arranged marriages would not do; kings and princes were invited from far and wide and in a ceremony, the princess in question could choose her husband from among them.

Anna

Elder Brother.

25

INSIDE THE FORT

The palm-tree insignia, Vandhiyathevan soon found, was every bit as powerful as the wonderful magic rings he had heard about, in the many fantasy tales of his childhood.

The hour was early that morning, and a great many people were crowded at the fort's gates, jostling with each other for entrance: milk and curd vendors; flower, fruit and vegetable sellers, artisans and craftsmen, clerks and other employees; the sentries at the gates felt the full extent of their authority and made sure everyone else felt it too, as they let them in through a smaller entrance set within the huge gate.

The instant Vandhiyathevan displayed the insignia, however, they bowed from their waists, showed him the greatest deference and actually opened one of the massive gates for him.

Vandhiyathevan entered Thanjavur, thus, in style.

And oh, the incidents that happened, once he set foot in this venerable city! One wonders about the alignment of planets and stars at that moment, but what was it that distinguished this, from many others? So many events followed one upon the other in such quick succession and with such an impact that his entrance, eventually, became a turning-point in the very history of the Chozha empire.

As for our hero—he stood awestruck for a while, after he stepped inside the fort.

Kanchi, ancient capital city of the Pallava Empire, had been subjected to a great many invasions; its buildings and residences presented a dilapidated appearance, falling apart with every day and often coated in mildew. Beautifully carved and decorated buildings once, were now practically in ruins. Aditha Karikalar had done his best to renovate a few upon his arrival, but even they stood out like fresh flowers dotting withered trees, and exaggerated the city's desolation.

Now, Thanjaipuri, on the other hand—ah, everything here, every *mandapam* and mansion was new, gleaming with the sheen of innovation. Residences jostled with each other; some glowed white, pristine in their finish, while still others were of burnt red brick, glittering like precious gems set among radiant pearls and dazzling diamonds. Many boasted luxurious gardens courtesy the rich, red soil. Trees such as *Punnai, Asokam, Arasu, Thennai, Aal,* Jackfruit and Neem spread about branches, their emerald leaves changing various tints of green in the sun, providing a refreshing sight for the eyes, and the mind. Truly, it seemed as though this was a celestial city, planned and executed by the divine architect Mayan himself. Such was its beauty and presence that one felt a burst of happiness even walking through its streets; a strange sense of unexplained, but entirely pleasurable pride.

The presence of a great many guards at the gates and the numerous conditions imposed on those who wished to enter had given Vandhiyathevan the impression, somehow, that he would find a largely empty city within.

He could not have been more mistaken: the streets well nigh burst with surging crowds. Horses and horse-drawn chariots rattled along the avenues in style, while the earth shook with the thundering steps of elephants, swaying majestically through thoroughfares like large, black hillocks, the bells around their necks tinkling in all directions. The shrieks of milk, curd, flowers, vegetable and fruit vendors almost shattered his ear-drums; the golden peals of the *alatchi* bell announcing the hour blended with the rhythm of loud *perigai* drums. Musical instruments sounded from unexpected corners, mingling with the melodious songs of young women—a festival atmosphere prevailed everywhere; enthusiasm and delight pervaded every space.

Now this—this was truly the very epitome of a city! And perhaps this was how the capital of an Empire that was rapidly enlarging upon its territories would look, with spirit and an energy that infected everyone.

The last thing Vandhiyathevan wished to do was display his ignorance about a city of these dimensions; anyone he asked for directions to the palace was sure to look him up and down in derision: *So you're new, are you?* Why, they might even stigmatize him a country bumpkin! He would find his own way—surely it could not be very difficult.

Sadasada! Padapada!—fluttered gaily patterned flags, *makara thoranams* and pretty buntings upon large mansions wherever he looked, fighting madly with the brisk west wind. Tiger and palm-tree emblems were to be found in profusion—but above them all towered one tiger flag, larger and more impressive than any in the city. This, Vandhiyathevan guessed, must clearly be the Emperor's, and began to plot his next course of action as he walked in its general direction.

Obviously, he must deliver the palm-leaf, but it was equally important that he pass on Aditha Karikalar's verbal message as well. He could not accomplish all this without Chinna Pazhuvettarayar's permission—but how was he to get it? God had graciously allowed him entry into the fort, but he couldn't possibly depend on divine intervention for everything, could he? No, he must find some ruse to meet the Emperor himself; what would that be? The blood of generations of Vaanars ran hot through his veins—and it did not lack resourcefulness in the least. *Ah, my ever-fertile brain, you must help me hit upon the perfect stratagem. Come, come; make use of the creativity you've always drawn on! After all, it isn't just poets and writers who need such things to get by; men such as I, in the thick of royal affairs require an imaginative brain as well. Well—what ruse have you come up with?*

One of the first things he did as soon as he stepped within the fort, was to determine for himself that a certain old warrior lord was, indeed, absent.

"My man—has Pazhuvettarayar returned to the city, do you know?" he asked one of the guards by the wall.

"Whom do you refer to, *Thambi*? The Younger is in the city."

"Of course I know *that*! I'm enquiring about the Periyavar, who was lately on a visit to the mid-lands."

"Was that where he traveled to? That's news to me. I do know that the young queen's palanquin returned last evening, but the lord of Pazhuvoor hasn't, yet. News is that he will, tonight," confided the guard.

This was good hearing, indeed. All that he needed to do, now, was to seek an audience with the Emperor somehow, and deliver his palm-leaf to him. How, *how* was he to accomplish this?

The next instant, an idea occurred to him. Worry fell away at once; his face regained its enthusiastic smile; his eyes gleamed with the spirit of mischief.

As it so happened, he did not have to wander endlessly in search of the royal residence; all he did was to keep the large Tiger flag in sight and follow the roads; they led straight to the palace entrance. And what a palace it was, indeed. Such imposing columns; such richly decorated pillars that held aloft the front *mandapam*—it was doubtful if even Indra, King of the Devas possessed such an impressive edifice, or the great king Vikramaditya of famed Ujjaini! Why, each of the ornamented horses sculpted into the tall pillars seemed about to pounce on him, so realistic were they!

A great many paths ran through the city, culminating in the courtyard that led to the palace; each was guarded by two cavalry men and a sprinkling of the infantry. Most passersby, Vandhiyathevan noticed, did not even approach the guards; a few daring specimens did dare to stroll up—but once they had stared at the palace's entrance and the fluttering Tiger flag above, retreated strategically. Whenever it seemed like a large crowd would congregate, soldiers were swift to make a sign and disperse it. Even those who gathered made sure to never raise their voices but conversed in low murmurs, calculated to reach only each other's ears.

Vandhiyathevan, needless to say, hesitated not a whit. Where others faltered, he walked briskly, with the utmost of confidence, along the palace-path. The instant he reached them though, two horse-guards barred his way, their steeds almost nuzzling. A cluster of spears clanged towards him, sharp points glinting in the sun—that of the soldiers on horses, and on foot.

His magical ring, however, had its effect: the instant he displayed it, the soldiers seemed to deflate; their thinly veiled conceit evaporated. Three guards stared at the ring one, by one. "Very well. Let him pass," permitted another. Two spears parted at once; Vandhiyathevan swept past them right regally.

And yet—what of it? How many more such inspections was he fated to pass? How much more scrutiny? How on earth was he going to find Chinna Pazhuvettarayar? Whom was he supposed to ask for directions, and how? For there was no doubt that he could not see the Emperor without due permission from that worthy. And where would they keep an invalid Emperor in this sprawling, enormous complex, anyway? How was he to find *that* out?

Vandhiyathevan sensed a gaggle of men behind him, paused, and turned. Yes, a group stood by the guards, waiting for approval to enter. They were dressed extraordinarily well too, in expensive silks, pearl necklaces, large *makara* ornaments and *kundalams* in their ears. Some wore sacred ash on their foreheads; others had decorated it with sandalwood paste, *kungumam* and fragrant *javvadhu*. Why — they seemed like poets, from the looks of it. And so they were.

"The royal bards have arrived; let them through, please!" called out one of the guards—their leader, possibly—and added to another, "Chinna Pazhuvettarayar may be found in the central *mandapam*. Escort them there at once."

"Respected lords—should you receive any gifts, please take this path on your way out. If not, do not bother!" teased another, and laughter rang through them.

The fruit falls into the milk all by itself, as the saying went, mused Vandhiyathevan, listening to this conversation. All he had to do, to find Chinna Pazhuvettarayar, was just follow this poetic group; there would be no need to stammer, stutter or wander around, asking for directions in vain.

As to whatever came after that—well, he had brains, hadn't he? His fertile imagination would show him some way out. Not to mention lady luck as well.

Vandhiyathevan joined the tail of the departing poets, and went with them.

26

"ABAAYAM! ABAAYAM!"

Vandhiyathevan entered the principal or *aasthaana mandapam*, a little ahead of the poets. A man sat upon a high throne, majesty and pride limning every pore of his body, and it was not difficult for our hero to guess that this must be Chinna Pazhuvettarayar.

Quite a few people surrounded him, their palms covering their mouths in the ultimate sign of deference: one stood waiting with palm-leaves of the day in his hands; yet another was obviously the *kanakkaayar*, head clerk, eager to deliver accounts; the heads of security stood by as well, in anticipation of instructions. A few menials were in attendance, ready to perform any service that may be required while others stood behind his throne, fanning him with a white *saamaram*. Yet another awaited his master's pleasure with a small box of betel-leaves and areca-nuts.

Vandhiyathevan, second to none when it came to a proud mien, found himself setting his consequence a little aside in the presence of this warrior-lord. If anything, Pazhuvettarayar the Younger possessed a pride of bearing that was a notch above even his elder.

The moment he set eyes on our young man, however, his face brightened noticeably. "Who might you be, *Thambi*? Where do you come from?"

A soldier by birth and breeding, his interest naturally revolved upon war and battle and, in consequence, strong young men; he was bent on gathering as many as he could under his command, in his army. Thus, his enthusiasm at the sight of Vandhiyathevan.

"I come from Kanchipuram, Commander. Prince Aditha Karikalar bade me deliver this palm-leaf to his father," said Vallavarayan in his politest voice.

Chinna Pazhuvettarayar's face darkened at the mention of Kanchi. "What? What is that you say?" he snapped.

"I've traveled from Kanchipuram with an *olai* from Aditha Karikalar."

"Oh? Well, hand it over." His manner might have been negligent, but the warrior-lord's voice betrayed his tension.

"Very well," replied Vallavarayan as he took out the palm-leaf from his waistband. "But Commander, it's for the Emperor—"

Which comment Chinna Pazhuvettarayar considered not at all, as he took it eagerly, threw a glance at it and bade the man next to him, to read the contents out loud. "Nothing new, here," he murmured to himself, as he heard the message.

"Commander, my *olai* …" Vandhiyathevan's voice trailed away.

"What of it? I shall deliver it to the Emperor myself."

"It isn't—it's just that I was ordered to deliver it into the hands of the Chakravarthy myself."

"Ah—so you were to place no trust in me?" The Thanjai Commander's face was a perfect storm of fury. "Were those your orders from Prince Adithar?"

"Not at all. Those were *your* brother's, however."

"Wait—what? Where did *you* meet the Periyavar?"

"At the Kadambur Sambuvaraiyar palace, where I happened to spend a night. And it was he who gave me this insignia, as well."

"Why could you not have told me all this earlier? So, you stayed at Kadambur? And who else was present?"

"Quite a few lords from Mazha Nadu, the mid-lands and Thirumunaippaadi—"

"Now wait, just a moment. You may as well give this into the hands of the Emperor himself—else those blasted court poets will demand an audience with him and yap away forever. You may tell me the rest when you have given your message. Now, you—" and Chinna Pazhuvettarayar sought out one of the soldiers near him. "Escort this youngster to the Chakravarthy."

Vandhiyathevan followed his guide ever deeper, into the palace.

The magnificent Chozha throne, seat of an empire that stretched from east coast to west, surrounded by the rumbling oceans on three sides—had lately become a sickbed. And it was here that Emperor Paranthaka Sundara Chozhar lay, his frail body supported by cushions. A good deal of his time was spent in rest, imbibing copious doses of medicine; much of his royal duties had been delegated to others—but there were still dignitaries to whom he had to grant an audience, and various claims upon his time. It was important for the well-being of the empire that Ministers, Commanders and the Velakkara Regiment meet with him at least once a day.

The man who had earned the respect of his subjects with his valorous deeds on numerous battlefields—an *asagaaya sooran*; one so famed for his good looks that he had been named Sundara, and deemed an equal to Manmadhan, the God of Love himself, by his adoring people—now lay on a bed, feeble and fragile, as though a stiff wind might break him in half.

Vandhiyathevan stared at the ruler of the Chozha empire, speechless. His eyes brimmed, overcome by the sight. He approached very softly, and delivered the *olai* with the utmost respect.

"Where are you from?" quavered the Chakravarthy, voice faint with fatigue. "Whose *olai* is this?"

"*Prabhu*, I come from Kanchi," Vandhiyathevan's voice was husky with emotion. "I bring you this message from Prince Adithar."

The Emperor's face brightened at once. "Devi," He turned to his consort, the Empress Vanavan Maadevi, originally a princess of the Thirukkovilur Malayaman clan. "Your son has sent us a palm-leaf," and he began to read the missive. "Ah. His highness has built a golden palace in Kanchi," he said, and his eyes lost their lustre. "He wishes us to stay there, for a while."

His face grew even more pinched than before, if possible. "Devi, my grandfather, the illustrious Paranthaka Chakravarthy, gathered every speck of gold in his palaces and donated them all towards a beautiful roof for the great Lord who dances in Thillai; he transformed it into a golden *ambalam*. None of our family was ever remotely interested in building golden palaces for themselves—their fervour lay in raising beautiful temples for God. And here is Adithan, committing such a heinous act against everything sacred! Ah, how are we ever to redeem ourselves?"

The Empress, whose face had gained some colour at the mention of a letter from her son, fell even more, if possible. She turned away, unable to say a word.

Vandhiyathevan decided that it was time to intervene. "Your Majesty," he began, screwing up every bit of courage and swiftness of tongue he possessed. "Surely your son hasn't committed a grievous sin that fairly demands redemption? He has, after all, only obeyed the dictates of a loving son's heart. Parents are always as Gods to their children, aren't they? Is it not, then, a commendable action to have built a temple for his deities to dwell?"

A wan smile appeared on Sundara Chozhar's face. "I know not who you might be, *Thambi*, but you seem eminently sensible, and you possess an intelligent tongue in your head. But tell me this: a son may consider his parents as Gods but surely they are not so, to the rest of the world? Golden temples may only be dedicated to the omnipresent, and omniscient supreme power, worshipped by all, may they not?

"*Prabhu*—a son may consider his father a God but so do people, their king. I have heard tell, and read in our ancient epics and sacred texts that an Emperor is the very incarnation of Thirumaal, the One who Guards us all. I should say that in this case, your son's intentions in building you a golden palace were laudable in the extreme."

The Emperor threw a glance at his queen, again. "Did you listen to this intelligent young man, my dear? Ah, if our Adhithan has friends such as these, then we need not fear for his future, any more. Nor worry about his tendency to rush where angels fear to tread!"

Then he turned to Vandhiyathevan again. "*Thambi*—what matters now is hardly the merit or otherwise, of building a golden palace. You see how I am situated, do you not? I can barely move about, and a long journey is certainly out of the question. We are desperate to see him but at this moment, he is the one who will have to visit me. Come tomorrow, and I shall ensure that you have a reply."

A confused babble of voices and footsteps reached them at this point, and Vandhiyathevan realized that the court poets were about to enter the *mandapam*. Ah, if those men arrived, chances were that Chinna Pazhuvettarayar would accompany them—and he might as well bid farewell to any chance of passing across a message. Now he would just have to seize the moment and whisper a few words of warning.

Having decided all this within moments, Vandhiyathevan broke into hurried speech. "Chakravarthy, grant me a favour: kindly do listen to me: you must leave Thanjavur at once! Great peril surrounds you here— *abaayam*! *Abaayam*—!"

Chinna Pazhuvettarayar had entered the hall even as he spoke the last few words, the court poets following him. Vandhiyathevan's hasty warning fell on his ears.

His face bloomed with fury.

ॐ

Hidden Meanings and Explanations

"Yet another awaited his master's pleasure with a small box of betel-leaves and areca-nuts ..."

Amongst the numerous staff waiting upon Chinna Pazhuvettarayar is someone, rather incongruously, holding a betel-leaf box, commonly known as a *vetrilaippetti*. But the truth is, these items of luxury were ubiquitous among privileged people who chewed combinations of betel-leaves, areca-nuts and lime often; so common were men and women holding boxes containing these essentials that in time, their names were forgotten and they came to be known as *"vetrilaippetti"* themselves.

27

THE COURT POETS

Paraak! Paraak! Here come the court poets—the royals bards— those eminent men whose knowledge of divine Thamizh is as boundless as the oceans!—The distinguished descendents of great sage Agasthiyar!—Who have read the numerous pages of classics such as *Tholkaappiyam* end to end!—Who have well-nigh gobbled up epics like *Silappathikaaram*!—Who know more about the renowned *Thirukkural* than its very author!—Who may prescribe the rules of grammar to literature!—Who will quote classics until the world ends to grammarians!—Who, despite all these fantastic qualifications, can actually compose verses on their own! The truth of their talent lies in the fact that millions of termites may subsist for centuries on their numerous, wonderful and timeless creations!

These superbly talented men now gathered in a group before the Chakravarthy and chorused in one voice: "*Vaazhga*! Long live the Emperor Who Rules over the Seven Worlds! Long live Sundara Chozhar, Who Brought Pandiyan to his knees! May He who guards and cherishes poets live long! May the grandson of *Panditha Vathsalar*, the illustrious Emperor Paranthaka Chozhar, royal patron of arts, flourish forever and ever!"

Judging by the expression on Sundara Chozhar's face, he was not very happy with these grandiloquent expressions—but his natural courtesy and breeding made him attempt to rise and welcome them.

Chinna Pazhuvettarayar, observing this, stepped forward. "*Prabhu*, our poets' intention was not to discommode you in any way—but rather to seek an audience with your gracious Majesty. I pray that you lie in repose, and not inconvenience yourself."

"Indeed yes, Oh King of Kings!" exclaimed Nallan Saathanaar, obviously the leader of the poetic group. "Never shall it be said that we were the cause of Your Majesty's agitation!"

"I am very glad to see you, of course, after such a long time," acknowledged the Emperor, who cherished a great fondness for Thamizh. "I should be happy to listen to a few verses, if you will."

The group sat down on the jewel-toned *jamakkaalam*, the carpet laid in front of the throne. Vandhiyathevan decided to seize the chance and took his seat among them, as well. His message was not complete, and he did not really want to leave if he could have another chance at delivering it fully.

Chinna Pazhuvettarayar saw him—and his ire rose. It took a great deal of self-control to push down the fury that threatened to consume him, but he did it. His first instinct was to send the insolent boy out but then, wiser counsel prevailed: he would have more scope to understand the upstart's intentions if he were right here, under his nose, so to speak. Very well, he would appear to ignore him for a while—but once these dratted poets left, he would seize upon him and know exactly what tales he had been telling the Emperor.

"*Danger! Abaayam!*" The young man's voice rang in his ears, even now.

—

"My good friends, I have not had the pleasure of your company in a long while. My ears hunger for the taste of beautiful Thamizh verses," began Sundara Chozha. "Have any of you written a new song, perhaps?"

At once, one of the many masters of poetry gathered, sprung up. "*Prabhu*, this servant comes to your feet from the Buddhist *Palli*, the monastery in Ulagapuram that carries your illustrious name, and brings you welcome news: the monks are delighted beyond measure at your magnanimous grants; at the nobility of a Saivite who showers wealth on their *madams*. They are, however, grieved to know of your ill-health and have been praying endlessly for your recovery. Your gracious Majesty must permit me to recite one of their verses."

"By all means; I am waiting to hear it," assented the Emperor. The poet obliged at once, with a simple song that exulted in the grace and compassion of Sundara Chozhar, King of Nandhipuri, and prayed that his strength, large-heartedness and beauty live long:

"Pothiyan thirunizhal punidha! Nirparavuthum
Methagu Nandhipuri Mannar Sundara
Chozhar vanmaiyum vanappum
thinmaiyum ulagir chiranthu vaazhgenave!"

"Excellent!" His compeers erupted in praise, once the poem ended.

"It is indeed astonishing that Buddhist monks should be capable of such gratitude," wondered one particularly staunch Saivite poet.

"True, for the service I rendered the Ulagapuram Buddhist monastery was meager, in my opinion," admitted the Emperor.

"Ah, never that, Sire. Who among us who has experienced Your Majesty's compassion and bounty can help but sing its praise? Why, even Indra, Lord of the Devas, the Sun God, and Siva Peruman have known that great felicity!" put forward one worthy.

"But how is this?" An amused smile twisted Sundara Chozhar's lips. "Surely all these divine entities could not have had occasion to find themselves beholden to me?"

"Your Majesty must permit me to recite this poem," requested the bard.

"Certainly."

"Indiran erak kari alithaar—
Pari ezhalithaar
Senthiru menith thinagararku—
Sivanaar manathup
Painthugilerap pallakalithaar—
Pazhaiyaarai nagar
Sundara Chozharai yaavaroppaargal ith
Thonnilathe!"

"Excellent!" "Marvelous!" The court echoed with loud applause, a great many signs of assent and numerous exclamations of approval at this extravagant verse.

Sundara Chozha looked at them, eyes bright with emotion. "Could one of you please elaborate on this song's meaning?"

Many rose at the same time and for a while, a confused babble grew, until everyone except Nallan Saathanaar took their seats again. The poet then began to explain:

"Once, Indra, Lord of the celestial Devas was engaged in furious battle with the demon Vriddhaasuran. So fiercely raged the combat that the Deva actually lost his famed and powerful elephant, Airaavadham. He searched high and low for a suitable replacement, but could not seem to find a single one in the whole world. Finally, desperate for a mount, he came down to Emperor Sundara Chozhar of Pazhaiyarai, and petitioned him for an elephant that was as powerful as his lost mount. To which the gracious Emperor replied that he was very sorry, but there was none that was the equal of the Airaavadham. "But I have a great many that are far superior!" and he led the way to his elephant enclosure, where stood thousands of the magnificent animals like large, dark hillocks. Devendran stared at them at a loss for words, for he knew not which to choose! Sundara Chozhar took pity on the stupefied lord of the Devas, and chose an elephant himself—but Indra was struck again, by anxiety: How was he ever going to ride such a mammoth? Not even his famed Vajrayudham, his signature weapon could control such a mount! And then, Emperor Sundara Chozhar came to his rescue again and gifted him with a splendid goad as well, to assist him!

"Yet another time, the Sun God, Surya Bhagavan, Who rules the sky with His dazzling red and gold rays, was bound in fierce combat with the dreaded snake-king Rahu. The evil demon tried his best to swallow Surya in one gulp, but the God's brilliant beams almost blinded him and he couldn't. His terrible venom, *Kaalakodi* did, however, kill all seven horses harnessed to the Sun God's chariot, and Surya Bhagavan stood bewildered—for how was He to shower His rays upon the world every day, without chariot and trusty steeds? And then, Emperor Sundara Chozhar, the very epitome of compassion, approached Him with seven of his best stallions and requested Him to nurture the world with His life-giving light. Surya Bhagavan duly appreciated this signal service from one who was His own regal descendent.

"And there is the time when Siva Peruman and His divine consort Parvathi Devi were to be wedded in Their heavenly abode of Kailasam. The bride's party arrived with Her *seer varisai*: the traditional, elaborate wedding-gifts that usually accompany the new wife—save for one thing: a palanquin. The entire bridal party broke out in worried speech: soon, a wedding procession would have to take place—and there was nothing except for the bull, for the newly married couple to ride in! Sundara Chozhar, who learnt of this situation, sent at once for his pearl-encrusted palanquin from Pazhaiyarai. With great deference and devotion due to God, he made a present of it on the occasion of Siva Peruman's own wedding. Who, I ask you, can possibly be the equal of Emperor Sundara Chozhar for compassion and benevolence, in this vast world surrounded by roaring oceans?"

Said Sundara Chozhar, listening to this involved and colourful explanation, broke into a merry peal of laughter. Long months of illness and suffering had lined his wan face; not even his consort, Empress Vanavan Maadevi had heard him utter a chuckle in all this time. Her husband's joy served to lift her sagging spirits a little. Even her maids and assistants were cheered at the sight.

Chinna Pazhuvettarayar, who had remained standing all this while, now stepped forward. "I believe I have committed a grievous error," he said, bringing his palms together. "Will Your Majesty forgive me?"

"Ah, is that Thanjai's Commander? Now what is this heinous error for which you beg my pardon? Perhaps you snatched the elephant and horses I graciously donated to both Indra and Surya Bhagavan? Or is it the palanquin that you looted from poor Siva Peruman's bride treasures? You *are* capable of such devious acts, you know." And the Emperor was consumed by mirth, again. This time, the court poets joined him—but it was Vandhiyathevan, perhaps, who seemed to appreciate the joke a little too much and laughed the most. Chinna Pazhuvettarayar noticed it and sent a scorching glance in his direction, before turning to the Emperor again.

"My mistake, Your Majesty, was this: I gave a great deal of credence to the royal physicians all this while, and kept our poets from visiting you. I believed their company would be detrimental—but I was mistaken. Their presence amuses you; this court has witnessed your laughter after aeons, I should think. Even the gracious Empress, Udaya Piratti and her maids smile at your happiness. And I delighted in it as well. It was an unforgivable crime, was it not, to have prevented such a pleasurable exercise all this while?"

"You make an excellent point, Commander—and have proven the truth of my words as well. I did ask, did I not, to disregard the physicians and allow the court poets to meet me, instead of barricading me against them?"

The royal physician judged this the right moment to rise, cover his mouth with his palms in extreme deference and launch into a long and involved explanation, but the Emperor did not seem very interested in it. Instead, he turned towards the poets.

"Does anyone here know the creator of such a wonderful verse?" he asked. "Do tell me, if you do."

"Ah, now *that* is what we could never find out," lamented Nallan Saathanaar. "Sire, if we ever do, we have resolved to award him the grand title, the *Chakravarthy of Poetry*, and carry him around in a decorated palanquin on our very shoulders. Alas—our efforts have so far, yielded no result."

"Not surprising in the least," was Sundara Chozhar's sardonic reply. "Any poet who can possibly stack so many outrageous lies one upon another in these silly verses certainly wouldn't be willing to reveal his identity, would he?"

The poets stared at one another, nonplussed at this remark. Not one of them could think of a suitable reply.

It was at this moment that our Vandhiyathevan threw himself valiantly into the breach. "Ah, *Prabhu*, they're not quite lies. After all, should ordinary people utter such things, they're classified as rank falsehoods— but the very same statements, made by royal strategists would be lauded cunning ruses worthy of Chanakya! As for bards, they would consider it imaginative, and call it by various beautiful and confounding poetic terms such as *ani alangaaram* or *il porul uvamai—*"

"Excellent!" The court poets turned towards him as one and expressed their approval in no uncertain terms. "Well said!"

The Emperor stared at Vallavarayan as well. "Ah, you are the young man who brought me an *olai* from Kanchi, are you not? Well, well, you certainly have rendered my arguments futile with your intelligent answer." Then, he turned towards the poets. "My learned friends, there is no need to expend a great deal of your valuable time in trying to find this elusive poet, and confer upon him the title *Chakravarthy of Poetry*—for he bears, already, the crushing weight of the Chozha crown upon his head and struggles to live with titles such as *Emperor of Three Worlds*, or even worse,

Seven Worlds, King of Kings, and other such grandiose appellations. I am not sure he could survive one more!"

And if I were to tell you, dear readers, that the poets who listened to this unexpected claim almost drowned in a sea of amazement—well, you will simply have to believe it. After all, it could be my imaginative and creative turn of phrase, and an example of various beautiful poetic terms such as *il porul uvamai,* or *ani alankaram,* could it not?

༺ೖ༻

Hidden Meanings and Explanations

Kalki's Notes

In years bygone, before this story took place, the Chozha lands were once under Pallava rule and Pazhaiyarai was known by the name Nandhipuri. This explains why Sundara Chozha was sometimes referred to as the King of Nandhipuri.

Udaya Piratti

It was the custom, sometimes, to refer to the Emperor's royal consort by this term.

28

AN IRON GRIP

Once the wave of amazement washing over everyone like an unexpected flashflood subsided a little, Nallan Saathanaar spoke up, a good deal of hesitation in his voice. "Then, the poet who composed the song, *Prabhu,* was it—?"

"—the Emperor of Three Worlds who lies before you this very moment, unable to even move his legs," supplied Sundara Chozhar.

"Ah!" A clamour of exclamations and surprise rose among the bards. Some shook their heads and bodies in various strange contortions, uncertain of how to express themselves; others sat still, unaware of their own feelings.

"Honoured bards," Sundara Chozhar himself, continued his tale. "Once, poets and learned men of words were gracious enough to visit me in Pazhaiyarai—perhaps some of you were there as well. Each sang in praise of the greatness of my ancestors and the Chozha dynasty. They sang about me, too, heaping praises that I gave away such-and-such a thing, or showered riches on someone else. Young princess Kundhavai was by my side, then, and when the poets left with their rewards, she expressed enormous admiration for their wonderful songs. I argued that I was a great deal more talented than them, and could sing just as well. That was when I composed this little verse on the spur of the moment—and then I petitioned her gracious Highness for a reward. My little girl climbed on my back, said "Here's your prize!" and delivered two smart slaps on my cheeks! Ah, I remember it as though it happened just yesterday. And yet, it has been more than eight years ..."

"Wonderful!"—"Astonishing indeed!" Exclamations of amazement and delight burst forth, from the assembled poets.

Kundhavai!—the very word sent a thrill of exhilaration through Vandhiyathevan's veins. Many were the tales he had heard of this young princess's beauty, refinement and intelligence. And here, in front of him was the fortunate man who had fathered her; the elderly woman by him, her mother. Ah, the pride in the Emperor's voice as he spoke of his beloved daughter—how his voice shook at the very mention of her name—!

Vandhiyathevan's right hand moved of its own volition towards the band of silk around his waist and felt around it; within, was the precious *olai* he was supposed to deliver to Kundhavai. And then his fingers stopped, paralyzed. His heart stuttered with shock. *Ayyo—the olai—the olai is missing! Where could it be? Could it have fallen somewhere? Perhaps it slipped out when I handed over the palm-leaf meant for the Emperor? But where, then? Perhaps in the aasthaana mandapam? What if Chinna Pazhuvettarayar got his wretched horrible hands on it? Ah, the peril of it falling into his clutches— what a terrible misfortune!—how am I to get out of this one—?*

Now that he knew that the *olai* meant for her had dropped God knew where, the court and its poets were the last thing on Vandhiyathevan's mind. He could barely sit still; none of the conversations around him really made any sense. Not that he cared, anyway.

Meanwhile, Sundara Chozhar had gone ahead with his recital, to the admiring bards: "I suspect that Kundhavai regaled someone with this silly verse of mine—probably Eesanya Bhattacharyar from Pazhaiyarai's Thirumetrali Temple. And he, perhaps, spread it around for a laugh at my expense—!"

"*Prabhu*, even if you were, indeed, the author of this piece—what of it? It is truly a wonderful little verse. In addition to being the Emperor of this world, you are now the Chakravarthy of Poetry as well!" commented Nallan Saathanaar.

"And yet, were I to compose one now, I would not stop at just giving away elephants to Indra, horses to Surya, or palanquins to Siva Peruman. Remember the tale of Markandeyan who appealed to the great lord to save his life? Well, Siva Peruman duly obliged and kicked away the God of Death but his pitiful mount, the buffalo, expired from the ire of the deity. And Pazhaiyarai's Sundara Chozhar, who heard of Yama's terrible plight, wandering without a steed, duly donated one to Him! And now, Death travels upon His mount majestically, seeking me. Not even Thanjai's Commander, Chinna Pazhuvettarayar, can stop Him and His precious buffalo, can he?"

Even as the words fell from the Emperor's lips, tears began to flow down the sallow cheeks of Udaya Piratti. Some of the poets gathered began to sob themselves, unable to bear the sorrow.

Chinna Pazhuvettarayar, it seemed, was the only one to maintain some semblance of courage. "*Prabhu*, I am prepared to battle even Yama, in the course of my service to you!" he announced.

"I entertain no doubts on that score, Commander. I do know, however, that no man is capable of winning against Him. All we can do is pray that we have the strength to face our fate without fear. After all, didn't one of Thamizh's greatest poets sing, "I do not fear Death?""

A poet rose at once, and began to recite the famous verse of Appar's, that sang of his willingness to face extreme torture and even death, fearlessly, in the face of persecution upon his faith:

"*Naamaarkkum kudiyallom,*
Namanai anjom

Naragathil idarppadom
Nadalaiyallom
Emappom, piniyariyom—"

The Emperor interrupted, at this point. "Such devotion; such complete conviction! Ah, who but one who has glimpsed God could have sung with such indomitable spirit? Saint Appar suffered terribly from the dreaded *soolai* disease—but Iraivan cured him completely of his stomach ailment. No wonder he sings so exultantly, that he fears pain, illness and Death no longer. My friends, far better that you sing such beautiful verses extolling the divine, rather than praise of pitiful creatures such as I. Great men of God like Appar, Sundarar and Sambandhar have sung thousands of songs brimming with devotion in beautiful, chaste Thamizh—how wonderful it might be, to gather them into a complete collection? Why, a lifetime would not suffice to learn, sing and rapturously lose oneself in them all!"

"If it pleases you, King of Kings, we shall be honoured to begin this sacred task at once."

"No—I am afraid that such an enormous undertaking could hardly be accomplished in my time. Later, however …" and the Emperor's voice trailed away as he lapsed deep into thought.

The royal physician tiptoed up to Chinna Pazhuvettarayar and murmured something into his ears. Sundara Chozhar, who glanced at the whispering duo, stared at his audience, eyes wide and puzzled, as though he had come out of a trance. He seemed, at that moment, a gaunt, pitiful creature, snatched just that instant from the gaping maws of death.

"Sire, you did desire to listen to a song from the Sangam era. These learned men may leave once they have recited one, may they not?" queried the Commander.

"Ah yes, of course I did," sighed the Emperor. "It seems to me that my mind is losing its battle with awareness, along with my body. Please—do continue."

At a sign from Chinna Pazhuvettarayar, Nallan Saathanaar of the poets stood up. "Oh King of Kings, chief among your ancestors, perhaps the most famous of them all, was the Emperor Karikal Peruvalathaar, who hoisted the Tiger flag on the very summit of the Himalayas. The beautiful city of Poompuhar—known, also as Kaverippoompattinam—was the capital of the Chozha Empire during his prosperous reign. Ships would dock at that sea-port with so many goods and produce that it was an onerous task to keep count. Here is a song by a poet belonging to the Sangam era and to those glorious times, describing Puhar's immense wealth, international trade and prosperity—through the goods that reached the globally famed port from various countries:

> *"Vadamalai pirantha maniyum ponnum,*
> *Kudamalai pirantha vaaramum akilum*
> *Thenkadal muthum, kunakadal thukirum*
> *Gangai vaariyum Kaavirip payanum*
> *Eezhathu unavum kaazhagath thaakkamum—"*

[*Gold and precious gems from the mountainous lands of the North; Sandalwood, akil and other fragrant incenses from the hills of Podhigai; pearls and corals from the southern seas; produce from the banks of rivers such as the Ganga and Kaveri; food-grains from Eezham and goods from far-flung places such as Kadaaram ...*]

Sundara Chozhar signed the poet to stop, at this point. "During the glorious times of Karikalar, it was Chozha Nadu that received food and grains from Eezham—you allowed in these poets to impress that upon me, didn't you, Commander?"

"Yes, Sire," came the voice of Chinna Pazhuvettarayar—admittedly, in a markedly feeble tone.

"You have made your point. Reward these bards, please, and send them on their way."

Thanjai's Commander turned towards them and delivered the royal dismissal, upon which they left, chanting praises. "*Vaazhi!*"

Already listless and rather panicked at the sudden disappearance of the *olai* meant for Kundhavai, Vandhiyathevan decided that he would make his escape as well and sidled up to them, hoping to slip into the middle of the crowd.

He was doomed to disappointment, however. As he neared the entrance, a strong hand crept out and clutched his wrist in an iron grip.

Now, Vandhiyathevan was a courageous young man in the normal way—but that grip shook him, right from the top of his head to the tips of his toes, and paralyzed him into standing still.

He looked up—and saw that the hand belonged to none other than Chinna Pazhuvettarayar himself.

The court poets streamed out of the *aasthaana* mandapam.

29

"OUR HONOURED GUEST..."

The poets' departure was the sign for the royal physician to approach the Emperor with some kind of a medicinal concoction. Vanavan Maadevi, princess of the Malayaman clan, received it from him gently and proffered it to her husband.

Chinna Pazhuvettarayar, who had kept his patience somehow, until this time, now hastened to his side, dragging Vandhiyathevan by the hand. "*Prabhu*? Has the new medicine had any effect?"

"The physician certainly swears by it; so does Her Majesty. I, however, must admit that I feel nothing of the sort. To confess the truth, Commander—all this is a pitiful waste of time and energy. My days are numbered; Yama nips at my heels. At this very moment, I know he seeks me in Pazhaiyarai and once he realizes that I no longer reside there, he will knock at my doors here—"

"You must not speak so, *Prabhu*—witness, if you please, how your words sink our spirits! Your ancestors—"

"Ah, you remind me, of course, that none of my ancestors feared Death. But if I were to have the good fortune of embracing a valiant end in a battlefield like my forebears, Commander, neither would I; nor would I bemoan my fate. I would, in fact, welcome it with open arms and an enthusiastic heart. My uncle Rajadithyar embraced death as he plunged into war, in Thakkolam; he carved his name into the annals of Chozha history and gained pride of place for eternity as He Who Embraced Death on his Elephant. As for me—I shall gain the noble title of Sundara Chozhan Who Feebly Welcomed Yama on his Sickbed, I suppose. Yet another uncle of mine, Emperor Kandaradhithar, was solely immersed in worship of Siva Peruman; death held no fears for him. He went on pilgrimages to lands along the western seas and attained the Lord's Feet, earning the sobriquet: He Who Embraced Death in the West. I claim no special devotion towards God; neither am I in any position to make pilgrimages. How many more days am I fated to lie abed, a sore trial to both myself and those around me? And yet, something tells me—I am not long, for this world—"

"Sire, the royal physician is confident that your health is in no danger; the astrologers are of the same opinion. And yet, this young man spoke of danger a while ago, did he not?"

"Ah, the youngster from Kanchi? Yes—I do remember him saying something about peril. What were you speaking of, *Thambi*? My state of health, perhaps?"

Vallavarayan stared at the Emperor, brain racing at the speed of lightning. Were he to admit that he did, indeed, warn the Chakravarthy of danger, he was done for; every worst suspicion would be aroused, and *he* would be the one courting peril in every form. Very well: now, if any, was the time to put his creativity to good use. He would have to play around with words and sounds; cannily employ Thamizh grammar to change the long to the short— transform *nedil* into *kuril*—and hope that he could pull off this particular ruse.

"Your Gracious Majesty, who am I to speak of danger in your exalted presence? Our valiant Chinna Pazhuvettarayar guards this formidable fort; the royal physicians are always at hand and here is our empress, caring for your noble person, the very incarnation of Savithri Amman, willing to drag her husband from the doors of death. What sort of danger could possibly dare to accost you, here? No; all I cried out, Your Majesty, was *Abayam*! *Abayam*!—I simply wished to submit a prayer at your illustrious feet; to beg your indulgence, your compassion. Grant me sanctuary, gracious Highness. I am but a stranger here—the last of our once hoary Vaanar clan; its only representative. Thus far, I have served under your son and gladdened his heart. Now, I petition you, Sire, to consider my request and grant me at least a fraction of the lands my ancestors once ruled over. Oh King of Kings, all I can do is prostrate myself at your feet—and pray that a boon be granted to this ignorant servant. *Abayam*, Your Majesty, this orphan begs your protection!" And Vandhiyathevan stopped to take a breath, after his nonstop speech.

Judging by Chinna Pazhuvettarayar's pinched expression, he was far from happy with this effusion. The Emperor's face, however, which had been haggard and drawn, now relaxed into a smile. The Queen's face showed her pleasure, as well.

"It would seem that Goddess Saraswathi showered this young man with Her divine Grace, and wrote on his tongue the very day of his birth," marveled the Empress. "He has a way with words, hasn't he?"

Well, he had come this far—no harm in seizing the day, was there? Vandhiyathevan decided that he would make the best of the situation. "Your Gracious Majesty—I appeal to you, *Thaaye*, to address my wants and further my cause with the Emperor. I am an orphan, you see, a man with no relations—I shall have to swallow my pride and speak for myself. I have heard tales from our epics that Goddess Parvathi appealed to her lord Siva Peruman, and the Goddess Lakshmi to her consort, Thirumaal, on behalf of their devotees. I plead with her Majesty to speak for me— pray, grant me at least ten villages of my ancestor's lands, and I shall consider myself fortunate beyond belief!"

Sundara Chozhar could not help but feel delighted and impressed at his well-mannered, submissive speech. "I find myself liking this young man a great deal, Commander," he addressed Chinna Pazhuvettarayar. "As for Devi—I believe she is considering adopting him as a third son, perhaps! About his request—we may grant it, I suppose? There should be no impediment, should there?"

"I do not quite see where my opinion ever enters this issue, Sire. Surely it is Prince Aditha Karikalar whose consent or otherwise is required, at this juncture?"

"Sire, I've petitioned the Crown Prince, but he bids me ask the Pazhuvoor lords. Now that I'm here, Thanjai's Commander wishes me to submit myself to the Prince. And here I am, caught in the middle—"

"Never fear, Child. We shall find an opportunity to hear them both out," promised the Emperor. Then, he turned to Chinna Pazhuvettarayar. "This youngster, I am sure you are aware, brought me an *olai* from the Prince. Nothing new, I am afraid: just a message, informing me that he is constructing a gold palace. Apparently, he would like it if I resided there, for a while."

"It shall be as you please, Sire," came the Commander's answer.

"Ah, *you* shall carry out everything as I please, of course. But my legs—my ridiculously weak legs refuse to accede to my wishes the same way. Journeying to Kanchi at this time is impossible—and I simply cannot even conceive of traveling in closed palanquins, like women. The very thought is disgusting. All I can do is send a reply to Adithan, bidding him here—"

"Surely the Prince is required to stay on in Kanchi for the time being? Our foes in the north are still powerful, aren't they?"

"Parthibendran and Malayaman are more than capable of taking care of them. I do not quite know why, but something deep within whispers to me that the Prince must be by my side, now. And that is not all—I wish to send a message to Eezham, asking the Ilango to return home, as well. I need them both with me, to discuss something very important. Besides, you will get an opportunity to communicate your objections to sending food to Ilankai, while Arulmozhi is here—"

"Forgive me, Sire, but as far as sending food to Eezham is concerned, neither mine nor the *Dhanaadhikaari*'s is the objection. Rather, it is the people of Chozha Nadu who protest at such a drain on our resources. The last harvest yielded disappointing results, Sire, and there was barely enough for our own people. When such is the circumstance, sending ship after ship of rice to Eezham seems to our people to be a colossal waste. At the moment, they are careful to keep their objections to a low murmur—but soon, their voices will swell to a shout. Why, they might even penetrate the walls of your palace and resound in your ears—!"

"Never would Arulmozhi embark upon something to which his people objected strenuously. In any case, it would be better if he does visit us, once. We must decide on sending a messenger to Ilankai as soon as Periya Pazhuvettarayar returns to us. Do you know when that is likely to be?"

"Tonight, certainly, Sire."

"Then I shall send a reply to Kanchi tomorrow. This youngster may carry it, may he not?"

"Someone else would be suited to the task, I think. The boy has traveled from Kanchi in one breath—perhaps it would be better if he rested for a while."

"Excellent. Why, he could even remain until the Prince comes to us."

The Empress chose to rise, at this moment. "Forgive me, Sire," apologized Chinna Pazhuvettarayar at once. "I have stayed talking far too long, today—and have forced Her Majesty to issue a warning."

"This young man is our guest, Commander. Please do ensure that his every need is taken care of," instructed Malayaman's daughter. "Ah, had the Emperor enjoyed good health, he might have stayed in this very palace!"

"Rest assured that I shall take care of him, Your Majesty," promised Chinna Pazhuvettarayar. "I shall take great care of him, indeed."

His hand rose almost without his knowledge, touched his impressive moustache—and twirled it.

ஜஸ்

Hidden Meanings and Explanations

Ilango

Prince, in Thamizh. The literal translation is "Young King." It's also used on occasion as a proper name.

30

THE CHITHIRA MANDAPAM

Chinna Pazhuvettarayar made sure to drag Vandhiyathevan along with him, when he left for the *aasthaana mandapam*. That young man's breathless explanation about danger had not really satisfied him. Had it perhaps been a mistake, he wondered, to send the boy off for a private audience with the Emperor? But what choice had he had? As Aditha Karikalan's man, he deserved every ounce of suspicion thrust upon him—but as someone who carried his brother's message, it was impossible to doubt him. Ah, but could anyone even presume to dictate caution to his elder brother, who knew everything there was to know about such things?

And yet—the Commander thought back to the moment he had strode into the Chakravarthy's audience chamber and seen the boy hesitate in front of the Emperor, looking rather nervous, his eyes almost falling out of his head. "*Abaayam! Abaayam!*" his voice seemed to ring out quite clearly. If he *had* indeed been talking about "*Abayam*," surely he could not have heard "*Abaayam*" in its place?

In any case, it would be better to keep the youngster with him for a few days, and make enquiries to his brother. A warrior such as this one would do very well for his personal entourage, to tell the truth—he would be of great use. And why not procure a part of his lost ancestral lands as well, while he was at it? Lads like these, once they were the recipients of such magnificent gestures, prostrated themselves at your feet for eternity. And if, by some chance, he was confirmed as the enemy, then steps could be taken to address such an eventuality as well.

Whatever the outcome, I would do well to wait until my brother returns, he mused. *And then—we shall see.*

The moment they reached the *aasthaana mandapam*, Vandhiyathevan began to look about him eagerly. He stared hard at the ground where he had handed over the *olai* to the Commander, wondering if, perhaps, there was another, equally important palm-leaf, somewhere. Ah, if it was gone—then the world possessed no greater fool than him! Lost, forever, would be the opportunity to meet the Chozha dynasty's most beautiful, world-renowned princess—and he would have failed in carrying out one half of Aditha Karikalar's commission.

Chinna Pazhuvettarayar glanced around, and narrowed on one of the men standing guard. "You—escort this young man to our palace. Find room for him in our guest quarters and make sure his every need is met. And stay there until I return."

The moment Vandhiyathevan departed with his escort, another soldier approached the Commander, deference limning every pore of his body, and handed a palm-leaf. "This *olai* was found on the floor, on the way to the Emperor's audience chamber," he murmured. "Perhaps it fell from the waist of the young man who just left?"

The Commander took it eagerly, opened the *olai* and ran his eyes through the contents. His brows rose in a threatening frown to almost half his forehead—and a terrifying expression flitted across his rather harsh countenance.

"Ah, an *olai* to the Ilaiya Piratti from her devoted brother Aditha Karikalan: *Hadn't you asked me for a reliable person to carry out certain tasks on your personal account—a warrior who wouldn't flinch at performing the direst duty?—I'm sending such a one. You may entrust any mission to him without compunction, for his loyalty and courage are beyond question.* Hand-written by the Crown Prince himself, too! There is a mystery afoot. I wonder if my brother knows anything of all this? I must exercise the greatest caution over this young man!" mumbled the Commander to himself. He called the man who had scrounged about for the *olai* in the first place and murmured a few instructions in his ear, after which the soldier departed at once.

—

Vandhiyathevan was shown every honour and luxury worthy of a highly eminent guest in Chinna Pazhuvettarayar's palace, where he was given a bath, and new clothes. All his life, he had entertained a passion for dressing well, and our young man made sure to enjoy the richness he was surrounded in. Swathed in the latest fashion, he was next offered the proverbial *arusuvai undi*, a six-flavoured feast fit for a king—yet another opportunity the famished young man made excellent use of, even forgetting, for the moment, his worry over the missing *olai*.

Chinna Pazhuvettarayar's men escorted him to the palace's private art gallery, the *chithira mandapam*, when he was finally done. "Do take a look at the paintings that adorn these walls until the Commander returns," said his guards, while three of them retired to the front of the *mandapam* and sprawled on the floor with abandon, trading gossip and playing their favourite dice-game, *chokkattaan*.

Thanjaipuri, already famed as the Chozha's brand-new capital city, had also gained renown far and wide in those days as the center for arts and sculpture, just as Thiruvaiyaaru had gained a staunch reputation for classical dance and music.

The *chithira mandapam* in Chinna Pazhuvettarayar's palace, in particular, was of some note; Vandhiyathevan entered it now, and gazed in stupefaction at the great many beautiful paintings that decorated the walls, losing himself in the brilliant colours and their execution. Such was his admiration for them that he forgot himself, and even the important mission he was engaged in.

In particular was he fascinated by the series of pictures that illustrated the history of ancient Chozha kings, and various important events in their personal lives. Many of the paintings in the *mandapam* were of the Chozha dynasty's famed rulers in the last century—and these were also the ones to which he was most attracted.

We would like, at this juncture, to gently prod our readers' memory with a précis of the hundred or so odd years of Chozha history, as its illustrious kings ruled from Pazhaiyarai and Thanjai. Such knowledge would prove extremely useful in understanding and appreciating the rest of this story.

We have mentioned, prior to this, Vijayalaya Chozhar who sported ninety-six scars as the greatest of ornaments on his noble, battle-worn body.

Chozha monarchs took the royal titles *Parakesari* and *Rajakesari* by turns; once *Parakesari* Vijayalaya Chozhar's reign had come to an end, his son and heir *Rajakesari* Aditha Chozhar came to the throne, and proved a worthy successor to his illustrious father. One of his first accomplishments was to join the Pallavas, defeat the Pandiyas, and regain the Chozhas a good deal of their lost footing in the political landscape. Next, he declared war on the Pallava king; Thondai Mandalam soon became a vassal of the valiant Aditha Chozhar as he fought a decisive battle, leaping upon the hapless Aparajitha Varman who came to battle on his richly decorated royal elephant, and sent him to his death. Kongu Nadu was swift to enter his territories as well. Aditha Chozhar proved to be a great devotee of Siva Peruman; to him goes the credit of having established a great many Siva temples all along the course of the sacred river Kaveri as she sprung from her source, in the Sahya Hills, until she tumbled into the oceans.

Parakesari Paranthakar followed Aditha Chozhar to the throne and ruled for forty-six long years; next to the glorious rule of Emperor Karikala Peruvalathan who bested the north and planted the tiger-flag atop the Himalayas, he was easily the greatest to follow in his footsteps. After all, did not various glorious titles such as Veera Narayanan, Panditha Vathsalan, Kunjara Mallan and Soora Sigamani attest to it? In addition,

he bore the magnificent name of *Maduraiyum Eezhamum Kondavan*—
He Who Conquered Madurai and Eezham; even during his time, the
Chozha Empire had stretched from Kanya Kumari in the south to River
Krishna, in the north. The Tiger-flag fluttered with glorious abandon in
Eezham too for a while; to this Emperor must be attributed all the praise
due to one who had sheathed the Thillai Chitrambalam Temple in pure
gold. Towards the end of his rule, though, the Empire met some of its
gravest dangers: the Rashtrakuta kings who had acquired some notoriety
in the north, gained steadily in strength and made inroads into Chozha
territories. What was more worrisome was that they had begun to taste
some success in their endeavours.

Paranthakar the First had three sons: the first, Rajadithyar, was a warrior
among warriors who spent a great deal of his time in Thirumunaippaadi
on the northern front, in daily anticipation of an invasion. He it was who
brought the magnificent Veera Narayana Lake into existence, in honour
of his father.

At Thakkolam, near today's Arakkonam was fought a bloody battle
as the Chozha and Rashtrakuta armies clashed furiously. It was here
that Rajadithyar demonstrated his incredible valour in the battlefield,
destroyed his enemies in one fell swoop and embraced a warrior's death.
Having given up his life as he fought atop a war elephant, like the Pallava
King Aparajitha Varman, he was graced, in the inscriptions and copper-
plates that followed, with the title *Yaanai Mel Thunjiya Thevar*—He Who
Embraced Death on an Elephant.

By rights, had Rajadithyar survived the war, it would have been
he who eventually succeeded Paranthaka Chakravarthy on the Chozha
throne. His descendents would have followed him as heirs to the Empire,
as per the dictates of justice.

That, however, was not to be. Prince Rajadithyar had died—and died
without issue, to complicate matters—which meant this his younger
brother Kandaradhithar acceded to his father's request, and ascended the
throne.

Like his father and grandfather before him, he was filled with the
fervour of devotion to God and a deep, unflagging love for Thamizh,

as well. Unlike them, however, he lacked the desire and passion to rule, much preferring to spend a majority of his time in worship of both deity and Thamizh. So well did he immerse himself in such pursuits that he composed hymns in praise of Siva Peruman, much in the manner of those staunch Siva devotees, the Naayanmars. Known collectively as the *Thiruvisaippaa*, here is a song that marks the last of it, and which he has sung, referring to himself:

Seeranmalgu Thillai chembon
Ambalathaadi thannaik
Kaaraar solaik Kozhi Vendhan
Thanjaiyarkon kalandha
Aaraavin sork Kandaradhithan
Arunthamizh maalai vallaar
Pera ulagir perumaiyodum
Perinba meythuvare!

Vijayalayar's successors might have ruled from Thanjai and Pazhaiyarai, but none had forgotten their antecedents, or that they hailed, originally, from the city that had once been their capital, Uraiyur. This city sported another title, "Kozhi," which explained why they took pride in referring to themselves as Kozhi Vendhar, or Kings of Kozhi.

Kandaradhithar might have ascended the throne and ruled in name—but there was no doubt that it was his younger brother, Arinjayar, who took the reigns of the Chozha Empire in his capable hands and administered, in full. The prince had accompanied Rajadithyar while he camped with his army in Thirunaavalur and other such bases; he had been a part of the ferocious campaign against the Rashtrakutas, and managed to convert what had seemed certain defeat, into victory for the Chozhas, in Thakkolam. Not to mention the fact that he made sure the Rashtrakutas did not venture further south, past the river Then Pennai.

All these were the factors that contributed to *Rajakesari* Kandaradhithar making a very important political decision: he declared his younger brother Crown Prince, along with the caveat that the latter would succeed his brother on the Chozha throne, when the former's rule came to an end.

Yet another reason did exist for his conclusion: Kandaradhithar had been married earlier, but his wife had passed away long before he was crowned Emperor; the thought of re-marriage had never entered his heart for many years, after. Brother Arinjayar, however, had a son who excelled in not just learning and martial arts, but beauty as well: in addition to being named after his grandfather Paranthakar, he enjoyed the title Sundaran, one that had been granted lovingly, by the people themselves. It seemed only natural to Kandaradhithar that such an excellent young man should succeed Arinjayar, after his time. He resolved that such would be the case; ensured that royal court officials such as the *Saamantha Kanam*, those associated with the armed forces such as *Thandanaayakkas* and various representatives of the public were made aware of, and assented to his decision. Accordingly, once the required formalities were fulfilled, he made it known to his subjects as well.

And yet—fate played its hand, once these momentous events had happened; a rather strange event occurred in Kandaradhithar's life. He chanced to meet, at this late date, the young princess of the Mazhavarayar clan; her beauty, grace, virtue and deep devotion to Siva Peruman impressed him and despite his rather advanced years, he married her. A son was born to them in due course and the happy couple named him Madhuranthakan, showering him with love and affection.

Neither Emperor not his consort, however, had any mind to change arrangements already made, with regard to the Chozha succession. Both were immersed in devotion to Siva Peruman and had no desire for a life of pleasure; they wished to raise their son the same way. Firm in the belief that ascension to the magnificent Siva Peruman's eternal celestial empire was of far more merit than to a puny, earthly kingdom, they strove to ensure that Madhuranthakan was deserving of a place in a heavenly abode, rather than on the hollow throne ruling a small part of the earth. Kandaradhithar, thus, took great pains to assure those around him, once more, that the Chozha *samrajyam* would pass on to Arinjaya and his son after his time, and no one else.

Thus it was that the Chozha throne bypassed Rajadithyar who was supposed to have ascended it; Kandaradhithar, who did ascend, but had no great desire to rule—on to Arinjayar and his descendents, who, it seemed, were destined to inherit an empire.

Parakesari Arinjayar, however, did not rule the country for an extended period of time; not long after Kandaradhithar ascended to Siva's celestial abode of Kailasam, his younger brother followed his footsteps to heaven. In accordance with their wishes, the lords, officials and people of Chozha Nadu decided, unanimously, to crown Arinjayar's son as the Emperor and so it was done: *Rajakesari* Sundara Chozhar duly ascended the throne and appeared properly cognizant of the great honour and good fortune granted to him. He ruled well, with a firm and just hand; ensured that the lost territories of Thondai Mandalam and Pandiya Nadu were annexed and a part of Chozha dominions once again, and drove away the Rashtrakuta forces from the shores of the Then Pennai, once and for all.

His sons, Aditha Karikalar and Arulmozhi were phenomenal warriors in their own right and seemed poised to overtake their own father when it came to goodwill and popularity. They were swift to assist their father however necessary; went to wars, took initiative and fought battles at the forefront at a very young age.

And Jayalakshmi, Goddess of Victory, stood by the Chozhas, granting success at every single step.

31

"THIEVES! THIEVES!"

Vandhiyathevan gazed at the portraits of every Chozha Emperor from the victorious Vijayalayar to Paranthakar, also known as Sundara Chozhar, with a great deal of admiration and pleasure. Ah, the valour and courage of each of these rulers! The great deeds they had accomplished; the wars and battles they had fought, standing at the forefront without a care for their own lives! Why, he hadn't heard such tales of daring even in the numerous epics that abounded in the country. Chozha Nadu was fortunate indeed, to be ruled by a dynasty such as this; indeed, so were the other lands under their dominions, at present.

Fairly dazzled by these Emperors and their greatness he might have been, but for all that, Vandhiyathevan hadn't failed to notice something rather important, about all the portraits: each Chozha had had the Pazhuvoor clan by him, providing extraordinary assistance, aiding in battle and otherwise, to the best and more of their abilities.

A Pazhuvettarayar had been the first to lay siege and set foot into the Thanjai fort when it had still been occupied by the Mutharaiyars. When Vijayalayar floundered in the battle of Thiruppurambiyam, having lost both his legs, a Pazhuvoor King hastened to his aid, hoisting the Emperor onto his capable shoulders, his timely support allowing his liege-lord to perform a great many valorous deeds. A Pazhuvoor scion had placed the crown on Aditha Chozhar's head at his coronation. And when that Emperor leapt from his elephant to send Aparajitha Varman to his death, a Pazhuvettarayar it was, who had bent down, offering back and shoulders in aid. These sturdy and hardy warriors had been at the forefront of many of Paranthaka Chakravarthy's battles, holding aloft the Chozha standard and tiger flag with a proud mien. As Prince Rajadithyar lay mortally wounded in the battlefield, it was a Pazhuvettarayar who gathered the bleeding prince into his lap, delivering the welcome news: "The Rashtrakutas are in retreat!" More of the same staunch, unflinching service had been provided by them to the Emperors Arinjayar and Sundara Chozhar as well.

Vandhiyathevan noted all these and more evidence—quite blatant, at that—of the Pazhuvoor clan's royal service, and was promptly immersed in speechless amazement. There was reason enough, it seemed, for the brothers Pazhuvettarayar to exert their authority over all of Chozha Nadu; neither could it be wondered at that Sundara Chozhar did not attempt a single decision without their expert advice.

What was obvious, on the other hand, was that he, Vandhiyathevan, was in serious difficulties at the moment. There was no doubt that Chinna Pazhuvettarayar entertained the gravest suspicions about him, and it was only a matter of time before they were proven right. The truth about the palm-tree signet ring would be out—and then the fat would truly be in the fire! Vallavarayan had heard a great many harrowing tales of Thanjavur's gloomy dungeons, under the direct supervision of its Commander. Perhaps Vandhiyathevan would find himself clapped into them—and then he may as well bid farewell to any hope of escape. It was common knowledge that even if anyone did manage to get out alive, it would only be as a blubbering, brainless idiot in skin and bones, wholly devoid of sense!

Ah, how was he to escape such a predicament? One thing was certain: he would have to come up with some ruse and leave this city before Pazhuvettarayar the Elder returned.

Even the overwhelming desire to meet the young queen of Pazhuvoor had deserted our young hero; all he wanted that very moment, with every fibre of his being, was to flee this city and its terrible dungeons, life and limbs intact. He might not have the *olai* but he could deliver his message to Kundhavai Piratti in person—and who cared, frankly, whether she believed him, or didn't? How, *how* was he going to make his way out of this wretched city?

Abruptly, he remembered something: what on earth had become of his old clothes? There could only be one reason for why his new hosts had confiscated those tattered garments, given him rich, dazzling attire, wined and dined him—check his robes! Of course, it was all obvious now: the *olai* meant for Kundhavai Devi must have fallen into the Commander's hands; no doubt about it. *Now* he knew why he had grabbed Vandhiyathevan and held his hand so hard, preventing the young man from slipping away with the poets. The reason for the three-man strong escort was clear as well. What he needed now was a ruse—any ruse, to get away from this terrible toil—something, anything, before Pazhuvettarayar returned—think, think—ah, yes! Here was a ruse! No time to waste; to think was to act. He would give it all he had. On guard—*Vetrivel! Veeravel!*

Vandhiyathevan peeped out of the decorated window of the *chithira mandapam*. Chinna Pazhuvettarayar approached resplendently on his horse, surrounded by his entourage. Ah, now was the time to carry out his plan; not a moment to pause.

The trio playing *chokkattaan* up front put a stop to their game and rose; obviously, they had heard their master's impending arrival, as well.

Vandhiyathevan walked up to them. "Beloved brothers, where are my old clothes? Do you know?"

"What on earth do you want with those filthy garments?" queried one of the menials. "We've obeyed our master's instructions and dressed you in new, expensive silks, haven't we?"

"I don't need these. Do return my old clothes to me soon, and I shall be content."

"We've sent them out to be washed. They'll be returned to you when they're done."

"Absolutely not—I need my old garments at once. Thieves, all of you—I'd stashed some money in them, and you've obviously been trying to steal it. Return my things at once, or else—!"

"Or else what, *Thambi*? You'll chop our heads and pack them off to Thanjavur, will you? But we *are* in Thanjai now, you know. You'd do well to remember that."

"*Adei*—will you return my clothes at once, or not?"

"Only if they exist, *Thambi*. You see, we dropped the whole smelly bundle in the river Vettaru. They'd be crocodile feed by now—and whoever heard of getting anything back from a reptile's stomach?"

"Thieving bastards! So you're mocking me, are you? Just wait till I report you to your master!" And Vandhiyathevan began to cross the threshold, when one of the men approached at a rapid pace to bar his path. The Vaanar warrior delivered a resounding punch and the man fell on his back, gasping aloud. Blood gushed out of his nose.

Another came at Vandhiyathevan, hands outstretched, as though he wished to wrestle him to the ground. Our young man promptly grabbed one of the hands, thrust a leg neatly between both of his opponent's limbs and gave a neat twist; the soldier shrieked a pain-filled "*Ammaadi!*" and sat down with an abrupt thump. By this time, the third was almost on top of Vandhiyathevan; the warrior turned his legs and aimed a neat kick at the soldier, who felt the full force of the blow and crashed down with a scream.

The three fallen men recovered within moments, rose and circled Vandhiyathevan for another attack—very warily this time, it must be mentioned.

By this time, the sounds of horses clattering up to the entrance of the palace could be heard. Vandhiyathevan saw his chance, set up a loud yell of "Thieves! Thieves!" and fell upon his would-be assailants. The latter tried to restrain him, in vain, while Vandhiyathevan kept up his terrible screeches. "Thieving scoundrels!" he bellowed, again.

This seemed to be the cue for Chinna Pazhuvettarayar to enter the scene. "What is the commotion, here?" he demanded.

32

An Inquisition

Vandhiyathevan ceased to fight the moment he saw Chinna Pazhuvettarayar, and began to walk towards him. His assailants scrambled forward and hung on to him in a bid to stop his progress. The young man cared not a whit and took four steps forward. "Not a moment too soon, Commander! These thieving scoundrels not only stole my clothes, but tried to kill me as well. Ah, is this how you treat your guests? Am I to believe that this is the best example of Thanjai's manners and morals? I am, if you please, not a random visitor, but an honoured guest of the Emperor—you did hear Her Majesty's words, didn't you? I'm not quite a nobody as you're well aware—I'm an emissary of the Crown Prince himself. If your wretched men could treat me, a royal messenger thus, what might be the fate of ordinary mortals? Frankly, my lord, I'm surprised you have such rascals in your service. We wouldn't even let such men cross our thresholds, in Thondai Mandalam—we'd sentence them to death on a sharp *kazhumaram*, first!" And Vandhiyathevan paused to take a breath, after his breathless exposition.

As for Chinna Pazhuvettarayar … he had not quite recovered, yet, from Vallavarayan's almost effortless handling of the three stocky men who had attempted to strangle him; visions of his martial prowess still clouded his memory. Ah, a warrior such as this would be a shining ornament to his own regiment! He *must* get this young man to join his ranks, somehow. "Patience, *Thambi*, patience," he soothed, voice practically dripping with tranquility and goodwill. "I find it rather difficult to believe that my men could have been quite so stupid. I shall make enquires, shall I?"

"That, precisely, is my desire as well, Commander. Interrogate them thoroughly, my lord, and deliver me justice," shot back Vallavarayan. "Not to mention my clothes and valuables as well."

"*Adei*, you idiots—leave that lad alone, for a moment. What were my instructions to you, and what is it that you have accomplished, now?" chided Chinna Pazhuvettarayar. "Why on earth did you lay hands on him?"

"We carried out every word of your command, *Yejamaan*: we escorted this young man here, treated him to a luxurious oil-bath, new clothes, dazzling ornaments, and a meal fit for a king. Then, we brought him to the *chithira mandapam*. He spent some time gazing at the portraits—and then, suddenly, came to us, asking for his old clothes," explained a man. "And then he practically pounced on us!"

"But you—three bulky men—could not handle that boy's blows, could you?" Chinna Pazhuvettarayar's hard eyes glowed blood-red with rage and mortification.

"If we hesitated, Master, it was only because he was a royal guest. Give us leave now, and we'll tear him into pieces—"

"Enough of these tall tales, idiots! Well, *Thambi*? What about you?"

"Give them the leave they ask for, I say. And give me leave as well, Commander. It's been quite a while since I grappled with Chozha foes; my shoulders practically ache for the exercise. I'd be delighted to teach them a lesson on perfect behaviour towards royal guests!"

"Admirable, my boy," Chinna Pazhuvettarayar smiled a little. "But you would do well to reserve your teaching instincts for genuine Chozha traitors. The Chakravarthy is ill, after all, and orders are to allow no disputes or altercations of any kind within the fort, that his peace might be undisturbed."

"In that case, kindly ask these men to return my garments and belongings at once."

"Where are they, you three?"

"Master, we have kept them safe, as per your orders."

"Ah, how they lie, these immoral idiots, Commander—and right to your face as well! A few moments ago, they swore that my clothes had been delivered to be washed, and now they declare they are "kept safe," as per your instructions," exploded Vandhiyathevan. "Beware, my lord—they'll brand *you* a thief in a little while!"

"Why, you dimwitted nincompoops," glared Chinna Pazhuvettarayar, at his hapless men. "All I said was to dress this young man in new attire—I never mentioned a thing about the old, did I? Be that as it may, do ignore them, *Thambi*; they blabber uselessly at the best of times. But why do you care so much about those ancient clothes? Er—did you, perhaps, store valuables in them?"

"A few gold coins for my journey, yes—" before Vandhiyathevan could continue, Chinna Pazhuvettarayar cut in. "Those would be of no account, *Thambi*. I shall supply you with all the gold you may need."

"I'm Crown Prince Aditha Karikalar's envoy, Commander. I'm not in the habit of receiving money from outsiders—"

"In that case, I shall make arrangements to deliver your own clothes and money to you, never fear. But—you had nothing else in your possession, did you?"

Vandhiyathevan spent a moment in thought; Chinna Pazhuvettarayar was quick to notice his pause. "I did carry something else—something that was very important, indeed. I hope your men haven't laid a finger on it. If they did, they're done for—!"

"Such fury in one so young! Perhaps that is why you forget where you are, and to whom you address these words. I shall ignore your heated retorts for the sake of your youth. But what was this precious article?"

"I'm afraid I can't reveal that, Commander. It's rather confidential."

"Indeed? Thanjai can harbour no secrets that I cannot know of, *Thambi.*"

"This, however, is a secret Aditha Karikalar entrusted to me."

"The Crown Prince is the *Vadathisai Maathanda Naayakar,* the Chief of the Northern Armed Forces; his authority may be enforced only north of the river Paalaaru. Here, however, it is the Chakravarthy who rules supreme."

"The Chakravarthy's authority extends to wherever the Tiger-flag flies high, Commander. Surely there can be no two ways about that?"

"For that very reason, there can be nothing that I may not know of; no secrets within the confines of this fort. The Emperor's well-being and security depend on it, you see—"

"Commander, the whole of Chozha Nadu owes tremendous gratitude to you and Periya Pazhuvettarayar, for guarding the Emperor's sacred person so jealously. I heard the Chakravarthy himself praise you today in the audience chamber, my lord—he mentioned that even Yama, the God of Death feared to set foot in Thanjai, bowing to your rule, here. Rare words, don't you think?"

"Certainly I do. Who knows what terrible fate might have befallen the Emperor, had we not brought him from Pazhaiyarai to Thanjavur? Those Pandiya traitors may have even carried out their perfidious plans."

"Ah, *you* say so, as well! Everything I've heard so far must certainly be true, I suppose."

"And what is it that you heard?"

"That there's a heinous conspiracy being evolved against the Emperor. And that there's another, being woven against his beloved sons as well."

Chinna Pazhuvettarayar ground his teeth, hard as *vajram,* and bit his lips. All these moments of conversation with this boy—and only now had the realization come to him, very slowly, that *his* had been the defeat, in this cunning war of words. He had traded barbs with this lad, hoping to catch him out in a lie—but all that had happened was that the Commander of Thanjai had been forced to pacify Vandhiyathevan, supplying halting explanations to assuage the boy's suspicions! Well, that would not serve any more. Enough was enough. This conversation would end, now.

"You need not worry your head about such things, *Thambi*. I and my brother are more than capable of destroying every conspiracy against any member of the royal family," he said, curtly. "All you have to do is submit your request—you wish your old clothes back. That is all, is it not?"

"My old garments—and whatever I carried within them."

"Which you have not exactly revealed, so far."

"I shall, since you insist—but I may as well tell you that the consequences must devolve upon you. Prince Aditha Karikalar presented me an *olai* for the Chakravarthy, yes. He asked me to deliver another, as well."

"Did he, now? To whom? You never dropped a hint as to this until now."

"As I mentioned before, it was supposed to be confidential, Commander. I'm revealing it now, as you insisted on knowing. The other *olai* was meant for Ilaiya Piratti Kundhavai Devi, in Pazhaiyarai."

"Oh? In that case, you certainly cannot leave for Kanchi right away, even if you do receive the Emperor's *thirumugam* tomorrow. I wonder what exactly prompted the Crown Prince to send an *olai* post-haste to Ilaiya Piratti?"

"I'm afraid I'm not in the habit of reading confidential missives, Commander. I didn't, however, have any objection to your reading the *olai* meant for the Chakravarthy, so I shall not have any, to this either. That responsibility as I mentioned earlier, rests upon you. What I do want are my old clothes and belongings, as soon as possible."

"Rest assured that you will certainly receive them. I shall ensure it myself," snapped the Commander, and began to walk away. Vandhiyathevan followed him. Chinna Pazhuvettarayar, who had noted his presence, communicated a message to his men with a look, upon which five or six armed warriors stepped in front of Vallavarayan, spears barring his way. There was no point in picking a quarrel with them, felt the young man, and gave in, resigned to a wait.

Thanjai fort's Commander returned in a little while—and behind him came a man, carrying Vandhiyathevan's old clothes on an elaborately decorated platter, for all the world as though they were precious jewels parading in a wedding procession.

"Here are your clothes, *Thambi*," waved Chinna Pazhuvettarayar. "Do inspect them to see if everything as it should be."

Vandhiyathevan took the Commander at his word and duly carried out a thorough scrutiny. He unraveled his waistband, to find that it contained a great many more gold coins than before. The *olai* meant for Kundhavai Devi was within, as well. But how on earth did so much gold find its way in here? And how had the *olai*, missing the first time, suddenly re-appeared? Well, there was only one explanation; it must have fallen into the clutches of Chinna Pazhuvettarayar, who had stuffed it in just now, post Vandhiyathevan's persistent questions. *I wonder why*, mused the young man. *And why is there so much more gold than I need? Ah, he's a wily one, Thanjai's Commander.* There was more to this than met the eye, and Vandhiyathevan wondered just how much more Chinna Pazhuvettarayar would put him through, before he was done. There was no doubt that he would have to be very careful indeed and never let his guard down for a single moment.

"Everything is to your satisfaction, *Thambi*?" enquired the Commander, solicitously. "Gold and precious belongings included?"

"In a moment, my lord," Vandhiyathevan replied and began counting the gold coins. He piled the excess number in a heap, and pushed them away. "Commander, I'm a scion of the Vaanar dynasty; a messenger of the peerless warrior Aditha Karikalar. I neither crave nor need anything that isn't mine."

"Your honesty is to be commended, but I rather think you may need this for your journey. Now, when exactly do you wish to leave? Today? Or will you take your ease and wait until tonight, to meet the Elder?"

"Certainly I shall stay tonight. I have no desire to leave until after an audience with Periya Pazhuvettarayar, my lord. Meanwhile—you'd better command your men never to lay a hand on my belongings," warned Vandhiyathevan, raking in the gold coins in their entirety and binding them up, carefully, in his waistband.

"Delighted, I am sure. I can assure you that you will meet with no further iniquity, from my men. You may ask, and receive whatever you wish."

"Well, I do cherish one great desire—to sightsee this beautiful Thanjai city. I may, mayn't I?"

"Certainly you may. Two of my men here shall be more than happy to show you around. A word of warning, though: do not venture outside the fort, for the gates will be closed at sunset, and you will not be able to return, no matter how hard you try. You are free, however, to wander where you will, within the city." And Chinna Pazhuvettarayar called forward two of his henchmen, murmuring something into their ears.

Vandhiyathevan, watching, him, did not find it very difficult to guess what the whispered message might have been.

෫ௐ

33

A Maid in a Tree!

With two of Chinna Pazhuvettarayar's men flanking him on either side, Vandhiyathevan set off in state, on his grand tour of the city of Thanjavur. That his escorts were to prevent his escape was obvious; equally evident was the fact that the sentries at the fortress gates had received orders to not let anyone leave the city, that day. Nevertheless, Vandhiyathevan determined to do so before midnight—he would have to, if he wished to slip out of the terrible fate of meeting Periya Pazhuvettarayar. Lingering any more would reduce his chances of escape considerably—nay, his very hope of staying alive!

His mind came up with a variety of strategies to make his way out, even as he wandered along one street after another, gazing at the sights. The first order of the day was to slip from the clutches of his two demon-like guards and then, from the fort—but how on earth was he to manage it? For the life of him, he could not evolve a suitable plan that would answer all his purposes.

To tell the truth, it wouldn't present a great deal of difficulty to overpower these men; he could flip them over his shoulder in an instant and slither into the crowds—but *where*? It was common knowledge that the Pazhuvettarayar brothers had strengthened the Thanjavur fort beyond belief; people were prone to say that not even a breeze could enter its confines without their permission. Why, even the Emperor had mentioned, this morning, that Yama himself quaked with fear about breaching its borders. How was he, a lone man, to manage it, then? All he had to do was lay a finger on his guards and they would set up a yell that would banish him straight to the city's dungeons. That, or he would lose his life in an instant. No, attacking his sentries was not the solution; he would have to strategize his escape; first from these men, and then, from this blasted city. Well—no fort worth the name had ever existed without a secret passage of some kind, had it? The stronger the fortress, in fact, the more the chances of a secret passage, somewhere. But how was he to discover it? Who would possess information of that kind? More importantly, even if they did, would they ever divulge it to *him*?

Even as he walked along, revolving and discarding one scheme after another, his mind recalled the young queen of Pazhuvoor. Ah, if there was anyone in this wretched stronghold who might extend a helping hand, it would have to be that gracious lady. Admittedly, this was a bit of a stretch, but he could use Azhwarkkadiyaan's name to get into her good graces. Things should proceed quite easily after that—but he would have to find Periya Pazhuvettarayar's palace first, to make headway along this circuitous route. And even then, he would have to give the slip to these men, who mustn't suspect his intentions of visiting the Ilaiya Rani. If they did, they would march straight to Chinna Pazhuvettarayar with the news, and that would truly be the end of it all. But oh, here was another terrible thought: what if Periya Pazhuvettarayar himself arrived home as he, Vandhiyathevan, was in his palace? He would not only be guilty of entering a ferocious lion's den, but sticking his head into its mouth as well.

Seemingly immersed he might have been in the city's sights, but for all that, Vandhiyathevan had not failed to make use of his eyes and mouth;

questions poured out of his lips in an unending stream. "What's that?"—
"And this?"—"Whose palace is that?"—"What's this building?"—"Is that
a *gopuram*?"—"What about this mansion?" His ears pricked up every
time, wondering if he would get "This is Periya Pazhuvettarayar's palace,"
or "This is the Pazhuvoor Ilaiya Rani's mansion," for a reply. His eyes
swung in all four directions, eager to take in anything and everything.
And as they did, one thing entered his sight and affixed itself in his brain
very well: Thanjai might possess wide avenues thronging with people
and vehicles—but it also accommodated a great many tiny alleys, little
alcoves, nooks and crannies, not to mention gardens thick with leafy
trees. It would not be terribly difficult, Vandhiyathevan mused, to dart
into one of those little lanes, scramble up a tree and hide inside some
sprawling estate. It would even be possible to stay concealed for a day or
two—but what was important was to make an escape without anyone
noticing, and to ensure that no one looked for him. Either of which
would certainly prove impossible if Chinna Pazhuvettarayar sent out a
swarm of his seemingly endless supply of soldiers, to conduct a search.

Or Vandhiyathevan had another option: beg for asylum at someone's
home. And who else but the Ilaiya Rani would take pity on him, in
this vast Thanjai city? He'd simply have to use all the powers of his
considerable imagination and spin a story so fantastic that she'd have no
choice but to believe him. And the first step towards accomplishing all
this would be to escape the clutches of his guards—

*Ah, what's this commotion? Who's shouting? Who are these people and
why are they going about in such crowds? Thanks be to God— there's no
doubt You are on my side, this instant! For I can see a way—here's the ruse I
need, the perfect tool to make my escape—*!

Vandhiyathevan had just arrived at a junction in one of the many
lanes that cut through a large avenue, and stumbled upon the sight of
a large crowd passing by, chanting in victorious voices that pierced the
heavens, clashing cymbals and other instruments. It was easy to see that
this was the Velakkara Regiment, on their way out of the fort after an
audience with the Emperor. What if he simply blended in with them—
ah, surely there couldn't be a better way to effect his escape?

He was quite sure that his persistent escorts would certainly never let him get away quite so easily; they would pursue him even through the chaotic regiment. And it would be no easy matter to slip through the imposing gates, either; surely no sentry worth the title would be quite so stupid as to let him just walk away? They *would* stop him— but on the other hand, what other choice did he have? He would have to be a fool indeed, to ignore this godsent opportunity to make his way out.

He turned, as usual, to the guards by him, asking who the passing men were and what they did here. Once he received the answer that "they were the Velakkara Regiment," he began plying his escorts with questions. He wished, he prattled on, to join this brave band of soldiers, and wanted to approach them, see them at close quarters—and began inching his way towards the noisy clan. A little later, he exclaimed, airily, that he wished very much to see the men who played the *thaarai* and *thappattai* instruments at the front—and promptly mingled with the crowd.

Even as the regiment moved forward, Vandhiyathevan shifted with them, going forwards and backwards, this side and that, yelling victorious chants in an enthusiastic voice that threatened to drown out even the Velakkara soldiers. Some of the latter stared hard at him, wondering at his identity; some pegged him for an idiot, excited at the sight of a crowd; others looked amused, obviously thinking he had indulged in spirits just a little too much. No one, however, tried to stop him, or push him away.

His escorts stayed by the sidelines, frankly nervous about mixing with the boisterous crowd. Somehow, he was sure to step out, somewhere, they consoled themselves, and assuaged their conscience by standing aside, peeping through the crowds occasionally.

At that moment, a young woman carrying a basket of curds, paused by an alley, to allow the Regiment to pass. One of the soldiers minced up to her. "I am very thirsty, Amma—may I have some curd?"

"Not curds," that young lady, not to be outdone, spat a retort. "But I can certainly deliver two sound slaps to your cheek!"

"Will you, now?" shot back the soldier. "Then you may as well give me those!" He stepped closer to the young woman who shied away and suddenly, took to her heels. The soldier set off in pursuit; two more men broke away from the regiment, haring after their mate. As every one of the runners began to set up shouts and yells, darting here and there, no one quite knew what the commotion was about; only that there was a great deal of entertainment involved.

Vandhiyathevan, watching all this, came to a sudden decision. As we have seen quite a few times before, to think was to act for our young man; the word hesitation had no place in his adventurous life. And once he had come to conclusion, to pause and reflect was alien to his very nature. Accordingly, he acted.

"Run! Run!" he shrieked, and took off after the soldiers in pursuit of the young curd-seller. "Catch her! Get her!" The lass ran for a while, and into a narrow alley—but when her pursuers entered it, panting, they could see nothing of her. She had vanished! The soldiers, however, seemed to have decided that enough was enough; they gave up their sport and returned to their own.

Vandhiyathevan, however, did not.

He ran for a while along the curd-seller's lane and scurried around two or three more corners. Then, and only then did he slacken his pace somewhat, and fall to a walk.

We know, don't we, that the Velakkara Regiment usually left the fort at sunset? The day ended earlier in the little lanes Vandhiyathevan walked through; they were already shrouded in darkness. Sometimes, he strode along streets with stone walls or *madhils* towering on either side; at others, just a simple fence, interspersed with foliage. No matter; Vandhiyathevan did not stop for an instant, uncaring of his direction. Small lanes and alleys, no matter how circuitous, would have to end in the outer fort walls at some point. He would decide his next course of action once he had reached his destination. He had the whole night to think up a dozen different ruses, didn't he?

Night fell completely, in a while—and Vandhiyathevan's path did end in a fort wall. In fact, he knew that he had reached an impasse in his journey only when he butted, slightly, against solid stone, in the thick of the night.

He could not really guess, however, at its height or other dimensions; for all he knew, it may well be the outer fort-wall itself. In which case, the best option at the moment was to squat at its base. The moon would rise soon, and he would know more in its pearly light. Certainly, no better place could be found to hide away in this sprawling city. His erstwhile escorts would have returned to Chinna Pazhuvettarayar by now and delivered the news; the Commander would have sent his men out, at once, in pursuit. He might even have suspected Vandhiyathevan of having made his escape with the Velakkara Regiment; it was certain that soldiers would be wandering the thoroughfares, looking for him both within the city and without. Let them tear their collective hairs out, by all means. Let them search for him endlessly and embrace defeat. *I shall dupe them all and make my escape out of this fort right under their very stupid noses, or my name isn't Vandhiyathevan—nor am I a scion of the famed Vaanar clan!*

Moonrise would, however, present difficulties for him too; Pazhuvettarayar's soldiers would find the light an ally, as well. They might even run him to earth here—ha, much good that would do them. Not a whisper of Vandhiyathevan would they find here, if their quarry chose to hide within these dense groves!

He leant back against the stone wall and slid down, to sit on the ground. Running around endlessly all day, the strenuous exercise and his own youth conspired to make him drowsy; his eyelids drooped. The west wind stirred the trees nearby; branches rustled against one another, soothing him with a pleasant, shushing lullaby that calmed his senses. Vandhiyathevan fell asleep.

By the time he awoke, the moon had risen and climbed a little, up the eastern sky. Pale light dappled the ground amidst tree branches and leaves, and Vandhiyathevan managed to take in a little of his surroundings. He remembered the day's events, took stock of himself, and was frankly astonished that he had actually managed to fall asleep under such circumstances. Even more amazing, however, was the reason for his awakening. What exactly had roused him? Hadn't it seemed like a voice? Human? Or an animal's? A night-bird's call, perhaps? *Had* he, in fact, heard a voice?

Vandhiyathevan craned his neck and peered above, to gaze at the wall towering over him in the patchy moonlight. This, he decided, could not really be the fort *madhil*; those were usually much, much higher. Was there, perhaps, a smaller wall within a larger one? Or was this the outer wall of some sort of palace's garden?

Still craning his neck, Vandhiyathevan rose—and his heart skipped several beats. His intestines seemed to uncoil themselves and climb up, choking his throat. Sheer terror stifled him for a moment. There, on a branch above the wall—*what* on earth was it? Memories of every single tale of *vedhaalams*, apparitions that haunted trees, flooded his mind.

But—could ghosts speak in a human voice? A young woman's too? This particular spirit seemed to possess such capabilities, at any rate. Vandhiyathevan decided that he would listen carefully, before he came to unjust conclusions.

"Well, *Ayya*? Did you fall asleep against the wall? How many more times am I supposed to call out to you?"

Ha—not a misplaced apparition haunting trees; this truly was a young human woman, talking from a branch. Was all this a fantastic dream? Surely such things didn't happen in real life!

"Of all the ridiculous—! You still look half-asleep. Here, I'm sending down a ladder. Climb up carefully, will you? I don't want you slipping and breaking your neck."

And the lass pulled up a slender bamboo contraption from her side and pushed it outside, leaning it against the wall.

None of this made any sense to Vandhiyathevan, of course—but when had he ever refused to make use of a godsent opportunity, a rare chance that practically offered itself to him, thus?

What must happen would happen; he would deal with anything that fate threw at him. Climbing up the ladder was the priority, now. As to what came after—he would confront it when he reached the top of the wall.

He had climbed almost three-quarters up, when the young woman spoke again. "I never knew anyone for being so late. There's the Ilaiya Rani, the young queen, waiting endlessly—and here you are, snoring against the palace wall!"

Vandhiyathevan almost fell off the ladder in shock. Fortunately, he grabbed hold of a random stone that jutted out of the wall and managed to right himself in the nick of time.

The Ilaiya Rani! Surely it couldn't mean—yet, who else could it be, but the young queen of Pazhuvoor? How on earth could she have possibly known that he, Vandhiyathevan, was squatting at the bottom of her wall? Truly, she must possess some sort of magic that allowed her to see such things! She certainly did seem intensely interested in meeting him, didn't she? But stay—perhaps—perhaps he had climbed up a ladder meant for another?

No matter. Vandhiyathevan had stepped forward; there was no going back. He would see this right to the end—and that wouldn't be too long, now.

He approached the top and the young woman put out a hand, pulling him up. Moonlight bathed her face—but by this time, Vandhiyathevan had lost all capability of feeling any surprise whatsoever. How else could he have not fallen off the wall, even after seeing that this lass was none other than the young curd-seller, pursued so hotly by the Velakkara Regiment that very evening? Truth be told, nothing, no matter how peculiar, would amaze him anymore tonight.

"Come—are you going to squat on that wall and gape forever? Pull the ladder in and climb down, quick!" And the young woman slipped down the tree swiftly.

Vandhiyathevan obeyed. He had landed, it seemed, in some sort of elaborate garden. In the distance rose a large palace's many *gopurams*, gables and towers, shimmering in the pearly moonlight like something out of a fairyland.

He cleared his throat, intending to ask whose this was—when he was silenced by a peremptory "Hush!" from the young woman, who signed him to silence with a finger on her lips, and walked forward.

Vandhiyathevan gave in, and followed her.

34

The Latha Mandapam

The young woman walked swiftly along a narrow path that meandered through an almost impenetrable mango-grove, and Vandhiyathevan followed her swiftly. No easy task, this; so dense was the foliage, the luxurious growth of bushes that he stumbled often. Once, when he hesitated, having almost run into a tree, the lass turned back to stare at him. "What are you dawdling there for? Surely you haven't forgotten the way? You've eyes that can pierce the darkness, haven't you?"

Vandhiyathevan simply brought a finger to his lips and returned her own answer: "Hush!"

Scrabbling noises and muffled commotion outside the palace walls reached them at that moment—it sounded like men scuffling about.

Man and girl walked on a little distance. A few moments later, Vandhiyathevan gave a low chuckle.

The young woman turned and raised an eyebrow. "See anything that amuses you?"

"Nothing I see—only what I can hear."

"And that would be—?"

"Don't tell me you didn't hear the footsteps of those who were pursuing me, hotfoot. I couldn't help laughing at the thought of their intense disappointment."

She looked suddenly fearful. "Someone's pursuing you? But why?"

"Why else did you think I was squatting at the bottom of a wall, bumbling about like a sightless loon?"

The wind rustled through the trees, unsettling heaving branches; a stray ray of moonlight fell on Vandhiyathevan's features. The girl gaped at him, face wreathed in perplexion.

"What on earth are you staring at?" he queried.

"I was wondering if you were, well—*you*."

"If I weren't I, who else would I be?"

"Well, you had a large moustache the last time you came, didn't you?"

"But how intelligent, my girl. A man like me, who makes his living climbing on and off walls at night—do you really think I could survive without a disguise to suit every occasion?"

"And you look, well—younger, too."

"As to that, a man in good spirits always drinks from the fountain of youth."

"You're in good spirits? Why?"

"The gracious and bountiful condescension of your beautiful Maharani would ensure the happiness of anyone."

"Don't you dare mock her. She may be the young queen now, but there's no doubt that she will become a Maharani, someday."

"My sentiments, exactly."

"Ha, you agree, do you? And what's to stop you from arguing that she became one only because of your magic and tricks? Why, you wouldn't even hesitate to demand half the empire from her!"

By this time, Vandhiyathevan had learnt a good deal of what he intended and stayed silent, choosing to spend his time, instead, in furious thought.

Who, he wondered, was he really about to meet? The young queen of Pazhuvoor? Equally, it could be Chinna Pazhuvettarayar's daughter, who had lately married Madhuranthaka Thevar. His escort was leading him towards the palace, obviously under the firm belief that he was some sort of magician and now, he was about to meet this mysterious "Ilaiya Rani"—but how on earth was he to conduct himself in her presence? Ah, be still, my beating heart! As long as you retain your courage, there's still hope. After all, there would be no dearth of clever ruses he could use, to make his escape—his brain had never failed to help him out of precarious situations. Why on earth would it betray him now, especially against a woman?

They approached a large palace, but went neither to its front entrance, nor the back. Instead, they seemed to be making straight for an appendage that jutted out from the building proper—a sensual, beautifully carved and decorated *latha mandapam*, in fact. On closer inspection, it became clear that this artfully embellished gallery was actually built as a passageway that connected two enormous palaces, both of which seemed to be markedly different: the one on the right shimmered against the night sky, lit with glowing lamps, filled with the echoes of human voices and sounds of occupation. The palace to the left, however, had not a single lit lamp, even a tiny one. Its walls rose to the sky, pale in the moonlight, but it remained shrouded in silence and darkness.

Once they were at the *latha mandapam*, the girl signed to Vandhiyathevan to stay where he was. It was only when he obeyed, that the young man drew a deep breath—and promptly took in the presence of flowers around him. Such fragrance—such a deep, overwhelming scent! Why, they wreathed around him, rose to his very brain and almost overpowered him with their heady perfume!

The young woman entered the gallery and obviously engaged in conversation—for a sweet, feminine voice immediately joined hers. "Do you even need to ask? Show him in at once; I've been waiting an age!"

That voice—it wound intoxicating tendrils through his senses and turned him giddy with pleasurable anticipation. The Pazhuvoor Ilaiya Rani, no doubt. In an instant, he would be in front of her; how was he to handle the situation? And she—what would her reaction be, once she saw that the man who stood in front of her was not the magician she awaited, but the one who had rammed into her palanquin? Would she be taken aback with surprise? Perhaps she would be delighted? Or—or would she choose not to reveal any emotion?

But stay—here was his young guide, back at the entrance to the *latha mandapam*. She was gesturing for him to enter.

Vandhiyathevan walked to where she stood, and peered within the gallery. In an instant, the scene entered his brain through his eyes, and seared itself into his memory.

A lamp glowed bright, affixed to a stand of burnished gold, sending its rich, vivid radiance into all corners of the gallery. Some sort of incense had obviously been blended with the oil; a sweet fragrance threaded its way throughout. An ornate *saprakooda* couch stood, strewn with fragrant flowers; on it reclined a young lady, majesty and grace limning every part of her.

It was indeed, the young queen of Pazhuvoor.

If she had seemed lovely in the stark light of day, within her palanquin—she appeared to be the epitome of exquisite beauty at night, a very Goddess come down to earth in her divine glory, seated on her couch, her stunning profile thrown into relief in the golden radiance of a lamp.

Said lamp's dazzling light; the gently soothing incense; the Pazhuvoor Ilaiya Rani's striking beauty—all these served to send Vandhiyathevan off-kilter, his senses reeling, brain fuzzy with the sheer magnificence of it all.

Careful, Vandhiyatheva! You dared to touch liquor only once—but you still remember, don't you, the terrible power it had over your faculties? The way it rendered you senseless, weak and inebriated? You swore never to touch a drop again. Remember your pledge—and steel yourself. Do not succumb to this intoxication, far, far more powerful than those of spirits!

Nandhini, young queen of Pazhuvoor, gazed at him, her soft coral-red lips parted a little in surprise, revealing pearly white teeth. Her temporary speechlessness served to assist Vandhiyathevan's cause, to tell the truth.

He laughed gently, and gazed back at her. "My lady, your maid entertained the strangest suspicions about me—she wanted to know if I *was* a magician, or not. And how do you think she chose to address it? She turned to me and asked, *Are you,* **you***?*" He chuckled again.

Nandhini smiled. A flash of lightning dazzled Vandhiyathevan's vision; a sweet shower of honey seemed to drench him.

"She's certainly prone to a variety of strange fancies, I'm afraid. Vasuki, why do you still stand here like a tree? Return to your place—and if you hear the slightest footstep, slam the door closed."

"As you wish, *Amma.*" And Vasuki retired, walking along a pathway that led within the *latha mandapam* towards the brightly lit palace; reached her place by the dimly lit entrance, and sat down.

Nandhini lowered her voice a little. "She didn't quite believe that you were a magician, you say? Silly little fool. More than half the ones who call themselves so are deceivers, I tell you. But you—you truly *are* one. What sort of spell did you weave to suddenly spring up here?"

"Nothing quite so dramatic, my lady. All I did was climb a ladder by the wall."

"*That,* is quite obvious—what I meant was, what sort of charm did you use to fool this young woman?"

"I turned on the full force of my charismatic smile on her, under the light of the beautiful moon. Failing that, I was hoping to show her the palm-tree signet ring you kindly bestowed upon me."

"So you do have it safe? Surely you could have just walked through the front entrance in broad daylight? Why skulk around in this stifling darkness?"

"If you wouldn't think it amiss, my lady, I should like to inform you that your brother-in-law Chinna Pazhuvettarayar's men are thieving rascals. First, they tried to make away with my clothes and belongings; next, they followed me around the city without leaving my side an instant. Ah, the devious ruses I had to employ, just to slip their nets of surveillance! I managed to escape, run through all the alleys and by-lanes I could think of, wriggle through nooks and crannies and finally made my way to your palace, wandering all around it. That's when I clapped my eyes on the ladder against the wall, heaved a sigh of relief that you had remembered this pitiful creature, and tried to aid me. This, I now know to be a mistake. Accept my apologies."

"There doesn't seem to be a need to offer any."

"But—why not, *Ammani*?"

"You weren't quite that far off, in your assumptions. Do you know why I wished to consult a magician?"

"I'm afraid not. I confess I have no knowledge of either sorcery or astrology."

"I've been thinking of you ever since last morning, you see. I wondered why you hadn't come to visit me, yet. And that was why I wanted to confer with a magician."

"Surprising, indeed."

"What is?"

"What you said, just now. Because—I've been thinking of you ever since last morning, as well!"

"Do you believe in past lives? The threads that bind us from one birth to another?"

"What exactly does that mean?"

"I've heard it said that sometimes, when two people are bound by friendship, or some sort of relationship in one birth, that bond continues in their next births as well."

"Until yesterday, I would've laughed at such an idea. Now, though—I find that I'm beginning to believe in such things."

For all outward purposes, Vandhiyathevan was merely spouting a convenient lie but in his mind's eye, it must be admitted, flashed a memory of the young woman he had encountered at the Kudandhai astrologer's home. Nandhini, however, had no way of knowing his innermost thought processes, had she? The young queen of Pazhuvoor assumed Vandhiyathevan to be talking of her.

"But that wasn't why you wished to visit me, was it? There was some mention of a message from Azhwarkkadiyaar Nambi—"

"Indeed, yes, *Ammani*. Delivering it was certainly my first intention. Once I set eyes on you, however, I simply forgot—everything."

"Where did you meet Azhwarkkadiyaar? What was his message to me?"

"A little outside Veera Narayanapuram—he was, at that moment, trying to establish the superiority of Vaishnavism with the strength of his staff. Periya Pazhuvettarayar's grand procession passed us on their way to Kadambur, at that moment and doubtless, sounds of his argument must have reached your ears, for you put out a slender golden hand, and pushed aside the silk-screen of your palanquin. That was when Azhwarkkadiyaar recognized you, and wished to send a message. He believed I would be able to pass it on, as I stayed at the Kadambur Sambuvaraiyar Palace that night—but much to my misfortune, I couldn't gain an audience with you until outside the Thanjavur fort—and that was only because your palanquin knocked into my horse!"

Nandhini had been gazing at some point above her, all this while; Vandhiyathevan could not gauge her thoughts or emotions from what he could see of her expression. When he finished, however, she turned to him.

"Indeed," her face was wreathed in an exquisite smile. "The palanquins I climb into always happen to be wickedly troublesome, don't they?"

৯৯

35

THE MANDHIRAVADHI

Somewhere in the distance, large and festive *ekkalams* blared to the high heavens; *perigais* thundered their steady beats, echoing around the fort. Human voices rose high, uttering cries of victory and welcome. The fortress gates opened and closed with a crash, while the ground shook with clip-clopping horse-hooves and stomping elephant feet.

Vandhiyathevan was quick to notice the change in Nandhini; obviously, the sounds had attracted her attention. As if to add to it, the maid guarding the entrance stood up, startled, and tiptoed up to her. "*Amma*, it looks like *Yejamaan* has returned—"

"I know—go back to your place."

Nandhini turned her attention to Vandhiyathevan, once again. "The *Dhanaadhikaari* has entered Thanjai, apparently. He will seek an audience with the Emperor, ask after his health, confer with the Commander, and arrive here, straightaway. You must leave before he does. Now—what message from Azhwarkkadiyaar?"

"*Ammani*, that staunch Vaishnavite claims that you're his sister," Vandhiyathevan opened his gambit. "Is that true?"

"You doubt it, do you? Why?"

"How on earth could anyone believe that a beautiful parrot and a hideous monkey were born to the same mother?"

Nandhini laughed gently. "He's right in a way—we did grow up together, part of the same family. He was as affectionate to me as if I were his very own younger sister. A pity that I have been such a disappointment to him!"

"Oh well, in that case—well, this is the message he wished me to deliver: that Krishna Bhagavan awaits you. The Veera Vaishnavites of this world still wish, with great eagerness and piety, to see the glorious sight of you wed Lord Kannan."

"Hasn't he given up that particular fantasy yet?" Nandhini heaved a deep sigh. "If you ever happen to see him again, kindly tell him this from me: I am not worthy enough for a fate such as the devout Andal, who married the Lord Himself. Ask him to tear out all memories of me from his heart."

"That, I won't accept for a moment, my lady."

"What won't you accept?"

"That you are not worthy of Andal's destiny. That poor girl had to sing, dance, tie up various flowers into fragrant garlands, weep floods of tears and practically beseech God to marry her, but that won't be the case with you. All Krishna Bhagavan has to do is set eyes on your lovely face, and he'd give up his wives Rukmini and Sathya Bhama, beloved Radhai, abandon all the Gopika women he usually runs behind—and lift you straight up onto their thrones!"

"*Ayya*, you seem an adept at *mukasthuthi*," Nandhini peeped up at him. "I'm afraid I don't really favour such tactics."

"Kindly enlighten me about the meaning of the word *mukasthuthi*, *Ammani*."

"Flattering someone straight to their face, of course."

"In that case, turn around and sit with your back to me, please."

"Whatever for?"

"I shall then be able to flatter your back, won't I? Surely there's nothing untoward about expressing appreciation that way."

"You're uncommonly clever with your words."

"*Now* who's adept at *mukasthuthi*?"

"Why don't *you* turn around and show your back to me, as well?"

"Be it a battlefield or the company of fair women, my queen," Vandhiyathevan said, grandiloquently. "I make it a point to never show them my back. You may flatter me to my face, by all means."

Nandhini went into a merry peal of laughter. "Say what you will, but you *are* a magician, a *mandhiravadhi*. Do you know how long it's been since I laughed aloud?"

"A very dangerous thing to do, however, my lady—making you laugh aloud, I mean. Lotuses bloom with laughter in their ponds—and bees fall unconscious at their beauty!"

"Not just a magician then. You're a poet too, are you?"

"Praises don't flatter me; insults don't faze me either."

"Insult?"

"You called me a poet just now, didn't you?"

"What of it?"

"I've been called *monkey-face*, when I was a boy. Today is the first I've been called so, after a long time, and by your coral lips no less."

"They called *you* that? And who were these wonderful wits?"

"Never mind. None of them are alive, now."

"Be that as it may—I'm not one of them. All I meant was that you seemed able to sing verses quite well."

"I do possess some little ability in that direction, I confess—but only against my enemies, my lady. That they may die through my word, if they cannot embrace death with my sword!"

"Great Lion among Lesser Poets! You haven't told me your name, yet."

"My own name is Vandhiyathevan. Vallavarayan happens to be my title."

"Of royal descent, then?"

"None other than the hoary old dynasty of the Vaanaadhiraayars, my lady."

"And what of your kingdom, now?"

"The sky above; earth below. Today, you see, my lady, I am an *Eka Chakradhipathi*—sole Emperor of the whole world and all that I survey."

Nandhini spent a few moments, subjecting Vandhiyathevan to a careful scrutiny. "Not quite an impossible task, after all," she said, finally. "You could recover your ancestral lands, you know."

"But how can that be? Surely there's no way of regaining anything that's vanished into the stomach of a tiger? They're all part of the Chozha empire, aren't they?"

"I can, however, make it possible for you to retrieve them."

"Pray do not, *Ammani*. I've never particularly been enamoured of ruling kingdoms—but what little ambition I may have cherished vanished completely, when I saw Emperor Sundara Chozhar, today. To live a life thus, dependent on others even for a morsel of food, day after day—I may as well be an independent man, master of myself, even if I never know where I am to get my next meal."

"Precisely my opinion!" exclaimed Nandhini. Then, she seemed to remind herself of something. "Why, by the way, are Chinna Pazhuvettarayar's men pursuing you?"

"He entertained grave suspicions upon my person, you see—not unlike your own loyal maid."

"Indeed? What about?"

"For one thing, how did I come by the palm-tree signet ring?"

The faintest shadow of nervousness flitted across Nandhini's face. "And—where is it, now?" she asked, in a startled voice.

"Here, my lady. Surely you didn't think I would lose it?" And Vandhiyathevan showed her the insignia.

"How did he know that you had it?"

"I'd entertained a great desire to seek an audience with Emperor Sundara Chozhar, you see—and I used this ring to gain entry into the palace. Later, of course, the Commander demanded to know how I'd gotten my hands on it …"

"And your answer?" Her voice revealed her terror.

"Certainly not your name, my lady. Only that Periya Pazhuvettarayar had given it to me—in Kadambur."

Nandhini released a deep sigh. Her face and voice seemed to lose some of her panic. "Did he believe you, do you think?"

"Not fully, I suppose—else, why should he send his men after me? Perhaps he wished to produce me before Periya Pazhuvettarayar, and see if he could wring the truth that way?"

"You need have no fears about the Elder," Nandhini smiled a little. "I shall see to it that he doesn't make a meal out of you."

"Your ladyship's influence over the Lord of the Chozha Treasury is renowned all over the world, *Ammani*—but I have a great many urgent tasks to accomplish outside this fort, which is why I crave your indulgence, in helping me escape."

"Urgent tasks, you say? What sort?"

"Too many to list them all, my lady. Conveying your answer to Azhwarkkadiyaar, for instance. What may I tell him?"

"To forget that he ever had a sister named Nandhini."

"I *could* tell him that, I suppose—not that it would be possible."

"What wouldn't be?"

"Forgetting you, of course. I've only seen you twice so far, and *I* would be hard put to rout you out of my memory. How do you expect a man who's known you all your life to do the same?"

Subtle shades of triumph blossomed across Nandhini's fair countenance. She cast her exquisite eyes on Vandhiyathevan's face, the sharp gaze spearing his heart like a lance.

"And why, pray, were you so eager to seek an audience with the Emperor?"

"Who wouldn't wish to see for himself a man who is famed for his looks? I have heard of kings who desired, more than anything, to be the greatest in courage and nobility, to expand their empires and fame; they ask their subjects to pray for the same. And yet, do you know what humble petition the Buddhist monks lay at the feet of Lord Buddha, when it comes to Sundara Chozhar?

"… *Sundara*

Chozhar vanmaiyum vanappum

Thinmaiyum ulakir sirandhu vaazhkenave!"

Vanappu! Beauty, you see. Naturally, I wished to see the king who is praised as much for his looks, as for his valour and strength, this Manmadhan of the Kali Yugam, for myself. It has been my ambition for many months, now."

"Indeed; the Chakravarthy is a very vain man. And his precious daughter is even more conceited—"

"His daughter? Who would that be?"

"That supercilious, arrogant little idiot who lives in Pazhaiyarai—Ilaiya Piratti Kundhavai Devi, I mean."

Vandhiyatheva, you lucky wretch, murmured the young man to himself. **Here** *is the ruse you sought, manifesting itself before your very eyes. Use it wisely and well, my man.*

Hitherto, Nandhini had been reclining on her couch, the very embodiment of languid grace. Now, suddenly, she sat up straight. "*Ayya,* here's a proposal of mine. Will you agree to it?"

"Pray tell me, *Ammani.*"

"Let us make a pact, if you will: aid me and in turn, I will assist you. What do you say?"

"My lady—you're the queen of the *Dhanaadhikaari* of the Chozha empire, who happens to be one of the most powerful personages in the land. There's nothing in this country that you cannot accomplish. I, on the other hand, possess not the slightest bit of influence. How would it be possible for me to aid you in any way?"

Wondering if these words were heartfelt or mere lip-service paid by a talented courtier, Nandhini trained the power of her lovely eyes on him, searching, it seemed, right into his very heart.

Vandhiyathevan gazed right back at her, not fazed in the least.

"I find myself in sore need of a trustworthy aide. A loyal and dedicated man. If I were to procure employment in this palace—would you accept?"

"I'm afraid I've accepted the very same commission under yet another lady. If she refuses my services for some reason, then I shall be delighted to offer them to you."

"*Another* woman? Who on earth is she, that she dares to compete with me?"

"The one that you addressed with such fondness, a few moments ago: Ilaiya Piratti Kundhavai Devi."

"Impossible—lies, lies, all of it! It can't be—I won't believe it. You're playing some sort of joke on me –!"

"My queen, so many people have confiscated and read this *olai* that it can't make any difference if *you* do, as well." And Vandhiyathevan proffered the palm-leaf Aditha Karikalan had written to Kundhavai.

Nandhini took the *olai*, held it under the lamp and read the contents without a word. As she finished, eyes flashing lightning shot sparks of sheer wrath that, to Vandhiyathevan, resembled a ferocious cobra's forked tongue, slithering through its fangs. Despite himself, he shivered.

"*Ayya*," she turned to the young man, face and form suddenly full of majesty. "You wish to escape this fort with your life intact, don't you?"

"Yes, *Amma*. Which is why I seek your gracious assistance."

"Perhaps—but on one condition."

"Pray tell me."

"Deliver your *olai* to Kundhavai—but her reply, whatever that might be, must be delivered to me. Do you agree?"

"A very dangerous stipulation, my lady."

"You prided yourself on never being afraid of peril just a while ago, didn't you?"

"True—but then, running headlong into danger must entail some sort of reward, mustn't it?"

"Reward? So, you wish for an incentive, do you? You'll certainly get one. The prize that you might never have conjured up, not in your wildest dreams. The reward that even Periya Pazhuvettarayar, the most powerful man in the Chozha empire, has awaited desperately for years—performed a veritable penance in fact, but to no avail. Should you choose to accept this commission, such a remuneration will be—yours." And Nandhini fixed her exquisite eyes upon him again, her limpid gaze carrying every promise of breathless romance; employing the divine *mohanastram*, calculated to fell any man worth the title with devastating effect.

Poor Vandhiyathevan stood rooted in front of her, dizzy beyond comprehension. *Be still, my heart—be strong,* he mumbled to himself, disjointedly. *Do not forget yourself—or take leave of your senses!*

And, as though to lend him assistance when he most needed it, an owl cried out just at that moment, in its most hideous voice.

Once—twice—thrice—the hoots came, regularly.

The hairs rose up on Vandhiyathevan's body. His skin prickled.

Nandhini gazed at the garden beyond, in the direction of the hoots. "It looks like the real *mandhiravadhi* has arrived," she murmured. Then, she turned to Vandhiyathevan again. "Not that I need his services anymore—but I shall speak to him anyway. Who knows? He may aid you in your escape, somehow. Now, follow my instructions, and conceal yourself in the darkness."

And she pointed in the direction exactly opposite the one her maid was stationed in.

36

"DO YOU REMEMBER?"

Nandhini walked to where the *latha mandapam* opened out to the garden, and clapped her hands thrice.

Darkness flitted across her face—but was it stark, naked fear, or merely the gloom of trees that cast long shadows in the moonlight? It was impossible to tell.

Ancient, colossal tree trunks, with vines winding around them could be seen for a little distance from the *mandapam*. Beyond, the garden was a large blob of deep darkness.

The magician appeared from behind a tree, cleaving through the pitch blackness, pushing away masses of plants and creepers.

Nandhini returned to her *saprakooda* couch and reclined gracefully, her beautiful face now clothed in tranquility.

The *mandhiravadhi* entered the mandapam; the lamp's golden light fell full on his face.

Ah, familiar features, these—where have we seen him, before? Why, he appears to be one of the men who had gathered by the Thiruppurambiyam monument at midnight; who had shaken out a bagful of gold coins. The one who had growled out, "Kill Azhwarkkadiyaan the instant you set eyes on him!" Indeed, this was Ravidasan.

The man seemed to be simmering with wrath even as he walked in; the moment he set eyes on Nandhini, who lay on her couch, looking the very epitome of serenity, his cat-like eyes seemed to well-nigh explode with fury. He took his seat on a convenient *manai* opposite, and glared at her. "*Hroom—hreem—hraam!*" He muttered a few chants. "Bhagavathy—Sakti—Chandikeswari—!" he bellowed.

"Enough! My stupid maid has fallen asleep at her post, I suppose. Say what you wish to at once!" snapped Nandhini. "*He* has entered the fort."

"Why, you wretch!" Ravidasan hissed, very like a ferocious snake.

"Who?" asked Nandhini, calmly.

"You, you ingrate! Devious, wretched Nandhini, who remembers nothing—the Pazhuvoor Ilaiya Rani, most ungrateful of women! You sly, scheming little witch!" And Ravidasan pointed an accusing finger at her.

Nandhini stayed silent.

"You appear to have forgotten quite a few things that ought to have been etched in your memory, woman," continued Ravidasan. "I shall take it upon myself to recall them."

"What's the point of raking up those old stories, now?"

"*Why*, you ask me? I shall tell you—once I have finished."

As though realizing the futility in stopping him, Nandhini heaved a much put-upon sigh and turned away.

"Listen, Rani! Three years ago, in the cremation ground on the banks of the river Vaigai, burnt a funeral pyre. It was midnight, and none of the customary rituals and rites that usually accompany such a final act were performed for this one; nor were priests present. Twigs, sticks and dried leaves were scrounged from the forest floor and heaped; men brought out a corpse that had lain concealed behind a tree, and placed it on the pyre.

They lit it and the fire burnt merrily, catching upon the logs. That was when a few men dragged *you* from within the forest's gloom. Your hands and legs were bound; your mouth was gagged with an old cloth. Your lovely tresses which you now wear so elegantly, knotted and strung with fragrant flowers, were flowing down your back and all over the ground in a straggly mess. Those who brought you out were prepared to throw you onto the pyre as well, and burn you alive. "We shall wait until the fire grows!" swore a man. They left you on the ground for the time being, while each swore a terrible oath. You might have been unable to speak, but your eyes and ears were open; you watched and listened for all you were worth. Once they had finished pledging themselves to their cause, they approached you—and you, silent and wide-eyed until that time, tried to use your hands desperately, to sign something. You rolled your eyes, wriggled your brows, and one of them saw it. "She seems to want to say something," he pointed out. "Another of her old stories, I expect. Throw her into the fire!" snapped another. "No, let's listen to what she has to say, before we burn her. Remove her gag," ordered a man. Since he happened to be their leader, his men obeyed." Ravidasan paused. "Do you remember your words then, woman?"

Nandhini answered him not; nether did she turn to acknowledge him. Disgust and sheer terror painted her lovely face at that moment but also, along with them, shone a terrible, steely resolve. Two pearly tears trembled in her limpid eyes.

"So, you do not wish to speak, do you? Fair enough, I shall recite the tale myself. You, my girl, swore that you would assume the same cause as the men around you; that you would pledge yourself to exact the same revenge. This, you argued, was because *you* had more reason than any of them, to do so. You would use your beauty and brains, and assist the men however you could, and renounce your very life the instant your purpose was achieved—this was what you swore. The others did not believe a word, but I did—and I saved you from being burnt to a crisp." Ravidasan stopped his narration. "Do you remember all this—any of it?"

Nandhini turned a little, to glance at him. "Remember? Remember, you ask? Every word is etched in fire, in my very heart."

"Later, one day, we were walking in the dense jungle along the banks of the broad Kaveri, all of us. Suddenly, we heard the thundering hooves of cavalry approaching. We decided to split up and hide in the forest—but you were the only one to deliberately disregard us. You stood where you were, and allowed yourself to be captured by those soldiers. Their leader Pazhuvettarayan caught sight of you and promptly fell head over heels for your charms. He wedded you, and I bore the brunt of my comrades' anger—they believed that you had betrayed us. I resolved to get hold of you alone, somehow, and I did. I promised myself that I would plunge my trusty knife in your treacherous heart. But you begged for your life again. You swore that you were here to carry out your pledge, and that you would lend us every aid possible from within this very palace. Now—isn't all this true?" barked Ravidasan. "*Isn't* it?"

"Why wouldn't it be? Why do you insist on repeating old history again and again? Tell me what you wish now, and be done with it."

"No, you do not remember any of those old times—you have forgotten your past, every single bit of it! You are lost in the luxuries of this Pazhuvoor palace—you dine upon lavish six-flavoured feasts; drape yourself in fine clothes and expensive jewelry; laze on *saprakooda* couches and silk mattresses and travel in ivory palanquins! You are a queen now, my lady—how could you ever remember where you came from?"

"*Chee!* Who cares about silks, mattresses, clothes and ornaments? Do you really think I live for such paltry objects? Not I!"

"Or, perhaps you have fallen for a beautiful face? The charms of some young idiot who passed you by in an alley? These little romances may have taken your mind from a revenge that is far more important, might they not?"

Startled and a little self-conscious, Nandhini flushed crimson. "Such nonsense," she spat, making a swift recovery. "Lies, all of it!"

"Indeed? I intimated you of my arrival today, a good while ago—and yet, you did not send your *thaathippen*, your handmaiden to receive me at the usual place. Why?"

"I did—but someone else climbed up the ladder meant for you. That silly maid of mine mistook him for you and led him straight here. How is that my fault, pray?"

"Who cares? Had I hesitated a moment more at that wall, I might have been mincemeat. The soldiers pursuing that young idiot of yours were almost upon me. It was all I could do to escape them—as it was, I had to scramble into the foliage adjoining this palace garden and plunge into a pond, holding my breath for God knew how long. And then I made my way here, dripping wet—"

"Serves you right. You dared suspect me of betrayal, did you? Consider your sins washed away by a dip in that smelly pond."

"Woman, answer me this: did you really not lose your wits and heart to that handsome young man?"

"Good heavens, what a horrible idea! Who on earth would ever admire a man for being handsome? The shameless people of Chozha Nadu might praise their king for his good looks, but a man's true beauty lies in his battle scars, doesn't it?"

"Well said—but if this is what you truly believe, what was that young man doing here?"

"I've told you; Vasuki mistook him for you, and led him here."

"You even gave him your signet-ring—a favour you would not extend me. Why?"

"To lure him here, of course. I wished to speak with him. Now that I have, I shall retrieve it—"

"You did, did you? Why? What were you two lovebirds cooing about, all this time?"

"I was cooing, as you put it, with a very important purpose in mind. He will prove useful to our cause, you'll see."

"You little witch! Proven yourself to be the stupid woman you are, have you? Betrayed us and our sacred cause to some silly boy we do not even know—"

"Cease your foolish ravings. Why do you screech so? I betrayed nothing. If anything, I learnt a great deal from him."

"And what would that be?"

"He carries an *olai* from Kanchi to Pazhaiyarai, to the tigress who resides there. He showed it to me, too. I was instructing him to bring her reply to me—which was when you barged in."

"Damn your palm-leaves and writing tools! What earthly use are such things to us?"

"That's all *you* know. We've sworn an oath to destroy those tigers by their very roots, but all you think of are the males; you forget that a dynasty may continue through its women as well. And that's not all: who do you think holds the reins of Chozha Nadu, now? A pathetic Emperor who is paralyzed and stays in bed all day? Or the princes in Kanchi and Ilankai?"

"That would be the man who has the honour to call you his wife; *Dhanaadhikaari* Pazhuvettarayar, of course. The whole world knows this!"

"Wrong again. Certainly the world thinks so; why, even that batty old man entertains such foolish notions. I'm not surprised that you've been fooled into believing it as well. In truth, it's that little tigress at Pazhaiyarai who rules the land with an iron hand. She sits in her pretty little palace, pulling strings like a master puppeteer, and everyone dances to her whims and fancies. There seems to be no one who will take her down—but I will make sure she learns her lesson. And that's why I put that young man to good use."

Ravidasan considered her, a hint of surprise and grudging respect in his eyes. "Cunning, aren't you? How do I trust you, though? Where is the proof that all this isn't just a convenient lie, made up for my benefit?"

"I shall surrender that young man to you; lead him out of this fort through the secret passage. Make sure to blindfold him before you do. Wait in the vicinity of Pazhaiyarai, and make sure he brings Kundhavai's reply to me without fail. Should he try to deceive you or escape, you have my permission to kill him."

"Not on my life. You and he may go to hell for all I care! Chinna Pazhuvettarayar's men are seeking him within the city even as we speak;

they will expand their search outside the fort in a while. Team him with me and I shall be sure to be caught along with him. No—let us just discuss the purpose of my visit here."

"Which you haven't revealed, yet, I might add."

"Arrangements are complete, regarding our men travelling to Kanchi and Ilankai. Of course, things will be difficult for those journeying towards the island; they will have to exercise extreme caution and cunning—"

"How am I a part of these problems? Don't tell me you need more money? Good grief, is there no limit to your ceaseless greed for gold?"

"We require it in such vast quantities for our cause and not for ourselves, as you well know. Why else do you think we have left you here, whole and well? The men we are sending to Ilankai will need coins of the island's currency; Chozha coins will not serve their purpose—"

"All this prevarication for such an ordinary request! I have your precious gold coins ready, as you can see." Nandhini bent down, pulled out a bag from underneath her couch, and handed it to Ravidasan. "This bag contains all the Ilankai coins you need—now leave! He'll be here soon."

She stopped him, as Ravidasan prepared to leave. "Wait a moment— at least escort that young man outside the fort. He may seek his path however he may. I have no great desire to show him the secret passage." She rose on the words and glanced towards the darkened palace.

It lay wreathed in inky blackness, and nothing was visible. Nandhini signed with her fingers and clapped her hands lightly, to no effect.

She and Ravidasan walked along the *latha mandapam*, following the passage that connected the gallery to the gloomy mansion, towards its entrance. There was no one to be found, not in all the four directions.

Vandhiyathevan had, quite simply, vanished.

37

The Clash of Lions

The good people of Thanjaipuri cherished a wholesome, somewhat unique regard for the Pazhuvoor brothers. Hadn't it been those great lords, after all, who had brought their old city new lustre and welcome pride?

It is only natural that a procession of elephants, horses, palanquins and even the odd camel or two attracts a great deal of attention; people throng to see such events, gape at the opulence and drink in the festivities. Small matter, then, that Thanjai's residents accorded the same degree of importance every time Periya Pazhuvettarayar entered or exited the fort; they ranged themselves on the sides of the roads, raising chants of victory, shouting out blessings; showering the entourage with flowers and puffed rice.

It was also the norm for Chinna Pazhuvettarayar to arrive at the fortress gates and welcome his brother, whenever the latter returned home after a visit.

Their embrace, once they set eyes on each other, was a sight that inspired majesty and devotion, as though the very Nilagiri and Podhigai hills were clasping each other—such was their stature and splendour. As for the times both set off in procession through the wide avenues of the city, on their respective elephants or horses—ah, one needed ten thousand eyes to digest the magnificence of such a picture.

Some considered them equal to the *asura* siblings, Hiranyan and Hiranyakshan; others were prone to call them Sundhobha Sundhars. There were those who swore that the affection that existed between them was not unlike that between those epic heroes, Raman and Bharathan, while still others considered them warrior brothers equal to Mahabharata's Bhima and Arjuna.

Today however, matters were vastly different: neither Periya Pazhuvettarayar's grand entrance, nor the suitably pompous performance delivered by his faithful entourage, served to stir up any excitement. The streets remained devoid of delighted welcome; not many people were present, for that matter. Even more important: Chinna Pazhuvettarayar was conspicuous by his absence.

Periya Pazhuvettarayar, however, chose to disregard this flouting of convention, and proceeded straight to his younger brother's mansion. Thanjai's Commander must have been unavoidably detained by something important. Perhaps the Chakravarthy's health had taken a turn for the worse—or perhaps—perhaps a certain *significant event* had finally happened?

Plagued by all these and more doubts, Periya Pazhuvettarayar's impressive retinue reached the Commander's palace far sooner than usual.

The younger arrived at the entrance to welcome the elder, his face plainly shrouded with worry and anxiety. He bowed respectfully; the brothers embraced. Then, they entered the palace—and made for the *mandhiralosanai* chambers, meant for supremely confidential council.

Once in private, the Periyavar came straight to the point. "You do not seem to be your cheerful self, *Thambi*. Has something occurred—is it the Emperor? He is well, is he not, Kalanthaka?"

Chinna Pazhuvettarayar, whose given name this was, nodded. "As much as he ever is, I suppose. Neither terribly ill, nor well."

"Why do you seem ill at ease, then? I did not receive your customary welcome at the gates—and the city seems less enthusiastic than usual."

"Something *has* occurred, *Anna*—a very insignificant event, I must admit. But more of that, later; what about your own affairs?"

"A complete success, of course. Every single one of the invited guests arrived at Kadambur; all agreed unanimously that your son-in-law Madhuranthakan deserved to be the successor to the Chozha throne. Raised the very roof with victory chants, I must say. And if those in question will not listen to reason, your royal champions are very willing to raise swords and fight for our cause. Witness the sight: even Kolli Mazhavan and Vanangamudi Munaiyaraiyar submitted completely to our decision—what more could we possibly need? As for Sambuvaraiyar, that man is eager to put his men, fortress, ramparts and wealth at our disposal, if it will aid our mission; his own son Kandamaaran is straining at the leash, frankly. Who cares about the mid-lands and Thirumunaippaadi, when we have all of Chozha Nadu within our grasp? What else need we worry about, pray? The only objection, if any, might arrive from Pallavan Parthibendran, Thirukkovilur Malayaman and Kodumbalur Velaan— and of these three, the last is in Ilankai and poses no threat. What could the other two possibly do? Turn the whole world on its feet? All that is required, now, is to confront the Emperor soon and be done with it."

"Excellent—as far as the lords are concerned. What of the people, though?" Chinna Pazhuvettarayar drew out. "If they should object—?"

"The people? Good God, what of them? Since when have royal affairs ever involved the subjects of the land? Should they ever be so presumptuous as to interfere in such things, it is our sacred duty to crush their impertinence. I do not, however, anticipate an uprising. All that needs to be said is that the Emperor desires Madhuranthakan as his heir—and that will shut the people up. They might be stirred into protests, I admit, were Arulmozhi Varman here, but fortunately, the boy is in Ilankai and unlikely to wreck our plans. And our beloved people do not harbour the same amount of affection for Aditha Karikalan, as you well know. As for your son-in-law, it would be an easy matter to gain him their loyalty: he has already made a name for himself as a devout young man with plenty of character—and do we not know that he is blessed with a countenance fairer than both of Sundara Chozhar's precious sons? Those learned idiots who always shriek that "the face is a reflection of the heart," would be sure to sing his praises. I should be amazed, I will admit, if I did not hear "Long live Emperor Madhuranthakar!" from all quarters, soon enough. No matter—surely there is nothing for you to fear as long as I am by your side?"

"Yes—but what about the Velakkara Regiment? How do we counter them?"

"Those warriors may have sworn a blood oath to protect Sundara Chozhar's sacred person, but not his sons, surely? And even if they should object, for some strange reason, your fortress battalion can break them, can't they? Drag the whole lot in a *naazhigai* and stuff them down the dungeons, I say."

"Pazhaiyarai is likely to pose the biggest threat by far, *Anna*. Who knows what sort of a terrible strategy that old hag and young demon might hatch, between them? We must bend our energies in destroying those, surely—?"

"*Thambi*, you aren't insinuating, I hope, that I must exercise more caution over two weak, defenseless women, than hardened warriors? What earthly havoc could they wreck? And if they should happen to drum up something, I possess more than enough trickery and magic to counter them, never fear."

"The Emperor has commanded both his sons to return to Thanjai—"

"Aditha Karikalan certainly won't. Arulmozhi Varman might give some credence to his father's orders—in which case we must make sure to stop him, using force if necessary. Neither of them must set foot in Thanjai until we have affirmed Madhuranthakan as the Crown Prince and set him on the Chozha throne, complete with every authority and power due to that position, if then. However, you may leave all these to my care. Now, to return to your concerns—what was this insignificant issue that worried you so much?"

"There was this young man who arrived from Kanchi, bringing palm-leaves to the Emperor and Kundhavai—"

"You have confiscated the leaves in question and imprisoned him, I hope?"

"Er, no. He mentioned meeting you in Kadambur—apparently, you commanded him to hand over the *olai* to the Emperor. Is that true?"

"Lies, all of it! There *was* a young man in the Kadambur palace, to be sure; an uninvited guest who called himself Kandamaaran's friend—but the dratted boy never mentioned an *olai* of any kind. I mistrusted him the instant I set eyes on his cunning face. Surely you did not fall prey to his scheming ways?"

"I am afraid I did, *Anna*—only because he mentioned your name."

"Why, you absolute idiot! What dim-witted blunder did you commit now? You did not allow that young scoundrel to deliver his *olai* to the Emperor? Without even taking a look at it?"

"I did, but it seemed to contain nothing of importance; only a message asking the Emperor to visit the Golden Palace in Kanchi. That young man, though—once he had delivered the *olai*, he went on, saying something about "danger" …"

"All this, and you did not imprison him?"

"No—although I did suspect his motives."

"What on earth *did* you do, then?"

"He said he wished to sightsee Thanjai, and I sent him with two escorts. But he gave them the slip and vanished. I was preoccupied with flushing him out, which was why I could not even come to welcome you home. I have sent out a warning to the city, as well—"

"*Chee*! What kind of a brainless idiot falls prey to a boy who is barely a man, without even a moustache? Fool that I was, I named *you* Kalanthaka Kandan, *He Who Vanquishes Death*; I strove to use every weapon in my armoury to make you the Commander of the Thanjai fort—ah, how well you have repaid my efforts! How dare you stand in front of me and admit that you were made a fool of by a scheming rascal of a boy? You ought to be ashamed of yourself!"

"It was not just your name that he mentioned; he showed me your signet ring as well. Did you give it to him?"

"Not on my life. What sort of a bumbling nincompoop did you think I was? *You*?"

"That may be, but he did possess the Pazhuvoor signet-ring, and so I will swear on all that is holy. What is more, he displayed it to the fortress guards as well, who let him in. If he did not receive it from you—then there is only one other source he could have gotten it from."

"And who might that be?"

"Can you truly not guess? I mean the Ilaiya Rani, of course—"

"Careful, boy! Guard your tongue—else I will cut it out, myself!"

"Do, by all means; you have my leave to chop off my head, if you so wish. But I have every intention of revealing what I have yearned to say, these many days: a vicious cobra may be a bewitching creature, and you may have considered it a thing of great beauty when you took it in—but remember that it will sink its fangs in you. Some day, that snake will ruin us all! Do not lose yourself to her wily charms, *Anna*—throw her out, and we may all be safe!"

"Kalanthaka Kanda—now that you have been so good as to share your much-vaunted opinions; give me leave to return the favour. I have yearned to speak my mind as well, and here is what I wish to say: you have my permission to deliver advice, share your concern; remonstrate with me, should you find any of my actions questionable. You may do all these—save criticize the lady who has done me the honour of accepting my hand in marriage. Speak a word against her, and I shall strangle you with the very hands that raised you. The slightest accusation, and I shall stab you to death with the very hand that taught you to wield a sword. Careful, now!"

Those two brothers, famed for their mutual affection, seemed like lions at that moment, ready to fling themselves at each other's throats;

willing to rip their eyes out. Their war of words rang through the chamber, echoing from every corner, very like the deafening roar of a ferocious jungle beast. They might have been supposedly engaging in a private conversation within the council chambers but their growling threats permeated the walls, falling on the startled ears of those outside like the roar of distant, terrifying thunder, the words muffled and indistinguishable.

Their entourage awaited their lords' pleasure, quivering. What sort of storm was about to break over their heads, now?

38

NANDHINI, THE COQUETTE

It was well past midnight and into the third *jaamam*, when Periya Pazhuvettarayar finally returned to his own palace.

The west wind whirred through the silent streets, whipping up the fine dust in dizzying eddies—but the storm raging in his steely heart, whirling with a furious frenzy, flung up far more than just dirt and filth.

Ah, the things he had said to his beloved brother! He wished he had not been quite so brutal, now. After all, there was no doubt that his *thambi* held him in the greatest esteem, and his accusations—unjust as they were—had been borne out of great concern and worry. Still, a vastly suspicious fellow, his brother; why pile these allegations on Nandhini, for pity's sake? The pitfalls of human nature, which committed grievous blunders and always sought to escape by making someone else the scapegoat! Such tactics were always used by weak, spineless cowards—but why must Kalanthakan fall prey to the same pathetic ruse? All this, after having let that rascal of a boy slip through his fingers too! Then he finds a way to point fingers at his *madhani*, his own sister-in-law and how this could possibly reflect well upon his courage and personal integrity, was a puzzle he could not fathom. What sort of a man even indulged in such things?

Well, he *had* apologized for his unseemly words, at any rate. There was no point in dwelling upon that conversation, was there?

And yet—could there possibly be an atom of truth to his claims? *Had* he, after all, fallen for a pretty young woman at this ripe old age? After all, hadn't he just addressed the harshest words to one who had fought by his side, shoulder to shoulder, in a hundred battles; shrugged off mortal danger to stand by him, his own younger brother—and all in defense of a girl he had dragged out from a forest! Was she indeed worthy of such loyalty? He knew nothing of her origins, after all; her speech and behaviour, it must be admitted, were peculiar at times.

Chee, how can I let my thambi's heedless words influence me so? Unjust indeed, to suspect Nandhini's motives. Her deep and abiding love for me is evident in everything she does—witness her mellow speech, and the utmost respect with which she treats me! As for wifely duties—was there ever a woman who showed as much interest in her husband's office as Nandhini? Why, she even troubles herself enough to offer suggestions and comments, aiding me in every way possible!

*Such petty issues aside—**how** she must have loved me, to wed a doddering old man of more than sixty! Devendran himself, king of the Devas, would fall all over himself to claim the hand of one so beautiful that she inspires celestial dancers to intense jealousy—as for the kings of this mortal realm, who might baulk at the good fortune of wedding such a sundari? Ah, the very Sundara Chozhar would have had no two thoughts about it, had she ever caught his faltering sight! And here I am, suspecting her—ah, how incredibly unmerited! I have heard tales, of course, of old men who spent every moment of their lives in hell, entertaining unlawful doubts about their wives' fidelity; I have laughed at such incidents myself. And yet here I am, caught in the same terrible toils; making a laughing stock of myself!*

Still, it would not hurt to question her about certain issues; there are a few of her activities that warrant inquiries. She wishes me to grant my signet-ring often; to what end? Why does she spend so much time in that God-forsaken latha mandapam? And what, of course, of that mysterious magician who visits her at all sorts of odd hours—and to which she admitted, herself? Why would she need his services anyway? Whose heart does she wish to conquer, that she must make use of such tactics?

All this aside, there is another, perhaps the most burning of all questions: how long is she going to keep me from her side, like a brahmachari yet to taste the delights of marriage? Every time the subject crops up, she conceives a fast or ritual that prevents our union—but never, not once, has she ever explained what exactly the worship entails! Ah, all this does seem very like the cunning strategies often used by wily women who detested their husband's advances! Well, no more of it; I have given way to her whims far too much. Tonight, all this and more must be discussed and put an end to, come what may!

Periya Pazhuvettarayar arrived at his palace entrance to a rousing welcome by his closest aides, servants and maids but search as he might, swiveling his eyes in every which direction, the one woman he wished to see above all else was conspicuous by her absence: the Ilaiya Rani. Upon enquiries, it was discovered that her ladyship was still in the *latha mandapam.*

What in the heavens is she doing there, well beyond midnight? A spark of anger burnt within him. Was his faithful wife playing him for a fool, perhaps? Had she devised some unique way of ignoring him, the willful woman?

Periya Pazhuvettarayar hastened towards the gallery, not a little peeved by what clearly seemed an attempt by her to incense her lord and master. He reached the corridor connecting the palaces in time to see Nandhini returning, maid in tow. The moment she set eyes on him, she stopped, choosing to gaze at something—no doubt vastly interesting—in the garden, shrouded in inky blackness. The maid had stopped at a little distance.

Pazhuvettarayar drew close to the Ilaiya Rani; she continued to fix her lovely eyes upon the dark foliage, seemingly unaware of his proximity. She neither acknowledged him, nor condescended to receive him.

Thus it was that the lord of Pazhuvoor, who had strode forward with every intention of subjecting his young queen to a furious diatribe—found that *he* had to pacify *her*.

"Nandhini, my dearest, you seem annoyed. Why will you not look at me, my love?" And he placed his hand, strong as a Vajrayudham, on her slender shoulders—gently, it must be said.

His wife grasped his iron-like arm, and shoved it off her. Ah, could a limb as soft and delicate as the flowers in his garden possibly possess such strength?

"You deigned to push me away with your dainty hands! Life could not bless me any further, my heart's dearest—you have accomplished what no warrior from the Vindhya hills to Thirikonamalai would have even dared think of. That, my dear, is my greatest good fortune, but you have not yet revealed the reason for your anger. Will you not speak to me?" pleaded that great warrior, veteran of a thousand battlefields. "My wretched ears yearn for the silken softness of your voice, more exquisite than the sweetest honey, my heart."

"How many days has it been, since you left?" demanded Nandhini. "Four—you've condemned me to four days, alone!" Her lilting voice held just the slightest hint of a sob—and Pazhuvettarayar, who had wielded a hundred swords and spears unflinching, found his steely heart melting like wax in a flame.

"And this is what upsets you, my dear one? You could not bear my absence for a mere four days? But I might have to leave for the battlefield; we might have to live apart for months on end—what would you do, then?"

"You believe me to be a cold-hearted wretch who would stay away from you for months, while you went to war? Perish the thought. I shall follow you thither, of course, like a shadow at your heels—"

"Here is a jest, indeed! What sort of a war do you think I could wage, with you by my side? Dearest, many are the injuries this chest has borne; my shoulders have taken more arrows and spears than can be counted—those scars number sixty-four, or so, many lavish praises upon me. But you—ah, if the tiniest thorn were to prick your exquisitely delicate skin, my life, then my heart would splinter into pieces; it would have accomplished what a thousand battles and weapons have failed to achieve, thus far. How, *how* could I possibly take you with me, into battle? I cannot even bear to see you stand all this while, on these unforgiving stone floors! Come, my queen, pray, do recline upon your beautiful, flower-laden couch, that I may look upon your exquisite countenance. Do not think, fair one, that these four days have wrought anguish upon your spirits alone—for I have suffered as well; every moment of your absence is an aeon to me. But now—ah, now I may gaze at your divine radiance until I quench my terrible yearning!" And he clasped her soft hands, leading her gently to the *saprakooda* couch.

Nandhini brushed away her tears and glanced up at him. The lamp's gentle light caught her lovely face, throwing her golden radiance into prominence—and the ravishing smile that bloomed upon it. The Chozha empire's *Dhanaadhikaari* gazed at her, struck by the pearls that peeped amidst soft, coral lips. *Ah, were they within my grasp, I would sacrifice all three worlds, just for a hint of this wondrous countenance—but as I lack these magnificent possessions, I shall have no compunction in placing my body, soul and worldly assets at her dainty feet. And yet, this celestial maiden demands nothing of me!*

Such were his dizzy thoughts, as he drank in her lovely form. Gone, forever, was any intention of ever taking her to task, demanding explanations, or reading her a lecture on appropriate behaviour; he was now willing and ready to prostrate himself at her feet, and carry out the most trivial task. Slavery of any kind is demeaning—but there is nothing that denudes a man of his dignity and senses as mindless submission to a beautiful woman.

"You've been away from me for four long days—why didn't you come home at once? Your brother was far more important to you, wasn't he?" retorted Nandhini, her face bright with mock anger; eyes darting lightning looks of playfulness.

"Not quite, my dear. I did want to come to you, straight as an arrow and true. I was detained, however, by that young idiot Madhuranthakan;

I had to make sure he returned safe home, through the secret passage. That was why I stayed so long at my brother's palace—"

"I cherish the greatest regard for your abilities, *Ayya*; I am deeply interested in all your concerns—indeed, I consider myself fortunate to be involved in any of them. There is nothing I wish more than for you to succeed in your every endeavour. Yet, I can't help but loathe the fact that a man traveled in *my* closed palanquin—and that every man, woman and child believes me to be a part of your retinue, wherever you go—"

"You do not believe that *I* welcome such a state of events either, do you? Never!—and yet, we *have* undertaken an extremely important task; I shall have to put up with a great deal for its eventual success. Besides, surely you have not forgotten that conveying Madhuranthakan in your palanquin was your idea in the first place? And was it not you who suggested that he use the secret passage to enter and exit the fort—?"

"I did, and in this, I believe only to have carried out my duty. Isn't it, after all, the sacred charge of a wife to aid her husband in any way possible? It's true that I put forward this ruse, but when I think of how it may have acted against you—"

"But that was not all, was it, my dear? Why, I remember well the Madhuranthakan of yore—the pathetic boy who smothered himself in sacred ash and spent hours mumbling *Om Namachivaaya*, over a string of rudraksha beads—making endless pilgrimages from one temple to another—the perfect son to his equally pious mother! I remember too, the monumental efforts we took to persuade him towards the Chozha throne, all to no avail. But you spoke to him twice—and he changed his mind in an instant! You might not believe it, but the lad now dreams of an empire that stretches from Imayam to the very tip of Ilankai; from the very heavens to the ends of the earth! Why, he can barely even wait for our efforts to come to fruition; he would like to ascend the throne this very instant! I do not know what sort of spell you wove over him, my heart—and speaking of which, you appear to possess a great many magical tricks up your sleeve yourself; why do you wish for the services of another? People talk, you see—"

"—and it is your divine duty to chop their unruly tongues. I have confided to you before, of my reasons for consulting a magician; should you have forgotten, I shall remind you again: that petty little snake in Pazhaiyarai must be taught her lesson. You are men, after all, my lord; you go to battles and settle your difference like warriors; "Women—such weak, defenseless creatures!" —*that* is what you think; war against one is the height of dishonour, to you. And yet, my king, a single woman may wreak more havoc than a hundred men. A snake knows its own kind; you know nothing of her, but I know Kundhavai's evil mind like my own. Ah, the temerity of that witch, to have scorned both you and me! Such things may have slipped your magnanimous mind, my lord, but it didn't mine. Never, *never* shall I forget her cruel words as she addressed me, in the midst of a hundred women: "*I shall never understand why you chose to marry that doddering old man! He may have lost his mind in his dotage, but what possessed you to lose yours? Where did your wits go begging?*" Ah, how can I ignore such vicious barbs? "*You fairly dazzle our eyes like a celestial maiden come down to earth,*" said Kundhavai. "*Any prince would consider it an honour to claim your hand in marriage and make you his queen—why must you choose an ancient, bumbling buffalo for your husband, you poor girl?*" My lord—never shall I forget those malicious words—not until my last, dying breath!"

And Nandhini began to sob, almost beside herself, after her breathless exposition. Hot tears coursed down her cheeks, flowing in a deluge and soaking her heaving bosom.

39

SPINNING WORLDS

He *had* married again at a ripe old age—and a ravishing young woman, at that. People were bound to gossip, and bandy ribald comments about his latest escapade. Periya Pazhuvettarayar had not exactly been unaware of the disparaging remarks that had flown about his nuptials and those who made them; that Kundhavai Piratti had been one, had come to his attention as well. No one had, however, made it their business to repeat her exact words so blatantly—and now that he had them from Nandhini herself, Pazhuvettarayar's wrath knew no bounds. His heart thudded furiously in his chest; flames of sheer fury scorched him, like the boiling heat in an ironsmith's forge. *Gup—gup* came his heated breaths in shuddering sighs, finding no other outlet for his burning hatred; Nandhini's hapless tears only served to rouse his towering rage.

"Is that what she said of me, my heart's dearest? Did that wretched witch truly call me an old buffalo? Well, she shall know my wrath, that little pest," he ground out, teeth gnashing. "I shall crush that slender body of hers like a petty vine under a buffalo's terrible hooves! See if I won't! I shall—I shall …" he stuttered to a stop, too angry to be coherent, face twisted in fury; his countenance so harsh it could not bear to be seen.

Nandhini used her considerable charms to calm him down. "*Nadha—* my husband, I knew you couldn't bear to see me slighted in any way," she spoke in a soothing voice, twining her delicate fingers, soft as the petals of a flower, with his iron digits. "And yet, how can one ever conceive of a magnificent lion, trained to splinter an elephant's brawny skull and drink its blood in a gory battlefield, fighting with a little cat? Kundhavai is just such a one—a spitting feline. And yet, she's powerful in magic—that's how she has everyone dancing to her tunes in this Chozha Empire, with her spells and trickery! There's only one way she can be overpowered, and that's with magic that will counter her own evil ambitions. Should you object to this, my lord, all you have to do is tell me," she sobbed again, "and I shall leave this palace this very day—"

The flames of fury died down; in their place rose waves of undeniable passion and ardour. "No, my dearest, pray do not even say such a thing— you may consort with a thousand magicians if you so wish, but do not leave, my heart! You are as life to me—nay, you *are* my very life! And what would this pitiful body be, devoid of your life-giving love, my beloved one? Ah, my spirit burns every moment I am away from you, every time your fasts and rituals force us apart. I die even as I am alive, my love. Tell me; how may I gain your affections? You know so many tricks and spells—will you not grant me one, to please you?"

"But why would you need such pathetic aids, *Nadha*? Pray leave such paltry devices to me, a feeble woman. Your valiant hands, used to swords, spears and glorious battle, need never have recourse to such things."

"Ah, my body thrills at your very voice; when your coral lips address me "*Nadha*!" I can hardly bear the exhilaration. Your radiant face strips me of every semblance of sanity. I carry swords and spears, you say, and must fight as a warrior, and I do; I destroy my foes with every weapon I possess—but alas, they are useless to me now! How do I wage battle against Manmadhan, my beloved one, with mere metal? Of what use are my trusty knives in this pretty *latha mandapam*? For it is *you* who possess all the weapons in this war of hearts. Why do I need tricks and charms, you ask—I shall tell you: to assuage the terrible fire that consumes my body and soul, and has done so, for days! Teach me a spell that will slake my thirst, I beg of you—or grant me the precious boon, my dearest one, of the pleasure of your intimacy! I give myself to you, heart's delight, but ask only one thing: release me from this terrible prison; save my life! It is now two years and more since we were bound by the holy vows of matrimony—and yet, we have not begun to live as husband and wife. You describe rituals and fasts, ceremonies that require you to stay away—and banish me to the terrible wastes of isolation, to eternal torture that batters my soul. Allow me, your lawfully wedded husband, by your side or end my torment: poison me with your own hands—!"

"*Ayyayo!*" Nandhini covered her ears with her palms. "Pray—*pray* do not distress me with such cruel words, or I truly might carry out your wishes—a few drops of poison and I shall end my life. And then you may be happy, free of the taint of my existence—"

"Never, my heart, never shall I repeat those hateful words; forgive me, most beloved one. Live a happy life without *you* by my side, you say? I am more than half demented, as it is; with you gone, I shall descend into complete madness—"

"Forgive me, my lord, but why? I see no need for your anguished existence, marred by terrible fits of lunacy; why should you? We are bound for an eternity you see; we became as one, the day we joined in matrimony. We are now one soul; we possess one spirit, merely constrained by two bodies. Every beat of your heart echoes in mine; every thought in your consciousness finds clarity in my being. My soul is but a mirror that reflects yours. Should your brows gather in a frown, my eyes tear in distress; I turn queasy at the faintest twitch of your moustache. With such unity of thought at the very core of our beings, surely there's no reason to invest such meaning in a pitiful body—a carcass that, moreover, will rot and die, some day; that will burn to cinders and turn to dust—"

"Stop—cease at once—my ears blister at your cruel words!" Periya Pazhuvettarayar cried out and continued breathlessly, before Nandhini could speak. "A pitiful body, you say? A carcass that might rot and burn? Do not—*do not* utter such terrible words; let your coral lips and honeyed voice never resort to such malicious speech. A mortal body, fated to turn to dust—is that what you truly think you are? Never, my life, *never*. The world has seen the birth of thousands of women; a hundred thousand still live upon its surface—and Brahmmadevan may well have made them of mud, stone, or even lime; moulded their ugly forms with coal and soot. But you—ah, do you even know how he gave shape to your wondrous form, my heart? He chose the most fragrant of the *mandhara* flowers strewn on the ground in Devalokham, the abode of the Devas; he came down to Thamizhagam next and gathered charming red lotuses; he then returned to his celestial abode and placed those sweet blooms in a precious bowl of divine ambrosia. He waited until nectar and blossoms blended into a glorious concoction; then, he added pearly, radiant moonbeams; descended to earth, and asked for the melodies of generations of *paanar* musicians. They played upon the beauteous *yaazh*, which Brahman added, as well. And this was the magnificent blend that he eventually used, to mould your divine beauty—"

"You speak as though you were by Brahma's side while he gave shape to my form, *Nadha*. Pray, why am *I* to be the subject of such overwhelming praise? Many are the wonderful ladies who occupy your *anthappuram*; gently bred princesses with whom you've led a wedded life for many long years. I on the other hand, have had the pleasure of your acquaintance for little more than two—"

"Nandhini!" Pazhuvettarayar cut in, before she could continue. His heart churned with emotions that threatened to overpower him; perhaps he wished to seek relief by speaking of them, and thus releasing some at least of his pent up feelings. Roaring flames almost engulfed his soul; he wished, perchance, to quench them with a shower of words. "Ah, you speak of the many women in my *anthappuram*—the ancient Pazhuvoor clan depended upon my marriage for its future; I believed it to be my sacred duty to wed them. Some of those idiots turned out to be barren; others bore me only girls. *If this was God's will, then so be it*, I reflected, and made peace with my lot in life. I gave up the very thought of women and pleasure, choosing, instead, to devote all my time to royal affairs. Chozha Nadu deserved all my attention, I believed; nothing and no one else commanded so much of my heart. It was at this time that we fought our final, decisive battle against the Pandiyas. Many were the commanders in their prime, young men yearning to wage war; yet, I could not find it in me to stay away from the battlefield. In the end, my presence did serve an excellent purpose; such a magnificent victory might not have been ours, otherwise. Once I had decimated the Pandiya forces and raised the glorious Chozha flag in Madurai, I journeyed towards the Kongu country. I was returning, making my way along the wide banks of the Kaveri—when I first saw you, in the midst of dense jungle.

"I could scarce believe my eyes. I closed, and then opened them again—but there you were, among the trees. *Surely this is a forest nymph; she will disappear when I approach*, I thought, as I stepped forward. You, however, did not. I wondered if you were some sort of angel, like those mentioned in our *puraanams*; a celestial being cursed to fall from heaven and walk this earth—certainly, you could not be a lowly human being; nor know the human tongue. I came even closer, and asked, *Who are you, woman?*

"When you replied, it was in perfect Thamizh: *I am an orphan, my lord; I offer myself to your gracious protection; grant me refuge*! I took you up in palanquin at once, I admit—and in those moments, my heart began to race with thoughts I had never given rein to, in all my life.

"It seemed to me that I had seen you before, somehow, somewhere—but try as I might, I could not remember *where*. And then suddenly, a veil lifted in my mind's eye, revealing the truth. It was not in this birth that I had met you, you see, but in many others, before. Those memories now came flooding into my heart, like a veritable deluge! Once, you were born as the beautiful Akalikai; I was Devendran, king of the Devas, and I came down to earth in search of you, braving even the most ferocious curses of your husband, a sage; Then, I was the Maharaja Santhanu, hunting along forest paths—and I stumbled upon you, a beauteous maiden; you were the revered River Ganga, of course, and had taken human form and I fell in love with you; yet another time, I found myself re-incarnated as the merchant Kovalan in the city of Kaverippoompattinam and you were the faithful, loyal Kannaki; I lost my mind for a while, caught in the wily illusions of this sickening world and forgot you—but the fates were kind to me again; the veil lifted and memories of you returned. I took you to Madurai; left you safe in Ayarkudi, while I went to the markets to sell your *silambu* ornament for money—there, betrayal cost me my life. And *that* is why I was born again, as a warrior in a Chozha clan, that I might take my revenge against those traitorous Pandiya kings—and I promptly did so, when I chopped Veera Pandiyan's head. I destroyed his wretched clan and was on my way home—when I caught sight of you. And that was when I knew, my dearest, that I had met my mate, my beloved Kannaki, whom I lost all those centuries ago—!"

Nandhini had sat with her face slightly averted, through all of Periya Pazhuvettarayar's fanciful ramblings about his various incarnations; her lord and master had not had the opportunity to see the plethora of expressions flitting across his wife's face. In this, it must be admitted, he was fortunate. Had he done so, it is doubtful if he might have continued with his fairy-tales, spanning across aeons.

"I'm not sure if your examples are all that appropriate, *Nadha*," Nandhini turned to him, when he finally paused to take a breath. "You see, they appear to be a little too inauspicious for my taste. Let's just say that you are the very incarnation of Manmadhan; I'm Rathi, and be done with it." Her face blossomed into a happy smile.

The Pazhuvoor lord's countenance brightened as well; pride and delight fought for supremacy in his eyes. A man might be hideous in the extreme—but surely even he would be exhilarated, when described as "handsome" by the woman he loves? Periya Pazhuvettarayar could not help preening himself either, at Nandhini's lavish praise. "You are entirely justified in calling yourself Rathi, my beloved, but it would hardly be appropriate to name me a God of love now, would it?" he demurred, as though the very thought was repugnant to him. "Your love for me prompts you to admire me so, I am sure."

"*Nadha*, I beg to disagree. To me, you *are* Manmadhan—a warrior's good looks lie in his battle prowess, after all, and there's not a single man in all of the southern lands to match your valour. All the world knows this. And then, there's also the fact that a true man always aids damsels in distress—and I am the best example of that, as you can well see. You knew not my name, my caste, clan or whereabouts; yet your heart was magnanimous enough to grant this orphan a refuge. To this day, I have known nothing but comfort; you have showered endless affection upon me, a hapless girl. Know this—I shall not make you, my lord and master, wait for very long. My fasts are almost at an end—"

"My heart's delight—*pray* do tell me what these precious rituals are, that I may do all in my power to complete them as quickly as I can, for your sake," begged the Pazhuvoor king.

"None of the descendents of that vainglorious Sundara Chozhan, who believes himself to be the handsomest man on earth, must succeed him. Kundhavai, that conceited, arrogant woman, must be taught a sharp lesson; her pride must be destroyed—"

"Consider these tasks done, Nandhini. Adithan and Arulmozhi Varman will *not* ascend to the throne in Thanjai; Madhuranthakan will be Sundara Chozhar's heir; the lords and kings of the Empire are agreed upon this—"

"All of them?" Nandhini demanded, stressing the word. "Truly?"

"Well—barring two or three, the rest certainly have. Malayaman, the Kodumbalur Velir and Parthibendran will not comply, of course, but no matter; they are of no account—"

"Be that as it may, it behooves us to exercise the greatest caution until our task is done, isn't it?"

"Indeed it does and I, for one, have made sure that all possible precautions are taken. If at all there *is* a mishap, it would not be mine, but another's. Why, something of that sort happened even today, I hear: a young rascal from Kanchi gave Kalanthakan the slip, and delivered an *olai* to the Emperor himself—"

"Ah—and here you've been singing your precious brother's praises all this while! Haven't I told you, time and again, that he is sorely lacking?"

"In this case, perhaps, yes. He alleges, besides, that the boy even showed him our signet ring."

"Excuses, excuses—always supplied to cover up failures. And so—was nothing done to capture this young man?"

"Why not? Our soldiers have flung their nets within this fort and without; the hunt is on. He is sure to be ensnared soon enough. I assure you, my dear: our mission is unlikely to be compromised by any of this idiot's machinations. Madhuranthakan will ascend the throne, upon the Chakravarthy's death—"

"*Nadha*—I believe it's almost time to finally reveal the purpose of my penance …"

"That, my dearest, is what I have been imploring you to do, for quite a while."

"All my fasts, rituals and sacrifices will serve no purpose, should Madhuranthakan—that young idiot who leers at women—ascend the throne …"

"What else, then? Come, reveal your heart's desire, and I shall make sure it is fulfilled."

"When I was very young, my king, a famous astrologer took a look at my birth-chart. He prophesied that I would suffer a great many ills until I was eighteen—"

"And? What else?"

"—but once I crossed this year, my stars would change. The planets would re-align themselves. I would ascend great heights of prosperity, and occupy a magnificent position—"

"And he was right. Who is this wonderful astrologer? Tell me, that I may perform a *kanakabishekam*, shower him with gold coins at once!"

"*Nadha?*"

"My heart?"

"The astrologer mentioned one other thing. May I disclose that, as well?"

"Certainly, my dear. I insist upon it!"

"He prophesied that my husband, the man who claimed my hand in marriage, would wear a glittering crown and ascend a throne fit for an Emperor among Emperors; he would be the magnificent ruler of an Empire that claimed the unwavering allegiance of all fifty-six kings of our land. You *will* fulfill that prophecy too, won't you, my liege?"

Pazhuvettarayar gazed at her, perplexed beyond belief. Nandhini and the beautiful *saprakooda* couch on which she reclined began to weave, in front of his dazed eyes. The *latha mandapam*, its pillars, and the gloomy garden opposite began to tilt crazily. The tree-tops, bathed in the pearly light of the moon, began to whirl around; the stars in the night sky and the palaces in either side swiveled dangerously.

The whole world spun.

40

THE PALACE OF GLOOM

Meanwhile, what of Vandhiyathevan, who vanished without a trace? We saw in the beginning, that he shielded himself within the inky gloom of the dark palace. For a few moments, he strained to listen to Nandhini's conversation with the *mandhiravadhi*—but not a word could he hear, much to his disappointment. Not that this concerned him too much. Involved as he had been in talking to the Ilaiya Rani, he had not failed to sense his faculties deserting him; a certain drowsy acquiescence wending its way through his mind, almost drugging him into obeisance. He knew it for what it was, now: an illusion calculated to make him drop his guard—but this meant that he could no longer afford to return to Nandhini's presence. No, far better to leave at once, without laying himself wide open to her charms! The Pazhuvettarayar brothers were terrible enough, but getting snared in the Ilaiya Rani's toils was a peril he could not risk. His wits did not desert him in the presence of those warrior-lords; his shoulders set to combat with a whim; his hands never strayed far from the sword at his hip. Wits or war; he was prepared for both. The young queen, though—ah, his wonderfully flexible mind deserted him in her presence; her seductive airs robbed him of any semblance of intelligence, and as for his knife-wielding abilities, the less said about his nerveless hands, the better. Heaven knew what disaster might befall him if he ever returned to her.

That magician, besides—what on earth was she doing, hobnobbing with men of that ilk? What sort of wicked spells did they weave? As for her hatred towards Kundhavai, good grief—how could he ever forget the way her eyes fairly glittered with malice at the very mention of her name! Who knew—Nandhini was quite capable of ignoring their conversation and handing him back to the tender mercies of Periya Pazhuvettarayar; women were well-known, after all, for their impulsive natures and brash decisions. Now, if he could just escape without ever catching her eye, but how? The only way out was possibly through the garden and over the wall—and what if the men pursuing him lay in wait, still? Was there no other way? At all?

Where have your wits gone begging, Vandhiyatheva? What of your famed luck that has never deserted you thus far? Think, think now—use those brains of yours—swivel your eyes in all four directions—ah, here's that gloomy palace—and why is it shrouded in such darkness, anyway? Was there anyone, or anything within? Perhaps a way out, through another entrance?

Should he enter its gloomy precincts anyway? After all, it might prove useful at some point, mightn't it?

But how on earth was he ever going to get in? What a massive door, to be sure—and such a huge lock, too! Ah, the heaviness of these objects, and such an enormous width—but wait, what was this? A door within a door? *Wonder of wonders—it opens at my touch! Well, what more can I ask for? If this isn't good fortune, I don't know what else is. Time to enter this mysterious place and gauge its secrets!*

Vandhiyathevan pushed open the tiny door, set so cleverly into the larger one that it could barely be seen, and stepped into the dark confines of the palace. His first thought was to make sure that Nandhini never knew his whereabouts; he pushed the door shut, noiselessly.

As shadowy as the palace already was, this seemed to deepen the gloom. Vaguely, he remembered catching sight of several large stone pillars in the dim light through the open entrance—but now, of course, he could not see a single thing. Ah, such stifling darkness—surely no one could even imagine such inky blackness—*chee*! Pull yourself together. *Of course* it was pitch black; isn't it always so, when one moves from light into gloom? A little while here and his eyes would grow accustomed to the interiors; he would be able to see the columns again, dimly, no doubt. Experience had taught him this—and yet here he was, frightened at darkness! Ridiculous, indeed.

I may as well begin walking a little, instead of imitating some of the pillars I saw, he mused. *I shall stretch out my hand and feel my way—one of those blessed structures ought to be here, somewhere—*

For a while, Vandhiyathevan stumbled along, hands in front of him, like a blind man. And found his fingers brushing a pillar, just as he had expected. Ah, this was a worthy specimen of stone, indeed—quite magnificent. *I shall simply feel my way around it*, he thought, and walked further.

He felt another column on his path—but still could not see a single thing, for some reason. Surely there must be some faint illumination, by now? Had he suddenly gone blind? No, that was silly!—people did not simply lose their sight for inexplicable reasons, did they? Well, he would walk further. No, he encountered no further pillars but there was a strange feeling of descending—wait, here is a stair! Thank heaven he had not lost his footing and fallen headlong—but how long was he supposed to stumble along this way, without a chink of light?

Cold fingers of dread suddenly clamped around Vandhiyathevan's heart. He really could not take a step more—he would have to return, back to the *latha mandapam*. Far better to face Nandhini and accept whatever scheme she came up with, rather than stagger endlessly in this gloom. It didn't matter *what* promise she demanded; he would give it— and then, well, things were apt to take care of themselves.

With this very creditable intention, Vandhiyathevan retraced his steps—or tried to, at any rate. *Was* he truly on the right path? How could he ever know, in this inky blackness? Nothing barred his path this time; where had all those enormous pillars gone? Would he never be able to find the entrance? What if he had to spend the whole night rambling all over this terrifying palace? Good God, what disaster had he let himself in for—?

Wait—what was that sound? *Sadasadasada*—it sounded like fluttering wings. Where was it coming from? Bats, perhaps? Hardly surprising, if so; those creatures were known to inhabit gloomy, dark places like these—no, no, these weren't just bat-wings; there was the faint sound of footfalls as well. Someone was walking around here—but who? Were these men? Or—or …

Vandhiyathevan's thoughts froze; his tongue cleaved to the roof of his mouth, which went dry in an instant.

Someone seemed to brush against his face. He gathered all his strength, swung his hand and sent his fist crashing into it.

His valiant arm ached fit to break; cradling the abused digits, Vandhiyathevan felt for his presumed attacker—only to see that it was a formidable stone column. Not only had he almost walked into one of those huge pillars, but actually tried to engage in battle with it! Vandhiyathevan might have laughed out loud—had his hand not been almost exploding with pain, that is.

His fears might have receded a little, but he was not free of them completely.

For he could still hear those terrible footfalls—sometimes they sounded far off; at others, as though they were coming straight for him.

Vandhiyathevan stood rooted to the ground, listening for all he was worth; his eyes swung around to the direction of the footsteps, and stared hard.

Ah—light! There was light, ahead—getting brighter by the moment—approaching him! Smoke accompanied the light as well; someone was arriving with an oil-torch. Was it Nandhini, perhaps, in search of him? That wouldn't be a bad thing—but what if it was someone else? It would be wise to conceal himself; after all, there was no dearth of hiding-places here.

The torch glided nearer; by its light, Vandhiyathevan saw that he was in a vast hall littered with massive stone columns; each had terrifying *bhoodaganams*, other-worldly genie-like creatures carved into them. A staircase seemed to climb towards the hall and curve upwards; the torch-light, he saw, appeared to move up from the base of said stairs—well, Nandhini was certainly out of the question, then; it could not be her.

Perhaps—was this, perhaps the way to the famed dungeons of Thanjai that he had heard so much about? Did it exist under this very palace? Was one of its infamous residents coming up, now?

Perspiration dotted every pore on Vandhiyathevan's skin; so many were the terrifying tales he had heard about the dungeons of this fort-city. He sought a particularly large column and slid behind it at once. As courageous as he was, even warrior Vallavarayan's limbs quaked at that moment.

Three shadowy forms moved up the staircase—and all happened to be human. One carried a spear; another, a torch. The one in the middle however, held nothing in his hands. Terror released its hold on Vandhiyathevan; intense amazement took its place when he caught sight of their faces in the steadily brightening torch-light. For the front-runner was none other than his dearest friend, Kandamaaran!

As for the man in the middle … Vandhiyathevan felt a surreal feeling settle over him, as though he were watching the strangest illusion—for it looked startlingly like Nandhini. The next instant, he saw that this was not true; this was a man; the beautiful prince Madhuranthakar in fact, whom he had barely peeked at, in Kadambur Sambuvaraiyar's palace. The third was unfamiliar—some sort of a servant or soldier, no doubt.

Vallavarayan's mind spun at an astonishing speed; within moments, he had unraveled the mystery of the trio slinking their way along this pitch-black staircase: Pazhuvoor's young queen had entered the fort a day ago; Periya Pazhuvettarayar, the night before. Both had left and returned to the city in full view of the public—but Madhuranthakar was a different matter; his movements could not, of course, be known. Thus, the secret passage—and this was probably the real mystery behind the palace of shadows.

As for Kandamaaran—once he saw Vandhiyathevan off on the banks of the Kollidam, the Kadambur scion had probably joined Periya Pazhuvettarayar, who had promptly co-opted him into his own personal service. One of those duties had likely been escorting Madhuranthaka Thevar through this secret passage—ah! He did remember now that Kandamaaran had made obscure references to a task in Thanjai: "I may find myself there soon enough—I have a commission to execute ..."—doubtless, this was it.

What would his dear friend think now if he, Vandhiyathevan, suddenly appeared in front of him?

The next instant, he changed his mind. Presenting himself to Kandamaaran was the last thing he could do; the way situations were, and considering the oath he had sworn, one of two things was bound to happen: Kandamaaran would be forced to kill him, or Vandhiyathevan would. Either, of course, was out of the question. Why on earth must he allow such complications to arise?

By this time, the secret triad had climbed the stairs and vanished out of sight; the light dimmed steadily, as well. Vandhiyathevan considered following them for a brief moment, and swiftly changed his mind. Doubtless, they were on their way to Chinna Pazhuvettarayar's palace and what was the use, pray, in Vallavarayan returning there? He may as well place his head in a lion's gaping jaw, having barely managed to escape it once, already. There was no point in returning to Nandhini's *latha mandapam* either; Periya Pazhuvettarayar might have arrived there, by now—and danger lurked in every corner. What else could do? As to that, why not climb down these very stairs himself?

To think was to act. Our young warrior stepped gingerly onto the stairs, and began his wary descent.

41

The Vault

Vandhiyathevan descended into the gloomy secret passage, making sure every step was slow, but sure—and most important, that he did not fall headlong into the pitch-black void. The stairs went down for while—then leveled out—more descent—level again. He spread out his hands, hoping to reach the walls, but found none. Suffice it to say that this was a vast passage, indeed. A while later, the steps ascended and then seemed to curve—*appappa*! How much further was he supposed to go? How long was this path anyway, and how long must he stumble along this inky blackness?

Ah—what was this now? The darkness seemed to be retreating a little! Very faint light appeared to meet his vision. Now, where could it possibly come from? Moonlight, perhaps, from somewhere in the roof? Chinks in the windows of this massive hall? Or was there a lamp stashed away in a hidden alcove, light escaping its prison?

No, nothing of the sort! Why, what sort of sorcery was this that met his eyes—? Was such a scene truly unfolding in front of him? Or had his brain finally scrambled itself for good?

The *mandapam* through which Vallavarayan was making his way happened to be built on a massive scale—carved from the very rock, and made into a fantastic underground chamber. This explained why the ceiling was so low that it often brushed his head. And as for the light—it certainly was not errant moon or lamp light, seeping through the roof or chinks in the walls. No, these strange rays came from something that lay in small heaps all along the walls, on the floor, or spread about in an untidy mess. Ah, and what a sight they did make, to be sure!

Pearly beams danced off unearthly objects on the ground: beautifully finished crowns set with gorgeous rubies, emeralds and diamonds; there, on the other side, chains of gold, rich strands of pearls; necklaces gleaming with the fire of precious stones. And oh, that large vessel, now? Good God, it was filled to overflowing with white pearls glowing with understated sheen—like beautiful *Punnai* buds! Large, round, heavy pearls! Gold coins brimmed over that pot in the corner, glinting like the rays of the late evening sun. Here were gold bars—why, this seemed, in truth, to be the precious treasury of Thanjai! Hardly surprising, in that case, that it lay concealed under a gloomy palace right beside the Treasurer Periya Pazhuvettarayar's own mansion. Ah, and here Vandhiyathevan had been led, by God knew what good fortune—for hadn't it been the combined grace of both Goddess Bhagyalakshmi and Adhirshta Devathai, Lady Luck, that had brought him in here? Hadn't he learnt of one of Chozha Nadu's biggest secrets, through no great effort on his own? All that was necessary now, was to divine how to make the best use of it. Forget that—he didn't even want to *leave* this place. All his desires devolved to a pin-point: weaving through these treasures. Hunger and thirst would turn alien to him; he wouldn't even feel the urge to sleep! What lay in front of his dazzled eyes were the fruits of over a hundred invasions by thousands of Chozha soldiers; the result of their sweat and blood. He had heard monumental tales of those famed riches, the *navanidhis* or the nine treasures—and all of them seemed to be here, at his very feet! Why, not even Kuberan, the lord of all worldly wealth could hope to beat a treasure trove such as this! Why on earth would anyone leave it all alone?

Vandhiyathevan wandered among the treasures, powerless to tear himself away. He fingered the delicately fashioned crowns in one corner; took up the necklaces that lay in another—the next instant he dropped them, strode over to the brass pot, plunged his arm into the pearls and watched as they dripped through his fingers, thunderstruck. He ploughed through another pot full of gold coins, gazing at them in wonder.

Then—he caught sight of something else that seemed to glow dully, spread out in an expanse, in a corner, and went to investigate it. It defied explanation at first and Vandhiyathevan bent down, peering at the heap. The next instant, he jumped away, stunned.

Ayyo—good God, it was a skeleton! A human being who had once possessed skin, flesh, blood, nerves, hair, eyes, face and ears—and was now just a pile of bones. And—oh, it seemed to be moving—was it coming to life? Was it jingling and jangling, very like the gold coins he had touched a few scant instants ago? Was it—was it—trying to tell him something? Every hair on Vallavarayan's body prickled with terror. Had he finally, gone quite mad?

Chee!—Of course not. The skeleton was as lifeless as ever; it was just a rat, trying to ease its way out from under it. Here it is, running over my foot. Ah, now that I see, the skeleton is quite still on the ground—but it is true, isn't it, that it's been trying to tell me something? Run away—do not tarry here. For I too, was a human being like you once, a living, breathing man— but I lingered here too long and died, lost in this tomb! I am fated to crumble to dust. Do not repeat my mistake—run, run!

This bag of bones is perfectly right to warn me—should I stay, I shall share its fate. I must leave at once, at once for if I don't, I'm done for!

In vain did Vandhiyathevan try to find a way out—to no purpose. There seemed to be no path of escape; neither could he find the way he had come. No matter where he went in this wretched underground vault, the demon of darkness welcomed him with its gaping maw; the corners were especially terrible. As for peering down—he felt as though he were slipping into hell itself; it seemed to descend forever, into unfathomable darkness. The stairs he had taken must be around here somewhere; all he had to do was run into them.

Vandhiyathevan wandered endlessly through the hall, hoping to stumble against them. On one of his endless circuits, he almost ran into a heap of gold coins. He stared hard at what seemed to be a web of some sort—ah, a spider's web, shiny and delicate, spreading its tendrils over the coins. Almost in spite of himself, it set off a train of thoughts within him.

He had heard elders speak often of the perils of land, women, and gold; of the way they spun complicated webs of allure, waiting for men to commit the gravest sins—much like a spider that awaits its prey. And a fly arrives from nowhere, fascinated by the trap and alights on it—whereat the spider draws in its hapless prey, and swallows it whole. Such were the three great temptations of mankind: they lay in wait so man would get caught in their toils, and once he did, there was no escape whatsoever.

As for Vandhiyathevan—strange indeed, that he had managed to encounter all three the very same day! There had been the young queen of Pazhuvoor, Nandhini, at first, who had tried to ensnare him with her considerable beauty; not satisfied with that, she had tried to overpower him with wily words about the Vaanar dynasty's ancient lands, and held aloft the vain hope that she might procure them for him. And now, here was the vast treasure of Thanjai, enticing him with its gleaming, glittering attractions in a bid to swallow him whole! He had managed to escape with his wits intact from the first two—now he would have to walk away from the third as well.

After all—why *must* he concern himself with vast kingdoms, wealth and the lures of willful women? This great land, with the sky as its marvelous roof was his palace in every way; and wasn't there a famous verse, a unique, fulfilling philosophy that he'd heard from his Thamizh ancestors often: "*Yaadhum Oore; Yaavarum Kelir*"— *All the countries on earth are my home; everyone here is my family*? And in truth, the earth *was* his and its residents, his friends. What could be better than to visit them all, hopping from one kingdom to another of his own sweet will? He would spend his life traveling by rivers that overwhelmed their banks with fresh floods; glory in luxurious forests where trees sprouted new leaves in the spring, and birds of every feather and colour flitted across the heavens; gaze with delight at deer, peacocks, hills with summits that touched the very skies; stand in awe by vast oceans as their waves crashed onto the shores—thus would he live, eating what he could, wherever he found food; sleep where the urge overtook him. Ah, *this*, indeed, was the sort of life worth living! And a wonderfully satisfying one it would be too. Why on earth would anyone want to give up something like this, so easily within his grasp, and choose a life fraught with conspiracies, perils and desires that were more dangerous than death itself? Somehow, he would have to escape this wretched chamber; then the palace of gloom and Thanjavur itself. Never would he allow himself to be caught in their toils again—

—but wait. Was that the sound of a door opening? Were those footsteps again? Ah, would there never be an end to the night's mysterious happenings? Nor the terrors, apparently.

It seemed to Vandhiyathevan that the footfalls, this time, seemed to come from very far away—and from two different directions to boot. He sharpened his ears and listened as keenly as he could; his eyes cleaved through the inky blackness in all four directions, straining to see something, anything. And in a while, he had his reward.

It was as though a *koothu* was playing itself out on a stage set very far away, and those acting their roles were minute figures upon it— from where he stood, Vandhiyathevan watched events unfold at a considerable distance, on what seemed a slightly elevated plane.

A torch appeared from one side of the *koothu* stage; another shifted aside the screen, and appeared from the opposite. The two drew closer and closer to each other. Two dark, hefty figures came to light in one; two more, in the other. One of the latter was tall and majestic while the other, petite and slender. The two parties approached each other evermore, and Vandhiyathevan's eyes almost bulged with the strain of identifying them. By dint of great effort, he was successful: the figures on the left were Kandamaaran and his escort; the ones to the right were Periya Pazhuvettarayar and his young queen, Nandhini Devi.

What would happen, Vandhiyathevan wondered, when these two parties ran into one another? Some sort of catastrophe? Or would they meet in a convivial fashion and leave way for the other? He almost forgot to breathe as suspense gripped him, watching the two groups converge.

Considering the way they stumbled about with some confusion, an unexpected meeting appeared to have been the last thing on their minds; both parties seemed amazed and perplexed at running across each other in the dark—but contrary to Vandhiyathevan's fears, nothing disastrous occurred. Periya Pazhuvettarayar asked something of Kandamaaran, to which that young man gave an answer. Vallavarayan could hear none of their exchange, however. The Pazhuvoor lord made some sort of sign and pointed towards the secret staircase, to which Kandamaaran reciprocated by bowing low with deep reverence, and proceeding towards said stairs. Periya Pazhuvettarayar watched him walk way, and then made a gesture to Kandamaaran's menial, who still held aloft the burning torch. That worthy bowed in turn, accepting the command with his palm over his mouth. He followed Kandamaaran almost at once, while the Pazhuvoor lord and his consort went on their way, to the left.

All these events, almost like something out of a mysterious shadow-tale or a fascinating street-play had happened within the space of a few moments and, Vandhiyathevan guessed, by the steps that led down to the underground chamber. Ah, what a fortuitous coincidence, then, that he hadn't dawdled about by the staircase and had wandered instead, into the chamber itself! What a terrible state of affairs would it have been if he had ended up between these two parties? Thankfully, that possibility had not come to pass and he was safe.

Now what, though? He would still have to find a means of escape. There was no doubt that Kandamaaran was making his way back, having escorted Madhuranthaka Thevar to his residence; he, Vandhiyathevan, had probably veered off his own course and ended up in the treasury. Following his friend now would doubtless lead him to the door that led outside the fort—and once there, he would come up with a ruse to bluster his way out. Why, he could even ask Kandamaaran for assistance or, if the worse came to worst, take him on and his servant in a bout.

Either way, following the Kadambur prince was the best option, now.

The torch seemed to approach the chamber at first. Vandhiyathevan sucked in his breath and stood stock-still. Then, it seemed to move away and by its light, he saw the steps by which he must have descended into the vault. He went down them once again, and climbed up with noiseless feet, making sure he kept the light in his range of vision, taking the greatest care never to alert his friend of his presence. Up and down he went, marveling at the curves and twists in the path, the dead-ends and endless loops that seemed designed to confound anyone—good heavens, no one could hope to follow it in the dark and make it outside, safe and sound! Long live Kandamaaran—but how and where could Vallavarayan ever repay this aid, rendered unbeknownst?

There was no way he could have guessed that an opportunity was about to present itself, in a matter of moments.

The end of the secret passage was in sight, at last; a vast stone wall rose in front of them, at an impressive height. It was almost impossible to suppose that it concealed some sort of entrance and yet—there *must* be one, mustn't there?

Kandamaaran's guide shifts his torch from his right hand to the left, places his free hand on the wall and does something—he seems to twist some sort of a bolt. A cleft appears on the rocky surface; a thin line that grows larger by the moment, rapidly reaching the dimensions of a full grown man. The guard points to it and says something; Kandamaaran gives a reply and places a foot outside the door. The other is still within the fort; his back is now visible.

But ah—what is this? The guard seems to be pulling out a small, curved dagger from his waistband and—good God, he's stabbed Kandamaaran! That wretched bastard—a scoundrel who plunges daggers in unsuspecting backs—!

Vandhiyathevan darted out of his hiding-place and sprang forward. The guard sensed movement, and turned the same instant.

The torch's flickering light fell full, on Vallavarayan's wrathful countenance.

42

The Mark of a True Friend

Vandhiyathevan's first impulse was to save Kandamaaran, somehow—but he retained enough of his wits to know that he would share his friend's fate, should he attempt to do so. No, what he had to accomplish first, was to take care of the villainous guard—he sprang forward and wound his arm around the man's neck. He swatted away the torch with another, which promptly rolled on the ground and began to smoke, its light shrinking. Vandhiyathevan tightened his grip on the guard's neck, gathered all his strength and delivered a mighty push. The guard staggered and fell, his head smashing onto the wall of the secret passage.

He lay as though dead but Vallavarayan, once he had approached the man cautiously and ascertained that he was indeed unconscious, took the precaution of tying up his hands with his *angavasthram*.

All immediate danger at an end within a matter of moments, Vandhiyathevan hastened towards Kandamaaran. His dear friend's body, he found, lay half within the secret passage and half without, the dagger stuck in his back; his spear lay beside as well. Vallavarayan stepped out and dragged clear Kandamaaran's body, picking up the spear; the passage closed at once. The massive walls stood silent, clothed in shadows, guarding their eternal secret from prying eyes.

Judging by the stiff winds that almost blew him away, Vandhiyathevan guessed that he was finally outside the fort. Trees loomed upon the horizon, not to mention the enormous battlements and fort ramparts, which meant that moonlight was meager indeed.

He hoisted Kandamaaran onto his shoulder, scooped up his spear and took a step forward—only to feel the earth slipping away under him, almost carrying him away in a landslide. He stuck the spear in the ground and with considerable effort, halted his downward progress. Then, he craned his neck and peered down.

Amidst the thick shadows thrown by ramparts and trees on the ground could be seen flowing water—and, Vandhiyathevan spied, in the dim light, that it whirled and tumbled forward at great speed. Thank heavens, then, that he hadn't put his foot right into it—or he would have somersaulted straight into disaster! God had, indeed, saved him, but that treacherous guard—ah, what was the point in thinking of him now? Doubtless, he had only carried out his master's instruction: to stab the Kadambur prince in the back and dispose of the body by throwing it into these floods. Had Vandhiyathevan not been inordinately surefooted, both would be tumbling into the water's depths, by now. And even had Vallavarayan managed to regain his footing, Kandamaaran was sure to have gone to a watery grave.

The Vaanar scion had learnt, before this, of the River Vadavaaru that almost hugged the Thanjavur fort walls at one point—well, this must be it, then. And though the river was not supposed to be swollen with floods, it might well have been considerably deep at this point by the fort; who knew? Vandhiyathevan dipped his spear into the waters, testing the depths—and found, to his horror, that even fully submerged, it did not strike the bed. Ah, those wretched, bloody rogues—!

But there was no more time to be lost in reflecting upon these betraying idiots; he and Kandamaaran had to make their escape right away.

Vandhiyathevan stepped forward, taking the greatest care that he did not lose his footing along the river banks; Kandamaaran on his shoulder and his spear gripped tight in his hands. His injured friend groaned and moaned twice or thrice which was, frankly, rather encouraging.

He trudged on for a while, gritting his teeth, until the fort-walls seemed to move away; the forest began to creep in along the banks. Thorns lay aplenty underfoot, which made the going difficult but oh, what was this—a large tree, right in the river! Of great height as well; the river must have scoured its roots and weakened them; it lay almost to half the river's breadth.

Vandhiyathevan climbed onto it and staggered along its length, trying to keep his balance on a trunk that wove a little from one side to another, in the waters; its branches and leaves thrashed helplessly amidst the swirling currents. The wind howled around him as well. He made his way to the end of the tree and stuck his spear into the waters again— thanks be to Lord Murugan! For the waters were not quite so deep here. He stepped off the tree and into the river, treading gingerly, feeling his way across troughs and crests in the bed, making sure he withstood the winds and raging floodwaters through the sheer force of his mind, and perseverance.

His body shuddered helplessly sometimes, with the strain of it; at others, it seemed as though his friend might slip and fall into the river. And yet, Vandhiyathevan braved all ills and finally scrambled onto the shore. He staggered for a while along the banks, trembling in clothes that were drenched to the waist, still hefting a Kandamaaran who was of not inconsiderable height and weight. A little later, the densely clustered trees gave way into a small clearing and he stopped, lowering his precious burden slowly to the ground.

First in the order of things was to take a respite, for the moment—but he wished to know if there was still life in his friend's body. For, what was the purpose in lugging along a corpse? Far better to take that wretched guard's course and throw it into the river—no, no, Kandamaaran was still alive; his chest rose and fell with heaving breaths; a tumultuous pulse thudded in his wrist.

So far, so good—but now what? Removing the dagger was out of the question; blood would gush out and kill him. No, what Kandamaaran needed at once was medicine; his wounds had to be dressed with skill—but these were hardly tasks that could be accomplished by him alone, were they? No, Vandhiyathevan needed assistance, but who else would—

Wait, what about Sendhan Amudhan? His home and garden were on the banks of the River Vadavaaru, weren't they? Bound to be somewhere nearby, surely? Kandamaaran might have a chance of survival if Vandhiyathevan managed to drag them both to Amudhan's home. What did he stand to lose, anyway?

Vandhiyathevan bent towards his friend, prepared to heft him onto his shoulders again and stopped—for Kandamaaran's eyes were open. "Why, Kandamaaraa—you're awake! Do you recognize me?" Delight and amazement suffused his countenance.

"Very well indeed. You're Vallavarayan, of course; how could I forget such an excellent friend? You're the kind that stabs a man in the back, aren't you?"

"*Ayyo!*" The last words lashed at Vallavarayan like a vicious whip. "But I wasn't the one who—" he stopped abruptly, as though remembering something.

"Of course not; all your knife did was caress me like a feather—you bastard! *You* were the reason I hurried down the secret passage at all—I wanted to get hold of you before Pazhuvettarayar's men did—to prevent anyone else capturing and torturing you. I swore that I would find you somehow, and enlist you in Chinna Pazhuvettarayar's Fort Guards Regiment—and here you are, betraying the friend who wished to help you! Is this the mark of true friendship? Have you forgotten all the times we clasped hands, swearing to protect each other? Now you—you've destroyed everything! Ah, how eager I was to tell you of—of the stunning changes that were about to sweep through this Chozha Empire—how I wished to warn you about—but how am I ever to trust anyone again?" Kandamaaran closed his eyes, slipping into oblivion. The effort of such hurried and furious speech had doubtless drained his strength.

"Surely there's no lack of people to trust?" Vandhiyathevan mumbled. "Who on earth would rely on the Pazhuvettarayars, anyway?" For all that, however, tears started in his eyes. He blinked hard and concluded that he had been wise to stay silent, after all. Then, he heaved Kandamaaran upon his shoulder and resumed his journey.

The scent of blooms engulfed him thickly, in the stillness of the night; he had been right to assume that Sendhan Amudhan's home must be nearabouts. And within moments, he did reach the *nandhavanam*— but oh, what a difference between his first visit and this one! Now, that beautifully kept garden looked like the ancient Ashokavanam destroyed by Lord Hanuman in a fury; like the exquisite *madhuvanam* wrecked by the *vaanarams*, the monkey-kind of Ramayana. Ah, it did seem like Periya Pazhuvettarayar's dutiful men had descended here as well, in search of him—and paid their respects in due fashion, heaping destruction. To think of all the trouble to which Sendhan Amudhan and his dear mother had gone, maintaining this wonderful, rich little garden! And now— everything was in rack and ruins.

Abruptly, Vandhiyathevan remembered his own precarious state— and all thoughts of sympathy for the flower garden vanished. What if those wretched spies and security guards lurked about, still? Well, he had no choice but take them on. Thank heavens at least for his horse, though, which stood tied to the tree ... wait, what if this was a trap as well? No matter; there was nothing he could do but relinquish Kandamaaran into the care of these excellent people and fly upon his steed—which would, God willing, halt only in Pazhaiyarai.

Vandhiyathevan tiptoed across the garden, towards the hut. At the entrance, he bent forward and tapped Sendhan Amudhan, who lay fast asleep on the *thinnai*. The boy jerked awake, startled—upon which the warrior laid a swift hand over his mouth. "You're the only one who can help me, *Thambi*," he spoke, in a low voice. "I find myself in terrible difficulties. This is my dear friend, Kadambur Sambuvaraiyar's son Kandamaaran. Someone stabbed him, you see. I saw him on my way out and brought him with me."

"Why, those rogues!" exclaimed Amudhan. "They've stabbed him in the back too, brave warriors!" He paused for a moment. "I shall care for him as much as I can. Several groups of soldiers barged here in search of you and wreaked havoc on our beautiful garden—see, there's almost nothing left of it. Never mind, though; it matters nothing if *you* manage to escape. Thankfully, they've left your horse alone—now get on it and leave!"

"That, *Thambi*, is my intention as well—but oughtn't we to do something about saving my friend's life?"

"Don't you worry about that; my mother knows her way around medicines. She's well-versed in handling wounds such as these." And Sendhan Amudhan tapped gently on the door, twice. It opened at once, and his mother stood in the entrance.

They carried Kandamaaran into the house slowly and laid him in the *koodam*, the hall. Sendhan Amudhan signed to his mother in the gentle light of a hand-held lamp; it seemed that she understood him. She gazed keenly at Kandamaaran; glanced at the dagger in his back and left swiftly, returning with rags and a few medicinal herbs. Then, she looked meaningfully at the two of them.

Sendhan Amudhan gripped the Kadambur prince tight. Vandhiyathevan gathered himself, placed a hand on the dagger sticking out of his friend's back, and pulled it out.

Blood gushed out of the wound. "*Oh*!" Even unconscious, Kandamaaran screamed in agony.

Vandhiyathevan covered his mouth swiftly.

Sendhan Amudhan pressed down on the bleeding wound as hard as he could.

His mother dressed the injury efficiently, with fresh herbs. Kandamaaran groaned pitifully, again.

Footsteps thudded in the distance—men running towards the hut.

"Go—now!" Amudhan admonished. "Quickly!"

Vandhiyathevan picked up the blood-stained dagger and spear, and then hesitated. "*Thambi*—you do believe in me, don't you?"

"I believe in God. And I do like you. But—why do you ask?"

"I require your assistance again. You see, I'm new to these parts, and don't quite know my way around. I wish to reach Pazhaiyarai at once and deliver a message to Kundhavai Devi. Would you be able to guide my way a little?"

At once, Sendhan Amudhan turned to his mother and signed something, to which she signified assent. The lady, it seemed, was not unduly perturbed by the night's happenings. She signed to him, in addition, that she would take care of the injured man as well.

They left together; Thevan on his horse while Sendhan climbed on behind him. Vandhiyathevan set his steed to a quiet trot, careful not attract the slightest attention. A little distance, and he set the horse galloping. The animal tore through the night, carrying its burden.

Five or six soldiers descended upon the hut the instant the steed set off; they banged on the door furiously. Amudhan's mother opened the door, and stood framed by the entrance.

"What was the noise we heard just now?" yelled a soldier.

Amudhan's mother quavered some sort of vague, blubbering response.

"What's the point of asking this deaf mute?" snapped another. "We'd better go in and see for ourselves."

"She's barring our path, isn't she?"

"Where on earth is that flower-boy?"

"Swat away that mute and get into that cottage!"

Amudhan's mother howled something more in her own, unique tongue, and tried to shut the door in the man's face. Four or five of the brawny soldiers pushed themselves through, making it impossible for her to do so. She shrieked something and abruptly, let the door go—upon which two or three lost their balance and practically rolled in through the entrance, falling at her feet. The others trampled over them, in their haste to enter the hut.

"Here he is!" yelled one.

"Finally!" crowed another. "Got himself into our clutches, did he?"

"Grab him before he runs," instructed another. "Tie him up!"

The mute woman blubbered wildly.

"Good God—what's with all the blood?" echoed a soldier.

Amudhan's mother held aloft the lamp and pointed to the injured man in its feeble light. "Beh! Beh!"

"*Adei*—this looks like someone else!"

"Beh—beh!"

"Is this the man who came here last night?"

"Beh—beh!"

"Where's your son?"

"Beh—beh!"

"Quiet, you dumb corpse! *Adei*—look at this one carefully. Does anyone recognize him? Well?"

"Not him."

"Of course it's him!"

"No—never!"

"Beh—beh!"

"Whoever he might be, we must take him to the fort at once. Come, carry him!"

"Beh—Beh—Beh—Beh!"

"Shut up, *saniyane*!"

Four of the brawny men hefted up Kandamaaran. "Beh—Beh—Beh—Beh—Beh—Beh!" bawled the woman, without a pause.

"Wait—are those horse-hooves?"

"Half of you carry this one—the rest, go and see who that is."

"This one isn't going any where. Come, all of you!"

They dropped Kandamaaran, and ran out as one.

Amudhan's mother's unearthly shrieks followed them all the way out. "Behbeh! Behbeh! Behbeh!"

43

PAZHAIYARAI

Our hero Vandhiyathevan is destined to undergo a great many difficulties; fall in and out of a score of perils before he can set foot in Pazhaiyarai—so we request our readers to kindly make an entrance into this fair city, before he does.

Now gaze at it, if you will, from your vantage point on the southern banks of the River Arisilaaru. *Adada*, surely this is more than just a city? Is it not the very embodiment of a beautiful ornament that adorns the Goddess of Thamizh's shapely forehead? Is it not, dear reader, a dazzling pendant, a *netrichutti* set with exquisitely lovely green emeralds, rich, red rubies and dazzling blue sapphires?

Ah, the rivers, streams, ponds and canals that surround this pretty city fairly brim with water; their surfaces filled to overflowing with flowers of every colour. Coconut and *Punnai* trees dot the landscape, the lush greenery offering cool shade. Strands of golden blooms hang from *Konrai* trees in profusion—and amidst nature's prolific creations rise incredible mansions and palaces, their golden towers and temple *gopurams* cleaving through the sky, such is their height.

Appappa! The number of smaller cities that all make up one magnificent metropolis! Here are Nandhipura Vinnagaram, Thiruchathi Muttram, Patteechuram, Arichandhrapuram—these and their temples together form part of Pazhaiyarai, the capital as a whole. Four temples dedicated to Siva Peruman adorn the city in each direction: Vadathali, Keezthali, Metrali and Thenthali. Four settlements meant exclusively for brave soldiers, *veerapuris*, as their reputation says, dot the city as well: Ariyappadai Veedu, Pudhuppadai Veedu, Manappadai Veedu and Pambaippadai Veedu. And in the midst of them all, standing tall, piercing the very heavens with its numerous towers, galleries, pavilions and balconies was the Chozha Royal Palace—but was it just one complex? Certainly not! In the time of Vijayalaya Chozhar, perhaps—but in the intervening years, every Chozha prince, his royal consort and princess had added his or her own dwelling and now, ah, one would need a thousand eyes to just take in the glorious sight of scores of new palaces around the original. Not even ten thousand poets could, with all their considerable talents, hope to describe a fraction of their beauty.

Why, hark at poet Sekkizhar Peruman's divine words on the city, two hundred years later:

> *"Therinmeviya sezhumani veedhigal sirandhu*
> *Paaril neediya perumaiser pathi Pazhaiyarai ... "*

The streets—avenues—people—ah, was there any other city to rival its merits? And if it had been thus in the poet's times, how much more magnificent would it have been during the reign of Sundara Chozhar?

And yet—our first visit to this exquisite capital is not attended quite by the same festive spirit that is described so fulsomely by these divine poets. For we were not so fortunate as to witness the grandeur of this metropolis when it was the principal seat of Emperor Sundara Chozhar, when he ruled from this city, the centre of the Empire.

Once the Chakravarthy, struck by ill-health, left for Thanjai, the many royal visits from foreign territories; kings and princes who paid obeisance and likewise, ambassadors, ministers and commanders, gradually tapered off into almost nothing; similarly absent were the *parivaarams* that invariably formed part of their retinue.

The normally effervescent four padaiveedu settlements looked considerably empty; more than half the soldiers were presently involved in the Eezham war, eager to display the best of Tamil valour to the world. The rest were off fighting in the northern frontiers, or exhibiting martial skills in Madurai. This meant that the settlements were populated by the infirm, women and children, for the most part.

The Velakkara Regiment that had made their home in Mazhavarpadi had uprooted their families and moved to Thanjai as well, which meant that the part of the city that accommodated their residences now sported a vacant look.

Ministers, royal *samanthakars* and officers involved in the everyday working of the government had all shifted to Thanjai as well, their families in tow.

For all the considerable decline in the number of residents, Pazhaiyarai's streets have not lost their pomp and splendour, yet. Its wide avenues well-nigh burst at the seams with people hurrying about their business: temple *sthapathis*, sculptors, devout Saivites, those who sang the divinely beautiful *Thevaram* hymns or *Odhuvaars*; temple officials and servants, tourists from many corners of the land who have journeyed all the way to visit the temples or partake in their celebrations.

Today, in particular, is a day of auspicious festivities, a *thiruvizha*, it would seem. Men, women and children parade in their finest dresses and ornaments. People throng the streets, congregating in certain corners, and in their midst are costumed people, singing and dancing—ah, how interesting! Surely we must know what parts they play? Why, here they are, dressed as Krishna, or Balarama and the Gopalas! Ah, here is a scene where Krishna holds aloft a mammoth mountain and Indra, Lord of the Devas falls at His feet, doesn't he? And over there, amidst another crowd stands Lord Brahma, complete with four heads, paying obeisance to

Krishna—ah, *now* we understand. Today is Sri Jayanthi, divine Kannan's birthday, and that is the reason for this gaiety; these festivities. Not to be outdone by street-theatre displays, there are *uriyadi* sports as well, where pots are tied to poles high up; onlookers try to hit them to much glee, while showered with turmeric-water by the uproarious public. All these in the vicinity of the Nandhipura Vinnagara Temple—but oh, what is this?

> *"Kanden Kanden Kanden*
> *Kannuk kiniyana Kanden!"*

Ah, who sings with such ecstasy, of gazing at the Lord? Where have we heard this voice, before? And indeed—here stands our old friend Azhwarkkadiyaar Nambi in all his Vaishnavite glory. A few have gathered around him already; some listen devoutly, attracted by the verses; other have begun a crude heckling. We fear for these naïve onlookers, wondering how Azhwarkkadiyaar's trusty staff will handle their thick skulls.

But stay—some sort of commotion at the entrance to the Vinnagara Temple. The chariots and palanquins by the side of the street are brought to the massive front-door; several ladies emerge from within the temple, obviously part of the royal family. And indeed—these are the high-born princesses and queens who adorn the many imperial residences of Pazhaiyarai.

At the forefront, leading them all is Sembian Maadevi, renowned through the Chozha Empire as Periya Piratti; princess of the ancient Mazhavaraiyar clan and royal consort of the devout Saivite, Emperor Kandaradhithar. Age might have marked her, and somber attire announce widowhood—but how regal her features; how radiant her countenance! Behind her walks Arinjaya Chozhar's consort, scion of the Vaithumbarayar dynasty, Kalyani. The exquisite loveliness of her finely chiseled features is obvious, despite her advancing years—how much more beautiful must she have been in her youth? Surely there is nothing to wonder at, then, that her son Sundara Chozhar is known universally for his good looks?

Following in her footsteps is another of the Chakravarthy's queens, a princess of the Cheraman clan, Paranthakan Devi.

In their wake arrive maidens, celestial nymphs who appear to have descended upon earth straight from the heavens: Kundhavai Piratti, Vanathi, and princesses of various Thamizh clans, with whom we have been acquainted, before.

Chozha kings have worshipped at the feet of Siva Peruman and Goddess Durgai from the times of Vijayalayar; that did not mean, however, that they abhorred Thirumaal, or other faiths and religions prevalent in the country. Far from form it, in fact, which might explain why all had assembled in full regalia at the Vinnagara Temple—to celebrate Kannan's birthday, no doubt.

It was as Periya Piratti was about to climb into her palanquin, that Azhwarkkadiyaar's song fell upon her ears. Was that, perhaps, why the Vaishnavite sang at the top of his voice? It seemed to have achieved its purpose, though, for Sembian Maadevi immediately called him to her side.

Azhwarkkadiyaar duly obeyed her summons, standing in front of her, head bowed, hands folded.

"Well, Thirumalai? I have not seen you for a while," began Periya Piratti. "Were you on a pilgrimage, perhaps?"

"Indeed, yes, *Thaaye*—I did visit a great many holy sites. Thirupathi, Kanchi, and Veera Narayanapuram to mention just a few. What was more—I heard and saw a great many wondrous things too."

"Our Palace tomorrow—and you may recount your many adventures in detail."

"I'm afraid not, *Amma*. I shall have to leave this very night."

"In that case, you may come this evening."

"Of course, *Thaaye*. Your wish is my command."

The many palanquins and chariots began to roll away, towards the palaces.

Kundhavai Piratti pointed towards the rotund Azhwarkkadiyaar and murmured something to her coterie; the lovely maidens broke into merry peals of laughter. Azhwarkkadiyaar turned in the direction of the mirth, hoping to see its cause.

Princess Kundhavai's exquisite eyes met the Vaishnavite's, conversing in a code obviously known only to them.

Azhwarkkadiyaar bowed a little in her direction—a sign that he had understood her surreptitious message.

Sembian Maadevi's impressive palace lay at the very heart of a sprawling complex of royal residences in Pazhaiyarai; in its principal council chamber, its *sabha mandapam*, sat the gracious queen, on a gold throne studded with nine precious gems. Following the devout path of religious saints such as Karaikkal Ammaiyar and Thilakavathiyaar, she seemed the very epitome of austerity, draped in spare white silk, her features adorned with sacred ash and *rudraksha* necklaces, but no other ornaments. Surrounded by almost limitless wealth—*the Ashta Aiswaryam*, or the eight great riches—she proved, to those who saw her, that it was possible to live the life of an ascetic entirely devoted to God, even amongst dazzling treasures. No bejeweled crown graced her head; nor any of the jewellery associated with royalty—and yet, her regal presence, radiant countenance, and an undeniable majesty announced: here was a queen among queens, a woman born to rule, who had married into royalty and held all in her sway. Gazing at her, it was easy to understand why every member of the Chozha royal family fell in with her every wish, held her in such great esteem, and never gainsaid her, at any time.

For all that, however—it seemed that something had happened to mar the serenity that surrounded her; the aura of piety seemed to have suffered a blemish. Her son, the pious Siva devotee, Madhuranthaka Thevar had gone against his mother's wishes, nay, her express command, and married into the Pazhuvettarayar clan. Rumours had floated in, moreover, that he aspired to the Chozha throne—all these, not unnaturally, had served to ruffle Sembian Maadevi's composure a little.

It was the norm for Periya Piratti's *sabha mandapam* and palace courtyard to overflow with enthusiastic temple sculptors, and echo with the hymns of *Thevaram* singers who made eager journeys to meet their royal patron. Devout Saivites and Thamizh poets often traveled great distances to display their knowledge, and receive appropriate gifts in return. No less were the crowds of priests marching in with offerings, once their daily worship at the temples was done.

That day, it was the turn of sculptors and devotees from towns such as Thirumudhukundram (Vridhaachalam), Then Kurangaduthurai and Thirumazhapaadi to petition the queen about commencing re-construction of their respective temples in stone; many carried elaborate sketches and toy temples that displayed the modifications, schemes, and plans each had visualized.

Having promised to duly begin the *thiruppani*, the sacred work on the first two temples, Periya Piratti turned to the rest. "Mazhapaadi?" she queried. "Which would that be?"

"The one where our beloved Siva Peruman asked for Sundaramurthy Nayanar Himself, gracious lady," supplied the town's resident. "It is here that the Lord holds court!"

"Pray, what is this incident you speak of?" inquired the Mazhavarayar princess.

"You see, *Amma*, Sundaramurthy Nayanar, great Saivite that he was, went on a great many pilgrimages. On one such journey, a river barred his path," began the man from Mazhapaadi. "But just as he was about to ford it, a voice suddenly rang out: "Sundaram! Have you forgotten me?" Sundaramurthy stopped, startled—and realized that it belonged to none other than Siva Peruman Himself, who had claimed him, heart and soul. He turned to his disciples and asked. "Is there a temple for my lord, hereabouts?" to which they replied. "Yes, *Swami*—the temple of Mazhapaadi is concealed behind those *konrai* trees."

"At once, Sundaramurthy made his way to the *konrai* trees, flourishing with fragrant blossoms—and in their midst, nestling among the foliage was a little Siva shrine. Sundaramurthy worshipped at this temple, and sang the most beautiful verses in its honour. He marveled at the grace and compassion of the Lord who, just as He had claimed him once, had called out to Him again, in Mazhapaadi. "*Swami*, what sort of a question *is* this?" he wept, intensely moved. "How could I ever forget You? And if

I ever did, whom could I ever worship, in Your place?" He set these, his heart's outpourings in the following beautiful verses:

"Ponnar Meniyane!
Pulitholai Araikkasaithu
Minnaar Senjadai Mel
Milirkonrai aninthavane!
Manne, Maamaniye,
Mazhapaadiyul maanikkame!
Anne unnaiyallal
Ini yaarai ninaikkene?"

"Great Mother—that shrine, the one to which Sundaramurthy sang such moving verses, still stands among those *konrai* trees, small and insignificant. It is this temple that we seek to rebuild."

"So be it," assented Sembian Maadevi.

Azhwarkkadiyaar had arrived with a companion, by this time. Both stood at a little distance, watchful spectators of the abovementioned events, their senses on high alert.

44

"THIS IS ALL HER DOING!"

A sculptor stepped forward at this point, a descendent of the artisans who had once worked in Maamallapuram, turning it from a port into a fantasy world of indescribable sculptural beauty. He had fashioned a tiny model for the stone re-construction, the *katrali* work to be done on existing temples, and poured into it every ounce of the considerable imagination he possessed. This, he now displayed, to the queen.

Periya Piratti gave her fulsome admiration, even going to so far as to call the model to the attention of Azhwarkkadiyaan's companion. "Well, *Battar*? Do you not see how beautiful this structure is? Indeed, my heart yearns to shape Thamizhagam's most significant Siva temples in this new, exquisitely lovely fashion."

"Surely there can be no obstacle to carrying out any of your wishes, *Thaaye*?" concurred Eesana Siva Battar. "We could construct Siva *sthalams* that have the honour of a *Thevaram* hymn this way—the moment people set eyes on it, they shall know that it is a "*Paadal Petra Sthalam*," that it has been sung by our great saints."

"Indeed, yes! We must make an effort to gather all the verses by Appar, Gnana Sambandar and Sundaramurthy; every temple purified by their presence, every *aalayam* that has had the signal honour, the divine good fortune of having a hymn dedicated to them, must cleave the very sky with magnificent *gopurams*, re-built with stone that will last centuries. I have harboured these two ambitions close to my heart for so very long—but I am plagued by doubts that they may never be. Had my lord and master not journeyed to the west and ascended to the feet of God—had he lived a little longer, all my desires might have been fulfilled ..."

"But—nothing has occurred to suggest otherwise, has it, *Thaaye*? Has not the Chakravarthy issued an edict, after all, that every single one of your commands must be carried out in an instant? Both his sons have always made it clear that they will divine your heart's deepest desires and accomplish them, whatever they might be, even before you have given expression to them; when such is the case—"

"—perhaps, but my heart is not at peace these days. Strange things I hear too—apparently, some people are concerned that I am draining the royal treasuries with my penchant for stone renovations. *Why does Siva Peruman need so many temples*, they ask, I am told. It does not worry me that strangers speak so; but to hear that the Prince in Kanchi might harbour the same sentiments—"

"*Thaaye*," Even as Periya Piratti recounted her feelings, Azhwarkkadiyaan stepped forward. "This servant is one among that number, I must confess."

The queen gazed at him with considerable surprise; the others stared, obviously startled and not a little perturbed at his presumption.

"My soul burns, *Amma*!" continued Azhwarkkadiyaan in a tone that fairly exploded with sparks of fury. "How can anyone stomach this injustice? And how can you, held to be the very Goddess of *Dharma*, ever countenance such a grievous wrong?"

"Ignore my brother's coarse words, Your Highness," soothed Eesana

Siva Battar, who stood by Thirumalaiyappan. "He is often prone to such fits of fury, I am afraid. Please, forgive him."

Religion, in those days was a vastly different affair from what it is in the present: Saivism and Vaishnavism were yet to undergo segregation. Devout followers of Vishnu co-existed with fierce Saivites, often in the same family. One priest was quite likely to perform worship and rituals at both a Siva Temple and Thirumaal's holy abode; Eesana Siva Battar was one such enlightened, broad-minded soul. Thirumalaiyappan happened to be his brother once removed; both cherished deep affection for each other, despite their differences—which explained why Battar craved pardon for his brother's transgression.

"Peace, Thirumalai, and speak calmly," smiled the Queen. "What is all this talk of injustice now?"

"Just this, Your Highness—ah, the number of temples, *gopurams* and magnificent complexes for a God clothed like a phantom; who carries a skull and begs alms for offerings! How many reconstructions and model temples! And yet, there is barely a one for Vishnu Murthy, who guards all the worlds!" lamented Thirumalaiyappan. "Not even a stone construction of an old, existing temple?"

"*Amma*, it is entirely natural that temples nestled in massive complexes, magnificent arenas and *ambalams*, beautifully carved chambers and golden roofs be built to house the Peruman who performs a glorious cosmic dance to cherish and nurture numerous worlds. As for Thirumaal, what does He do but sleep endlessly? Surely all He requires is a tiny room, preferably dark, without even a lamp?" queried the Battar. "Why build enormous temples furbished with delicate alcoves and divine sculptures?"

"The One who sleeps endlessly as you deride him, *Anna*, is the one who guards the world," retorted Azhwarkkadiyaan. "He who pressed Mahabali into the nether lands with his foot!"

"And yet, this Perumal who measured the three worlds, as you exalt, is the one who went digging through the earth to seek our Siva Peruman's divine lotus-feet in a vain bid to find them—which He could not, if you

remember, try as He might, descending into the very Pathaala Logam!"
quipped Eesana Siva Battar.

"With a frame as large as that all that, why does your Sivan require a
temple, I ask you?' barked Azhwarkkadiyaan. "Surely the temple would
collapse into ruins should He ever attempt to enter it?"

"Cease your quarrel, both of you," laughed the Mazhavarayar princess.
"Thirumalai, what *is* all this talk about no temples for Thirumaal? Who
said any such thing? Why could you not make a courteous request for the
Vinnagara temple you wish to see rebuilt?"

"*Ammani*—recently, I had the opportunity to visit the sacred Veera
Narayanapuram Vinnagaram, named after your illustrious father-in-
law, the Emperor who ruled the Three Worlds, the noble Paranthaka
Chakravarthy; it is here that Thirumaal guards the massive Veera
Narayana Lake, massive as an ocean, without a moment's respite during
either day or night. It was here that I noticed, much to my dismay, that
the great Lord's temple walls, built with brick and mortar, were beginning
to crumble. Such can only bode ill for the hundreds of residents of
the region, gracious lady—for don't we all know that the lake will be
destroyed, should the temple walls fall? Pray rebuild the Vinnagaram
with stone, I beseech you!"

"Very well; so be it," promised the gracious Chozha queen. "You shall
tell me more—but now, it is time for our visitors to leave."

Eesana Siva Battar and others duly took the hint and dispersed.

The next instant, Sembian Maadevi lowered her voice. "Thirumalai,
your pilgrimage—what were the holy sites you visited? What were the
things you heard? Reveal all to me, please, in detail. I know you have
something of grave import; was that not why you interrupted me, just
now?"

"News of enormous consequence, yes, and I would have awaited
your pleasure before revealing them—but Your Highness began to speak
of the Kanchi Prince, and I deemed it far more necessary to halt that
thread of thought. Who amongst those here were genuine devotees, and
who, merely spies? We know nothing of them, after all. Strange events

are afoot all over the country; the blade of betrayal might cleave us at any moment, from anyone," warned Thirumalaiyappan. "It behooves us to be extremely wary."

"Indeed—and it is even worse that members of the same family, bound by flesh and blood are now in the appalling position of suspecting one another," sighed the Periya Piratti. "When I think of Aditha Karikalan himself—ah, how loyal he was? Why, he cherished such love and respect for me, a hundred times more than what he felt for his own mother—but even *he* doubts my intentions, now. Ah, Thirumalai, how I wish I had left this dreadful world with my lord! But he bid me stay—he would not let me leave—and delivered a great many responsibilities into my hands as well," she mourned. "What an unfortunate creature I am!"

"Your noble husband, *Amma*, was a saint who foresaw the past, present and future. Was he not like the very incarnation of the illustrious King Janakar, ruling the Chozha Empire in this wretched Kali Yugam? These lands are fortunate, gracious lady, that he bid you remain after his passing—for it is now *your* sacred responsibility to save the Chozha Empire from destroying itself through civil unrest; prevent a lineage that spans a thousand years from butchering its own sons and brothers. And that is a task only *you* can accomplish!"

"Not quite, Thirumalai. My own son does not heed my words; how may I expect anyone else to do so, then? But stay, you mentioned something about spies, did you not? Who could spy on me—and why? Perhaps you suspect Aditha Karikalan of such deeds?" queried that pious lady, steeped in devotion to Siva Peruman. "Ah, does he now distrust me so much?"

"I'm afraid I heard his words with my own two ears, Amma—else, I wouldn't have dared to believe that Prince Aditha Karikalar entertained even the slightest suspicion of you—"

"Did you? And what was it that you heard, Thirumalai?"

"They were seated by one of Maamallapuram's stone temples, and that was where I heard them speak—"

"Whom do you mean by *they*?"

"One was Prince Aditha Karikalar; Thirukkovilur Malayaman was the second, and the third happened to be Parthibendran, of the Pallavas. They were deep in conversation; I managed to overhear them as I lay hidden in a dark stone shrine. Malayaman and Parthibendran were furious; they spoke in enraged tones of the Pazhuvettarayar brothers concocting a conspiracy with your son Madhuranthaka Thevar, and imprisoning the Emperor. Malayaman declared that you must have been a part of such an evil plot; the others assented. Parthibendran put forward the plan that they must all march towards Thanjavur and free the Emperor; the others assented to this as well—but the Prince wished to make one last attempt to bring his father to Kanchi, without recourse to bloodshed. That was when they decided unanimously on a course of action: send an *olai* to the Chakravarthy through a trusted messenger. From what I could gather, this envoy was no ordinary man—a warrior of rare resourcefulness, great intelligence and courage; one who was capable of both delivering messages *and* spying. I tried to engage him in conversation once, and believe me when I say, *Amma*, that he slipped away from every one of my verbal traps like an eel. Cunning as he was, he tried to wring information out from me, while not revealing anything in return. Even the Kudandhai astrologer tried his hand at extricating something from him, to no success. I've heard, through reliable sources, that he actually did manage to seek an audience with the Emperor and deliver the *olai* …"

"And then? What was the Chakravarthy's answer?"

"Apparently a reply was promised the next day—but the Pazhuvettarayars appear to have grown extremely suspicious of the messenger. Somehow, he managed to escape all their nets, their brawny soldiers, and fled the city overnight!"

"In that case, an extremely resourceful man, no doubt. And what about you? Once you left Kanchi—"

"My first intention was to arrive straight here. I stopped at the Veera Narayanapuram Vinnagaram, however, to worship at the feet of Thirumaal—where, by the grace of the Lord, I practically stumbled upon an immense secret …"

"*Another* one?"

"Indeed, *Thaaye*. You see, the Sambuvaraiyars hosted a very grand banquet at the Kadambur palace that very night and what was more, Periya Pazhuvettarayar was the guest of honour. Not to mention the fact that the Ilaiya Rani's palanquin was a part of his retinue, as well."

"This is all *her* doing, Thirumalai—this terrible calamity that stares Chozha Nadu in the face, it is the work of that young woman! Were you able to meet and speak with her?"

"That, *Amma*, is precisely what I *couldn't* do. Ah, the years I spent, raising that vicious snake as my own sister, acting upon your orders—the lands I wandered, gathering rare Prabandha *pasurams*, beautiful hymns and verses that I taught her with such care! My soul burns when I think of what she is; she refuses to even see me, now that she has become Pazhuvettarayar's queen—"

"I am afraid your sorrow serves no purpose, Thirumalai—for such is this world, and its people. We plan a great many things but in the end, well … go on. What happened in Kadambur, next?"

"I trudged there, certain that it was Nandhini in the palanquin and revolving various ways and means I could either meet, or send an *olai* to warn her, at the very least. I braved the greatest peril as I scouted around the towering fort walls, and found a way to clamber into the palace grounds—and that was when I stumbled upon a truly great mystery, a secret that turned my world upside down—"

"You, Thirumalai, are easily the most aggravating man I have ever known. Always, always you begin your tales this way and rouse us to fever-pitch, but never do you reveal a single detail! What *was* this precious mystery, pray?"

"Forgive me, *Thaaye*—my natural hesitation in even speaking of such things made me reticent. We have all supposed, thus far, that Periya Pazhuvettarayar squires his young queen around, wherever he goes—but that's not true at all. For it is not the Ilaiya Rani who travels in that closed palanquin—"

"No? If it isn't the Ilaiya Rani, who else could it be? Another woman? Is there no end to that old man's lust?"

"It—it wasn't a woman at all, *Thaaye*."

"Not a woman? But what sort of man travels in a closed palanquin?"

"Forgive me, *Amma*—but it was none other than your beloved son, Madhuranthaka Thevar."

Sembian Maadevi sat still for a few moments, startled and shocked beyond measure.

"Dear God," she murmured, to herself, finally. "Do I truly deserve such a cruel punishment for my crime?"

Later, Azhwarkkadiyaan recounted the secret meeting that had taken place in Kadambur Sambuvaraiyar's palace that night; the speeches made, and the conspiracy hatched.

It is impossible to describe Periya Piratti's desolation and misery, as the narrative progressed. "*Ayyo*, was it for *this* that I raised my son a pious man, devoted to Siva Peruman? Must this be my reward?" she lamented. "Must you be the reason the magnificent Chozha Empire falls to rack and ruin? Must *you* be the cause of such infamy, the reason this ancient dynasty reaps such misfortune?"

When she spoke, moments later, she had managed to compose herself. "Visit me once more, before you leave, Thirumalai. I must think things through—and consult with Kundhavai as well, about preventing this disaster, somehow."

"Far be it from me to suggest this, *Amma*—but you would do well to preserve your own counsel, regarding these matters."

"Surely you do not suspect even her motives?"

"It is only natural to do so. Isn't she, after all, Aditha Karikalar's beloved sister?"

"What of it? Were you to tell me now, Thirumalai, that the sun rose in the west and set in the east, I might believe you; my mind might even be swayed by your forceful arguments that Thirumaal is the greater God and Siva Peruman is naught—but not a word will I believe, against

Kundhavai. The palace midwife placed her in my arms the very instant she was born; I have raised her ever since, with the greatest care and affection—even more, perhaps, than my own daughter, had I borne one. She, for her part, returns my love with all her heart; the dear girl considers me her parent and her respect for me cannot be denied—"

"Permit me to ask you a question, *Amma*: did Princess Kundhavai ever mention to you the fact that she visited the astrologer of Kudandhai?"

"No. What of it?"

"She did not recount to you then, of a certain young man she met there, of Vaanar descent; nor that she ran into him once more, on the banks of Arisilaaru?"

"She did not. But Thirumalai—these questions seem irrelevant. What is their purpose?"

"That the princess harbours a secret not known even to you, *Amma*. That young man, the Vaanar warrior, happens to be Aditha Karikalar's messenger I warned you about—in fact, it wouldn't be amiss to call him a spy."

"It matters not the least, Thirumalai. Even if, as you, say Kundhavai has her secrets, and does not trust me with them—I have no doubt that she has her reasons. I may as well give up my life, rather than doubt her!" announced the illustrious Kandaradhithar's royal consort.

"*Ayyayo*! Pray do not even conceive of such an idea, Amma," remonstrated Azhwarkkadiyaan. "It may be that your trust isn't misplaced—indeed, I hope it's so. Be that as it may, the Princess has expressed a desire to meet me; I shall inform her that *you* wish to meet her, as well."

ॐ

45

THE RUNAWAY SPY

Two thousand years ago, the Chozha king Karikal Peruvalathan raised the banks on either side of the Kaveri; they remained in excellent repair and held the river in check for years. Then, for a period, the Chozha reign's brilliance dimmed; their power diminished; others who had lain in wait for just such a circumstance such as the Pandiyas, the Pallavas, Kalappalas and Vaanars rose to prominence. The Kaveri, stumbling without her *kaavalan*, her king, began to break her banks, shifting without direction and overwhelming the lands.

There were, of course, occasions when she did more than just wash over fields; sometimes, Ponni changed path altogether. And then, the river's course often shifted drastically: Old Kaveri became the New Kaveri, and the reverse was true as well. So radically did her route change that dry beds often transformed into *nansei* or rich, fertile lands while depressions were altered into lakes, waves lapping greedily at the shores.

One such lay to the south of Pazhaiyarai's many Chozha dwellings, and its proximity to the palaces made it one of their chief adornments.

Originally the result of Kaveri's periodical change of course, Chozha kings had deepened the natural depression, widening its banks and making sure it always brimmed with water. In addition to beauty, there was another advantage: the artificial lake acted as a natural barrier, an immense protection against outsiders encroaching upon the many royal residences along its banks, particularly *anthappurams*. No one could cross unless by ferry, and even this was a privilege accorded only to those on familiar terms with royalty.

Many were the beautiful *uthiyaanavanams* or royal gardens that lined the banks of the pretty lagoon; many, the royal ladies who promenaded along their pretty paths, admiring the greenery without fear of being spied on. Here, they could discard their inhibitions, forget royal protocol and dance like peacocks, or lift their voices in song like nightingales. They could descend into the water and swim in its cool depths, or ply boats and entertain themselves with playful games.

It was considered the norm, when a king embraced death and another ascended the throne, for the new ruler to build a palace for himself, while the queens and offspring of the departed king continued to dwell in existing abodes.

Of all the royal palaces in Pazhaiyarai, next to Sembian Maadevi's splendid edifice, it was Princess Kundhavai's royal residence that rose to meet the heavens, awing subjects with its magnificence and exquisite beauty. Had it not, after all, been Emperor Sundara Chozhar's seat once? And now that the Chakravarthy had moved to Thanjai, his daughter reigned supreme in his place.

Of all the royal gardens that dotted the landscape, Princess Kundhavai's *uthiyaanavanam* was, not surprisingly, the most beautiful. Luxurious banyan trees grew along the many paths, their numerous vines anchored to the ground; tiny bushes found a place, as well. Flowering creepers wound fragrant tendrils around sturdy tree trunks that curved in search of sunlight while cozy little arbours, covered with said creepers made perfect niches to enjoy the landscape.

Kundhavai and her coterie of friends spent most evenings in these luxurious gardens. Sometimes they whiled hours together, laughing as they traded choice pieces of gossip. At others, they separated into little cliques of two or three, sharing secrets amongst themselves.

Of late, though, it had become the norm for Kundhavai and Vanathi to wander into the gardens all by themselves. One such day found them both in conversation under a shady banyan tree, swinging together upon a creeper tied to one of its branches. The tinkling laughter of women vied with the gentle, delighted notes of bird-song that fell from the trees around them.

The two princesses, however, saw no reason to laugh; neither did they seem to relish the mirth of others in the vicinity. As to the question of whether they were sunk fathoms deep in talk—well, that was not true, either.

A woman's voice rose in song from an arbour nearby. It was Kannan's birthday, after all—and so she sang, naturally, about the blue-tinged God.

The moon showers its gentle rays upon the earth, one night. The melodious notes of Kannan's flute waft through the air, falling upon the ears of a young woman. Her heart is lost to Him, and His musical notes wound her. Wrung by despair, she sings her deep unhappiness—and a parrot, in a tree nearby, tries to offer consolation:

Woman:

Who is this lout, that plays a flute?
Heartless, this painful moonlit night?
Alone am I, a maiden, yet no mate
Cruel, cruel, to thus scorn my plight!

Parrot:

He plays upon his flute, his notes so true
That the earth and skies may dance in bliss
Do they burn, my doe, pierce and taunt?
Such strange whims—pray, what is amiss?

Woman:

Welcome, welcome, my little bud—

> *Let me garland you, with pretty Punnai blooms,*
> *For are you not here, as my spirit wilts*
> *To console my heart; my soul, to soothe?*

Parrot:

> *In truth I come from afar, fair maiden,*
> *To speak of Kannan, who wanders lovelorn,*
> *In despair he sank, as you left his side,*
> *Sweet butter now sours, once love was born!*

Kundhavai shook her head, seemingly in despair, having listened to the latter part of the song carefully. "A precious God our wonderful Thamizhagam has been saddled with," she remarked, once the verses came to an end. "Plays upon his flute; gobbles butter by the pot and spends his time romping with women! How on earth is anything worthwhile supposed to get done, pray?"

No reply was forthcoming from her companion, which prompted Kundhavai to turn to her. "Well, Vanathi? Why this silence? Surely Kannan's beautiful flute hasn't struck you dumb as well?"

"*Akka*? Were you speaking to me?" blinked Vanathi. "What was it that you asked?"

"What was it that I—good heavens, my girl, where have your wits gone begging?"

"Nowhere, *Akka*. They've been here, with you."

"Why, you little imp. Playing off your pretty tricks on me, are you? Your heart isn't here at all, my child—shall I tell you where exactly it *is*?"

"If you're so certain, why not?"

"And why wouldn't I be? Isn't it on the battlefields of Eezham? Fluttering around my young brother, that innocent young boy, scheming with ways to snare him with your spells?"

"You *are* half-right, *Akka*—my heart does escape to Eezham often, I admit. Not to ensnare him with my spells, though. All I can think about is how horrifying the battle must be; how terrible his living conditions, and—*how* he must suffer, the wounds his body might have sustained—

where and how does he eat and sleep and oh! These are all I can think about. My mind revolves endlessly around his afflictions in war—while I lie here on soft cushions, dining off silver plates on fine food, dressed in silks and gold! I can barely stand it, *Akka*. If I had wings I would fly to Ilankai this very instant—!"

"And do what? Be even more of a nuisance, I suppose?"

"Never. I shall emulate the ladies from our epics, Subadhra and Sathyabhama—just as they drove chariots for their lords Archunan and Krishnan, so shall I, for mine. And when his foes fire their treacherous arrows at him, I shall intervene and bear them upon my heart—"

"All of which courageous deeds he shall just stand by and watch, I suppose?"

"Well—well, if such things aren't quite to his taste, then I shall await his return, in camp. I shall anoint his wounds with rejuvenating salves and unguents; spread soft mattresses for him to rest upon; prepare the finest meals I can, to tempt his palate. I shall play upon my *veena* to soothe his bodily pain, and sing, lulling him to sleep with my music ..."

"None of this is ever likely to happen, Vanathi. You may as well reconcile yourself to it. Chozha men do not let their women accompany them to battlefields, ever."

"Why not, *Akka*?"

"Because, my dear, they fear us women, far more than wounds!"

"But why? What could women possibly do, to them?"

"Nothing, of course—but what if our fearsome foes catch sight of your exquisite beauty, fall at your feet and surrender in hordes? Our men wouldn't have a chance to display their valour, would they? Chozhas don't ever wish to be known as a tribe that lets their women win wars for them."

"*Do* such things happen, *Akka*? Truly? Are foes quite so silly as to surrender at the sight of a pretty woman?"

"Well, why not? Vanathi, my girl—remember that young warrior we saw at the Kudandhai astrologer's home and later, on the banks of the Arisilaaru?"

"Yes. What of him?"

"The way he stood upon the threshold, as though drugged, at the very sight of us? Do you remember that as well?"

"Indeed I do—but I beg to differ about his inebriated state at the sight of *us*, *Akka*. If memory serves me right, it was your exquisite face that made him quite so giddy; he didn't even spare a glance for the others."

"You've certainly learnt to spin fabulous tales, Vanathi. This isn't a joke at my expense, is it?"

"No, never. *Akka*—I wish to ask you something. Will you promise to answer me truthfully?"

"Let's hear this wonderful question of yours first, shall we?"

"Why were you thinking of that young warrior, just now?"

"Why, you brat! And why shouldn't I, pray?"

"Do, by all means—I never took you to task about that, did I? It's entirely natural, in fact, that you should. I've been worried about him, myself. About what might have befallen him, you see."

"You have? Why would that be *your* concern?"

"No? But if we happen to meet someone, and think of him often— wouldn't it be natural to wonder what became of him?"

"There's nothing even remotely natural about *that*. And we oughtn't to let our wits wander in such chaotic fashion either; we must rein in our hearts—hark, Vanathi! There's the sound of a *parai*—a public announcement! What does the voice say? Listen carefully, will you?"

Indeed—a *parai* thudded loudly at a distance in the streets, interspersed with human shouts. A little attention to the voice, and ah, this is what it announced:

"An enemy spy entered the fort of Thanjavur with a counterfeit signet ring, learnt royal secrets and has made his escape. Furthermore, this spy has caused grievous bodily harm to two men as well, in his desperate bid for freedom. A young man, well built, with the wits and sly tricks of the *asura* Indrajith himself, he is named Vallavarayan Vandhiyathevan. Those who grant him refuge will be sentenced to death. Those who apprehend him and turn him over to the authorities will receive a reward of a thousand gold coins. Announced, hereby, as per the supreme authority of the Thanjai Fort Commander, Pazhuvettarayar Kalanthaka Kantar!" The *parai* pounded *Dum! Dum! Dadum!* in accompaniment.

Kundhavai's slender frame trembled, for some reason.

"Devi?" A maid ran up, at that moment. "A Vaishnavite by name Azhwarkkadiyaan seeks an audience with you. A very urgent matter, he says."

"I shall be there in a moment." Kundhavai slipped off the creeper-swing and hurried away.

46

THE MASSES MURMUR

Azhwarkkadiyaan's journey from Periya Piratti Sembian Maadevi's palace to Princess Kundhavai's royal residence took him through the streets of Pazhaiyarai, and what he saw as he wove his way through the crowds, filled him with delight. Today happened to be Kannan's birthday—ah, how enthusiastic were this city's residents, as they indulged in celebration and worship. There was no doubt, no doubt at all, that Vaishnavism was here to stay in Chozha Nadu, and would only grow from strength to strength. As to Saivism's own popularity, it would have been surprising in the extreme if it hadn't occupied pride of place here: Chozha kings had been establishing Siva temples around the country most diligently, in the last hundred years or so; the *Thevaram* songs of Saivism's three greatest saints were sung there often, ensuring, thus, that the campaign reached the masses; elaborate chariot festivals were held as well, resulting in a good deal of celebration. All this, however, had not sounded the death knell for Thirumaal or his fame—for Kannan, said to be the ninth and most complete incarnation of Vishnu Murthy had so captured popular imagination; his many adventures and divine *leelai*, indeed his life, played out in Mathura, Gokulam and Brindavanam had made sure that he stayed in their hearts forever. The Bhagavada groups that abounded here; the many street-plays and the sheer number of artists intent on portraying Kannan's life—*Ammamma*! Impossible indeed, to describe them all, for they seemed to have multiplied since the last time we visited this fair city. The crowds they collected at every corner, their thunderous applause and shouts of approval added to the festive air and indeed, more artists and actors were trickling in steadily from the many villages surrounding the city, in the hopes of just such audiences.

One such street-play group seemed to have arrived just that instant, complete with a contingent that consisted of Vasudevar, Devaki, Krishnan, Balaraman and Kamsan; their songs, dance and witty dialogues seemed to be far superior to that of others, thereby attracting more attention than the rest, Azhwarkkadiyaan's included.

Kamsan and Krishnan were engaged in a verbal battle at the moment and the Vaishnavite paused to watch the fascinating performance. Played by a young boy, Kannan's many accusations against his ruthless uncle were listed with an endearing lisp. "Come and fight me!" the child cried out, finally—and Kamsan responded with appropriate outrage.

"*Adei*, you cunning little rogue, Krishna!" he yelled with a truly creditable assumption of fury, voice ringing out like a peal of thunder. "Playing off your pretty little tricks on me, are you? Ha— none of them will work! I shall kill you now, you and your precious brother Balaraman and your father Vasudevar. And see that Vaishnavite over, there, covered with sacred *naamam* signs applied with sandalwood paste? I'm going to throttle *him* as well!"

The crowd gathered around the troupe glanced at our Azhwarkkadiyaan, and began to laugh. The actors donning the costumes of Krishnan and Balaraman darted looks at him as well. Quite a few members of the audience sidled up to the Vaishnavite and began to cackle at him. "Kek-kek-kek!"

A wave of anger slammed into Thirumalai at the blatant heckling; he wanted, more than anything, to swing his staff at these idiots and deliver a few choice blows—especially that ridiculous Kamsan. But what was the point in trying to bash his head? None of his trusty blows would have the least effect; Kamsan, in keeping with his costume, wore a wooden mask with a horrifying moustache, and terrible teeth painted in a variety of garish colours, over his face. All in all, using a staff on the people hereabouts wouldn't exactly be appropriate at this time. Thirumalai shook his head and regretfully, slipped away from the crowd. The man who played Kamsan, though—*how* he had yelled his dialogues! Now, where exactly had Azhwarkkadiyaan heard that voice? For he *had* heard it—of that, he was sure. The question was, where? And to whom did it belong?

Mulling over these questions as he walked along the streets, Azhwarkkadiyaan noticed something; a gradual change in the people he was passing by. They appeared to have lost their recent enthusiasm—ah, why were they dispersing so quickly? What had caused this sea-change? Even the songs, dance and the melodious music had ground to a halt—instead, everyone had gathered into little cliques and appeared to be murmuring furtively amongst themselves. What were their secrets? And why were they walking away so rapidly, discussion at an end?

Dadaal! Dadaal!—Really, why were doors being banged shut in such quick succession?

The reason was revealed in just a few moments: the *parai* announcement about a runaway spy that had set even Princess Kundhavai trembling.

So depressing was this unexpected proclamation that it quenched the city's festive spirit at once. People looked pinched and drawn, staring suspiciously at those who walked past them all alone, or even someone with whom they claimed no acquaintanceship. Azhwarkkadiyaan himself was subject to a good many doubtful stares by passers-by, who hurried away the moment he caught their eyes.

Thirumalaiyappan guessed the reason behind this reaction, more or less; his quick brain put together the subject discussed by these little, secretive cliques he stumbled upon, by the roadside. Random words that fell upon his sharp ears only served to confirm his suspicions.

For, all talk seemed to revolve around the wretched Pazhuvettarayars and their tyrannical rule. But then—wasn't it entirely natural for the people of the city and residents of nearby villages to feel thus? After all, hadn't the brothers been the means of removing Emperor Sundara Chozhar from his principal seat in Pazhaiyarai, to Thanjai? A king, moreover, who had been immortalized by great poets, in verse, too:

"… Pazhaiyarai nagar Sundara Chozharai
Yaavaroppar ithonnilathe!"

Hadn't said Pazhaiyarai steadily lost its lustre with its lord's absence? Surely it would be a city radiant with festivities, dazzling a thousand times more, had Sundara Chozhar still been here: the many street-play troupes that entertained the general public would have gathered, finally, in the royal courtyard; the Chakravarthy would welcome them all and reward the many singers, dancers, the *paanars*, actors and poets as they merited. Ah, wouldn't it seem as though the whole of Chozha Nadu had gathered in the city to partake of its delights? Every shop and stall would be deluged by customers and do business a hundred fold—and wouldn't the streets resound with dance, song, sword-fights and *silambattam* performances when Venugopala Swamy began His divine procession from the Nandhipura Vinnagara Temple, that night?

Everything was ruined, now—by the Pazhuvettarayars.

This was not all; the good citizens of Pazhaiyarai nursed yet another massive grievance: their beloved Prince Arulmozhi Varmar, dearer to them than anyone else among the royals, was now in Eezham, fighting a desperate war; ten thousand men from the four Padaiveedu settlements of Pazhaiyarai had accompanied him thither as well, braving the wilds, terrible beasts, treacherous climate and wretched mountains, engaged in upholding Thamizhagam's pride and valour, raising high the standard of Thamizh integrity. Why, hadn't the young Velir of Kodumbalur marched to Ilankai, heading an army himself, before taking a spear to his chest and embracing death upon the battlefield? Hadn't the rest of his contingent fought to the bitter end as well, gaining honourable deaths? And here was young Prince Arulmozhi Varmar, leading his armies even now, seeking to soothe their grieving souls, fighting to uphold their honourable sacrifice and ensure that the tiger flag flew high. While these Pazhuvettarayars, symbols of wretched tyranny, were seemingly refusing to send him food grains and clothes, money and weapons that would mean their very survival! How unjust—had anyone ever heard of such things? What on earth were all the enormous granaries in Thanjavur for, overflowing with rice? What purpose, for that matter, did the royal treasuries, brimming with gold garnered from a hundred years of invasions, serve? What use were money and grains that could not be handed to Chozha warriors in their time of need? Surely the Pazhuvettarayars were not about to bundle and hoist them on their shoulders upon their deaths, to be carried to Yamalokham?

Such were the many muttering among the people of Chozha Nadu in recent times, and Thirumalaiyappan was well aware of them. Pazhaiyarai's citizens had more cause than the rest to be dissatisfied: ten thousand of the city's men might be fighting a war in Ilankai—but their families, women and children resided here still, didn't they?

It was only natural, then, that the *parai* announcement about a runaway spy and his apprehension, under the strict orders of the much-vaunted Pazhuvettarayar brothers found little favour with them. Far from it—it only served as an excuse for the city's residents to air their many grievances. *A spy indeed,* many spoke amongst themselves. *Which country is likely to be brazen enough to send one amongst us—when the tiger flag flies high, announcing its superiority from the river Vada Pennai to the tip of Kumari? Which king would ever dare to slip a spy into Chozha Nadu? No, this is just another of the Pazhuvettarayars' clever ruses; should they ever take a dislike to anyone, they brand him a spy and cast orders for his imprisonment! Drag him straight to their famed dungeons, no doubt. Still, such affairs are none of our business. These are powerful men with the authority to accomplish anything here, unjust or otherwise. Besides, branding someone a spy means that no local-body, not even the town's Panchayat will dare question them, doesn't it?*

Thus did the good people of Pazhaiyarai murmur amongst their acquaintances, discussing royal affairs in low voices—and

Azhwarkkadiyaan gleaned every bit of information he could with his trusty ears, supplementing the rest with his keen intelligence.

Such discontent certainly boded ill, however, and even as he wondered just how things would end for everyone concerned, Azhwarkkadiyaan found that he had reached Kundhavai Devi's royal residence.

The Chozha princess had always evinced considerable delight in conversing with him about worldly matters; the Vaishnavite had earned a name for himself as a seasoned traveler, and many a pleasant hour had she spent, enthralled, as he recounted his many adventures in the lands through which he journeyed. Keenly interested in learning about anything or anyone new, Ilaiya Piratti also enjoyed Azhwarkkadiyaan's recital of the many Azhwar *pasurams* he had routed out, not without great effort, and memorized. In consequence, her welcome for him was always a gracious one; she made sure to enquire after him and his, her countenance agreeable and good-humoured.

Today, however, the princess's features and speech seemed different. Kundhavai's expressive face indicated that her attention was elsewhere; her words, as she faltered uncharacteristically, revealed some agitation—a marked departure from her usual, composed self.

"Well, Thirumalai? I hope I see you well," she welcomed him. "And so—what news? Why an audience?"

"I confess there seems to be no need for one, *Thaaye*. Forgive me— but I assumed you wished to converse with me, as is the norm, about various worldly matters. Accept my apologies. I shall take my leave—"

"No, don't! Stay a while. I did wish to see you, after all—"

"It almost slipped my mind, *Thaaye*—but I have just come from the Periya Piratti's presence, and she bid me here with an important message; she wished to meet you—"

"Certainly. I've every intention of visiting her, in any case. Before that, however—do tell me about your journey: where have you been?"

"Everywhere from Kumari in the South, to Vengadam in the North."

"And—what did people talk about?"

"Most speak of the Chozha reign and its magnificence. Soon, they say, Chozha dominions will stretch from the river Ganga in the North and even the Himalayas; such is its power ..."

"And—?"

"Much is spoken of the Pazhuvettarayars and their valour. The principal reason for the Chozha Empire's present splendour and rapid ascendance, they say, is the Pazhuvoor lords' dauntless courage and—"

"Enough. What else?"

"Your brothers are held in great esteem and affection. Prince Arulmozhi Varmar, in particular, owns pride of place in their hearts; their love for him defies description."

"Hardly surprising, that. Anything more?"

"Many wondered why the Chozha Emperor's beloved daughter remains unmarried, yet. I was asked this myself, often."

"And what was your answer?"

"That the prince worthy of our beloved princess hadn't yet been born, in this world!"

"Upon my word—! Really, Thirumalai, if the one who's to wed me is yet to be born, I shall be a doddering old woman by the time he's a youth! Enough of me now if you please; is there anything else, at all?"

"Why ever not? Many have expressed the greatest astonishment, for example, at the news that the great Saivite saint, the most pious Madhuranthaka Thevar has entered quite abruptly, into the state of holy matrimony—"

"Your sister—the one whom you claimed was destined to become a great devotee of Thirumaal, a *bhaktha sironmani* like Andal—how is she, now?"

"What of her, *Thaaye*? Isn't she now Periya Pazhuvettarayar's young queen, mistress of his palace and all his wealth?"

"Not just his dominions, from what I hear—she's the dictator of the whole of Chozha Nadu, isn't she?"

"So it's been said, *Thaaye*—but why even think of her, on an auspicious day such as this? Speaking of Andal, I must tell you that I sojourned at Srivilliputhur for a while, and had the immense good fortune to learn a few of Vishnu Siddhar's divine songs. Listen, Amma, to one of them; it deals with the sacred occasion of Kannan's birth:

"Vanna Maadangal soozhthiruk Kottiyur
Kannan Kesavan nambi piranthinil
Ennai sunnam edhir edhir thoovida
Kannan muttram kalanthalaraayirre!

Oduvaar vizhuvaar uganthalippaar
Naaduvaar nambiraan engutraan enbaar
Paaduvaargalum palparai kotta nindru
Aaduvaargalum ayitru aaypadiye!"

[*Witness, fortunate ones, the joy of the birth of Kannan! For on this day, the beauteous city of Thirukkottiyur, resplendent with many exquisite galleries and maadams, devotes itself to celebration as oil and colours are strewn about the temple courtyard. They jump and run about in delight, His devotees; songs and music fill the air as they view their beloved Lord—and thus in their ecstasy, do we see Aypadi, before our very eyes!*]

"Such is Pazhaiyarai too, this day, *Thaaye*—just like the Ayarpadi of old."

"Perhaps, but Thirumalai—didn't you hear another sort of *parai*, a few moments ago? What was *that* all about, do you think?"

This, it seemed, was the moment Azhwarkkadiyaan had been waiting for. "Ha, a spy—one who has escaped, too! They're offering some sort of reward for his capture—but what do I know of such things, *Amma?*"

"Don't you? Not a smidgeon of suspicion as to his identity?"

"A smidgeon, yes—but I daren't even whisper it, *Thaaye*. Did you know—I was subjected to a good many hostile stares myself, on my way here. What if someone suspected me, and dragged me off to the dungeons—!"

"It would take extraordinary cunning to even get hold of you, Thirumalai; they'd need men with horns, as they say, in our ancient tales!

Tell me what you know—but only if you truly wish to, of course. Surely you don't think *I* might hand you over to the authorities?"

"Krishna, Krishna! Nothing of the sort. All I did was catch sight of a young warrior in Veera Narayanapuram. He said he was on his way to Thanjavur. Wouldn't let slip a word about his business there, but he did ply *me* with plenty of questions—"

"Really?" Kundhavai sat up, abruptly. "What was he like?" Agitation coloured her voice.

"Obviously well-born—even aristocratic, I should say. Certainly, a handsome young man. Possessed of a keen intelligence and physical strength—"

"What did he ask you?"

"About the Emperor's state of health, and who might succeed him upon the throne. The prince who is engaged in battle, in Eezham. Later, I learnt that he'd subjected the Kudandhai astrologer to the very same interrogation—"

"Ah! He did visit the astrologer, then?"

"Why, I do seem to recollect something about that visit—he practically ploughed through the guard at the door and made quite the entrance, I believe. But you, by good grace, did not know him for what he was—"

"My instincts were correct, then."

"Pray, what about, *Amma*?"

"I sensed, somehow, that that rough-and-ready young man was ripe for trouble ..."

"And you were proven right. I suspect him to be the runaway spy, and the one about whom the Pazhuvettarayars have made a *parai* announcement, in hopes of capture."

"Thirumalai—will you do me a favour?"

"Command me, *Thaaye*."

"Should you ever happen to meet that young man, at any time—"

"Shall I apprehend him and claim my reward?"

"Not on your life! Bring him to me. You see—I have a commission for him."

Azhwarkkadiyaan stared at Kundhavai Piratti for a while, as though struck with wonderment. "I don't think there will be any need for that, *Thaaye*. I shouldn't think I would have to seek him," he said, finally. "For, you see—I think he will find you, all on his own."

ॐ

Hidden Meanings and Explanation

Aypadi/Ayarpadi

Although legend says that Krishna Bhagavan was born in prison, he was raised by his adopted parents amongst the Gopa tribesmen, who were cowherds. Ayarpadi literally translates to "cowherd settlement," in Thamizh.

47

EESANA SIVA BATTAR

His audience with Princess Kundhavai at an end, Azhwarkkadiyaan made his way from her royal residence towards that of his elder brother, Eesana Siva Battar, situated in close vicinity of the Vada Metrali Siva Temple, approximately half a *kaadham* away. It said a good deal of Pazhaiyarai's splendour, that its dimensions and general magnificence could be glimpsed on the journey from the palaces to the temple.

The Krishna Jayanthi celebrations had almost come to an end, Azhwarkkadiyaan noticed. Even more surprising were the sights he witnessed as he strolled past homes, in residential areas: women had gathered in little knots and seemed embroiled in furious discussion. Each had garlanded a much beloved son or husband with *vanji* flowers, wishing him victory in the Eezham battlefield; certainly, every family claimed at least one courageous casualty in the numerous wars waged by the Chozhas in all four directions. Theirs were the families now shrouded in gloom; the women murmuring and muttering their woes in furious, dissatisfied tones. How was all this going to end? Thirumalaiyappan continued to walk, concerned.

Darkness had fallen, by the time he reached the temple. This indeed, was the celebrated shrine Appar had glorified in his songs; in his time, it had been surrounded by man-made hills riddled with caves and catacombs, constructed with painstaking care for the benefit of Thigambara Jain monks who conducted penances. Today, there still exists a village in Pazhaiyarai's vicinity called Muzhaiyur, to remind us of them.

Such *muzhais* or caves had risen high and completely concealed the Vada Metrali Temple within when Appar arrived for a visit, having heard a great deal about Pazhaiyarai's many spiritual merits. The sight of the shrine overwhelmed by Jain catacombs was enough to dismay the saint, who had divined, with his superior powers, its existence. He made a plea at once, to the then Pallava representative ruling the city, who took swift action by destroying a few of the caves, thus revealing the shrine again, to the public. Ecstatic, Appar sang at once in praise of Siva Peruman.

Chozha kings who ascended the throne later, took pains to renovate the simple shrine into stone, thus adding to its magnificence. And yet, the surrounding caves remained, almost like a thick *madhil*. Contrary to the rule of four entrances to a temple, this one boasted of only one, underneath its *gopuram*.

The easiest route to Eesana Siva Battar's home was through the Temple's main entrance and across its precincts; the alternative was a circuitous one that consumed a good deal of time.

Thus Azhwarkkadiyaan, stepped into the temple, on his way to his brother's home. He glimpsed a few devotees at the sanctum—much to his surprise, they seemed to be members of the theatre from earlier that day, colourfully costumed as Krishna and Balaraman. *Ha*, Azhwarkkadiyaan thought to himself. *Now, how did these people end up here, of all places?*

Eesana Siva Battar hastened out of the sanctum even before Thirumalai could complete his ruminations, grabbed his brother who had barely stepped into the temple's threshold by the hands, and almost dragged him outside.

"Why, *Anna*, what's this?"

"You wish to know, do you? I shall tell you, Thirumalai, and in such clear terms that they will permeate even your very thick skull: I have decided, henceforth, that our relationship is confined to the exterior of this temple. You, my fellow, are a blaspheming, Godless heathen—you who hate Siva Peruman with all your soul and do not hesitate to display your deplorable feelings for all to see! Your endless *Siva nindhanai* means that you do not deserve to set foot within a Siva temple. I have been patient far too long, Thirumalai, but I could not bear it any more—not after your despicable speech in the great Queen's presence! You are welcome to haunt my home and fill your disgustingly large stomach if you wish, but not a *foot* will you set inside this sacred temple. Disobey—and I shall transform into the wrathful Sandeswara Naayanar himself—!"

"But, *Anna—Anna!*" Eesana Siva Battar caught his beloved brother by the scruff of his neck and practically towed him out, seemingly in a towering rage. None of Thirumalai's pleas moved him, and before his distraught younger brother could go further, he had stalked back in and banged the huge doors shut, drawing the bolt securely.

"So that's how it is, is it?" Azhwarkkadiyaan loitered in front of the temple for a while, mumbling to himself. Then, he circled the whole precinct, Jain caves and all, two or three times, taking care to go left instead of right—to do so the other way around might end in a proper *pradhakshinam*, or a salutary circumambulation to the much-hated Sivan within—which the fierce Vaishnavite could not countenance at any cost. His painstaking observation did reveal something to him: every one of the manmade caves was closed. Later, he made his way to his brother's home, where he was made heartily welcome by the good Battar's wife, who relished Thirumalai's witticisms a great deal. Azhwarkkadiyaan did not disappoint: today, he was at his sarcastic best, regaling her with thrilling accounts and jokes and took care to eat the Battar and wife out of house and home. His gargantuan stomach finally filled and almost bursting at the seams with *prasadham* from the Sivan Temple, Thirumalai belched, waddled to the *thinnai* and sprawled upon it.

Somewhere between sleep and wakefulness, his mind wandered over the happenings of the previous day—and lit upon one particular event.

Thirumalai was ambling along the banks of River Kudamurutti, when his ears were assaulted by the thundering of horse-hooves, on the opposite side. Quick to think on his feet, he slunk behind a thicket of luxurious bamboo trees.

A horse careened on the shore, first, seemingly without direction; it seemed drenched—from sweat or having swum across the river, Thirumalai could not guess. A young man, almost a boy, was bound to it. He looked frankly terrified—but underneath was a streak of determination, as well. Four or five horses galloped up behind him, all bearing soldiers armed with spears; they were nearing the runaway steed with every moment. One of the men rose from his perch, his spear held aloft as if to throw it, but his cohort leaned over and stopped him.

The boy's steed passed under a thick cluster of bamboo trees at that moment; one of the slender branches, already dropping towards the ground, tangled in the youngster's tresses. The horse strained to move forward; the branch yanked at the rider's hair. Just as Thirumalai shuddered at the latter's fate, his pursuers galloped up and surrounded him. They took one look at his youthful, pale features, and appeared overcome by surprise and dismay.

Pelted with their sharp questions, their quarry stammered and stuttered his replies, none of which were very audible to Azhwarkkadiyaan. "Where's he? *Where?*" was a question repeated often, to which the boy sobbed and heaved pitifully. "He's gone—the waters took him—the floods swept him away!"

The men soon trussed him up, secured his horse and marched both long the banks.

None of this had made much sense to Azhwarkkadiyaan at that time —but now they seemed, finally, to reveal some of their significance.

In the midst of all this intruded the memory of the Balaraman and Krishna theatre troupe he had stumbled upon that day; in particular, the man donning the costume of Kamsan, his face veiled by a wooden mask.

Something about his body language and speech had seemed vaguely familiar. Now—now, he could see glimmerings of light, about the true identity of the so-called actor.

The first thing Eesana Siva Battar saw when he returned home late that night, upon the completion of the *ardha jaamam poojai* at the Sivan temple, was his erstwhile beloved younger brother sprawled upon the *thinnai*. "Thirumalai!" he called out. "*Thirumalai!*"—voice practically ringing with fury.

Azhwarkkadiyaan moved not a muscle, feigning deep sleep. The Battar gave him up as a lost cause, stalked into his home and banged the door shut in a way calculated to rouse the street: *Padaar!* His raised voice within reached even Thirumalai, sunk as the Battar was in some sort of discussion. It seemed to have developed into a verbal altercation—the subject of which, Thirumalai guessed, was himself.

The next morning found Eesana Siva Battar accosting his errant brother once more. "When will you begin gallivanting about the country, again?"

"Once your anger has died down, *Anna*."

"Do *not* call me that. You—I am no longer your elder brother and you, certainly, have no claim upon me as my *thambi*—you blaspheming scoundrel! *Neechan—sandaalan—*"

"Pray, why do you curse him so?" Battar's wife hurried up, quick to speak up for her brother-in-law. "What has he done now, that he has not done before? It is *you* who have turned into a Siva fanatic!"

"Quiet! If you knew what he spoke in the great Queen's presence yesterday—*Why does this Paramasivan, a mad ascetic dancing among skulls and ash in a cemetery need temples*, he asks! It was as though someone had poured boiling hot lead into my ears—and I hear that Her Majesty did not sleep a wink last night, the poor lady!"

"Thirumalai will repeat no such thing, in the future. Indeed, I shall make sure he learns from his mistakes. And why would he not, as long as we instruct him the right way?"

"Right and wrong ways, my foot! What he *must* do right away is journey to Rameswaram and beg the pardon of the divine Siva Peruman, worshipped by Rama himself, to wash away his sins. That, and only that will be the means of his redemption. And until he does, I shall certainly never set eyes on this heinous creature's face!" finished Eesana Siva Battar, in a magnificent display of temper.

Thirumalai's lips twitched—with the overwhelming impulse to return every one of his brother's taunts with interest, of course—but now was not the time. Should he speak a word out of turn, all his painstaking efforts would have gone to waste.

"Of course—why would he not?" butted in the Battar's wife, once again. "He will be certain to obey any command of yours. Come to think of it, would it not be an excellent plan to accompany him? So many years and not a child of our own—doubtless, we have committed a grave sin that must be remedied with worship. Thirumalai," she turned to her brother-in-law. "Why do we not all journey to Rameswaram?"

Eesana Siva Battar glared at them both, and stalked away. Some time later, he confronted Thirumalai again—but this time, in a somewhat tranquil frame of mind. "Our elders do say *Kobam, Paapam, Sandaalam*— anger leads to nothing but destruction. And I am afraid I have given way to wrath," he admitted. "You have not taken my hasty words to heart, I hope?"

"Not at all."

"In that case, stay here. I shall return once I have completed midday worship; there are a few important matters I wish to discuss with you, and upon which I require your opinion. You *will* stay here, won't you?"

"I've no intention of leaving you—now, or ever, *Anna*."

The Battar departed, satisfied.

"So that's how it is to be, is it?" Azhwarkkadiyaan mumbled to himself a few times—and then left, abruptly. He made his way around the Vada Metrali Temple and its caves twice or thrice, making sure to conceal himself at the slightest hint of sound.

His wait was not in vain. Within a few moments, one of the gates to the Jain caves creaked open—and Eesana Siva Battar peered out. He stared keenly in all three directions, before stepping out gingerly. Someone else followed him outside—ah, now who might this be? By the look of him, it certainly seemed to be the one who had earlier donned Kamsan's costume. But who *was* he? Ha, so this was the reason for the Battar's elaborate deception—his taunts and convoluted temper tantrums. Well, well, well!

The men from the *muzhai* began to walk swiftly; Azhwarkkadiyaan was careful to keep his distance, out of their eyesight, as he dogged their steps. They walked for a while before reaching a quay—the one upon the artificial lake that edged the royal residences, choppy with waves almost like an ocean. But this one happened to be situated in the west, at a great distance from the palaces.

The banks boasted a luxurious growth of thick trees; Azhwarkkadiyaan slunk behind one, and peered out from between two branches.

A boat bobbed upon the choppy surface; it looked, upon inspection, like a royal craft. A boatman waited upon the shore. The moment he spied the Battar and his companion, he dragged the boat closer, in readiness for them, apparently. The men promptly climbed in.

Once the little craft began to float away, the Battar's companion turned towards the shore. For an instant, his face was clearly visible—and Azhwarkkadiyaan recognized him at once.

Not that the revelation came as a surprise; he had arrived at an accurate conclusion as to the man's identity, by now. It was, in fact, none other than the valiant young man he had met in Veera Narayanapuram, and on the banks of the river Kollidam! Azhwarkkadiyaan had no doubt, moreover, that "Kamsan" had been the very same warrior, as well.

All that remained, now, was to discern the secret assignation of these two men—or, as Azhwarkkadiyaan swiftly amended himself, to confirm that his suppositions regarding their destination was correct, of course.

Among the many palatial residences that lined the royal avenue, nearly piercing the skies, one in particular, at the very end, lay silent and empty. Once the honourable seat of Sundara Chozhar's Chief Minister, Aniruddha Brahmaraayar, the palace was now under lock and key: the venerable minister was on one of his many state visits to Madurai, the Pandiya capital, providing much needed restoration to ruined royal administration; his family currently resided in Thanjai, which meant that none remained in Pazhaiyarai.

It was here that Azhwarkkadiyaan finally made his way. The palace guards at the entrance bowed in deference at his arrival, and opened the doors wide at his command. Once within, they closed and locked the doors from the outside as per his instructions.

Azhwarkkadiyaan crossed all three *kattus* or sections of the rambling residence and reached the gardens, where he swiftly routed out a slender track cutting across the luxurious bushes and many creepers that twined round each other, glorying in the lack of a gardener. He walked steadily along the narrow path until he reached Kundhavai's royal gardens, where he located a cunningly placed alcove and hid himself, swiftly.

Judging by what followed, not a single one of his painstaking efforts were in vain.

For something did happen—a dramatic event worthy of the poetic skills and elegant verses of masterful bards such as Mahakavi Kalidasa himself, and many such others.

The boat crept along the waters, edging towards the shore; when it stopped, Eesana Siva Battar and Vandhiyathevan climbed out, and began up the steps leading to the gardens.

At a little distance from the stairs waited Ilaiya Piratti Kundhavai Devi, majestic upon a marble seat placed most artistically, in her garden.

The travelers ascended steadily from the shores; Princess Kundhavai rose, the moment they reached the last stair. It was then that Vandhiyathevan raised his head and caught a glimpse of the gracious young lady.

He stopped short and stood still, transfixed at the vision in front of him.

A slender vine crept up just then, its delicate tendrils reaching between the young man and Kundhavai, as though seeking to obstruct their view. A beautiful butterfly, its dazzling, fragile wings fluttering in the sunlight, alighted gently upon it.

Kundhavai bent her radiant, golden countenance a little, gazing at the butterfly, entranced.

Vandhiyathevan, on the other hand, drank in her delicate, blooming beauty, unable to even blink.

The lake churned with restless, foaming waves.

Birds in the heavens ceased their restless twitters. Time and space, it seemed, stood still.

And aeons passed.

48

WHIRLING POOLS AND SWIRLING EYES

Aeons ago, God created the first man, the *Aadhi Manidhan*, who made his home upon a mountain slope. Sturdy rock caves guarded him from wind and gales; luxurious trees and foliage growing thick upon the mountain provided him with fruits that satisfied every one of his heart's cravings. Beasts of the jungle lived in perennial fear of him; he himself, led a life free of worry or fear, free as the birds that wheeled in the sky. And yet—yet, there seemed to be something sorely lacking. A yawning pit opened up somewhere in the region of his heart—a deep yearning, a lack haunted him every passing moment. He could not quite define it, but some sort of mysterious force seemed to drag him in directions unseen. He seemed to be seeking, at all moments, something he had neither seen nor experienced, thus far. By day, he allowed his imagination full rein over this object; by night, his subconscious took over in the form of dreams. *This marvelous treasure that I seek—this luscious karpagakkani—this strange force that tugs at me—how do I find it?*

When? The questions haunted him day and night, and his heart fluttered, aching for some sort of reprieve.

Meanwhile, God had given form to the *Aadhi Sthree*, the first woman, the same instant he created her male counterpart. She lived on the other side of the mountain. Fruits from trees quenched her hunger; fresh water from the mountain's sources slaked her thirst, and she lived in a cave that afforded excellent shelter. In other words, she suffered no want—for all intents and purposes. And yet, a fire burned deep within, tormenting her every moment; a mysterious force seemed to bind and tug her somewhere. But where did it wish her to go? And why did it possess her spirit so? These were questions for which she knew not the answers.

A towering mountain thus separated the world's first man and woman—preventing them from setting eyes on each other.

One day, the weather followed the vagaries of a scorching summer; a forest fire began to rage through the mountain in all directions. So swiftly did it cut across the vast swathes of vegetation, its tongue licking the plants and trees, that the man and woman knew there was no hope of escape. None, at least, through the jungle; the only way was to climb up to the summit. That was where they caught their first sight of each other.

And stood completely still, hardly daring to blink.

Forgotten was the forest fire, and even the reason for their sojourn to the summit. Gone was every instinct of hunger and thirst.

This. This was, they realized, the reason for their existence—to meet each other, at this very instant. This, then, was the mysterious force that had pulled and tugged at them. Within each other, they realized, lay the key to their hearts; within themselves resided the only means to fill the gaping emptiness that had made their lives miserable. And having found each other—there was no force on earth, they realized, that had the power to separate them.

High above in his celestial abode, Brahmmadevan, who had observed this magical meeting with some trepidation, realized that the good work had begun—and returned to his divine duties, duly satisfied.

It would be safe to say that our Vallavarayan and Princess Kundhavai resembled the first man and woman, at this very moment.

This was what they had sought, all their lives, whispered a voice, deep within their hearts. This was indeed, what they had waited for; the meeting that defined their very existence.

Unlike the *Aadhi Manidhan* and *Sthree*, however, princess and warrior were bound by the dictates of their society and culture; neither could ignore the difference in their respective statuses, which meant that they could not give in to their newfound, rapturous feelings. Their eyes, however, played an elaborate dance, sinking into each other one moment; shifting to flowers, trees, butterflies and the lake nearby, the next.

Eesana Siva Battar, having decided that enough time had passed in silent conversation, cleared his throat—which was when both realized that their meeting had been convened for another, far more important purpose.

"I believe you petitioned Eesana Siva Battar to seek a private audience with me?" Ilaiya Piratti's voice held a good deal of severity.

Her authoritative tone, calculated to snub pretension, touched Vandhiyathevan to the quick. He straightened to his full height in spite of himself. "I am not sure I may volunteer an answer without knowing your identity," he returned, very much on his mettle. "I wonder," he murmured. "Has Eesana Siva Battar led me here erroneously?"

"Indeed, I am plagued by such doubts as well. Who was it that you wished to speak with?"

"I requested the Battar to lead me to the Chozha dynasty's most lustrous light; Emperor Sundara Chozhar's illustrious daughter; young sister to the Crown Prince Aditha Karikalar; she who was born older to Prince Arulmozhi Varmar; Ilaiya Piratti Kundhavai Devi …"

"Well," Kundhavai smiled a little. "It is indeed I who bear the crushing weight of all those grandiloquent titles."

"In that case—surely you aren't the young lady I met in the Kudandhai Astrologer's home, and on the banks of the river Arisilaaru?"

"Yes, yes, guilty as charged, on both occasions, especially when it came to my mannerless conduct. You didn't expect to meet such a socially inept woman again, did you?"

"Hardly accurate to term this a second meeting, Devi."

"Why not?"

"Such a thing would be possible only if there were a parting, in the reckoning. But you—you were never far from my thoughts for an instant."

"I didn't quite expect Thondai Mandalam's citizens to be such adepts at conversation."

"You prefer, it would seem, to heap all praise upon noble Chozha Nadu, and bestow none upon the pitiful rest."

"I must confess that that is a crime often laid at my door—and with good reason. But you don't seem to profess much affection for Chozha Nadu, yourself."

"Not at all. I like these lands very well—except for two great perils that seem to accost unsuspecting men at every turn. A prospect that terrifies me, I assure you."

"Indeed, the swords and spears of Chozha warriors present a grave danger to anyone. Foreigners would do well to exercise considerable caution. Especially those with circumspect motives, such as spying, for example—"

"I beg pardon, but those weren't exactly the perils I had in mind, Your Highness. I possess a trusty sword and spear myself and what's more, I am even well-schooled in the art of their use—"

"How true!—ah, fortunate were we indeed, the damsels privileged to witness your mastery in action, upon the banks of the Arisilaaru! Why, your trusty weapon speared that hapless, stuffed crocodile with one swift stroke—a stroke so sure that it tore open the cotton packed inside completely!"

"Ah, but then, *Ammani*, I must confess to ignorance about the brave demeanour of Chozha Nadu's warrior princesses who shudder and quake at the sight of dead, stuffed reptiles. I didn't know, moreover, that Chozha warriors made a habit of attacking corpses; I believed the threat to be real, and used my wits. Hardly my fault, or my spear's—"

"Entirely the fault of that stupid crocodile, I assure you. For it breathed its last before brave Vandhiyathevar of the Vaanar clan could rip it apart and send it to a glorious death, didn't it? It deserved its terrible fate. But stay—if these weren't the perils you mentioned, what else?"

"The raging whirlpools in your rivers, as flashfloods thunder and roar through them—never to be trusted. The bane of my very existence! I can barely describe how they battered me senseless."

"You—in a raging whirlpool? But you hardly seem the type to even set foot in water, let alone dangerous flashfloods."

"One cannot refuse to climb a *murungai* tree, having wedded a ghoulish Vethalam, as the saying goes. And it would seem that having set foot in Chozha Nadu, getting snared in whirlpools and flashfloods is but a part of everyday life. And all this, I tell, you because of a silly young man and his idiotic scruples—would you believe me if I told you that he refused to utter a little lie?"

"This all sounds very mysterious indeed. Would you care to elaborate?"

"Why, so I will. The Thanjai Fort's Commander, Chinna Pazhuvettarayar sent his men to capture me, branding me a spy—me, your beloved brother's messenger! I, however, had no desire to get caught before my mission was accomplished; I beseeched the young man of whom I'd begged accommodation, to escort me—"

"Where did you stay the night, in Thanjai?"

"The home of a flower-seller, outside the fort. The poor woman was mute."

"Oh. And her name?"

"I must plead ignorance. But I do know her son's name. Sendhan Amudhan."

"I was correct, then. Proceed, please."

"I took the lad up on my horse and set out towards Pazhaiyarai, when I realized that some of Pazhuvettarayar's men were in pursuit. As I mentioned, I had no wish to get into their clutches before I could accomplish my task; when we arrived at the Kudamurutti, I instructed the young boy to carry on upon the horse, while I stepped down at that point. *They will believe me to be the rider and go after you,* I said to him. *Once they have you, they will realize their mistake. Should they question you about my whereabouts, tell them I fell into the river and drowned!* But that dratted boy appeared to have been a direct descendent of King Harichandra himself. *How may I lie that you drowned, when you're no such thing?* he asked. And so, my lady, I had to turn my lie into the truth—all for the sake of his testimony. I tied him to the horse well and good, and jumped headfirst into the river. *Ammamma*—the murderous whirlpools and treacherous swirls that haunt Chozha waters, especially by the banks! A terrible time I had, trying to escape them and swim to safety. In the end, I had to grab hold of a sturdy tree root and haul myself, somehow, on to land. But Devi—what did you think I saw, even as I was swirling around in those dangerous pools, half conscious, fighting for every breath and aching for land? What were my thoughts, do you think?"

"Pray, how may I know? Gajendra the elephant's divine salvation, perhaps?"

"No, never. I saw *kayal* fishes in the waters, my lady, caught in the currents and as helpless as I was. Those beautiful creatures, long, and sleek, reminded me of the eyes of Chozha women. Even those strangled by traitorous water currents may somehow make their escape—but a man ensnared by a Chozha damsel's exquisite eyes and their swirling beauty, I thought, may never free himself of their toils!"

"It's a common habit, I've noticed, to blame women and their beauty for the mistakes and weaknesses of others; men, in particular are constantly guilty of this crime."

"Indeed, I freely admit my sins," quipped Vandhiyathevan. "Why on earth wouldn't I?"

The melodious notes of a flute wafted over to them, from within the palace. *Kinikini—Thandai silambu* ornaments twinkled as feet danced upon the floor, while the *mathalam* thundered its beats with majesty. The many voices of young women rose in sweet harmony as they sang an *Aichiyar Kuravai*, a collection that was part of that famed epic, *Silappathikaaram*:

"Kanru kunilak kani udhirtha maayavan

Indrunam aanulvarumel avan vaayil
Konraiyan theenguzhal kelaamo thozhi!
Kollaiyanchaaral kurunthositha maayavan
Ellainam aanulvarumel avan vaayil
Mullaiyan theenguzhal kelaamo thozhi!"

[*Will you not know, my dear friend, of the presence of Maayavan who draws fruits from the trees in our groves, and enters our herds, by the exquisite notes of the divine flute at his lips, like the sweet perfume of jasmine and konrai?*]

Kundhavai and Vandhiyathevan stood rooted to the spot, spellbound by the song's beauty and devotion, until the very end. Instruments began to play again: the *mathalam* sounded its steady beat and anklets twinkled; a sign that the dance had resumed.

"The palace performs its *Kuravai Koothu*, no doubt," ventured Vandhiyathevan. "I had the fortune of witnessing one such in the Kadambur Palace—not that they were the same, of course."

"True; my companions learn their pieces even now. They will begin to look for me soon—and now, what brings you here?" asked Kundhavai.

"As to that, Your Highness—I am happy to announce that I have accomplished my mission, the task I set out upon, from Kanchi. Having braved whirlpools, traitorous flash floods and betraying eyes, I bring you this: your brother's *olai* to you, safe and sound."

And Vandhiyathevan held out the palm-leaves with a flourish.

৯৯

Hidden Meanings and Explanations

"One cannot refuse to climb a murungai tree, having wedded a ghoulish Vethalam ..."
Vandhiyathevan's referring to an ancient Thamizh proverb: *"Vedhalathirku vaazhkaippattaal, murungai maram erithaan aaga vendum."* The inference is quite clear: when committed to a cause, one cannot back out, but follow through, no matter the complications.

49

WONDER OF WONDERS!

Kundhavai Piratti received the *olai* Vandhiyathevan held out, and began to read it. Her face, marred by a frown and clouded over until that moment, began to relax. By the time she finished, her countenance glowed with a golden radiance.

"Well," she glanced up at the Vaanar warrior. "The *olai* is now in my hands. What, now?"

"My task is done, Your Highness. I suppose all that's left now is to return home."

"Not at all. I should say, in fact, that your mission has only just begun."

"I'm not sure I understand you, Devi."

"My brother, the Crown Prince states here very clearly that I may entrust you with any confidential assignment. Surely you aren't going to disregard his assurances?"

"I did, indeed, accept such a commission from him—but I appeal to your kindness: pray, do not burden me with missions of the utmost secrecy or importance, I beg of you."

"I'm afraid I'm the one who doesn't understand, now. Is it a common practice among Vaanar warriors to accept a commission, and then withdraw from carrying it out?"

"It's not in us to languish upon past laurels. Neither is it the Vaanar practice to remove ourselves from previously accepted assignments."

"Well, what then? Perhaps you nourish a wholesome hatred for all womenfolk?" A pretty smile hovered about Ilaiya Piratti's lips. "Or is it just me you dislike cordially?"

*Well, really. What **sort** of a question was this? Would the ocean ever nourish a hatred for the brilliant chandran, hanging low in the night sky? And if it should, why on earth would it ever try to reach for it with a thousand of its limbs, the sea-waves? Who could ever claim that the blue sky loathed beauteous Bhooma Devi, the Earth? Why else would it gaze down at her every night, hope and longing mingling in its thousand sparkling eyes, the stars upon the velvet sky? Could it ever be that dark clouds held the dazzling lightning in revulsion? Why else did they wish so desperately to clutch a power that cleaved them in half, and hold it in a close embrace? Did the bee ever loathe the flower? If so, why would it hover endlessly around blooms? Would anyone ever believe it if the vittil insect was said to abhor the gentle glow of a lamp? Else why would it fall into the light and sacrifice itself? What a question indeed, Devi. Dislike you? Why would your eyes, as they throw little glances in my direction, paralyze me into a state of ecstasy, if I truly did? Why do you think that tantalizing smile, at the edge of your lips, drives me to such madness, a sweet, sweet torture I can barely have enough of …?*

Such were the chaotic thoughts that chased through Vandhiyathevan's heart—thoughts that he could not, however, give voice to.

"You haven't answered my question yet, *Ayya*," the Princess began, again. "You believe, perhaps, that it's beneath the dignity of valiant Vaanar warriors to carry out a mere female's commands? Didn't the Crown Prince inform you of the contents of this *olai*, when he gave it into your possession?"

"On the contrary, Devi—I was well aware of his express wishes and everything my mission entailed, when I began. If anything, I'm inclined to believe that I didn't quite start my journey at an auspicious moment. I managed to make enemies all the way; I even had the supreme misfortune of a bosom friend turn into a foe. They pursue me even now, in all four directions. How may I carry out any task you may set me, under such circumstances? That, in truth, is the reason for my hesitation," explained Vandhiyathevan. "I don't wish your commission jeopardized on my account, after all."

"Foes in pursuit, you say?" enquired Kundhavai, worry seeping into her voice. "May I know who they are?"

"Well, the Pazhuvettarayars, for one thing—they've sent men in every corner, in an effort to apprehend me; my dearest friend Kandamaaran now believes me to have stabbed him in the back; Azhwarkkadiyaan, a certain fierce Vaishnavite fraud dogs my steps day and night. Not to mention the fact that the Pazhuvoor Ilaiya Rani has set a dangerous magician on my tracks. I've no idea when one or the other of these will ensnare me, to tell the truth."

Memories of his encounter with the self-same *mandhiravadi*, the night he escaped a watery grave in the floods accosted Vandhiyathevan, at that moment.

Continuing his journey during the day was far too dangerous, he decided, and had spent the hours skulking in bamboo forests and plantain groves, choosing to walk steadily along the river banks once darkness fell. Weariness overtook him sometime around the third *jaamam* that night, and he decided to take his ease in a ruined *mandapam*.

The moon shone its pearly rays upon the earth, turning night into day; some of its radiance reached even a little inside the crumbling edifice. Vandhiyathevan moved beyond the light, and lay down in the shadows. Sleep beckoned him. Even as he felt his eyes close all by themselves, he was shaken awake, rudely, by a horrible screech very near him. An owl.

Hadn't he heard the same screech during his conversation with the Pazhuvoor Ilaiya Rani, in her *latha mandapam*? Vandhiyathevan rose hastily. Deep in the darkness, two tiny spots of light seemed to train themselves on him. He took two paces towards the entrance—when the sound of footsteps stopped him.

Someone had just entered the *mandapam*.

Vandhiyathevan sidled behind a broken, ruined pillar and peered out. The moonlight fell on the newcomer's face—and the Vaanar warrior realized that he was none other than the *mandhiravadhi*; Nandhini's erstwhile visitor.

Much to his surprise, the magician seemed to make the pillar his target; Vandhiyathevan hoped that the man was unaware of his concealment, and would walk away.

His hopes were ruined. *The mandhiravadhi*, tiptoeing like a stealthy cat until he reached the pillar, suddenly fell on Vandhiyathevan and clutched his neck with a loud, inhuman shriek. "The signet ring!" he howled. "Give me the palm-tree signet ring now—or I will strangle you this instant!"

Vandhiyathevan could barely breathe—his throat felt like being crushed in a vice; his eyes startled out of his head as though they would pop out; he heaved and panted.

And yet, somehow, he reined in his panic. He caught hold of the old pillar, gathered his strength, and threw out his leg in a mighty kick. The *mandhiravadi* crumpled to the ground with a scream. The pillar chose to crash that moment; stones and rubble began to rain down from the roof. A terrified bat flapped its way out of the *mandapam*; so did Vandhiyathevan, as fast as his legs could take him. Only when he was sure of no pursuit did he stop, finally, catching his breath.

His legs shook and body trembled even now, when he recalled that night.

"*Ayya?*" Kundhavai's melodious voice shook him out of his reverie, somewhat, and restored equilibrium. "How long has it been, since you left Kanchi?"

"A week and a day, Devi."

"Wonder of wonders, then, that you've managed to earn quite so many enemies within such a short space of time. Pray, how did you accomplish such a feat?"

"That would prove to be a very long story indeed, Your Highness."

"You may recount it to me, nevertheless. My decision to entrust you with another mission depends, you see, upon knowing every detail of your journey, so far." She turned to Eesana Siva Battar at this moment, and called him aside. "The boatman—what sort of a person is he?"

"Deaf as a post in both ears. He wouldn't notice thunder if it tore his ear-drums, *Thaaye*."

"Excellent. Shall we embark on a boat ride, then? We would do well to row across the lake for a while; I wish to listen to his account in its entirety," remarked the princess, walking swiftly towards the shore.

A thrill of exhilaration coursed through Vandhiyathevan. On a boat—in company of the illustrious Chozha dynasty's exalted princess! What had he ever done to deserve this richness? He must have earned a great deal of virtue in at least seven past lives, to be the recipient of such excellent fortune! Now that the Gods had seen fit to bestow such largesse upon him, he would ensure that the unlooked-for expedition lasted a very long time indeed; Vandhiyathevan would describe his adventures in such terms, and with so many endless paragraphs that it never came to an end. Never let it be said that he ended a story far too quickly. Such strokes of luck did not always find their way to people—where was the need for any hurry?

Vandhiyathevan's instincts may have been creditable indeed—but he had reckoned without Kundhavai's own. The moment the boat began to glide over the waters and he began his account of the midnight conference in Kadambur Sambuvaraiyar's palace, the princess's impatience rose with every passing moment. "Well, what next?"—"And then?"—"What happened later?" she shot the questions, barely able, it seemed, to sit still. To his credit, Vallavarayan did use the considerable powers in his repertoire and lengthened his tale as much as he could—but the longest of them has to come to an end at some point, mustn't it? By the time he finished, the boat had completed its circuit upon the lake, and returned to the quay.

It was obvious, even as they climbed out and entered the royal gardens, that the *Kuravai Koothu* was still in full swing within the palace; instruments played melodiously, accompanied by the tinkling of *Thandai* anklets. A beautiful *Silappathikaaram* verse, set to an old tune, wafted towards them, as well:

> *Periyavanai mayavanai perulagamellaam*
> *Virikamala vunthiyudai vinnavanaik kannum*
> *Thiruvadiyum kaiyum thiruvaayum seyya*
> *Kariyavanaik kaanatha kannenna kanne!*
> *Kannimaithuk kaanbaartham kannenna kanne!*
>
> *Madanthaazhu nenjathu kanjanar vanjam*
> *Kadanthaanai nootruvarpaal naatrisaiyum potrap*
> *Padarndhaarana muzhangap panjavarkkuth thoothu*
> *Nadanthaanai ethaatha naavenna naave!*
> *Narayanavenna naavenna naave!*

[*What eyes are those that do not marvel at the great Lord, the Maayavan; He who holds the whole world upon a beautiful lotus, borne of His navel, in a gentle clasp? What eyes are these that even blink, as they gaze upon His feet, eyes and dark, divine Form? What tongues are these that do not sing in praise of the Great One Who foiled the evil Kamsan's devious plans; Who went as an envoy from the illustrious Pandavas to the hundred Kaurava brothers, to the glorious praise of thousands? What tongues are these, that do not chant the blessed name, Narayana, at every turn?*]

"Kanjanaar might have been devious in his *vanjam* indeed, making deceitful, terrible plans to vanquish Kannan," mused Vandhiyathevan, "But it can't be denied that he performed me a signal service."

"Did he, now?" Ilaiya Piratti raised her eyebrows. "What might *that* have been?"

"Assisting me in entering the city, of course," he returned. Then, he went on to describe the exact circumstances of said assistance:

Vallavarayan had guessed, quite accurately, that the Pazhuvettarayars' men would be lying in wait for him even before he arrived at Pazhaiyarai, guarding every single point of entrance and exit. The least sign of suspicious behaviour, and he would be carted off to prison at once. How on earth was he to enter the gates, under these troubling circumstances?

He stood mulling over this complex problem on the banks of the Arisilaaru, some distance from the city's principal entrance, when he caught sight of an approaching theatre troupe, complete with Kannan, Balaraman and Kamsan in their full regalia. Of these, the last-mentioned was the only one to wear a curiously fashioned mask, as part of his disguise.

A fascinating idea began to take shape in Vandhiyathevan's fertile brain.

Sauntering over to the troupe, he engaged them in random conversation. "Your precious actor, the one who's playing Kamsan—not very talented, is he?"

Unsurprisingly, "Kamsan" took instant exception to these flippant comments, and engaged Vandhiyathevan in a lively quarrel—and since when has our warrior ever walked away from one? He snatched away Kamsan's mask and wore it, in one audacious move. "Here's my challenge," he crowed. "I'm a far better dancer than you—and I shall prove it!" he yelled, flinging himself about with abandon.

The rest of the troupe agreed, carried away with his theatrics, even going so far as to say that Vandhiyathevan put on a much better show than their own member. This seemed to be the cue for the original Kamsan to tear off the rest of his disguise and stomp away, disgusted and furious.

"Who cares about *that* idiot?' Vandhiyathevan shrugged, superbly. "I'm here now—and I shall play Kamsan, if you wish." The theatre troupe did so wish, and bore him off promptly, delirious with joy at having found a true actor.

Every song and dance at Pazhaiyarai's street-corners at a jubilant end, Vandhiyathevan followed Aditha Karikalar's advice to the letter and met Eesana Siva Battar at the Vada Metrali Temple. The priest bade him wait in one of the Samana caves, before seeking Kundhavai Devi's permission for a private audience. Once this was given, he brought Vandhiyathevan to her, journeying upon the lake.

Ilaiya Piratti gazed at him, her exquisite eyes lovelier still, wide with astonishment. "It appears to me that Kotravai, the Goddess of Victory stands firmly by the Chozhas," she murmured, a little awed. "Indeed, it is Her grace that has sent you to my assistance, in these times of peril!"

"But—I haven't been assigned a task yet, Your Highness," protested Vandhiyathevan. "Nor a hazardous commission with which to prove my true worth."

"Fear not. The mission I have in mind is one that will make your previous perils seem nothing at all, in comparison."

Vandhiyathevan felt his heart swell, his body quiver, with pride. Ah, wouldn't he cross the seven roaring seas in this lady's service? Wouldn't he engage in battle with a thousand lions and tear them apart without recourse to a weapon? Even climb atop the insurmountable Mount Meru and pluck the very stars in heaven, at a single wave of her hand?

In the midst of the royal gardens stood a beautifully wrought *vasantha mandapam*; it was to this marble edifice that Kundhavai next made her way. The Battar and Vandhiyathevan followed her.

The princess reached into a tiny alcove; took out a palm-leaf and gold-handled quill, and began to inscribe the following message:

"Ponniyin Selva! Return home the instant you receive this message. More, you will know, through the bearer of this palm-leaf. You may trust him implicitly."

She signed this effusion with a tiny etching of an *aathi* leaf, and handed it to the Vaanar warrior. "You are required to leave without a moment's pause to Eezha Nadu; convey this message into the hands of Prince Arulmozhi Varmar, and escort him home, personally."

Vandhiyathevan's life, it seemed, was complete.

He stood still for a moment, buffeted by waves of sheer, unadulterated happiness, hardly daring to believe his luck. One of the two greatest ambitions, *manoradhams* he had cherished all his life, had just come true: meeting the ancient Chozha clan's magnificent princess, Ilaiya Piratti Kundhavai. And it seemed that his second would be achieved as well, by virtue of her: soon, he was about to have the supreme good fortune of meeting Prince Arulmozhi Varmar.

"A task my heart craves above all, Devi," he murmured. "I shall take your *olai* and set off at once." And he stretched out his right hand.

The *olai* was duly given; Kundhavai's beautiful fingers, graceful and slender as *kaanthal* flowers, touched Vandhiyathevan's fortunate ones, as she handed it over. A spark of energy burst through his body; his skin prickled with goosebumps; his heart felt like it might explode with ecstasy. A hundred thousand butterflies filled his vision, dazzling him with their delicate, exquisitely fragile wings; a hundred thousand nightingales warbled a glorious song of rapture; fragrant blooms descended upon him in veritable mounds, deluging him with colour and perfume, scattering in all directions.

Vandhiyathevan raised his head; his eyes met Kundhavai's for a long moment. A thousand words trembled upon his lips; his heart overrun with emotion. And yet—what power had mere words, to express his deepest feelings?

No matter. His eyes, it seemed, were able to perform this office for him, more than adequately. What they communicated to the Princess at that moment—the splendid poems they recited, the magnificent verses they extolled—ah, not even Kalidasa, great bards, or the ancient composers of epics such as *Muthollayiram* might have accomplished any such. What more needs to be said, then, of their beauty?

Salasalasala … dry leaves rustled somewhere in the distance, outside the *vasantha mandapam*. Eesana Siva Battar cleared his throat.

And Vandhiyathevan came back to earth with a thud.

Hidden Meanings and Explanations
Kaanthal Flower
Delicate red and yellow flowers; also the state flower of Thamizh Nadu.
Aathi Leaf
Associated for centuries, with the Chozha dynasty. Traditionally, kings wore *aathi* garlands on ceremonious occasions.

50

THE PARANTHAKAR INFIRMARY

The sun's rays bathed the wide streets of Pazhaiyarai the next morning, flooding them with light; the golden domes atop the city's splendid royal palaces dazzled with its red-gold brilliance.

A lavishly decorated elephant, resplendent with an *ambaari* on its back, made its ponderous way towards the front of Kundhavai Piratti's palace. The princesses themselves walked out within moments, onto steps meant for ascending such mounts, and made themselves comfortable. The animal began to stalk towards the Paranthaka Chozhar Infirmary, set in the middle of Padaiveedu settlements, thundering through the streets with its precious burden. The mahout walking by the side took matters into his hands at once and soothed the elephant, upon which it moderated its speed.

Tinkling bells heralding the arrival of the royals was enough to have the doors of various homes slammed open, and their residents to hasten towards the street. Their faces beamed as they encountered the princesses, and folded their hands with deference.

The avenues were swiftly crossed and soon, the elephant had arrived at the Padaiveedu cantonments—which presented a vastly different picture from other residential areas. Plump, well-fed roosters crowed all over the place, seeking combatants for a quarrel; rams, bearing their sturdy, curled horns proudly seemed to strut about, as though sending out a proclamation: *Who amongst you is willing to lock horns with me?* Ferocious dogs that seemed capable of ripping anyone's throats were bound to the entrance-pillars of homes with slender ropes or leather strips; little boys pranced through the streets, battling their peers with strong bamboo staffs; *Sadasada, padapada*! snapped their sticks as they slashed at each other, practicing the martial art of *Silambam*.

A good many homes displayed vibrant *kaavi* paintings upon their *thinnai* walls; for the most part, these seemed to depict the many adventures of Muruga Peruman or Chozha Emperors themselves— and even so, war and battle dominated the scene: the Lord chopped away head after countless head of Soora Padmasuran in one panel, while Durgai's execution of the evil Mahishasuran was illustrated in full and terrifying detail in another. Other walls glorified the many valorous exploits of Chozha warriors in the battlefields of Thellaaru, Thanjai, Kudamooku, Arisilaaru, Thiruppurambiyam, Velloor, Thakkolam, Sevur and many more such.

The princesses' majestic entry into the soldiers' settlements was the signal for the streets to break into pandemonium. Roosters flapped their wings, highly incensed, and flew towards the protection of the roofs; children called out to one another and ran to their homes, banging on doors to inform their families of royal visitors.

"Long live Ilaiya Piratti Kundhavai Devi!" Women, children and the elderly from practically every household lined the streets as the princesses went past, showering them with joyous blessings. "Long live Sundara Chozhar's illustrious daughter!" Some chose to follow the elephant and soon, this gregarious crowd grew ever larger, echoing with various blessings and chants.

We have mentioned previously, that the Padaiveedu residents numbered, amongst them, the women, children and parents of those soldiers presently in Eezham; Kundhavai had taken it upon herself to establish an infirmary, an *adhura salai* for their benefit, using funds from her own numerous landed property. The Chozha clan derived great pride in extolling the names and deeds of their forebears; the princess was no exception. Amongst her ancestors, one of the greatest was undoubtedly her grandfather's father, Emperor Paranthakar the first, and she had named the infirmary after him. It was her custom to visit often, and enquire after the health and well-being of the families of various soldiers, settled there.

The elephant stopped in the vicinity of the *adhura salai*; it bent its forelegs first, then, its hind legs. The princesses descended carefully. The mount's departure was the signal for the general population—comprising mostly the women and children—to surround the royal ladies at once.

"The infirmary is of benefit to you, isn't it?" enquired the princess. "Do the physicians dispense medicines to those in need, every day?"

"Indeed, yes, *Thaaye*," rose several voices in answer. "They do!"

"I suffered from a terrible cough for three months, Devi," recounted a woman. "The Vaidhyar's medicine cured me in a week."

"My willful son climbed a tree, fell and broke his leg, Amma," said another. "Our physician splinted his limb and bade him take medicine for fifteen days. His leg is now healed—he runs and plays about with his usual spirit. He has even begun to climb trees again!" finished the relieved lady.

"My mother's vision has suffered for a while now, Your Highness. She visited the infirmary for a whole month, and took her medicines," related one young woman. "I am happy to say now, that her sight is as well as ever!"

"Hear that, Vanathi?" murmured Kundhavai. "Ah, how enlightened were our ancestors! I wonder how they ever divined the precise herb that could cure a certain ill?"

"Undoubtedly, they must have had the benefit of second sight," was Vanathi's response. "How else could they have learnt all they did?"

"It might be true that they've discovered medicines for almost every physical malady—but alas that they shouldn't have found a single remedy for those such as you, dwindling away from mental afflictions!" mourned Kundhavai. "Now, what do you believe can be done about that?"

"Pray, *Akka*—kindly cease talking about my mental illness—it's no such thing! My friends tease me mercilessly as it is—"

"And that's as it should be, for you deserve every word of it. You've turned my own brother's head, haven't you? The poor boy used to enjoy the luxury of a carefree existence—and now he sends messages enquiring about your health through every envoy from Ilankai!"

Abruptly, a shout reached them: "Way! Way for the Vaidhyar! Way!" Guards cleaved a path through the surrounding crowds, and the most senior of the physicians presiding over the infirmary arrived, to welcome the princesses in state.

"You mentioned, I believe, certain wonderful herbs to be found in the forests surrounding Kodikkarai, didn't you, Vaidhyar?" asked Kundhavai. "I sent you a young warrior who might undertake a journey there and back—did he arrive?"

"Indeed, yes, *Thaaye*—that quick-witted youngster came yesterday, under the escort of Eesana Siva Battar. I have formed the intention of sending my son with him, too. My boy shall return from Kodikkarai, while your soldier appears to wish to journey to Ilankai as well—"

"Do we really need herbs from as far as that?" wondered Vanathi.

"Certainly, my lady—you do know the tale from Ramayanam, where the powerful Lord Anumaar flew over the seas, bringing the Sanjeevi hills, full of herbs, to save Lakshmanar's life—and it's said that a few fell from the mountain and onto the forests of Kodikkarai during his flight, which is why we still harvest such wonderful specimens from that region. Since the Sanjeevi Hills were in Ilankai in the first place, it is only to be expected that the best of herbs still be there. Should I manage to find the ones I need, Devi, I swear that I shall cure all the Emperor's ills myself, without doubt—!"

"May it be so, by God's grace. And so—where are those young men, now?"

"Within, *Amma*, and in readiness for their journey, upon your word."

The princesses entered the infirmary, escorted by the Chief Physician, taking in the sights of those waiting in the corridors for medicines, and those who had already had that felicity. Every one of them beamed at the sight of Kundhavai Piratti, vowing and declaring gratitude for their princess's kindness in setting up such an *adhura salai*, for them.

Two men awaited the ladies within the physician's room; one was Vandhiyathevan who, Kundhavai noted, amused, had dressed himself in the latest of fashions with the utmost care. Even Vanathi seemed to recognize him. "Why, *Akka*," she whispered into her companion's ears. "It does seem to be that young man from the Kudandhai Astrologer's home, doesn't it?"

"So it would seem," Kundhavai's tone was bland in the extreme. "What's more, he's visiting the Vaidhyar after barging into the home of an astrologer. Perhaps the poor man suffers from some hideous mental affliction, like you?" She turned to Vandhiyathevan. "You, *Ayya*, are the warrior who is willing to undertake a journey to Ilankai for herbs to soothe the Emperor, I believe?"

Whatever incomprehensible language Vandhiyathevan's eyes and lashes may have chosen for silent communication, his lips took recourse to the one in vogue among humans. "Indeed, yes, Your Highness. I'm on my way to Ilankai, true—and I may even have the felicity of meeting the Prince. Is there a message you wish me to convey to him?"

"Why, so there is. Kindly inform his royal highness, should you ever meet him, that the Kodumbalur princess suffers grievous physical maladies; she swoons often and stays unconscious for hours on end. Should the prince ever wish to see her in possession of her wits, he ought not to pause an instant in Eezham, but come home at once!"

"By all means, *Ammani*," and Vandhiyathevan turned his attention to Vanathi.

Kundhavai's flippant words threw the maiden into a morass of confused bashfulness; her beautifully chiseled features glowed, their exquisite loveliness enhanced, if that were even possible. She blushed painfully, striving to master the embarrassment that threatened to overwhelm her. "K-Kindly do not convey any such message, *Ayya*! If you must, do tell—do tell him that the Kodumbalur princess dines four times a day, dresses and revels in the kind hospitality of Ilaiya Piratti Kundhavai, if you please."

"By all means, *Ammani*," promised Vandhiyathevan.

"Well, upon my word! You've heard both our messages—yet, you assure us that you will deliver them faithfully! Surely only one of them can be true?"

"What of it, *Ammani*? My duty is deliver the messages of both the plaintiff and the defendant—it's the prince's responsibility, as the judge, to decide upon the veracity or otherwise of the statements," finished Vandhiyathevan, with aplomb.

"But don't, I beg of you, confuse the messages with those who gave them!" put in Vanathi.

Kundhavai turned to the Vaidhyar, apparently feeling that the conversation had gone on long enough. "Have you received the palm-leaves to be given to these men, from the palace's Thirumandhira *Olai* Official?"

"Of course, *Thaaye*. Two, to be accurate. One carried a general message: *These envoys are engaged upon a mission to secure herbs for the wellbeing of the Emperor; government officials on their path are to render whatever assistance necessary, in accomplishing their task.* The other was addressed specifically to the guardian of the lighthouse at Kodikkarai," explained the Vaidhyar. "Both are in the possession of these youngsters."

"Excellent. I see no reason for them to tarry, then," said Kundhavai. "Surely they may leave at once?"

"Why, certainly," assented Vandhiyathevan.

Easier said than done, however.

The whole cavalcade exited the infirmary. The royal elephant, *ambaari* at the ready, stood prepared to allow the princesses to mount. Two stallions, fleet-footed as the wind and fairly twitching for a gallop had been brought over from the palace as well, for the messengers.

And yet—it did not seem as though everyone concerned could begin their journey at once. Vandhiyathevan, for instance, seemed to be beset with a veritable plethora of doubts that had to be assuaged that very instant; Kundhavai, for her part, seemed to be plagued by a thousand perils that might endanger her messenger, and of which she thought it best to warn him. In particular did she instruct him about the dangers he might be expected to encounter, upon his journey.

The princesses ascended their royal mount.

Vandhiyathevan and his companion climbed onto their horses as well.

The elephant cherished no desire, it seemed, to move; Kundhavai indicated, with a sign, that it might be prudent for those who were to travel the longer distance to start.

Left with no further pretext to dawdle, Vandhiyathevan wheeled his horse—with a great deal of reluctance, it must be admitted. He craned his neck and gazed at Kundhavai one last time, eyes fairly brimming with eagerness and yearning.

Then, abruptly, he delivered a slap to his stallion, as though furious with it; that well-bred animal sprang forward, quite unused to such cavalier treatment. It sped away, kicking up a cloud of dust; the Vaidhyar's son had to gather all his considerable inexperience just to follow him.

Kundhavai fell into a reverie as the elephant made its ponderous way back to the palace. *Strange indeed, the vagaries of the mind,* she mused. *Why does my conscience, having rejected kings among kings, and the greatest of warriors with a flick of my finger, take such pains over an ordinary man? Why does my heart worry so much about his fate, and hope upon hope that he will succeed in his perilous mission …?*

"Such deep reflections, *Akka*," Vanathi's voice intruded upon her thoughts. "What are they, may I ask?"

"Nothing worth the mention, my dear. If you must know, I was wondering about that conceited young man, and why on earth I must needs choose him to send a message to my brother—"

"Indeed, *Akka*, you're very right. A vastly troublesome fellow, I thought. Even a master thief, if I might say so—"

"A thief, you say? But why?"

"Well, theives make away with such useless things as silver and gold in the ordinary way, but this one seems a vast sight more dangerous—I fear, very much, that he wishes to steal Chozha's Nadu's most precious deity in his capable hands!" twinkled Vanathi. "Surely you won't let such an eventuality come to pass?"

"Why, you insolent little brat," exclaimed Kundhavai, without heat. "So you think me the same as you? Not on your life, my girl!"

As the elephant progressed along its way, its occupants noticed, at one point, a great many women congregated upon the street. Kundhavai halted their progress at once, and leant out. "What is it?" she enquired. "Do you wish to apprise me of anything?"

"There has been no news until now of our men in the Eezham battlefield, *Thaaye*," one of the gathered women took a step forward. "Is it true that the Thanjavur authorities have prevented rice and grain from being sent to them? But how will they survive without food in those harsh conditions, *Amma*?"

"There's no cause for concern, I assure you," soothed Ilaiya Piratti. "No matter the schemes of those in Thanjavur, be aware that our soldiers receive their sustenance from the ports of Maamallapuram. Surely your beloved Prince wouldn't let his valiant men starve, when they're distinguishing themselves for the sake of Chozha Nadu?"

At any other time, the princess would have stayed longer, in a bid to assuage their lacerated feelings—but she wished for solitude now, battered and buffeted by strangely unsettling emotions.

The elephant marched on, towards the palace.

૪௳

51

MAAMALLAPURAM

We now wish our readers to make a journey to a seaport with which they are undoubtedly well-acquainted: Maamallapuram.

Three hundred years have passed since Mahendra Pallavar and his illustrious son, Narasimhar Pallavar transformed the rather drab harbour-city into a fantasy land of unimaginable beauty with wonderful, life-like sculptures.

These days, the port has lost some of its earlier splendour and dimmed, in consequence—an unwelcome change that sinks our hearts. Mansions and palace lie in a protracted state of dilapidation, the noble edifices crumbling; the streets and harbour no longer thrive with crowds of people. No more do the great warehouses exist; no more are there mounds of wares and produce littering the sands, ready for import and export.

We have seen, earlier, that the sea made its way inland, forming a deep, natural waterway that facilitated ships to enter and berth themselves with a good deal of ease. Now, however, the canal was shallow, sand having silted a good deal over the years; small crafts and canoes were the only ones that could find their way in, perhaps. Larger ships and boats would have to stay moored much further away, in the open sea; goods meant for export would have to be loaded onto smaller crafts, and transported to them.

It must be admitted, though, that despite this general dilapidation, Maamallapuram had also acquired a few merits: in particular, the temples on the beach, that capture our heart and eyes with their indescribable beauty. These are unlike those carved out by Mahendran and Maamallan out of sheer rock, but have been constructed piece by piece, with stone sourced from elsewhere, and seem to sparkle like wondrous crowns that adorn Samudhraraja, the Ocean King. *Adada*, one is bereft of words indeed, when it comes to describing the astounding form and beauty of these creations!

There is, in addition to the above, a charming Vinnagara temple in the midst of the city, dedicated to the Lord who Guards the Three Worlds as He reclines upon His snake-bed. This noble edifice, we learn, was renovated by the devout Parameswara Pallavan, he who considered both Saivism and Vaishnavism as twin halves of his soul, and as dear to him as his very sight. Thalasayana Perumal, who graces His devotees here, was visited by Thirumangaiyazhwar himself, who prostrated himself at the Lord's feet and sang hymns, overcome by a veritable deluge of devotion. We may deduce from his songs, in fact, that the Pallava *samrajyam* was a thriving, flourishing empire even in his times, judging by the many riches and splendours mentioned:

> *"Pulankoll nidhikkuvaiyodu*
> *Puzhaikkai ma kalitrinamum*
> *Nalankoll navamanik kuvaiyum*
> *Sumanthengum naanrosinthu*
> *Kalangal iyangum mallaik*
> *Kadal mallaith thalasayanam*
> *Valangoll manathaaravarai*
> *Valangoll en mada nenje!"*

A hundred years have swept by since the saint sang his songs; the Pallava *samrajyam* is no longer, and the sun of its magnificence has set a long time since. Kanchi, once known as peerless in learning, has lost its claim to that title as well; even *"kalangal iyangum kadalmallai"*—Kadal Mallai, once famed for its ships, commerce and trade, seems dimmed.

Time may have marched on and left its indelible mark on the city, but in one aspect, Maamallapuram remained almost unchanged: Time, for all its progress and prowess, could not ravage the port-city's beautifully wrought carvings. Images sculpted among the many rock faces, the temples and *vimanam*-chariots carved out of the boulders dotting the landscape stayed in the same, pristine condition they had been, three hundred years ago, when first carved. These days, more crowds thronged the lands to glimpse these marvels of human creation, than merchants to deal with the humdrum business of trade.

A beautiful chariot, designed to represent a *vimanam* and harnessed with two blood stallions rattled along the wide avenues of the city, in great style. The well-decorated horses; spacious, intricately carved and embellished chariot not to mention its roof, overlaid with gold and glinting in a way that rivaled the evening sun, were indicative of the fact that its three passengers could not be anything but royal.

And so it proved to be. One, warrior among warriors was Sundara Chozhar's firstborn, Aditha Karikalan, a man who had proven himself by venturing into battlefields at a remarkably young age, performing a great many valorous deeds and earning a reputation for himself as a veteran; who had faced Madurai's Veera Pandiyan in war, slaying him, hence earning the distinguished sobriquet, *The Kopparakesari Who Beheaded Veera Pandiya*. Almost immediately after one of the Chozha dynasty's greatest enemies had finally been routed out and the Pandiyas safe under their authority, Sundara Chozhar had fallen prey to illness; this prompted him to announce formally, without any further ado, that his firstborn was the heir to the throne and he duly performed a *Yuvaraja Pattabishekam* to enforce the edict. Aditha Karikalan was authorized from that day on, to make grants as he chose and style himself as the Crown Prince, on his own stone inscriptions.

The next few years saw him proceed to the northern lands hotfoot, with the praiseworthy intention of routing out Kannara Devan of the Rettai Mandalam kingdom, and freeing Thondai Mandalam from his clutches. Great were the valiant deeds he performed here as well, and his battle exploits were many as he trounced his foe, beating him into retreat well beyond the northern banks of the Vada Pennai. All these ferocious martial activities did mean, however, a frequent replenishment of resources; Aditha Karikalan made camp often in Kanchi, gathering the men, weapons and equipment necessary for warfare. It was at this point that the Pazhuvettarayars began throwing obstacles in his path; further battles along the northern front would only be possible, they proclaimed, once the war in Eezham had concluded. Other rumours began to float in as well, on the questionable activities of various people: it was learnt, later, that the Eezham forces had not fared any better than their mainland counterparts; food from Chozha Nadu had not reached them, and they suffered from its lack.

All these and more had served to turn Aditha Karikalan into a morass of fury and indignation, his warrior heart thudding in agony.

Certain momentous events occurred in the three hundred years before and after the time of our story; Thamizh Annai, the great mother, gave birth to men and women who carved a place for themselves in history with their ideals; accomplished such valorous deeds that they eclipsed heroes of epics and ancient legends. Warriors the likes of Veeman and Archunan, Dhronar and Bheeshmar, Gadothgajan and Abhimanyu appeared, and performed wondrous feats that stunned the world; each of their achievements in battle only seemed to add to the strength of their shoulders. Men advanced in years possessed the strength to break entire mountains with bare hands; youngsters not yet of age seemed able to journey to the heavens upon the winds, and pluck the very stars from their black depths.

Two such warriors now accompanied Aditha Karikalan, occupying pride of place in his chariot. One was Thirukkovilur Malayaman; lord of Malayamanadu, the name of which had, over the years, shrunk to Maladu. Often was it referred to, in popular usage, as Miladu, which explained another title of his: *Miladudaiyar*. Sundara Chozhar's second queen Vana Maadevi happened to be his much beloved daughter, which made him Aditha Karikalan's grandfather as well. The years had sharpened his intellect and added wisdom while not lessening his physical prowess in any way, thus likening him to the Kauravas's much revered guru, Bheeshmar himself. Great as the faith Aditha Karikalan had in this revered old man's insight, it cannot be denied that his old-fashioned theories and long-winded advice did, sometimes, test his patience sorely.

The last of the trio was Parthibendran. The scion of a branch of the ancient Pallava clan, he was slightly older than Aditha Karikalan. Lacking a throne, his only ambition was to distinguish himself in the battlefield with a great many courageous exploits; he had attached himself to the crown prince, as a result. His talent had made him the right hand of Aditha Karikalan in the decisive battle against Veera Pandiyan; it had earned, in consequence, the warrior's respect, and a staunch, intimate friendship. Ever since the fall of their hated foe, the two had become boon companions.

Rattling along the streets in state, their conversation, such as it was, revolved almost entirely around news from Thanjavur.

"I will *not* stand the Pazhuvettarayars' high-handedness an instant more, I tell you! They cross all bounds with each passing day. How dared—how *dared* they brand my personal messenger a spy? The sheer audacity of it! And to announce all over the city that he carries a bounty of a thousand gold coins upon his head? How do you think I can stand outrageous behaviour such as this?" Aditha Karikalan thundered. "My sword shrinks within its very scabbard with embarrassment—and here you are, counseling patience!"

"Quite the contrary—but then, I did warn you to reconsider sending Vandhiyathevan, of all men, on a sensitive assignment such as this," came Parthibendran's dulcet tones. "I knew that rash idiot would wreck and ruin it with his impulsive acts. A royal mission requires swift thinking and sharp intellect; certainly something more than just the ability to brandish a sword and spear, after all—"

The Pallava prince, it must be admitted, was neither a great admirer of Vandhiyathevan, nor of the crown prince's obvious partiality for him. Never did he miss an opportunity to point out that young man's faults, and took care to level criticism at his every act. His reaction at this juncture, therefore, came as no surprise.

"Didn't take you long to begin against him, did it? You've never been able to rest in peace unless you've managed to rage against Vandhiyathevan at least once," groaned Aditha Karikalan. "And as for wits—who else might be suited best for a mission such as this, I ask you? How does he lack for sense? My orders were for him to deliver my *olai* to the Emperor somehow, and he managed to carry it out. And that's why the Pazhuvettarayars are furious—where's Vandhiyathevan's fault in all this?"

"In not acceding to your commands, strictly," sniped Parthibendran. "I've no doubt he went above and beyond your instructions, poked his nose into what wasn't his business and managed to anger them in some way."

"Oh, be quiet. *Thatha*, why this profound silence on your part? Reveal your opinion, I beg you. What do you say to gathering all our forces, storming Thanjavur and rescuing the Emperor ourselves? Why not bring him to Kanchi? How many more days must I sit still, forced to watch those wretched Pazhuvettarayars guard my father like a prisoner?" growled Aditha Karikalan, plainly furious. "Just who do they think they are? And how much longer am I supposed to spend in mortal fear of them?"

Thirukkovilur Malayaman-Miladudaiyar, veteran of sixty-four blood-drenched battles, cleared his throat, preparatory to speech. By this time, however, the sea was well within their sight; white-tipped waves crashed onto the shore. "Let us alight from this chariot first," he ventured. "We shall make ourselves comfortable at our usual place, shall we, and speak to our heart's content? For, I am getting on in years, *Thambi*, and find it quite uncomfortable to speak in a rattling chariot, you see."

જી

52

OLD MEN, AND MARRIAGES

Small boulders dotted Maamallapuram's shoreline in plenty. Sometimes, the sea would pound upon them, the massive waves submerging them completely; at others, the tide would recede and reveal them to the sun, affording time to dry out a little. Not a single one had been ignored by the great sculptors of the port-city to spend eternity as faceless rocks; each had been turned into an exquisite work of art, large or small, depending on their size and now decorated the shores, forever a vista of sculptural beauty.

The Chozha prince and his companions approached two such boulders facing each other, and alighted from their chariot. Karikalan and Malayaman seated themselves on each of the rocks, obviously meant to be thrones fit for kings, while Parthibendran stood apart. Often, the sea surged over to them, washing their feet and reaching up to their calves. Sometimes, droplets of water splashed onto their faces as waves crashed over rocks, pearls showered by the ocean. Row upon row of boats cleaved the water at a distance, loaded with various produce and goods meant for trade. A good many of these were carefully removed from said boats and carried aboard large ships that lay further out at sea, their enormous sails unfurled against the wind.

"When I think of all the equipment and goods gathered so painstakingly for the Rettai Mandalam invasion being carted away wholesale to Eezham ..." murmured Parthibendran. "I can't stand it—my whole being burns!"

"Well, what else can be done, pray?" demanded Aditha Karikalan. "The best of Chozha warriors have been sent there, and they're heaping victory upon victory on battlefields, showering us with accolades. Why, they've actually managed to capture Anuradhapuram, pride of Eezham rulers and their principal seat for a thousand years—you know it always managed to dance away from our grasp—and hoisted our flag! Do you truly want warriors of such mettle to starve?"

"Not starve, no—when did I ever say that?" retorted the Pallava prince. "Of course, they must be sent grain—but from the Chozha port at Nagaippattinam. Or Sethukkarai, perhaps, in Pandiya Nadu. What's the necessity of carting them all from these drought-ridden, arid Thondai lands? Especially when we're on the point of setting out towards Rettai Mandalam? That, you see, is my objection—that we're forced to kick our heels just for the sake of sending them essentials."

"Precisely—I can't bear to sit still, either. And I fail to see what those dastardly Pazhuvettarayars are hoping to accomplish with these acts!" fumed Karikalan. "How long are we supposed to put up with such a state of affairs? *Thatha*," he turned swiftly to the old man, "Do open your lips and tell us what you think—why this blessed silence, anyway?"

"These waves crash ceaselessly onto the shore, thundering all over the place, my child—and your friend adds his bit, screeching above them," pronounced Malayaman Miladudaiyar. "How am I supposed to compete with them? I am getting on in years, after all."

"Do be quiet for a while, Parthibendra, and let *Thatha* give us his opinion," instructed Karikalan.

"Witness my lips seal this very instant!" retorted Parthibendran.

"After all, *Thatha*, poor grandfather, has had a great deal to bear—having to ooze at a snail's pace from his rock-fort in this doddering old age, just to meet us. My deepest sympathies for his efforts; of course, how dare I open my mouth in his venerable presence? This sea, now—mannerless creature that it is, dares to rave, rant and throw itself about just as it chooses, right in front of him! There seems to be no one capable of taking it down a peg or two," he shook his head. "Why—it's almost as though the Ocean King fears the Malai Nattu ruler not at all!"

"And yet, *Thambi*, Parthibendra, there was a time when he did," the old man answered calmly, choosing to disregard this flippant speech. "A time when the kings and emperors of this land shook at the mere mention of Thirukkovilur Malayaman—when rulers of vast lands, such as the Chalukyas of Rettai Mandalam, the Vanagovarayars of Vallam, the Gangars and Kongars slithered into their holes like snakes at the peal of thunder! Why, even Samudhrarajan, the King of Oceans knew his place and stayed subdued—but now, now that this feeble body of mine reveals its years, they've seen fit to shed their fears and show their true colours shamelessly. As for those wretched Pazhuvettarayars of the West who seek to rout me out—not on their lives! You mentioned a moment ago, didn't you, Karikala, that you were unaware of their true motives? Listen, young man, and I shall reveal it: their intentions are none other than to cause a rift between you and your brother. Their heinous objective is to weaken each of you, and ensure that you never join hands. To make certain that Arulmozhi Varman tastes bitter defeat in the wars at Eezham and to humiliate him; that you, therefore, develop a hatred of him and treat him with contempt. Then, of course, nothing else would do for the both of you to want to rip each other's throats, whereupon, this old man would be reduced to utter misery ... and this is what they wish—"

"Then they'd be certain to taste defeat, *Thatha*," Karikalan interrupted before Miladudaiyar could finish. "I've no intention of quarreling with Arulmozhi—in fact, I would give my life for him, if ever the need arose. Speaking of which ... sometimes, I wonder if I oughtn't to board a ship and leave for Ilankai myself—what difficult straits might my brother not have been reduced to, in those wretched lands? Meanwhile, here I am, with nothing better to do than eat and sleep myself into a stupor, in my pretty palace. My spear and sword rust in their place, and each moment seems an aeon! I can barely sit still here. Tell me, *Thatha*—may I board one of those vessels on their way to Eezham now? This very instant?"

"What an excellent suggestion, Your Highness," exulted Parthibendran. "Now this—*this* is more like it! You've merely given form to my own intentions, this many days. And not a moment more to lose either; let's leave at once. There's no point in asking *Thatha*; he's bound to counsel you to squat on your haunches and wait. *Don't decide anything on impulse*," he mimicked the old man. "Let's leave tomorrow—we'll round up half our Thondai Mandalam men, march to Ilankai, finish the war one way or the other, and then disembark at Nagaippattinam," he shot out his plans like water spluttering in boiling oil. "And then we'll descend like a ton of bricks upon those blasted Pazhuvettarayars and give them a hiding—!"

"You see what he says, Karikala? I warned you right at the beginning, didn't I? Now you know why I swore I wouldn't say a word unless this one kept his mouth shut, don't you?"

"As you wish, then, *Thatha*—I've shut up," Parthibendran snapped. "And you're free to speak your mind. Whatever that may be." And he closed his lips with his palms, in a theatrical gesture.

"You, Karikala, are a warrior among warriors; there haven't been many of your ilk even in these brave Thamizh lands, famed for their courageous sons. As an eighty-year-old and a veteran of many, many huge battles, let me tell you, my boy—I've never seen the likes of you, who dared to plunge into the battlefield all by himself, hacked his enemies and emerged triumphant. You were barely sixteen when you plunged into the Sevur battle—and never have I seen such, either before or after, as you waded through blood and gore, destroying foes, sword swinging now right, now left, dismembering and decapitating at a rate that heads simply rolled, everywhere! Why, I can see you still, if I close my eyes …" he paused. "So is your friend; a great warrior in his own right. And yet, the two of you are far too quick to anger, and as for your impulsiveness—this, exactly is why you fail at your tasks. You fail to think things through, and end up doing the opposite, the very thing that will serve your purposes the least—"

"You've given us this very piece of advice at least a thousand times, *Thatha*."

"And it has yielded absolutely no results—is that what you wish to say? Or perhaps you want me to leave for my home without another word?"

"No, not at all. Tell us, please, what must be done next."

"Send forth, right away, for Arulmozhi; make sure that the two of you are never separated an instant—"

"What on earth—what sort of advice is this? And what of the war in Eezham, pray, if my brother comes here?"

"The war, my boy, has now reached an impasse. Our troops have, at long last, captured Anuradhapuram, just in time for the rains, I might add, which will last for four months and during which time, nothing can be done in the way of an invasion except to retain what has been captured. A task, I am sure, our commanders are more than capable of undertaking. It is vital that Arulmozhi be here at this very moment, Karikala—I see no point in concealing the truth from you, anymore: the Chozha Empire that Vijayalayar wrought into being with blood and sweat is under threat of collapse; it is imperative that you and yours stand together at this dangerous time, and keep safe. We ought to do all in our power to gather our forces, for there is no supposing what peril we might find ourselves in, at any time—"

"But—*Thatha*, what's all this nonsensical talk? What's the need for me to fear anything, as long as I bear my trusty sword in my hands? And what does it matter if we're in the very thick of danger, anyway? I can take care of myself—surely there's no foe on this earth I can't defeat, no peril I can't face by myself—I need no one's support …"

"Spoken like a true warrior, Karikala—and there's no need to remind me of your valour; haven't I just said that I know you, my boy? And yet, there's no harm in casting our minds to that great saint Thiruvalluvar, and reflecting upon his wise words:

*"Anjuvathu anjaamai pethamai anjuvathu
Anjal arivaar thozhil!"*

Cowardice may be despicable, lad, but there's something to be said
for entertaining a healthy fear of that which is worthy of it. Quivering in
your place during war, when you're facing the enemy is contemptible—
and if I ever have the misfortune of being saddled with a boy of that kind
in my family, I shall cleave him in two with my own sword, in my old,
trembling hands, bereft of their legendary strength, without a moment's
regret! But of other things, my boy—such as treachery and appalling
plots hatched in the darkness of souls filled with hatred, and conspiracies
that terrorize an empire—these, you must and should fear. And take steps
to protect yourself from grievous harm. Royals, especially those in the
direct line of succession to the throne, who will one day rule the country,
must be especially cautious about such threats; there's no room or place
for indiscretion or carelessness. That will spell doom for the land, as a
whole."

"But—what are these inexplicable perils that you keep harping
about? Only if you share them in detail, *Thatha*, will we be able to guard
ourselves—"

"Certainly I shall; I was about to, anyway. A few days ago, the
Sambuvaraiyars played host to a mysterious midnight meeting at
Kadambur palace; from what I can see, quite a few big names were there:
Periya Pazhuvettarayar, for instance, and then Thennavan Mazhavaraiyar,
Kundrathur Kizhaar, Vanangamudi Munaiyarayar, Anjaatha Singa
Mutharayar, Rettai Kudai Rajaliyaar ... these were the names I could
gather. A good many others may have elected to be present as well—"

"Why, so they might have; what of it? Doubtless they watched
song and dance far into their precious midnight meeting; ate until their
stomachs burst; drank gallons of liquor and stumbled off to their beds
in a stupor. How does all this affect us? All these men you mentioned—
grey-haired with white beards trailing around their feeble waists in their
dotage—what on earth do you think they can accomplish, with their
whispering campaigns?"

"Considering your confirmed opinion of old men and their feebleness, Karikala, there does not seem to be anything more to be said. After all, I am getting on in years myself; far, far older than any of those I mentioned—"

"Pray don't be offended, *Thatha*—would I ever dare to class you with those doddering idiots? Do tell us what happened next."

"Ah, there you go again, implying that we cannot even fend for ourselves! Do not forget, my prince, that the feeble old man who heads them did, after all, enter wedlock just some time ago. Do not forget, Karikala, that there is nothing more dangerous than a young man who has married in his old age!"

A strange expression flitted across Aditha Karikalan's face at the very mention of said old man and his wedding; his eyes grew bloodshot, staring stark, as though a ferocious Goddess, a dark spirit thirsted for blood; his lips trembled, and the sounds of his teeth grinding were almost audible.

Malayaman, intent on his story, noticed none of this; Parthibendran could, and did.

"Need we talk of all that now, *Ayya*?" he intercepted, at this moment. "Why don't you relate what happened next at the Sambuvaraiyar palace?"

"I was about to—but I am, as you so kindly said, getting old ... my mind wanders so much these days that I went on to something else. Now listen, Karikala; Parthibendra, you must, too. The meeting I mentioned was attended not just by old, doddering men, but a few youngsters as well. One of them was Kandamaaran, Sambuvaraiyar's son. The other ..."

Karikalan was quick to notice the pause. "Well, who was it?" he prodded. "*Who*, Thatha?"

"The beloved son of your elder grandfather, Kandaradhithar. None other than your Chithappa, Madhuranthaka Thevan!"

Parthibendran and Karikalan stared at him for moment. The next instant, they broke into merry peals of laughter.

"But—what is it that I have said?" Miladudaiyar asked, querulously. "What do you find in this to amuse you? Or perhaps you are laughing at me again—"

"Not at all, *Thatha*; pray don't take offense. We found it hilarious that you chose to refer to Madhuranthakan as a 'youngster!' Isn't he, after all, even more elderly than all of you put together?" gurgled Karikalan. "The very symbol of pious old age, surely?"

"You *have* heard, I know, of youth returning to old men, at times. It looks like the years have rolled back for your uncle too. Until some time ago, he was touring the country, mumbling about renouncing the world and devoting himself to divine service and Sivan—but now, he's married wives one, two and three at a steady rate, I see."

"Well, and so he may, with my goodwill. He can go on gathering wives into his harem, for all I care. What of it?"

"But that *is* the problem, *Thambi*. You see, none of his marriages are affairs of the heart; they are political, all of them, and at the behest of those treacherous Pazhuvettarayars, to further their conspiracies—!"

"I see no need for beating about the bush any more, and these mysterious tales of plots and betrayals, *Thatha*. Do step right out into the open: what do those Pazhuvoor brothers wish? What on earth is behind their tours of the land, and these precious midnight conferences? What do they hope to accomplish with silly little Madhuranthakan?"

"Nothing much, I am afraid: merely to place him upon the Chozha throne, and ensure that neither you nor your brother inherits this empire," announced the old man in stentorian tones. "It is to this effect that they have almost imprisoned your father within the Thanjai fort—to secure his approbation for their heinous plan!"

53

MALAYAMAN'S FURY

It might have been true that the last, terrifying declaration uttered by Thirukkovilur Malayaman—as famed for his intelligence as his integrity, and equally renowned for his wealth of worldly experience—did not quite have the effect of sending Crown Prince Aditha Karikalan into a deep swoon ... but came quite close to it. The young man sat in his place, dumbstruck, and quite unable to do anything else. Beside him stood Parthibendran, gaping like a landed fish. Even the sea appeared to have quieted down for a brief while, and as for the vigorous chants of "*Elelo*!" from the men engaged in transferring goods from small-craft to the ships—even those seemed in abeyance, for now. All was silence.

Abruptly, Karikalan raised his head and stared at his grandfather, shaking himself out of his astonishment and feeling a flicker of embarrassment at having even given way to it, in the first place. "I've heard of such rumours floating around the cities, yes—but I've never given any credence to them, so far. You seem to be so very certain of your news ... can such a thing even be possible, do you think?"

"Why not?" queried Miladudaiyar. "Have you forgotten who ruled this empire before your grandfather? Wasn't it his elder, your *periya thatha*, Kandaradhitha Thevar? And who else might be said, pray, to have more right to rule this land than his son? More than even you?"

"No—never—not on your life! Whom do you think deserves the privilege of rule? An absolute and ineffable fool—someone who can't string together four words—cannot even grip a sword in his hands—who ought to have been a woman, but was born a man by a grievous error on nature's part—*that* one? Or a warrior among warriors who entered the battlefield at the tender age of twelve—the lion who beheaded Veera Pandiya with a single stroke of his sword—who has never, until this moment tasted defeat in any form—to Aditha Karikalar?" Parthibendran's words shot out like a volley of arrows. "My much revered and respected Miladudaiyar— have you finally and completely taken leave of your aged senses?"

Aditha Karikalan suppressed him with a few sharp, well-chosen remarks, and turned to his grandfather. "This empire doesn't really matter much to me, *Thatha*—my sword is capable of establishing ten such realms. Pray, tell me, though, how law and justice stand upon this matter. Had it been resolved right at the beginning that Madhuranthakan was to inherit the throne, I wouldn't have minded at all, but now that I've been declared the crown prince and my *Yuvaraja Pattabishekam* carried out in full view of this land and people—how can anyone expect me to just relinquish my claims? Would *you* truly agree to such a course of action?"

"I would not; not now, not ever. Should you ever decide to bestow this empire on Madhuranthakan yourself, in a fit of benevolence, my first instinct would be to cut you into a hundred pieces with this sword of mine—and then, I shall seek the woman who bore you in her womb for ten months, and scatter her flesh to the winds! And then I, I who brought your mother into this world—I shall kill myself with my own bare hands! Never—not until my body releases its last breath shall I allow this ancient Chozha kingdom to pass into anyone's hands but yours!" Miladudaiyar's faded eyes gleamed with the spirit of his growled speech; his aged, withered body trembled with the force of his emotions.

"Hear, hear! *That's* as it should be—wonderfully spoken, *Thatha*!" And Parthibendran practically sprinted towards the old man and folded him into a hearty embrace, eyes overflowing with tears.

Karikalan spent a few moments in silence, staring at the sea. "If these truly are your sentiments, *Thatha*," he began, finally, "why wait? Let's gather our forces and march towards Thanjai wholesale; descend on those dastardly Pazhuvettarayars and their cohorts—Mazhavaraiyar, Sambuvaraiyar, Mutharaiyar, Munaiyaraiyar and the rest; vanquish them in one stroke and capture the fort; bundle Madhuranthakan into prison and free the Chakravarthy. All we need, *Thatha*, is your blessing—for who on this wide earth can defeat me and Parthibendran, as long as we're together?" This, in a voice fairly brimming with pride and confidence.

"Not in direct combat, perhaps—but what about stealth and treachery? How would you withstand attacks from invisible enemies? The moment you approach Thanjai with your forces rumours will start flying about imminent war between father and son! Why, they would even spread word that the Chakravarthy had left this world, unable to bear such terrible tidings. And there would certainly be those ready to believe such horrible untruths. What then, Child? You would falter—for, would you be able to bear the heinous charge of gathering forces against your own father?"

"Siva Sivaa," Karikalan clapped his palms over his ears. "I can't—no!"

"There it is, then. That is what I meant in the beginning, when I warned you that grievous peril—*abaayam*—surrounds us. "

"Suggest some sort of *ubaayam*, then—a ruse to escape these terrors."

"Send a loyal messenger to Ilankai, first, and bring forth your brother Arulmozhi. He will not, I am sure, be so unconscionable as to leave behind his own men or the battlefield; someone must be sent, who possesses extraordinary powers of persuasion; the skill to present the situation and change his mind—"

"If you will permit, *Ayya*," Parthibendran stepped forward. "I should like to go, myself, and carry out this task."

"That is as may be; you and Karikalan may decide upon a course of action yourselves. I must insist on this, though: whoever you choose, eventually, cannot afford to behave like Vandhiyathevan, interfering in affairs not of his concern—"

"There!" crowed Parthibendran. "Hear that? What did I tell you?"

"Have you heard any news of him, *Thatha*?" enquired Karikalan.

"I must confess that I almost suspected him, once, of having joined our foes—but later, I decided that there was no foundation for my doubts. For they proved to be groundless."

"*Now* what do you say?" Karikalan challenged his friend, in turn.

"Pray, let him finish—there's no point in interrupting. *Ayya*, what sort of suspicions did you harbour against Vandhiyathevan, and how did you manage to absolve him of any complicity?"

"I learnt that he was present in Sambuvaraiyar's palace, the night of the midnight meeting—but I understand he had no part to play in any of those great men's machinations."

"But—how did *you* know all this?"

"For one thing, I never received an invitation to grace the Kadambur banquet, and that set my nerves on edge. I acted on my instincts, waylaid Kundrathur Kizhaar, who was returning home from the celebrations, imprisoned him in my mountain fort and questioned him carefully, upon which he divulged that Vandhiyathevan and Sambuvaraiyar's son Kandamaaran were friends—"

"True indeed; they were part of our armed forces and shared guard duty on the banks of the Vada Pennai, didn't they? I know that their friendship dated from those times—"

"However that may be, it was clear that the boy had been within the palace when the conspiracy was hatched, but I knew not the way to discover if he had been a part of it. Later, I absolved him of any blame when I learnt that he had escaped Thanjai fort, having stabbed Kandamaaran in the back—"

"Now *that* I shall never believe! No matter what harebrained scheme he may think up, Vandhiyathevan would never be cowardly enough to stab a man in the back, and he's certainly not the kind of bastard who would do that to his own friend—!"

"Even if he found out that that precious friend was now involved in a treacherous plot to betray his own lord and master? And if said 'friend' was eager to co-opt Vandhiyathevan's services and loyalty towards such an effort?"

"Whatever the temptation or cause, he would engage his foe in a fair fight, face-to-face; as to stabbing him in the back … no, I shall never lend any credence to that."

"Your confidence in your friend is a source of eternal marvel to me, *Thambi.* Be that as it may—that is the accusation leveled by the Pazhuvettarayars, who are now hunting him in good earnest. That is all I know—but I wish to tell you this: regardless of whether or not any stabbing took place, it seems obvious that there must have been some sort of altercation between Vandhiyathevan and Kandamaaran. That serves as proof, doesn't it, that your friend was blameless?"

"I assure you that there was no need to go quite that far, to establish his innocence. Should Vallavarayan ever decide to join hands with our enemies, this very earth, I believe, would collapse into anarchy. The seas would dry up into barren, arid deserts; the heavens would crash down! The sun would rise at night, and the entire Chozha clan would disintegrate into nothing—" Aditha Karikalan could barely speak for the haste and emotion that coloured his voice and features.

"I must say, I agree with his highness," Parthibendran put in heavily, at this point. "Vandhiyathevan meditating evil upon us and the empire— *that* I could never believe. If there *is* an accusation I must place upon him it's this: not for all the worlds can he resist the temptations of a beautiful young woman. He'd lose his head in an instant."

Aditha Karikalan threw a glance at his companion; his lips curved into a slight smile. "Pray, why else do you think I charged him with an *olai* to be delivered to my sister, Ilaiya Piratti, immediately after he'd done so to the Chakravarthy? Once he'd set eyes on the princess—ah, where would he find the means to escape? She'd have a faithful servant at her feet for life."

"Were *those* your instructions to that boy?" queried Miladudaiyar at once. "Ah, what a pity that I knew nothing of this—and have you heard anything from Vandhiyathevan, since he fled Thanjavur? What of news from Ilaiya Piratti?"

"I expect an *olai* any moment—but so far, I'm sorry to say, nothing."

"Once Arulmozhi is here, you shall send for your sister as well, and then, all will be well. We may entrust this empire with all its concerns, problems and ruses to Ilaiya Piratti, whose advice we shall all take to heart and follow with right good will. That should be the end of all our worries—"

"Good heavens, *Thatha*—you seem to be even worse than Vandhiyathevan, in this respect! "

"Indeed, and I am not ashamed to admit it. She took the scepter of this empire into her capable hands when she was barely two, my boy; her word was law to her parents, me and your grandmother; she has tyrannized us every way she wished—and that is how it has been, to this day; that is how I hope it to be. Her slightest wish has always been my command, as far as I am concerned. Do not consider her praises a slight against you, Karikala; they add to your consequence, if anything, and not otherwise. For there is none, either among men or women in this land, whose intelligence rivals that of Ilaiya Piratti Kundhavai!" exulted Miladudaiyar, voice fairly ringing with elation. "You know of the superior intellect of our Chief Minister Aniruddha Brahmaraayar himself, don't you? And if such a great man unbends enough to ask her opinion—well, what more can I say?"

"All very well, I daresay and I'm not denying any of it, but what's to say that Vandhiyathevan *would* have met Ilaiya Piratti first?" Parthibendran's dislike of the young man, never very far from his thoughts, now rose again in good earnest. "What if he'd run headlong and bumped into some other young lady before her, and fallen hard for her considerable charms? Such as that dazzling beauty, the Pazhuvoor Ilaiya Rani, for instance?"

The last few words, uttered in a low voice, escaped the old man; not so Aditha Karikalan, whose head snapped up in an instant. The crown prince turned and leveled a stare at the Pallava warrior that fairly flew with such sparks of fury that Parthibendran almost quailed.

"You youngsters," Malayaman judged it time to leave, and rose from his rocky seat. "Doubtless have a great many things to discuss, in privacy. You are leaving for Ilankai tomorrow, are you not? Well, then. As old as I am, I shall need all the time I have to return to my palace. You may converse freely, and come home as you choose."

He left, and the friends waited, watching as he moved away, slowly.

Then, Parthibendran turned to Aditha Karikalan. "Your highness— my prince! Something troubles you deeply, chipping away at your conscience; a sorrow that has lodged into your heart, allowing you no respite. I know for a fact that it has to do, somehow, with the young queen of Pazhuvoor ... your very face and form undergo such a complete transformation whenever either she, or Periya Pazhuvettarayar's marriage are mentioned; your eyes turn bloodshot and fairly spew fury. How much longer will you stifle this anguish—before it consumes you completely?" He approached close, eyes brimming with a sort of suppressed anticipation. "You've called me your closest friend a thousand times— and yet, you seek to shut me out of your deepest thoughts. Why? Why not admit me into your confidence; share what ails you so deeply? Will you not permit me to listen to you, and assuage your pain? How many more days must I wait by your side in silence, fated to watch you suffer endlessly, without the power to serve you?"

"My friend," Aditha Karikalan heaved a deep sigh. "My pain, as you say, has been a constant companion for years—but it is one that can never be assuaged. It lives within me, and must die only when I do—of absolution, there's none. Neither is there a reason for why I mustn't share it with you, and so I shall—but later, tonight." He rose. "Now, we must leave for the palace with the old man; it isn't fair to let him return, all alone."

જી

54

"DEADLIER THAN VENOM, IS SHE!"

The three warriors spent the night in one of the old edifices that had once belonged to the Pallava Emperors of yore. Once the last meal for the night was at an end, Malayaman left, eager to attend a performance of an Aravaan Tale recital, to be held by the *Aindhu Radhams*, the Five Chariots. Aditha Karikalan and Parthibendran retired to one of the balconies, upstairs.

Underneath, spread out the night-time vista of Maamallapuram. The crown prince stood watching it for a while, from his superior vantage position. Lamps flickered feebly, here and there, in a vain attempt to dispel darkness; the streets were mostly deserted. The last ceremony for the day, the *ardha jaama* poojai was done; massive temple doors slowly groaned shut. The sea roared dully, desolation and loneliness seeping in from afar. In the distance, by the Five Chariots, people surrounded the *villuppattu* artist as he sang and recited the tale of valorous Aravaan; dark, misshapen shadows beyond a ring of oil-torches.

"Old as the hills—and he's gone to listen to ancient tales and songs!" exclaimed Aditha Karikalan. "Men like him are hard to find these days, aren't they? Getting on in years, but for sheer determination and iron grit, there aren't many like the ancient ones."

"Good lord, your highness, not you too. Pray don't start on the glory of the past," groaned Parthibendran. "What did they accomplish after all, that we haven't, ourselves? And if it comes to that—I certainly haven't heard of any warrior who went into battle and performed the illustrious deeds you yourself did."

"It augurs well for you, Parthiba, that I know you to be honest; your lips do not speak the direct opposite of what your heart harbours. Else—I would have been forced to consider you my greatest enemy," Aditha Karikalan smiled. "Your extraordinary praises; the way you pander to my ego—! There's nothing more powerful when it comes to destroying a man, my friend. Nothing else that would assure his swift and inglorious descent into *Pathalam*, the goriest underworld!"

"Indeed, *Ayya*, if one were to praise and please a man with completely spurious motives; to raise him to the skies without just cause—ah, that, then would be false and pretentious. If you were to approach Madhuranthakan, that shameless Pazhuvettarayar slave, for instance, and tell him that he was a 'Warrior Among Warriors,' that would be *mukasthuthi*. And if you ever believed me to be guilty of such a crime, pray do not hesitate to cut me down with your own sword. Tell me— was any of what I said about you an exaggeration? A blatant untruth? Who among those ancients, after all, has even come close to matching your martial accomplishments? One could, perhaps, consider your great-grandfather, Rajadithyar, who embraced death on an elephant, as somewhat approaching you with respect to valour; even so, he couldn't have been greater …"

"Enough, Parthiba, for God's sake! Comparing me with Rajadithyar— how could you *even*—you and I, my friend, aren't worthy to speak of a man who destroyed the massive Rashtrakuta hordes, the scourge of millions, a terrible ocean spewing evil in its wake, with a miniscule army! And ascended to the heaven of warriors too, on the battlefield. Pit ourselves against him? Do we even dare? Ignore the Chozhas for a moment, if you will, and let's speak of your own ancestors, the Pallavas. Think of the legends they sired—are we ever to see the likes of Mahendra Varmar and Maamallar again? To think of Narasimha Varmar, who single-handedly crushed Pulikesi, a man who ruled an Empire from Narmadha in the north to Thungabhadhra in the south—and even erected a column of victory in Vathapi? And to mention us in the same breath as him! Do you think anyone in our lifetime, or after us, could ever bring into existence a fantasyland such as Maamallapuram? *Adada*, just look around you once, Parthiba. Cast a glance at the *villuppattu* recital over there, in the distance. Men who could turn ordinary boulders into such beautiful works of art; carve rocks into magnificent chariots; who could accomplish such great feats—imagine, if you will, what a joyous place Maamallapuram must have been, three hundred and fifty years ago. How *alive*! My skin prickles with goosebumps at the very thought. Don't you feel it too? Doesn't your heart soar, your shoulders swell with pride at the mere thought of your ancestors?"

"Some moments ago you accused me of *mukasthuthi*, your highness. It's slipped your mind, perhaps, that I've always leavened my praises with a healthy dose of criticism as well. It appears that this terrible passion for arts, crafts and sculpture that destroys people and their whole lives, has infected you too. My ancestors were afflicted by it, and thus, all their victories and triumphs lost merit. Maamallar did erect a *jayasthambam* at Vathapi as a sign of his momentous triumph; true. What of him, later? What did the great warrior do? Sit around sculpting rocks and drilling holes in the boulders strewn around him, of course! And we all know what happened as a result: the Chalukyas gained in strength, built an empire, gathered their massive forces and swept down south for revenge. Kanchi and Uraiyur were reduced to ashes; they descended even as far as Madurai. Had Nedumara Pandiyan not decided to make a stand and destroy them in Nelveli, all the southern lands would be under Chalukya suzerainty by now, wouldn't they?"

"Not at all, Parthiba. Remember history, my friend—have we ever heard of any one dynasty ruling endlessly, beyond all bounds of time?

Never! Even the illustrious Ishvaku clan, which boasted Lord Rama, died out. The Rettai Mandalathar rose to bring the Chalukya reign to an end. Empires and dynasties do have a habit of rising to tremendous greatness, and crashing to hollow depths; entirely natural, don't you think? There are kingdoms that have ruled for centuries, and disappeared without a trace. Take my own forebears such as Karikal Valavan and Killi Valavan, for instance; they ruled illustriously—but what do we know of them today, after all? Only their names and a little of what they accomplished; largely because a few poets managed to sing upon them. As for their verses—who knows if they were the complete, undiluted truth—or just outrageous lies spewed for the edification of the public, after a few enjoyable rounds of liquor? But the fabulous sculptures carved by Mahendra Pallavar and Maamallar—now *these* will stand the test of time for thousands of years, extolling them to the whole world. What have you and I done to even remotely be compared to them, I ask? To be sure, we've slaughtered tens of thousands of men; made sure battlefields were submerged under rivers of blood. But what else? What else, to ensure that our names stay on in history?"

Parthibendran sat still for a while, dumbstruck. Was this really Aditha Karikalan, speaking? Then, he heaved a sigh. "If these are truly your opinions, your highness, about wars and heroes … then, well—what can I say? You're distressed today; your mind is not at peace. Perhaps that's the reason for this disillusionment. Couldn't you possibly open your heart to me, *Ayya*?" He pressed on, eagerly. "Couldn't you possibly let me know the secret that's locked in your iron-heart?"

"And if I did, Parthiba—if I really did break open my heart to you … what, or who do you think you'll find in it?"

"That's what I wish to find out, *Swami*."

"Not my parents, Parthiba. Not my beloved brother and sister, dearer to me than my own life. Not even you and Vandhiyathevan, best of my friends. No—you'll find a woman. The very embodiment of evil. That wretched, accursed Ilaiya Rani of Pazhuvoor—that's whom you shall find. Ah, the trials and tribulations she's put me through! The torment I've been meted out by Nandhini, cruel, cruel Nandhini, more venomous than poison!" Aditha Karikalan's voice reverberated with barely controlled fury; each word burning like hot coals. "*She's* the one within my heart, breaking it every living moment—and I've never breathed a word of what I've undergone, all this time, to a living soul. No one, except you."

"I rather guessed this, *Ayya*. Whenever the Pazhuvoor Ilaiya Rani was mentioned, I noticed your face darken; your eyes turn bloodshot, and as for the agony I glimpsed in them ... well. But do tell me—how did such a fatal attraction ever find place in your heart? You, scion of a dynasty that reveres every woman as his own mother? Pazhuvettarayar too, has close ties with your family and has done so for generations; he's getting on in years as well. They might be our foes today—but surely that wasn't the case before? Your father and grandfather held him in the highest regard, I know. And to even think of the woman he married, with Agni Bhagavan as his witness—no matter how abandoned she is ... is that really the right thing to do?"

"It isn't, Parthiba, it isn't! Do you really think I don't know so? I suffer, because I *do*. You see—she didn't make a place for herself in my heart after her marriage to Pazhuvettarayar, but before. My heart was poisoned by her bewitching ways aeons ago. I tried—believe me, I tried to weed out her memories—but I couldn't. I know I speak as though she's the one to blame—but the truth is ... well, no one knows the truth except God. If anything, He's the one to be blamed for every ill. Or, perhaps, fate itself that made us meet, and then part in such cruel fashion!"

"Met her *before* she became the Young Queen of Pazhuvoor, your highness? But—how? When, and where?"

"That's a very long story. Are you sure you want to listen today?"

"Indeed I do. In fact, I shan't find peace until I do know the truth of it. You've asked me to leave for Ilankai tomorrow, haven't you? I'm not sure I can carry out my duty well, without listening to your story, and finding some way to soothe your heart!"

"Soothe my heart, is it? My friend, there's no semblance of peace for me—in this lifetime, at any rate. I'm not sure if I shall find it even in my next. But you clearly wish this; I shall oblige. I don't want you to leave for Ilankai, knowing that I harbour a secret that I cannot even trust *you* with!"

Karikalan paused, for a while. Then, he heaved a great sigh, and began his tale.

55

NANDHINI'S LOVER

I was twelve, when I saw Nandhini for the first time. Once I, my young sister and my brother were paddling boats in the little pond behind our royal palace, in Pazhaiyarai. We finished our play, moored our boats, and returned to the palace through the gardens. Somewhere along the way, the voice of our *periya paatti* Sembian Maadevi floated out to us. We made much of our elder grandmother, all of us; we'd grown up in her fond embrace, after all. We ran up to the little arbour where she sat, to tell her about our play. There were three other people in there, aside from her. One was a young girl around our own age. The other two were obviously her parents. They were speaking to Maadevadigal about their daughter. They stopped, and everyone stared at us, as we erupted into the little space. But I—the only thing I saw was the girl's large eyes, widening even more at the sight of us. I can picture the scene even now, so clearly, in my mind's eye ..."

Aditha Karikalan's voice trailed away. He raised his eyes to the heavens, and fell silent. Perhaps he glimpsed that little maid's face from long ago, once again, amidst those wispy clouds floating serenely in the night sky.

"*Ayya?*" came Parthibendran's voice. "Please go on."

Aditha Karikalan returned to earth, and continued his tale. "It was my sister Kundhavai who tumbled out the whole story about our boats and play. Maadevadigal listened patiently to her, and then pointed out the new girl. "Do you see her, my heart? How bright she looks! She and her people have arrived from the Pandiya country. They will be staying here awhile, at the home of Eesana Siva Battar. This young lady's name is Nandhini. Include her in your amusements sometimes, won't you? I am sure she will make you an excellent playmate."

"I realized, almost at once, that my sister was revolted at the very idea. *Anna, did you take a look at the girl we met just now? How ugly she looked, to be sure*! she muttered, as we made our way outside the arbour. 'Why do you think her face looked so terrible— just like a hideous owl? Why does *Paatti* wish us to play with her? Good heavens, how can I even look at her without laughing? What do I do?' she asked."

"I understood something very important, in that instant: women are born with jealousy in their hearts. No matter how exquisite she is, she can't stand to see another as pretty. My sister's beauty was famed amongst all our clan—but not even she could bear another girl's loveliness. What else could be the reason behind all her catty remarks? But then, I wouldn't let her alone either; I exaggerated the other girl's charms just to infuriate my young sister. We argued and quarreled about her, often; our young brother Arulmozhi would stare at us, puzzled, unaware of the reason for our animosity. Some time later my father left for the Pandiya War; I accompanied him. Together, we battled and triumphed many times over the Pandiyas, as well as the Ilankai forces sent to assist them. And then, finally, Veera Pandiyan ran from battle and concealed himself. At that point, we weren't quite sure if that was what he'd done, or if he'd fallen on the field. That was the signal for the Ilankai soldiers to retreat. We pursued them right up to Sethukkarai. Those who had managed to escape death at our hands hastened into ships, and left our shores hotfoot. My father wished to teach a lesson to the Ilankai king, who kept sending troops to assist the Pandiyas and caused us endless trouble; he decided to send a large force there, under Kodumbalur Siriya Velaar. It took some time to gather the ships, men and material required for such a large undertaking—but still, we stayed there for awhile until the vessels were loaded and sent on their way. We returned to Chozha Nadu only after having learnt that our men had disembarked in Maathottam, safe and sound."

"Two years had passed, by the time I returned to Pazhaiyarai. I'd forgotten the poor little priest's daughter who'd come to us from Madurai or thereabouts. But when I entered the palace and saw her and my sister—they'd changed beyond all recognition. They were very friendly, these days, I noticed. Not only had Nandhini grown—she fairly dazzled, dressed in silks and ornaments. This, I learnt, had been my sister's doing. Nandhini, however, refused to meet my eyes or speak to me, as in the old days. I tried very hard, I admit, to remove these hindrances; my greatest delight lay in her company, when I could bring her to overcome her bashfulness. I can't really explain why I felt this way—I certainly couldn't understand my exhilaration when I was young. During those days, my heart was overflowing with a sort of ecstasy, like the new floods that break the banks of Kaveri. I realized something else too: those around me didn't quite like any of this. Kundhavai began to detest Nandhini, ever since my return; my grandmother, Maadevadigal called me aside as well, one day: "She's a priest's daughter; you, however, are the son of the Emperor. You have both come of age. It is no longer advisable for you to be friends." I, who had revered her as a deity until then, and placed great faith in her judgment, now grew quite angry; I refused to heed her words. I went against her express command, searched out Nandhini, and took great delight in pursuing her friendship. Not that any of this lasted for long. I learnt, one day, that she and her parents had suddenly left for their village in Pandiya Nadu. Sorrow crushed me—and fury, as well. I locked away my misery, but made my sister the target of my anger. Thanks to God, though, it came about that I had to leave for the North, soon enough; I accompanied the Chozha armies that marched against Rashtrakuta forces that had invaded Thirumunaippaadi and Thondai Mandalam. That was when you and I met, and became inseparable friends.

"We battled the Rashtrakutas with the help of noble Malayaman; set them running north, beyond the River Paalaaru, and captured Kanchi. Bad news arrived, right at that moment, from Ilankai: our forces had been routed out and Kodumbalur Siriya Velaar had lost his life. The moment he heard the news, Veera Pandiyan, who had slunk away and curled inside a desert cave, crept out, snake that he was. He gathered his forces again, invaded Madurai, and raised the Fish Flag atop the fort. You do remember our fury when news came to us, don't you? Our anger, the way we wanted to crush this little up-start like an insect? We left at once for Pazhaiyarai. My father was already ailing; his legs had begun to lose feeling. All this notwithstanding, he was still prepared to set off for the battlefield. I barred his way, and flatly refused to entertain the idea; I swore a bloody oath in his presence: I would not return to Chozha Nadu without annihilating the Pandiya army, re-capturing Madurai, and lopping off that traitorous Veera Pandiyan's head as a prized trophy. You were there too, at that time. My father honoured my pledge and sent us both to battle, subject to the condition that we would accept the leadership of Kodumbalur Boodhi Vikrama Kesari, who had already marched thither with his forces. We agreed; on our way, we ran into Periya Pazhuvettarayar, who revealed his disgust at having been passed over to lead the attack, not to mention the indignity of Kodumbalur's King being delegated that responsibility. Adding insult to injury, indeed.

"Our war fervour convinced Senathipathi Boodhi Vikrama Kesari to grant us permission to conduct the war our own way. It wouldn't be too much to boast, my friend, that you and I managed to accomplish quite a few extraordinary feats, in that battle. We destroyed the Pandiyan army and annexed Madurai again—but that wasn't all. We weren't satisfied with sending those devils packing; we wished to raze them to their very roots. We commanded our soldiers to hunt down and kill every coward scattering in all four directions from the battle; one by one, mercilessly. We, on the other had, gathered an elite band of warriors, and set out to pursue the Pandiya King. It wasn't too difficult either; the Fish flag, fluttering aloft, showed us his direction; we followed, hotfoot. Our enemy was surrounded by his precious bodyguards, those wretched *Abathudhavis*, who guarded his person like a fortress. It must be admitted they were a shade more terrifying than even the famed Chozha Velakkara army; they had sworn a blood oath, after all, to never desert their king in distress, and to save him—at the cost of their own lives. If they couldn't, and the Pandiya king suffered grievous physical harm as a result, they would cut off their own heads in atonement. Those were the warriors we were ranged against. They carried out their duty well, I must say; we killed them all, to the last one. The corpses of those dead at our hands grew and grew, like a mountain—but not even amidst them could we catch a glimpse of the king. We'd been tricked by the Fish flag—for it was an elephant that bore it, standing by. Not a sign of Veera Pandiyan either on, or anywhere in its vicinity! Well. He was an adept at scampering from battlefields and concealing himself in dark corners, wasn't he? We suspected that he'd probably done so this time as well; split our army into several factions, and sent them in all four directions, to find him.

"You and your forces thundered along the twin banks of the River Vaigai, in pursuit. I wasn't sitting idle either: I descended into the riverbed, struck across the sands, and went south. I could glimpse the hoof-prints of a solitary horse, here and there. There were spots of blood, alongside its trail, as well. I followed both and by and by, came upon a small oasis of vegetation, in the middle of the Vaigai riverbed. Within was a tiny shrine, dedicated to Thirumaal. Beside it were one or two huts, belonging to the temple's priests. The little patch of land fairly bloomed with flowering trees, meant for the exclusive use of the deity. There was a tiny lotus pond as well, brimming with fragrant blooms. Perhaps you might remember, my friend, that I had declared that particular oasis off-limits to our soldiers, at all costs. Not just because I didn't want the deity's daily worship halted by the exigencies of war—but also because of the presence of someone, in the temple priest's simple home. The lady who had bewitched my soul; the queen of my heart.

"You see—I'd caught sight of Nandhini once, when I'd entered the oasis. She presented a different appearance, now: she'd bound her hair into a large crown-like knot, brought it slightly in front, and decorated it with a string of flowers, rather like Saint Andal. A garland of flowers hung around her neck as well. "What's all this in aid of?" I asked her. She'd sworn, she said, never to marry another human being, after our separation; that Kannan, the deity would be her husband, just as he was for Andal herself. This, I thought, was decidedly ridiculous. How on earth was a human girl going to marry God? Even so, this was not, I felt, the right time to descend into an argument with her. Once the war was done, I could enter in to all these and more. I asked her if she needed any help. "Please ensure that your soldiers do not barge into this little haven, by any chance. My old, blind parents are the only ones here; my hale and hearty brother has gone on a pilgrimage to Thirupathi." I promised that I wouldn't let any of my men set foot on her little island, and left. I made my way there twice or thrice, and did manage to see her. Ah, what I felt for her—my infatuation was now ten times what it used to be; a raging fire that consumed my heart! But I resolved to be patient; there was work to be done, first: I must return to Pazhaiyarai, with Veera Pandiyan's head. And in return, I would ask my father for Nandhini's hand in marriage.

"So far had I come, in my ruminations. Imagine my surprise and fury, then, when I saw those horse-hooves leading straight into that little oasis! I plunged further through the dense trees, and saw it tethered to one of them. The runaway must certainly be here, in one of these very huts. I crept up to Nandhini's dwelling, and peeped through a *palagani*. What I saw, then—ah, my friend—it is branded into my very mind's eyes, like the burn of red-hot iron onto my chest! Veera Pandiyan lay on a tattered rope-cot. Nandhini was giving him little sips of water, to quench his thirst. Her face glowed with unearthly beauty; tears trembled, like exquisite pearls, in her eyes. I couldn't bear it any more. I kicked the door open with a bang. Nandhini, who'd been dressing his wounds, stood up, and came forward. She prostrated full-length at my feet, and rose. "I beg of you, *Ayya*, in the name of the affection you once cherished, for me," she pleaded, folding her hands. "Do not harm him! He lies injured, here—let him not meet death at your hands!"

"What?" I spluttered. "What's he to *you*? Why would you beg me to spare his life?"

"He's my lover; my God," she answered. "A vision of mercy, who has promised to marry me!"

"I lost whatever shred of compassion I'd felt for an injured Veera Pandiyan, lying on an old bed. Ah, this bastard—this *sandaalan*—what a revenge he'd taken upon me! I wouldn't have cared if he'd stolen every last piece of my kingdom—but he'd succeeded in spiriting away my beloved, the one who'd taken my heart! How could I spare him? Mercy? Compassion? Never, never!"

"I kicked aside Nandhini, advanced upon Veera Pandiyan on his bed, raised my sword, and chopped off his head with one blow. Shame fills me even now, when I think about that brutal, inhuman deed. But then—at that moment—I was consumed, not just by the wrath of war, but a terrible, personal vengeance as well. Fury took over; I used its terrible power to kill Veera Pandiyan. When I stalked back to the doorway, I turned around, to see Nandhini. She stared back, unblinking. I swear to you that I have never before seen such a look in my life. You've heard, haven't you, of the six terrible emotions, the destructive forces, that rule our lives? *Kama; Krodha; Lobha, Moha; Madha; Maarchariyam?* I saw them all, raging like an inferno in her eyes, in that moment. Since then, I've tried so hard to divine the meaning of that glance—but I've never understood it, to this day!"

"By then, you and others burst in, having searched for me. You saw Veera Pandiyan's corpse, his blood-splattered head, and roared in victory. But I—I was conscious of only one thing. The weight of all the Vindhya Mountains, crushing my chest …"

ஜ

56

THE ANTHAPPURAM INCIDENT

Centuries ago, Mahendra Pallavar, ruling a flourishing empire from Kanchi, the capital, had made arrangements for the epic Mahabharatham to be narrated in every corner of the country; in a land where peace and compassion, advocated by Jain and Buddhist traditions, persevered, war-fervour was an absolute necessity, he felt, to draw out people from their stupor and ensure that their battle instincts were as well-honed as ever. Bharatha *mandapams*, meant specially for the re-telling of these epics sprung up at his command; the practice had continued almost uninterrupted in Thondai Mandalam, all these years. Vast numbers of people gathered at night, either in these *mandapams* or open-air clearings, to listen to their favourite stories. Songsters, *padinis* appeared by the dozens, possessed of the unique talent of taking the numerous stories and sub-stories from the Mahabharatham, weaving them into appealing songs and verses, and relating it to their audience in voices filled with vibrant emotion.

Archunan, wandering on one of his pilgrimages, happened to catch sight of Chithrangi, the Princess of Manipuri, in a garden a little outside the borders of her kingdom. They fell in love; in due course, a most beloved son, Aravaan, was born. The scion of a princess from a valiant clan among the hills, and Archunan himself, it was no surprise that Aravaan turned out to be a phenomenal warrior. News of the imminent Kurukshetra War reached him; he journeyed, forthwith, to join the Pandavas and offer his services. It was the custom in those days to choose a young man, a great warrior blessed with every gift known to humanity, and sacrifice him on the eve of battle, to ensure great victory. Talk, naturally, came up about this practice before war was about to begin, and Aravaan spoke up: "Here I am— sacrifice me; that you may be granted the victory you deserve." The Pandavas possessed none as valorous as he; left with no choice, they took him at his word and duly gave him up as *kalabali*.

The people of Thamizhagam lost their hearts to this brave young man, Veera Aravaan, who had offered himself with such goodwill for the sake of his own; shrines were built for him alongside the ones erected for Draupadi Amman; festivals were organized and celebrated with great fervour, in his honour.

Tonight's tale, beside Maamallapuram's Five Chariots, detailing his many sterling qualities and valorous deeds seemed to have to come to an end. "Long live Chakravarthy Sundara Chozhar, Lord of the Three Worlds!" Loud chants rose, cleaving the very air. "Long live the illustrious Kopparakesari Aditha Karikalar!" This was the cue for the audience to disperse.

"The story's over for tonight, I see," murmured said Aditha Karikalan. "Malayaman will be back in a matter of moments."

"Aravaan might be done—but what of you, and your tale, your highness?" queried Parthibendran. "That's not over, not by a long shot, is it?"

"Malayaman's vigour never ceases to amaze me, you know," said the crown prince, meditatively. "At his age too—and he stays awake until midnight, walking all the way to these clearings, listening to these stories. Imagine the will-power of that man!"

"I see nothing in merely staying alive for years and years," Parthibendran shrugged. "This place is fairly littered with doddering old men who can't get to sleep, and drag themselves to storytelling sessions to while away their time …"

"And you're comparing Thirukkovilur Miladudaiyar with those drooping men, who've done very little worth the while in their lives? Ah, the number of battles he's seen—dare we even suppose that we'll be alive at his age? And if, by some chance luck we were, I highly doubt if we'd be as able."

"Well, if you must know, your highness, it's not exactly difficult to see why those old-timers are striding around, fit and able, at their age—"

"It isn't? What's the reason, pray?"

"They never lost their hearts to petty little priest's daughters, for one thing; neither did they sit around moaning about their lost love or weeping at her very memory. And even if they *had* set their hearts on some woman—well, their methods were swift and efficient: they simply dragged her by the hair, flung her into their *anthappuram*, and that was it. Mission accomplished."

"Nandhini is no ordinary priest's daughter, Parthiba. There's some mystery surrounding her birth, I think—no, I'm sure …"

"Be that as it may, your highness—*what* does it matter? Who cares if she's the daughter of a priest, a king or no one? What does her parentage matter? Why, take that old fossil, Periya Pazhuvettarayar himself; he stumbles upon her on some God-forsaken forest-path— and what does he do? Drag her to his harem, of course, and throw her in, the ninth after eight women …"

"You know, I never could understand that, either …"

"You couldn't make sense of why an old man fell for her fatal charms and let himself be reeled into her wily net?"

"No—but why would a woman who professed her love for me—who then fell in love with Veera Pandiyan and tried to save his life—finally submit to this old man, body and soul? I confess I don't understand *that*."

"I'm afraid I do; all too well. What confounds me, though, is something else: having confronted that wretched Pandiyan, eternal foe of our Chozha dynasty—a dastardly coward who runs and hides from enemies at every opportunity, and yet dares to call himself *Veera* Pandiyan—you come across a woman who shelters him, begs for his life ... and then you leave her *alive*? I never could make sense of *that*. You could, and must have done one of two things: cut her into pieces that very instant, or, if you entertained scruples about killing a woman, truss her up like a fowl and throw her into our dungeons, at the very least. But you did neither ... ah, I remember, now: You dragged Veera Pandiyan's corpse out of the hut and flung it outside; we surrounded you, raving like maniacs, drunk with triumph. In the midst of it all, I couldn't help hearing someone sobbing from within the hut. "Who's that, weeping?" I asked; you replied that they were women of the priest's family, frightened out of their wits by what they'd witnessed. "Don't go in, any of you; there's no cause to terrify them further," you commanded. Flushed with victory, none of us were inclined to do so, anyway. We made our way back, carrying aloft Veera Pandiyan's head; you accompanied us as well. But you didn't really participate in the joy and revelry of the moment; you seemed rather drawn and fatigued. I asked you the reason; you brushed away my questions," recalled Parthibendran. "I remember wondering if you'd sustained some grievous injury that we knew nothing about ..."

"I had. Not physically, but in my heart of hearts; an injury that would never heal. I couldn't—I couldn't forget the sight of her, falling to her knees, shielding Veera Pandiyan, begging me to spare his life! Often and often would I anguish over her desperate plea: *Ayyo*, why couldn't I have granted her this wish? If my life could have brought her lover back, then willingly would I have sacrificed it—but it wouldn't. Nothing I did or could ever do, would make her happy, and I cursed myself for it; I went mad, knowing that I was the reason for her misery. We pride ourselves so much on our valour, Parthiba; we believe ourselves equal to anything; able to carry out any task. Nothing is beyond us, in this world! We look at ancient palm-leaves that announce: "Kings possess the essence of the great Maha Vishnu Himself, Guardian of the World; they are His representatives in human form"—and we actually believe it! But can we return a departed soul to its body? Has any member of any royal household ever been able to achieve such a miracle? We have the power to cause death in abundance, but no man has ever had the unique gift of bringing a corpse to life."

"And a good thing too, I should say. Imagine the catastrophic results, had you actually possessed such a unique gift! You'd have brought Veera Pandiyan back; he'd have slunk away and buried himself in some other mountain lair; the Pandiya War might still be going on, for all we know. And all, for the sake of a woman's tears!" finished Parthibendran, dramatically.

"You're a cynic, Parthiba; an unfortunate creature who can't appreciate women. You speak so, because you've no idea about love, or its power."

"Too right, your highness. I do cherish a wholesome hatred for women and all their works; that's also why I've never gotten myself into any twisted female's toils. Now, your beloved friend Vandhiyathevan, on the other hand—hah! *There's* a hot-blooded idiot who needs no prodding to fall in love! All he needs is the barest glimpse of a turmeric-endowed face, and he scrambles to do her bidding, a stupid leer on *his* face. That's why you like him so much, isn't it?"

"Back to Vandhiyathevan, are we? I did wonder if you'd forgotten him during our conversation."

"Ha, you never did appreciate my attempts to expose his true character. Well, I won't. What happened next? Didn't you ever see Nandhini again? Or ask her why a woman who'd pleaded and cajoled for Veera Pandiyan's life, actually agreed to marry that old fossil, Pazhuvettarayar?"

"Veera Pandiyan was finally dead; once you'd celebrated more than half the night away, everyone fell asleep, quite heavily. I couldn't. My eyes wouldn't even close. Every nerve in my body quivered with the need to find Nandhini again; to explain myself, and beg her pardon. But then the next moment, I felt a fury that consumed my very being; all I was conscious of, was to vent my terrible anger, as well. Whatever the reason, I *had* to see her; I would know no peace, else. I couldn't return to Chozha

Nadu until I did. At midnight, I rose noiselessly, ensured that none of you saw me leave the *paasarai*, and rode towards the oasis between Vaigai's banks. My heart thumped within my chest; my body quaked and shivered as though with a fever, and my legs trembled as I slipped off my horse. I crept, step by little step, towards the little Thirumaal temple. Every single hut in its vicinity had been torched and reduced to ashes. A man and woman, both old, squatted beside one of them in tears, lamenting their fate. I tiptoed closer—and recognition dawned: they were the ones who had brought Nandhini to the royal gardens, in Pazhaiyarai. The moment they set eyes on me, their grief and terror seemed to mount by leaps and bounds.

"They couldn't even speak, for the few first moments. I soothed and pacified them and then, they managed to gather strength, and answer my questions. Their first daughter lived, it seemed, across the river; she was pregnant and about to deliver, and they had journeyed to see her. Nandhini refused to go with them; knowing her willful ways, her stubborn nature and unaware of how to force her do their bidding, they left her to devices, and went by themselves. On their way home, they caught sight of a group of ruffians tying up a helpless girl hand and foot, trying to throw her into a funeral pyre. Such atrocities were not uncommon in times of war; terrified of even catching their eye, they hurried on their way, and returned home—only to find their huts burnt down. Nandhini was gone. The priest and his wife came to the end of their recital. "Great prince, where is our beloved daughter?" they cried, wracked with sorrow and worry. "What has become of her?" I had suspected for some time that they were not her real parents; now, I knew, for certain. Had they truly borne her, not for a moment would they have entertained the thought of leaving Nandhini all alone. Their distress didn't move me; I couldn't find it in myself to feel sorry for them. Nandhini's fate, though ... oh, the very thought seemed to cleave my heart in two! Sorrow had me in its fierce, unyielding grip. "Find your precious daughter's wretched pyre, and throw yourselves onto it!" I screamed. "Burn and die, you idiots!" I cursed them with all my grief-filled heart, and returned to camp before dawn. You were still deeply asleep; none of you had known of either my departure, or return."

"True; we didn't. And then, on top of all that, to keep such a thing to yourself so long ... the thought fairly turns my stomach. A fine way of treating your friend, your highness; keeping secrets from him. Not in my wildest dreams could I have suspected you of such—such treachery," Parthibendran scowled. "Why, in your place, I certainly wouldn't even have entertained the notion!"

"But you aren't, are you, Parthiba? I don't think anyone could be, in the whole, wide world. Who knows how you might have acted, in my place?"

"What's done is done, *Ayya*; there's no sense in re-visiting the past, or pointless argument. What happened, afterwards? When did you next see Nandhini? Was it after she'd become the Young Queen of Pazhuvoor, or before?"

"Had I managed to catch sight of her before, she *wouldn't* have become the Pazhuvoor Queen. We weren't even around, during the wedding; do you remember our disgust when we heard the news? My *Yuvaraja* coronation occurred a few days later; my father, Grandmother and others of influence didn't want any ambiguity about the succession—perhaps they suspected that someone might instigate Madhuranthakan to ascend the throne? Whatever the reason, I was made not only the heir, but also awarded the Parakesari title; I could now authorize stone inscriptions in my own name. *This vast Chozha Nadu is now yours and yours only, by right*, announced my beloved father; his heartfelt words were echoed by his ministers, courtiers, commanders and his subjects, with full force. Their resounding chants of victory pierced the very skies. Nandhini had completely faded from my memory during these times of joy and celebration—but something happened soon after the *Pattabishekam* that ensured that she would never, ever leave my heart.

"The ceremony had just come to an end; an ancient Chozha crown now adorned my brow. My father escorted me to the *anthappuram* that I may receive the blessings of my mother and my grandmother, not to mention the other royal ladies. Chief Minister Aniruddhar, my younger brother, and the Pazhuvettarayar brothers accompanied us as well. My sister and her handmaidens stood in a large group, mingling with the various royal mothers; all of them dazzled in their best ornaments and finest dresses. Their faces shone; their smiles brilliant on this joyous occasion; clearly, they'd been expecting our arrival eagerly. But my eyes were riveted onto only one person—or rather, one face. Nandhini's. My heart's dearest, whom I'd thought burnt to embers on a lonely pyre. But—how had she arrived here, in the palace's *anthappuram*? How had she managed to deck herself out in such fine garments and jewels, a queen among queens, eclipsing even those bred in luxury and majesty? And the light in her eyes …! Her exquisite features seemed enhanced a thousand times, from what I remembered. Her beauty almost blinded me. My heart raced; within moments, my besotted mind had built several improbable castles in the air: Was this day, the day I'd been crowned *Yuvaraja* to the Chozha empire, truly about to become the happiest, of my whole life? Was she who ruled my heart and dreams, finally about to be my queen in real life as well, my *pattamagishi*? Had the Gods bent their compassionate gaze on me finally, and wrought some sort of miracle—*indrajaalam*, perhaps, or some fabulous magic trick that made all my dreams come true?

"And then, my mother, Vaanamaadevi, took a couple of steps forward. "My child," she whispered, and embraced me warmly, bestowing her blessings. That very instant, something shocking happened: I heard someone scream. My father! Suddenly, he crumpled to the floor, unconscious. The place erupted in pandemonium; the others and I threw ourselves into raising the Emperor, and bringing him around. The royal women, except for my mother and Sembian Maadevi, promptly disappeared to their own quarters. My father recovered soon enough.

"I took my sister a little apart. How had Nandhini managed to arrive here, I asked. "Why, she's married Periya Pazhuvettarayar," revealed Kundhavai. "She's the Pazhuvoor Ilaiya Rani, now." I sustained a severe shock—as though a sharp spear had plunged into my chest. Many are the injuries I've borne, in battle, my friend—but nothing can ever equal the blow I received, just then. Nandhini—the wife of Periya Pazhuvettarayar!"

Aditha Karikalan pressed a hand to his chest. Clearly, his heart ached. Even now.

57

Maya Mohini

Karikalan's tale had not quite moved Parthiban in the beginning—but it must be acknowledged that now, as he wiped away eyes moist with tears, he was touched, despite himself.

"I would've never dreamt that love for a woman could lead to such devastating heartache," he admitted. "None of us even guessed, of course, that you'd sustained a shock such as this, the day of your *Pattabishekam*. We were rather surprised at your low spirits, to be sure; we tried to raise them by indulging in a lot of silly jokes and teasing, I remember."

"You did. You also tried to restore my happiness by reciting the glory of all my future achievements once I ascended a glittering throne—you expanded the Chozha empire from Imayam to Ilankai within the space of a day! Then you crossed entire seas and invaded kingdoms far away … oh yes, I recall all those conversations. I remember too, how distressed I was, at the very mention of such topics.

"Later, one day, Nandhini asked me to visit, at the Pazhuvoor Palace. Must I go, or should I refuse the invite? Conflict raged in my heart for a very long time; in the end, I decided that I would honour her request. My mind was besieged by a great many doubts and suspicions which I wanted clarified—I also wanted to know, I must admit, the truth about her birth. I even wondered if there was some connection between her presence in the *anthappuram* that day and my father's sudden, inexplicable loss of consciousness. You may remember, perhaps, that though he came around quite soon, my father was never quite himself again; his health too, wasn't what it used to be.

"If I could but just talk to her once—I cherished hopes that I might learn answers to the mysteries that tormented me. That, at least, was the explanation I gave myself. As to why I really wanted to meet her— ah, what else could be the reason but this, this insane, irresistible force that dragged me into her presence, this strange power that exerted all its considerable influence over me? Everything else was just a ploy; reasons I needed to justify my desire to see her. I obeyed the dictates of my heart, and Nandhini. Pazhuvettarayar wasn't in town; there were none in his palace with either the power or authority to forbid my entrance; none who knew, in fact, of our old friendship. Many concluded that the Prince, made newly heir to the throne was merely paying a formal visit to the royal mothers of the *anthappuram*, to seek their blessings.

"I met Nandhini in the *latha mandapam* in her palace garden. Parthiba—you've heard tales of many sea voyages from hardened travelers, haven't you? Do you remember what they said, about massive currents? That there are some spots in the ocean that churn and heave under their phenomenal power—that ships, once caught in their vicious toils, often splinter to pieces. That was my experience too, in Nandhini's presence—a helpless ship tossed and tormented, sucked into a terrifying whirlpool. My body, heart and soul shattered into a thousand shards; I was horrified by the words that came out of my mouth. *Ayyo, what am I blathering on about*, I thought, but I couldn't still my tongue, which seemed to have taken on a life of its own, and uttered a farrago of nonsense. Nandhini began quite formally, felicitating me upon my *Pattabishekam*.

"I see no reason for happiness, upon the occasion," I replied.

"Really? Why not?" she asked.

"Well, what a question! How could I, considering your treachery?"

She pretended not to understand me. Our speech grew more impassioned: I accused her of having betrayed my love, and allowing herself to encourage Veera Pandiyan's lecherous advances; I even managed to wound her about having married that fossil, Pazhuvettarayar.

"You began by destroying my love for you, your highness," she retorted. "Then, you killed the man who loved me, in front of my very eyes; it almost seems like you will know no peace until you've hacked *me* to pieces, as well. As you wish, then," she pulled out a small dagger from the recesses of the clothing, at her waist, and stretched it out. "What are you waiting for?"

"Kill *you*?" I asked, harshly. "Aren't you the one torturing me slowly, to death?"

"And then—and then, my lips uttered words that make me shrink with shame, when I think about them. "It isn't too late even now, Nandhini. Say the word; tell me that you'll leave this doddering old idiot and I'll give up my position, my claims to this throne, this instant! Let us leave this kingdom at once, sail to lands far across the great seas and live our lives in endless happiness!"

Nandhini listened to my intemperate, impassioned ramblings—and laughed. A terrifying laugh that chilled me right down to my marrow. My skin prickles even now at the very memory. "Journey across the seas, make our home in new lands—and do what, exactly? Chop firewood? Or did you, perhaps, envision us cultivating plantain trees for a living? That would be idyllic, wouldn't it?" she sneered.

"You wouldn't like that, would you?" I jeered, in turn. "The priest's daughter is now the Young Queen of Pazhuvoor, isn't she?"

"Oh, I've no intention of being satisfied with my present station in life," she murmured. "I've set my sights on something more; something quite ambitious—nothing less than the jeweled throne of this empire. You see, I wish to become the Chakravarthini. Tell me—are you able and willing to accomplish my desire? Kill the Pazhuvettarayar brothers in one stroke, throw Sundara Chozhar into prison, ascend the throne—and make me yours. Your Queen, your *pattamagishi*!"

"*Ayyo*, how could you even—what are you saying?" I stammered. "Such cruel thoughts—"

"What about killing an injured Veera Pandiyan in front of my very eyes?" she demanded. "That didn't seem cruel to you, I suppose?"

"My fury knew no bounds; sheer wrath bubbled through my veins, blinding my eyes and heart. I knew not what I was saying, except that I let loose a torrent of angry, vicious words that tore her characters to shreds. I was about to leave—but she still had something to say."

"Should you change your mind some day, your royal highness, do return," she crooned. "When your mind and heart are perfectly willing to make me your Chakravarthini—come back to me!"

"I left her, then, finally," finished Aditha Karikalan. "And that was the last I saw of her."

"Good lord, *Ayya*," Parthibendran, who had listened to this account with growing horror, astonishment and not a little loathing, heaved a great sigh. "What a terrible woman! Do such vicious demons actually exist in this world, in real life? A good thing that you never met her later."

"I didn't—but she never will leave me be. Nandhini's face and form—her every gesture haunts me every hour, every minute, Pallava—she flits around my consciousness during the day; tortures me in my dreams, at night. One moment, she approaches me with a lilting smile capable of bewitching entire worlds, eager to embrace me with a kiss; at another, with a gleaming dagger in her hand, intent on plunging it into my heart. Sometimes, she weeps and sobs as though her heart would break; at others, her screams shatter the world as she raves and rants, her long tresses flying loose, scratching her cheeks with her own nails until they're torn, dripping blood. She laughs and shrieks like an insane creature—and then transforms into a soothing, ministering angel, intent on whispering calm words of understanding. My God, my God—the torment I suffer at the hands of that terrible witch—how do I put my heartache into words? Do you remember my grandfather's words from this afternoon? Many were the reasons he outlined, for why I shouldn't visit Thanjai; but there's only one reason for my loathing to enter that city, and wishing my father to join me here, in Kanchi: Nandhini."

"*That's* your paltry reason? You're quivering with fear, afraid to set foot in the capital for the sake of a woman? What do you think she might do—practice some sort of deception and poison you?"

"Not at all, Parthiba. Your lack of comprehension pains me. I don't fear death at her hands—only the fact that she might induce me to do something against my very instinct. If I met her again, she's quite capable of commanding me: "Imprison your father—send your sister out of this very country—kill that old idiot, and take the throne by force! And I— Parthiba, I'm afraid that if I heard those words one more time—*I might want to obey her.* One or the other of us must die, my friend—that, or death must embrace us both," anguished Karikalan. "Else, I see no hope for peace in this lifetime!"

"Really, your highness—what's all this? Why must *you* die? Just say the word, and I shall postpone my journey to Ilankai. My first assignment will be to kill that witch. And if I fall a victim to *sthree hathi dhosham*, the curse of killing a woman—well, then, so be it."

"Attempt anything of the sort, Parthiba, and I shall consider you my greatest foe from that very moment. If any killing's to be done, I shall do it—with my own hands. I shall strangle Nandhini—and then kill myself as well! Not for a moment will I ever allow anyone else to touch her, or harm even the nail on her little finger. Forget her, my friend, and everything else that I said. Obey our grandfather's instructions; leave for Ilankai tomorrow, and bring back my brother Arulmozhi, somehow. Let's persuade him to stay here; grandfather and grandson can discuss the entire country's future together, and come to their respective conclusions. Meanwhile, you and I will journey to Ilankai; we shall set sail in magnificent ships on the eastern seas, and gain massive victories against kingdoms such as Saavagam, Pushpakam and Kadaaram. We shall plant the flag of victory upon those lands and then, we shall sail westwards. There are glorious empires there, aren't there—Arabia, Paraseekam and

Misiram? We'll give them a taste of Thamizh courage, shall we, and make sure the Tiger-flag flies high there, as well? Did you know that *karpu*, the silly vow of chastity that binds women here, has no place, in countries such as those?" Karikalan's voice was filled with wonder. "Kings can cast their sight upon any woman that takes their fancy, and bring them back to their *anthappuram!*"

Before Parthiban could think of and voice a suitable response to these glorious fantasies, Thirukkovilur Malayaman appeared on the scene. "Ah, there is nothing to equal Aravaan's wonderful tale anywhere in the world—not even in all those fabulous strange lands you spoke of, just now. But—why are you still awake, both of you, talking all hours of the night?" he enquired. "You do remember your proposed journey to Ilankai tomorrow, don't you, Parthibendra?"

"Precisely why we haven't been to sleep yet," quipped the Pallava prince. "We've been talking about it, all this time!"

BOOK 1 CONCLUDED.

About Kalki R Krishnamurthy

Most men manage to embrace a single vocation in their lifetime—but very few are successful in what they have chosen to do with their life. Even among these, Kalki Ra Krishnamurthy was something of a rarity, for he managed to be a freedom-fighter, a talented writer, traveller, poet, journalist and a veritable connoisseur of the fine arts. He formed a part of the elite breed of writers who could churn their reader's emotions with their passionate words, or rouse them to wrath with powerful expressions.

Born on September 9, 1899 in the village Buddhamangalam, in the Thanjavur District, to Ramaswamy Iyer and Thaiyal Nayaki, Krishnamurthy, as he was named, began his earliest studies in the local school, later pursuing his education in the Hindu Higher secondary school. His thirst for literature became evident at this stage, for he began to write short stories and essays, under the able tutelage of his Thamizh professor, Periyasamy Pillai.

1921 saw the launch of the Non-Cooperation Movement by Mahatma Gandhi, to which Krishnamurthy, like thousands of other students, responded in earnest by giving up his education and participating in the fight for freedom from the British Raj. In 1922, he was awarded the sentence of one year in prison, during which time he met two people who would provide him with encouragement and enthusiasm all his life: T. Sadasivam and C. Rajagopalachari (Rajaji). It was during his imprisonment that he produced his first novel, *Vimala*.

During October, 1923, he ascended to the post of Sub-editor in a Thamizh periodical, *Navasakthi*, edited by eminent Thamizh scholar and veteran freedom-fighter, Thiru. Vi. Kalyanasundaram, otherwise known as Thiru. Vi. Ka. The next year saw his marriage to Rukmini, while he translated Gandhiji's *My Experiments with Truth* into the famed *Sathya Sothanai*. He also published his first collection of short stories, titled *Sarathaiyin Thanthiram* (Saratha's Strategy). In 1928, he walked out of *Navasakthi*, and engaged in the freedom movement in earnest. Living for the next three and a half years in Gandhiji's Ashram, he was a part of the magazine *Vimochanam* (Release) edited by Rajaji, and it was from this period that his writing skills began to come to the fore. With Rajaji banished to prison, Krishnamurthy wrote rousing essays and short pieces in the magazine, for which he paid the price—another term of imprisonment for six months in September, 1930. Released on March 19th the next year, he took over the editorship of *Ananda Vikatan*, a humour weekly which was swiftly ascending to popularity. From this period, his fame increased phenomenally.

Writing under the pen-names 'Kalki,' 'Thamizh Theni,' 'Karnatakam' etc. his witty, precise and impartial essays attracted readers of all walks. His novels and short stories appeared as serialized versions in the magazine, among them, notably *Kalvanin Kadhali* (The Bandit's Beloved) in 1937, which happened to be his first novel, followed by *Thyaga Bhoomi* (The Land of Sacrifice), both of which were made into movies. In 1941, he left Ananda Vikatan to start his own magazine, *Kalki*, in which T. Sadasivam was instrumental.

He wrote *Parthiban Kanavu* (Parthiban's Dream) during this period, one of his first forays into novels based on a historical setting, with members of the Pallava and Chozha Dynasty as its principal characters. In 1944, *Sivakamiyin Sabadham*, one of the best historical novels ever to have been written in Thamizh was produced, for which Kalki (by which name he styled himself) journeyed to Ajantha and Ellora, so as to add the touch of realism and precision. He also wrote the screen-play for the hit-movie *Meera* starring M.S. Subbulakshmi, the legendary Carnatic singer. 1948 saw the start of *Alai Osai*, a novel set in the era of freedom-fighters, discussing the then political and social situation, and was considered by Kalki to be his best. It won for him the Sahitya Academy Award, posthumously. In 1950, he journeyed to Sri Lanka, which formed the base for his magnum opus, *Ponniyin Selvan*, which, according to many, has none to equal its stature as a superb historical novel till date.

Kalki performed many roles with consummate ease during his lifetime; he wrote stirring novels which explored human relationships and social conditions, subjects considered largely taboo in those days for society was, in general, above criticism and history largely confined to schoolrooms. His writings were in simplified chaste Thamizh, so that they would reach a multitude. He was one of the first writers to add a large humour quotient in his writings—at a time when many authors considered humour beneath their dignity or were unable to project it into their works, Kalki used wit to deliver his sharpest snubs and most pointed criticisms. The effort, not unnaturally, made friends for him even among those who sought to criticise him. At a point when the self-esteem of the Thamizh population was at its lowest ebb and honour, to most, consisted of identification with the British regime, Kalki strove to bring Thamizh Nadu's rich history and culture into focus—he was largely responsible for tearing away the cloak of convention, the stigma around Bharathanatyam, and made it accessible to the common public. Until that time, it had largely been left to the devices of courtesans, and learning it was not considered proper by the general public. Kalki brought the understanding that the Thamizh population had plenty to be proud of.

Kalki relished travelling; his love for the Thamizh countryside, its people, the language and their customs can be found in abundance in almost all his works. He was one of the first authors to promote research and precision in writing, for he actually visited many of the places mentioned in his novels and short stories.

As a freedom-fighter, he was among the most respected in the country—he did much to rouse the people from their self-imposed lethargy and diffidence. Occasional periods of imprisonment did nothing to extinguish his fervour; he made more friends who were willing to join hands in his quest, and his popularity increased.

Small wonder, then, that he is revered by many to be a veritable Leonardo Da Vinci of Thamizh Nadu—for he managed to accomplish much with little.

Translator's Note

The first of Kalki R Krishnamurthy's works that I ever read was Ponniyin Selvan. I was twelve when my mother decided that my Thamizh reading skills were now perfectly satisfactory, and that I could progress to a novel that spanned five volumes. Not that I agreed with her right away—I found the first volume quite difficult, and names like Pazhuvettarayar well nigh broke my teeth.

But these were minor quibbles. The tongue-twisting titles didn't stop me from following Vandhiyathevan's journey, slack-jawed, from Kanchi, to Pazhaiyarai and Thanjavur, towards Princess Kundhavai and the hero of this story: Arulmozhi Varman, also known as *Ponniyin Selvan*. I forgot to breathe when he went on his adventures; felt an adoring hero-worship for young Arulmozhi, was quite jealous of both Vanathi and Poonguzhali by turns, proud of Kundhavai (from whom I took my online pseudonym), and felt an intense affection for Chozha Nadu (which does happen to be my native land.)

I still do. The fields, lakes and temples Kalki described exist, to some extent, even today—if you turn off the smoothly paved, traffic-ridden national highways and meander into small, unexplored roads. But it's the spirit of the story, of an Emperor who dared to be different, and a man who aspired to success, that brought it all alive. Kalki's fascination for History kindled my interest as well; it was the catalyst, the tipping-point towards my own eventual career: a historical fiction-writer.

Ponniyin Selvan was Kalki's last completed work. They say, in some cultures, that an artist's last work is often his best, because his soul, when it leaves his body, enters his work. I'm sure that this is true of *Ponniyin Selvan* as well. Certainly, Kalki wrote a lot, but none of his other works have gained, perhaps, the kind of recognition this one did.

I've tried to infuse my translation with the liveliness and spirit of Kalki's own words. I hope you enjoy reading it, just as much as I enjoyed translating it.

Pavithra Srinivasan,
May, 2019
Chennai.

About Pavithra Srinivasan

Pavithra Srinivasan is a writer, journalist, artist, translator, columnist and editor – not necessarily in that order. She is fascinated with History, and writes children's fiction in The Hindu. She's also an organic farmer and lives in her farm in Thiruvannamalai District, Tamil Nadu, where taps are still seen as luxury items. She has to her credit two collection of historical short-stories for young adults, *Yestertales* (Vishwakarma Publications, 2017); *Little-Known Tales from Well-Known Times: Back to the BCs,* (Helios Books, 2012); two historical novellas *Swords and Shadows* and *I, Harshavardhana* (Pustaka Digital Media, 2016); the translation of Kalki's epic historicals, *SivakamiyinSabadham* (Helios Books, 2012, Tranquebar Press, 2015) and *PonniyinSelvan*, (Tranquebar Press, 2014); *Lock-up: Jottings of an Ordinary Man* (Tranquebar Press, 2017) – the novel on which the National Award winning movie *Visaranai* was based. She has translated Jeffrey Archer's short-story collection into Tamil, *MudiviloruThiruppam* (Westland, 2009) as also Amish Tripathi's acclaimed *Shiva Trilogy* (Westland, 2014, 2015), and *Scion of Ikshvaku* (Westland, 2016). Book 2, *Sita: Warrior of Mithila* (Westland, 2018) is currently under production.

Pavithra is a miniaturist – an artist who draws miniatures. Her work has been featured in The Hindu, Deccan Chronicle, and AvalVikatan. To get regular updates about her work, check out her Facebook page: https://www.facebook.com/pavithra.srinivasan

Lightning Source UK Ltd.
Milton Keynes UK
UKHW010632051022
409964UK00002B/281